Jackie Ashenden w[...]
alpha heroes who'v[...]
only to have it blo[...]
heroines. She lives in Auckland, New Zealand,
husband, the inimitable Dr Jax, two kids and two rats.
When she's not torturing alpha males and their gutsy
heroines she can be found drinking chocolate martinis,
reading anything she can lay her hands on, wasting time
on social media or being forced to go mountain biking
with her husband. To keep up to date with Jackie's new
releases and other news sign up to her newsletter at
jackieashenden.com.

Zara Cox writes contemporary and erotic romance.
She lives in the Garden of England—aka Kent—with
her hubby and two kids. She loves to read and travel. In
2017 she managed to visit her number one bucket-list
destination—Hawaii—and is now actively pleading
with her husband to live there! She loves to hear from
her readers. You can get in touch with her via Twitter
@zcoxbooks, on Instagram zaracoxwriter, or Facebook
zaracoxwriter.

BAD BOSS

JACKIE ASHENDEN

DRIVING HIM WILD

ZARA COX

MILLS & BOON

First Published in Great Britain 2020
by Mills & Boon, an imprint of HarperCollins*Publishers*
1 London Bridge Street, London, SE1 9GF

Bad Boss © 2020 Jackie Ashenden

Driving Him Wild © 2020 Zara Cox

ISBN: 978-0-263-27757-9

Printed and bound in Spain
by CPI, Barcelona

BAD BOSS

JACKIE ASHENDEN

MILLS & BOON

To those who are just a bit 'different'.
You're all heroes.

CHAPTER ONE

Morgan

I WANTED TO kill my boss.

And I did mean that quite literally. I wanted to put my fingers around Ulysses White's strong, powerful neck and squeeze the life right out of him.

Naturally, I didn't. Instead, I stood in front of his monumental black desk in his cavernous London office, with its view of the city and the Thames laid out beneath it like a supplicant before a throne, and stared at him instead.

'What do you mean, you declined my annual leave request?' I demanded, my fingers itching. 'My perfectly reasonable leave request.'

He didn't look up from the stack of papers he was signing, the early-morning sun glossing his night-black hair. 'Your leave request was inconvenient,' he said in his cold, dark voice. 'So I declined it.'

My jaw ached. There'd been many times in the years I'd worked for Ulysses that I'd wanted to strangle him, because he did induce that kind of urge. But I had to admit that I'd never actually wanted to do it more than I did now.

'You know that I've accumulated nearly six months' worth of annual leave?' I pointed out, keeping my voice very level, as Ulysses was never moved by emotion. Only logic. 'I have to use it or else—'

'I'll pay it out.' One strong, long-fingered hand signed yet another paper in his bold, slashing signature.

I bit down on the urge to tell him what to do with his pay out. 'That's not the point. The point is that I haven't had a holiday in years.'

'So? Neither have I.'

It was true, he hadn't. Ulysses didn't take holidays. He barely even took weekends. Managing Black and White Enterprises, the multi-billion-dollar company he'd begun from some brilliant crypto-currency speculation, along with his friends Damian Blackwood— my brother—and Everett Calhoun took every hour of his time.

He didn't seem to mind. Then again, Ulysses didn't seem to have feelings at all, so who knew? He was a man who lived and breathed numbers, and his brilliance with money had enabled him to push Black and White into the stratosphere. His brilliance with people, however, was non-existent.

That was where I came in. I was more than just his personal assistant. I was his heart, or at least that was how I thought of it. He was the brain, all cold logic and strategy, while I was the heart, dealing with his staff, his colleagues, his contacts—basically anything that required personal interaction, as he had zero inter-personal skills.

Don't get me wrong. I loved my job. It was always different, always exciting, always challenging. But Ulysses was demanding, and I worked long hours, and sometimes, just sometimes, I wanted some time off.

Such as now. My brother had got married the previous week, which had prompted a certain amount of soul-searching. He was blissfully happy with Thea, his new wife, and their happiness had made me look at the emotional wasteland that was my own life.

Probably overly dramatic, but still. I was twenty-six and single. I'd never had a boyfriend and never had the opportunity to get myself one, given Ulysses owned all my time.

Not that I needed a man to complete me but, if I was going continue to be the heart of Ulysses's company, I needed something more than work in my life.

I was lonely. I'd spent years telling myself that I was fine, that I loved working and living in London, that I didn't need anything more than the challenge of working for Ulysses and Black and White. But perhaps I wasn't as fine as I'd thought.

If my former man-whore brother could find someone to share his life, why couldn't I?

'I am not you,' I said. 'And I need a holiday.'

'Too bad.' Ulysses didn't look at me, continuing to sign his stack of papers. 'I need you here. Especially with Damian and Everett still away.'

Frustration coiled inside me, but I ignored it. Ulysses

was uncomfortable with emotional displays, which wouldn't help my cause.

'I'll be much more productive after a break,' I argued. 'And it won't be for long. I'm thinking a week would—'

'What do you want a holiday for?' Ulysses picked up another piece of paper.

It was a genuine question. All his questions were genuine. Ulysses didn't do sarcasm and didn't understand it when it was directed at him. So I used it a lot for my own amusement, not to mention to let off steam, because dealing with Ulysses was a whole thing.

'Why does anyone want a holiday?' I asked. 'To have a break from work, relax, do things they want to do and not things they have to do.'

He kept on signing those wretched papers. 'What do you want to do?'

I eyed him. Interesting. He never asked me personal questions. 'Oh, you know, have an actual life for a change.'

'You already have an actual life.' He scrawled across another page.

'But not one like any other woman my age.'

'How would you know? Plenty of women your age have different kinds of lives.'

I gritted my teeth. 'I want to meet someone, Ulysses. Go out on a date. And maybe even get laid for once in my life.' I said the last merely for effect, but I should have known that Ulysses would take it seriously because he took everything seriously.

'You don't need to meet someone,' he said. 'You have me. I'll take you on a date, if that's what you want.'

Because he wasn't looking at me, I rolled my eyes at this typical response. 'And I suppose you can get me laid too?'

'Yes.' He didn't miss a beat, signing yet another paper. 'I can do that as well.'

This would have been a joke with any other man. But Ulysses didn't joke.

I nearly laughed. 'You've got to be kidding.'

'No, I'm not kidding.'

Of course he wasn't. He didn't know how to kid.

An inexplicable jolt of electricity shot through me. 'So, you're seriously offering to take me on a date? And then what? Have sex with me?'

He signed the last paper and finally looked up. 'Yes. I believe that's exactly what I said. Do I really need to repeat myself?'

I was conscious of a strange, twisting feeling in my gut. A familiar twisting feeling.

Because although Ulysses White might have zero people skills, he got away with it, because he was, quite simply, beautiful.

Not in the way my brother was beautiful—Damian was all warmth, all charm—but in the way a perfect diamond was beautiful. Or an iceberg. Or a mountain. Or a statue.

His features were sculpted: high cheekbones and a sharp jaw, an oddly sensual mouth and straight nose. It was an intensely masculine face and yet there was a distance to his beauty. A coldness. His looks were the kind that prompted worship rather than a desire to touch; his beauty was so sharp, you'd probably cut yourself on it.

His eyes were as black as his hair and as cold as the rest of him, glittering like obsidian, and for a second I didn't know what to say.

He meant it. He'd absolutely take me on a date and then he'd have sex with me. Which would have been a lot more flattering if it had been about me. But it wasn't. He'd never shown the slightest bit of sexual interest in me, which was just as well since not only was he my boss, he was my older brother's friend, and Damian would definitely have words to say about it.

Not that I cared about what words Damian would have said.

Do you care about Ulysses showing interest, though?

That strange little pulse went through me again.

Ulysses was very attractive and I'd have had to be blind not to notice. In fact, when I'd first started working for him, I'd developed a bit of a crush. However, that had soon vanished when it had become apparent he didn't seem to notice that I was even a woman. I'd have thought he wasn't interested in sex at all if it hadn't been for the fact that he often got me to find him female company of an evening.

Yes, I managed his little black book, and he had quite the stable despite his consistent lack of charm or anything approaching romance. I'd once asked one of them what drew them to him, and I'd expected it to be about the money or the power. But, though those were indeed attractive, it was more because he was very, *very* good in bed.

A fact I hadn't realised I'd filed away until now.

I knew getting offended would be pointless, as he hadn't meant to be offensive. He was only being his usual literal self.

'No, you don't need to repeat yourself,' I replied, his literalism meeting my calm. 'But you do realise that sexual relations between us would be problematic?'

He gave me the frown he always gave me when I confronted him with something puzzling. 'Why?'

'You're my boss and sleeping with the boss is generally not a good idea.'

'I don't see the problem. If you feel you'd be more productive after sex, then it seems logical that I should provide you with it.'

My cheeks warmed, which was stupid, given I'd never had a problem with Ulysses's blunt honesty before. 'I didn't say that I would be more productive after sex. I said I would be more productive after a holiday.'

'Yes. A holiday involving meeting someone, a date and some sex.'

Damn. Why had I said that? I'd let my irritation get the better of me, which had been a mistake. It always was with Ulysses.

My cheeks got even warmer and he noticed, his gaze narrowing. 'There's nothing to be embarrassed about, Morgan.'

'I'm not embarrassed,' I said automatically.

'Yes, you are. Does the thought of sex with me bother you?'

My stomach twisted again, a certain heated fantasy taking shape in my head of his hands holding me down, not letting me go. Of me struggling to get away, but knowing he was too strong. Of knowing that I'd never be able to get away from him no matter how hard I tried…

I shoved the shameful fantasy away. Hard.

'Again, you're my boss,' I said. 'It isn't appropriate. Come on, Ulysses. You know HR has a policy about this kind of thing. I helped you write it, remember?'

He ignored that completely, his gaze unwavering and very, very direct. 'It shouldn't bother you,' he went on, as if I hadn't spoken. 'I'm very good at it.' He said the words without any discernible smugness or triumph. As if it was an undisputed fact, as certain as gravity and that humans needed oxygen to breathe.

'I'm sure you are.' I took no notice of the feeling that kept twisting in my gut. 'But that doesn't change the policy.'

'Then I'll rewrite the policy.' He put his pen down, continuing to stare at me with the kind of unwavering concentration he normally only gave to his study of the stock market. 'If you need me to prove it to you, I can.'

'Prove it to me?' I repeated blankly. 'Prove what?'

He pushed his chair back and stood up, and just like that I became aware of him in a way I hadn't been before—or, at least, hadn't let myself be aware of before.

Six-foot-four and built like a rugby prop forward, his beautifully cut charcoal suit enhanced powerful shoulders and a broad chest, a lean waist and long legs. Just like his face, his body was nothing but sheer male perfection.

He rounded the desk and, with a jolt, I realised he was coming straight for me.

'Ulysses?' My voice sounded not quite as shocked as it should have. 'What the hell are you doing?'

CHAPTER TWO

Ulysses

MORGAN'S DEEP BLUE eyes were wide with surprise, which was puzzling. She'd told me what she wanted and I'd told her I'd provide it. And I would, given I couldn't let her have her annual leave, not with Damian and Everett being gone and the Black and White Foundation—the charity our company had just launched—getting off the ground. I needed her with me.

'What do you think I'm doing?' I frowned as she backed away. 'I told you I'd give you what you needed.'

'Now?' Her voice sounded breathy and there was a distinct glitter in her eyes. I recognised that glitter, because I'd trained myself to look for it. The glitter of a woman beginning to feel sexually aroused.

'Of course now.' She'd said she'd be more productive with a holiday, a date and sex, so there was little point in waiting. I preferred to act immediately once I'd made a decision and this was the most logical decision to make.

She'd backed up to the meeting table near the windows, putting her hands back to brace herself against it, still looking up at me, blue eyes wide.

Her face was pale and yet there was colour in her cheeks. She had perfectly symmetrical features. I'd heard people call her beautiful, though beauty didn't interest me. What interested me was the small beauty spot near the left-hand side of her top lip, the one flaw in her face. The one break in the pattern.

It bothered me. I couldn't explain why. In fact, it had been bothering me for a while now, and the fact that I was bothered was an issue. It was likely to be some kind of sexual response, in which case the best way to solve the issue was to have sex.

Which made her confession about needing a holiday come with perfect timing.

I stopped in front of her, staring down at her. She wore a dark blue pencil skirt and a white blouse with a bow at the neck. The bow was loose, beginning to come undone, revealing the pulse at the base of her throat. It was beating very fast.

I studied her face, searching for fear, which I did when I was with a woman. Morgan wasn't wrong—sex was a good way to relax—but I preferred sex a certain way and, as that way could be misinterpreted, I liked to make sure that the woman I was with didn't have problems with it. Especially as making a woman come was the whole point.

I'd never feel the same things other people did, I simply wasn't built that way, but I knew what physical pleasure was and I could give it to someone else. I could feel what they felt in that moment. I could…connect.

It was addictive. I liked to do it as often as I could, and it struck me that it was something I could give to Morgan.

'Really,' she murmured. 'Must you be so literal all the time?'

She often asked questions like this, which didn't seem to require an answer, since the answer was obvious.

Nevertheless, I replied anyway, just in case it wasn't obvious. 'Yes. I don't know how to be anything else.'

I couldn't stop studying her face. I wanted to tell her that her little mole bothered me, but I'd learned that women didn't appreciate having such things pointed out. I didn't understand why it bothered them, given none of those things were flaws—or at least, they weren't to me—but I didn't want to say anything that would bother her. I didn't understand that urge either, as I generally didn't concern myself with other people's feelings. Yet for some reason the thought of Morgan's feelings bothered me.

Perhaps it was because she was Damian's sister and I felt an obligation to her. He'd asked me to give her a job a few years ago, also asking me to look after her, and I'd initially refused since I ran a company, not a baby-sitting service. But Damian had argued that I needed someone to help me when dealing with people and that Morgan was very good at dealing with people.

He hadn't been wrong. She was good. Good enough that I simply couldn't do without her.

'You could pretend,' she said.

'What would be the point?' I took her chin between my fingers, holding her securely.

She went very still. 'What are you doing?'

I examined her face once more, but there were no signs of fear, only some other expression that I couldn't identify. Her pupils had dilated and I could hear her breath catch.

Her skin was very warm and very soft against my fingertips, a sensual pleasure I hadn't expected.

'I thought I'd give you some proof that I'm as good in bed as I said I was,' I said, a trifle irritated at having to explain. 'It's logical to try something out before you commit yourself.'

She blinked, her mouth gone very soft. It was red and it made me feel hungry all of a sudden, as if I wanted to take a bite out of it.

Careful. Be very careful.

I'd have to be. Some women had no problem with my particular desires, a lot even shared them, but I had a sense it would be different with Morgan. It was true that she was my employee, and having sexual relations with an employee wasn't looked on with approval these days. But if both parties agreed, what was the issue?

Still, Morgan had brought it up, which made it an issue for her, and anything that was an issue for her was also an issue for me.

She blinked again. 'I didn't realise you were going to offer proof right now. Especially when I haven't said that I actually want to have sex with you.'

I frowned. 'Your pupils are dilated and your cheeks are flushed. Your pulse is also very fast. All of which indicates a certain level of sexual arousal.' Moving my thumb experimentally, I stroked the line of her lower lip, testing the softness of it and watching her reaction. If I wasn't much mistaken, that little sound had been her breath catching again. 'Yes, you like me touching you, I think.'

'Ulysses…' Her voice sounded husky and the flush in her cheeks had deepened. 'I don't think this is a good idea.'

'Why not?' Again, I stared at the little mole to the side of her upper lip. It was dark against her pale skin, an almost perfect circle.

'Because you're my boss.'

'You've said that before and I fail to see the relevance.'

'A date first.' She sounded breathless. 'That's what I said. A date first before the sex.'

She smelled of jasmine. I wasn't sure if it was her perfume, her soap or what, but I liked it. It was sweet and I'd always had a fondness for sweet things.

'What does it matter whether the date comes before the sex?' I didn't like dates, mainly because they consisted of pointless small talk, and I couldn't do small talk. Sex was much easier for me. I rubbed my thumb over her bottom lip again, feeling her shiver beneath my hand. 'I can't promise that I'll be an entertaining date, but I can promise that you'll climax many times in my bed.'

I didn't think it was possible for her face to get any redder, or for her eyes to get even wider, but it seemed it was entirely possible.

How interesting. I'd never flustered Morgan Blackwood before. She got impatient with me, and sometimes angry, but I'd never made her eyes go smoky the way they were now. I'd never made her blush. And I wasn't sure why that made me feel good, when it had never occurred to me to fluster her before, but it did.

'Ulysses,' she said again.

But I was tired of arguing. 'I'm going to kiss you,' I said. 'Do you agree?' I always asked. I had to be careful with emotional cues, as I tended to miss them, and since a woman's climax was dependent on her enjoying the sexual interaction I always made sure she was a willing participant.

Morgan was trembling slightly. 'I…don't know.'

'Why don't you know?'

'Because…this is very sudden.' Her gaze dropped to my mouth and it made my cock harden.

It was an intriguing sensation. I'd never considered Morgan as a sex partner, mainly because of my association with her brother and his request that I look after her. Also, it had never occurred to me. Sex I could get from any woman, so why would I complicate matters by getting it from her?

Yet now I was considering doing just that, and it was an interesting prospect. What would she be like in bed? Would her body go pink and would she writhe beneath me? What would her climax look like? Would she scream, like some women did, or would she bury her face in the pillow? Or would she be silent, closing her eyes and panting as it washed over her? Would she like to be held down—a personal fantasy of mine—or would she struggle against my hold? Would she find being restrained a turn-on?

'Your body doesn't seem to find it sudden,' I pointed out.

'No, but my head needs to catch up.' She took a breath. 'You do understand that, don't you?'

'Yes.' I paused. 'Do you need a seduction?' Some women did before they felt they could participate. 'Or would you prefer me just to take the kiss without asking?' Again, something else that some women liked.

Her pupils dilated even further. 'I…beg your pardon?'

Was that a fear response? I couldn't tell. Further testing seemed to be required.

'I could force you into a kiss,' I explained, watching her face carefully. 'Some women enjoy it. They find it adds excitement.'

She was trembling harder now, the pulse at the base of her throat even faster. Her eyes were very dark, only a sliver of blue showing around the inky black of her pupils. 'I don't know.' Her voice was slightly thicker this time, her gaze dropping once more to my mouth. 'I don't know what I like.'

Interesting. Well, she might not know what she liked, but I'd given her the opportunity to say no and she hadn't said it. And, given how she was looking at my mouth, it seemed clear that she wasn't averse to the idea of kissing it.

So I tightened my grip on her chin. 'Let's find out, then,' I said. And I bent my head and covered her lips with mine.

CHAPTER THREE

Morgan

I DIDN'T KNOW what was happening. One minute I'd been complaining about Ulysses not approving my leave request, the next we were talking about sex, closely followed by him getting in my face, taking my chin in one large, capable hand and insisting on giving me proof of his bedroom skills.

And I hadn't pushed him away. I hadn't even said no.

I'd just stood there and let it happen as he'd bent his head and kissed me.

If I'd ever imagined Ulysses's kiss—and believe me, I hadn't—I'd have imagined it as cold and as passionless as his icy black eyes.

I was wrong.

His mouth was firm and not cold in the slightest. In fact, it was warm, so very, very warm. And there was a gentleness to the kiss that I hadn't expected, his lips brushing over mine, lightly testing.

A shudder worked its way down my spine and my lungs felt empty of air. All my awareness zeroed in on his mouth and how it felt on mine, and how very different it was from any other kisses I'd experienced in my life.

Not that I'd experienced very many. I'd gone to an exclusive girls' school back in Australia, where I'd grown up, and had always been conscious that Damian had worked very hard to send me there. I hadn't wanted to squander the educational opportunity by messing around, like some of my friends had.

Once I'd left school, I'd gone straight to London and had ended up working for Ulysses, and the long hours had pretty much cemented my status as a virgin. Until a few years later, when I'd decided I'd had enough and had used a dating app to finally get rid of my bloody hymen.

The experience had been dull and kind of awful so I hadn't been in any hurry to repeat it, happy to remain boyfriend-less for the next few years. Until Damian had got married. Until I'd realised that I was lonely and didn't want to be lonely any more.

Until bloody Ulysses White had kissed me.

It wasn't like the one time with that guy—I couldn't even remember his name… Brian Someone-or-other—whose kiss had been tentative, hesitant and awkward. I hadn't wanted any of those things. I'd wanted passion and intensity. I'd wanted to be gripped and held tight, and kissed as if he couldn't get enough of me. As if he was desperate for a taste.

Ulysses's grip tightened on my chin, holding me with exactly the right kind of firmness, taking control effortlessly and with a practised mastery that left me shaking. He touched his tongue to my bottom lip, tasting, coaxing, and I found myself opening up to him, letting him inside.

It was wrong to let him kiss me like this, to let him take it from me without asking. But he'd asked me what I'd liked and I'd told him I didn't know.

I was a liar. I did know. I just hadn't wanted to say— not when the last time I'd voiced my fantasies it had turned out badly. Yet somehow he'd known anyway, kissing me exactly the way I wanted him to.

The kiss deepened and I nearly moaned. His mouth was hot and he tasted spicy and rich, like a good, smoky whiskey.

My hands lifted to his chest, my fingers curling in the crisp cotton of his shirt. There was an ache inside me, a pulsing pressure between my thighs, and I had no idea why, since I'd never felt anything like this around him before. Never, ever.

His tongue stroked deep inside my mouth, and my head fell back, allowing him to kiss me deeper. I shut my eyes, his sensual flavour unravelling every expectation I had, coaxing me to respond, to kiss him back.

But I wanted more. Wanted harder. Rougher. To be shoved back against that desk, his mouth taking and taking…

Are you out of your goddamn mind?

My fantasy came to a screaming halt, realisation hitting me like a bucket of cold water. My boss of nearly eight years was kissing me in the middle of the day, in the middle of his office, because he wanted to give me proof that he was good in bed.

Because he'd offered to have sex with me.

And I was letting him.

What the hell was I doing?

I went to push him away, but he was already doing it, letting go of my chin and stepping back. And my body was so behind my brain that I almost followed him, almost kept hold of his shirt to keep that masterful mouth on mine.

He frowned, then smoothed his shirt where I'd been holding it. 'Well?' His voice was its usual cold self, as if he hadn't just kissed me silly. 'Is that proof enough for you?'

I surreptitiously braced myself on the table behind me, my knees weak. 'Proof enough?' I echoed, my thought processes sluggish. 'What?'

His expression turned impatient. 'Proof enough that I know what I'm doing when it comes to sex.'

I tried to kick-start my stupid brain. Yes, that was why he'd kissed me. Because of what I'd said about a holiday. About meeting someone and dating and… Shit. Getting laid.

What had possessed me to say that? What had possessed me to stand there and let him kiss me?

You liked the kiss, though.

I shivered, trying to ignore how hot and sensitised my mouth felt and how his rich, spicy flavour lingered on my tongue. Trying to ignore how much I'd liked the firm way he'd held me and the confident mastery of the kiss.

Because, even if I'd liked it, I couldn't let anything more happen. He was my boss and, no matter what he said, sleeping with him would complicate matters. If I was going to meet a man, it had to be one who was not related to my working life in any way.

I leaned against the table, annoyed that I was the one getting all weak-kneed while he stood there in his usual way, as if nothing touched him.

I knew Ulysses did actually have feelings. He was highly uncomfortable in social situations, and when he was uncomfortable he got agitated and angry. Just as when he was involved in a project that consumed his attention, he'd sometimes hum under his breath, which meant he was happy. Or at least content.

But he didn't look angry now, and he wasn't humming, and that meant he didn't feel anything. It bothered me. Almost as if I wanted him to be as affected by that kiss as I'd been, which was ridiculous.

'Well?' he demanded, impatient with my silence.

'It was a…very effective demonstration,' I said, clearing my throat.

'Yes,' he agreed with his customary self-confidence. 'Of course it was.'

'But I'm still going to have to decline. I can't have sex with you, Ulysses.'

His frown became ferocious. He wasn't often thwarted, got irritated when he was, and he clearly was now. 'Why not?' he demanded. 'You were very aroused by that kiss, I could tell.'

I could feel my cheeks get hot again. 'You're still my boss.'

'So? I understand that complicates things for you, but it wouldn't complicate anything at all for me.'

I tried not to sigh. 'That's kind of the point. I don't want to go to bed with someone who doesn't really want me.'

His frown became a scowl, his black eyes focusing on me intently. 'You think I'm not sexually aroused by you?'

'Well, I—'

'Give me your hand.' He held out his commandingly.

I swallowed, having a good idea of where this was going. 'Ulysses...'

'Give me your hand.'

I extended my hand and, sure enough, he brought my palm down over the fly of his trousers. The wool was warm and smooth, and I expected to feel nothing but distaste for the hard ridge I could feel there. Yet instead of distaste electricity whispered over my skin. He was hotter than I'd expected, and so much harder. Long and thick...

Awareness filtered through me that it was his cock I had my hand on, and that there was no doubting the fact that he was hard. Very, *very* hard.

He might only have offered to sleep with me for the sake of my so-called productivity, but his body wanted me. Sure, he might have got hard for any random woman, but here, right now, that random woman was me.

And you like that. You like that a lot.

He was a powerful man, the head of a multi-billion-dollar company. He snapped his fingers and the stock markets fell or rose, depending on what he was doing. CEOs of other major companies rushed to do his bidding. He probably owned half of London.

And yet I, a little nobody from Sydney, Australia, held him in the palm of my hand.

'You see?' His obsidian eyes glittered. 'I'm hard for you.'

I wanted to pull my hand away and have him press his down on mine, holding it there. But that would mean giving in to those very wrong urges, so I left my hand where it was. Not that it was a bad place for it to be. The hard line of his cock burned against my palm and, inexplicably, I wanted to close my hand around it, see what he'd do if I did.

You know what he'd do.

A shiver ghosted along my skin, raising goose bumps. Yes, I did know. He wouldn't hesitate. He wouldn't be shy. He'd lift me up on this table and he'd push me down and I...

Crap. Stop. I wasn't going there with Ulysses, and certainly not with *that* particular fantasy.

'That's got nothing to do with me,' I said coolly, finally dropping my hand from him. 'That's only because I happen to be female.'

'Of course it's got something to do with you.' He

sounded irritated. 'I wouldn't have kissed you if you were male, because I'm straight.'

Literal. Always so literal.

'What I mean is that you're not attracted to me in particular,' I pointed out, trying to be patient.

'No.' Ulysses's stare was unrelenting. 'It's true that I wasn't attracted to you before. But I am now.'

'What? Just like that?'

'Yes.' His gaze roved over me. 'Do you want me to kiss you again? Or perhaps I shouldn't ask. You liked it when I did that just before.'

My mouth had gone dry. He was only this intense when he was focused on a particular project, and only when he was really interested in it. He'd never looked at me that way before, and I couldn't understand why I liked it. And I did like it. I *really* liked it.

Because no one has ever looked at you that way before.

It was true. Not even my single, solitary date. He hadn't looked at me as if I'd been fascinating, and he definitely hadn't taken a kiss from me. He hadn't taken hold of me at all, and when he'd touched me it had been hesitant. So I'd asked—awkwardly—if he could hold me tighter, kiss me harder, perhaps even hold me down. He'd been horrified, looking at me as if I'd been crazy, so I'd never mentioned it again. To anyone.

But I hadn't even had to ask Ulysses. He'd simply taken that kiss the way I'd secretly longed a man do, and his grip on my chin had been perfect. And I'd had the sense that I could have pushed against his hard chest and he wouldn't have moved. Wouldn't have let me go…

My breathing ramped up, the thought of him grabbing me and kissing me again exciting, though along with the excitement came a sense of shame. My one-night-stand had made me feel bad about what I'd wanted and part of me had agreed with him. Because, seriously, what woman got excited about the thought of being held down? Of struggling against a man far stronger and more powerful than she was? Of not being able to escape?

You do.

Yeah, but why? What was it about me? Maybe it was the whole wrongness of it, which was a whole can of worms I hadn't expected to open. At least, not right now.

God. I'd only applied for some bloody leave.

'You're not going to approve my leave application?' I pushed myself away from the table, struggling to get back on track.

'Of course I'm not,' Ulysses snapped. 'Not with the Black and White Foundation party coming up. I need you, Morgan, and there'll be no more discussion about it.'

Damn him. I shouldn't be surprised, though. When he made up his mind about something, he seldom changed it. And, as reluctant as I was to admit it, the upcoming party for Black and White Enterprises' new charity for underprivileged kids was a worthy cause. We wanted to thank the donors for their generosity and, as it was a purely social occasion, Ulysses would want me to handle it personally, because he couldn't.

'Now,' he went on in his characteristically impatient way. 'Answer the question, please.'

Right. The question. About kisses and whether I wanted him just to take them…

To be perfectly honest, I didn't want to think about that, because I knew the answer would be yes. And possibly want him to take more than a kiss. Which meant no, it wasn't happening.

'I'd rather not talk about this just now,' I said with as much dignity as I could muster. 'In fact, could we forget about the entire thing?'

But he showed no sign either of moving to let me pass or forgetting about anything. 'We can't forget about it. And it doesn't solve the fact that you said you wanted a holiday in order to be more productive.'

Bloody man. He wasn't going to let me sweep this whole embarrassing incident under the carpet, was he? And, yes, it was embarrassing. For me.

Oh, come on, you're intrigued—don't deny it.

I couldn't deny it. But I didn't want to confront that just yet, at least not while he was in my immediate vicinity. 'Fine,' I snapped back. 'I'll think about it, okay?'

And, before he could reply, I pushed past him and went out, slamming his office door behind me.

CHAPTER FOUR

Ulysses

I worked late that night, as per usual, but I found it difficult to concentrate. I kept getting distracted by the memory of Morgan's face after I'd kissed her. By the red flush in her cheeks and how pouty and full her mouth had looked. By that beauty spot above her mouth and how it bothered me. How it made me want to taste it.

The whole thing was annoying, especially the way she'd walked out of my office without answering my question. She hadn't come back either, and when I'd asked one of my secretaries to find her I was told she'd gone home with a headache.

Morgan never got headaches, though, which meant she'd excused herself from work for some other reason.

Normally I wouldn't have wasted my time trying to sort out what that reason could be, because my time was literally money. But Morgan's presence was vital and I didn't like that she'd absented herself without telling me.

Why had she done that? She often did inexplicable things, but I didn't tend to notice unless they actively impacted on me. Such as her way with people, and how she managed to make them smile, and how she talked to them so easily. She didn't get impatient and was able to navigate social situations with an adeptness I admired, because it wasn't something I could do myself. I had very few weaknesses but I didn't like social gatherings. People irritated me and I couldn't be bothered with the pointless small talk that seemed to be required whenever more than two people were in a room. Business topics I had no issues with, but when conversations included things like the weather, the traffic and how people were feeling that day then I got impatient.

It was all meaningless to me. All pointless. I didn't understand the jokes people made and I often had the sense that there were unspoken discussions being had that I wasn't a part of, discussions that everyone else could understand. Before Morgan had come to work for me, I hadn't attended any social gatherings, but since she'd become my assistant and handled those situations for me I could deal with them in a limited way.

What was especially irritating, though, was that the Black and White Foundation donors seemed to require a party to thank them for their donations. I wasn't sure why they needed to be thanked, as the cause was good, but Morgan had assured me that people liked to be acknowledged for their charity.

I'd been hoping Damian would be back so he could go in my stead but since he and Everett had seemingly both disappeared off the face of the earth it was left to me to deal with it.

Or rather, Morgan. Which meant I couldn't approve her leave right now.

I glared at my computer screen, unable to stop thinking about how she'd walked out of my office earlier that day. She'd gone very quickly, almost as if she'd wanted to get out fast. Was she angry with me for refusing her request?

She hadn't been pleased, but surely she understood how important the foundation was? I couldn't allow her a holiday, but I had offered to give her the other things she'd wanted. Or was it about something else?

She was confusing about the kiss.

I leaned back in my chair and swivelled it round so I faced the windows and the lights of London spread out beneath me. I liked looking at those lights. They showed me the patterns of the streets and I could map the entire city in my head. It was soothing.

Except the lights weren't soothing tonight. My cock was hard—irritating, given I couldn't concentrate when I needed sex.

I couldn't get the taste of Morgan's mouth out of my head.

She'd liked the kiss, and she'd liked it when I'd mentioned taking another one from her, and I didn't understand why she hadn't admitted it. I didn't understand why she didn't want to accept my offer of sex either, when it was clear the thought had excited her. I knew she had reservations about me being her boss, and that she needed some time to think about it, but she'd already had...what? A good six hours. Surely that was enough time?

I reached for my phone, deciding against a text and calling her instead.

The phone rang for a long time, which was strange, because normally she answered on the second ring. But this time she didn't answer until the tenth, and when she did she sounded tired. 'What is it, Ulysses? Can I not have a single evening without you in it?'

'I'm not anywhere near your evening. I'm here at the office.'

'Are you ever anywhere else?'

'Sometimes.' Surely that was obvious? 'Sometimes I'm at home. Why do you ask?'

She sighed. 'It's fine. I was just being sarcastic.'

I scowled at the lights outside. 'Well, don't be. You know I don't like it when you are.'

'Well, I don't like it when you kiss me out of the blue.' Her voice sounded less tired and more sharp.

'It wasn't out of the blue. I told you I was going to kiss you.' I began the process of mapping the city again, following the lights, trying to soothe the agitation inside me. 'You went home today without telling me.'

'I had a headache. I thought you wouldn't mind.'

Lies were difficult for me to pick up on, especially with people I didn't know, but I knew when Morgan was lying because her voice got very flat. And it was very flat now. 'You don't sound sorry,' I said. 'And you didn't have a headache. And, yes, I do mind.'

There was a silence.

'How do you know I didn't have a headache?' she asked.

'Because you've never gone home with a head-ache before.' I felt restless all of a sudden, impatient. I didn't want to talk about her headache or why she'd gone home. Those things were murky and difficult to grasp, especially when what I really wanted was to kiss her again. 'Have you thought about it?'

'Thought about what?'

'About whether or not you want to take up my offer of sex. You've had about six hours to think about it, which should be more than enough time.'

She was silent.

'Are you worried I'll require a relationship from you?' Perhaps that was what was causing her doubt. 'You needn't, if so. I don't have relationships with the women I sleep with.'

'That's…not what I'm worried about.'

'But you still haven't made up your mind?'

'Ulysses.' Her voice was now quiet. 'Why are you pursuing this so hard? Why not call one of your other women if you want sex so very badly?'

I studied the lights outside, uncomfortable at the thought of confessing this to her, though I had no reason to be. 'I don't want one of those other women. I want you.'

'Oh,' she said.

People didn't say no to me. They always did what I told them, gave me what I asked for, and there were only two people in the entire world who wouldn't do those things.

Damian and Everett were those two people.

But I was beginning to realise that there was a third. Morgan.

'This…wouldn't affect our working relationship, would it?' she asked after a long moment.

'Why would it?'

'No.' She sighed. 'I suppose it wouldn't with you.'

'Of course not. Sex has nothing to do with our working relationship except where it affects your productivity.'

'I'm beginning to wish I'd never said that,' she muttered.

'But you did say it.'

She was reluctant and I didn't know why. It puzzled me, irritated me. Her body had been ready, but her head hadn't, or so she'd said, and she'd needed time. Neither of those things should have bothered me. If she didn't want to accept my offer, then I shouldn't have given it another thought. I had plenty of other women who were happy to accept what I had to give.

But it wasn't other women that I wanted and I understood that now.

It was Morgan.

I shut my eyes, closing out the view of the lights and the fascinating pattern, concentrating on her voice. It was easier to talk to her on the phone, where I didn't have her face in front of me with all those expressions crossing it. Expressions that didn't match with her tone and that I couldn't interpret. With only her voice, there were no other distractions. I could parse the meanings in it.

'Tell me,' I said, because I wanted to know, 'Is it other sexual experiences that are making you reluctant? Have you not had physical pleasure before with a partner?'

Yet more silence.

Was she offended? I couldn't tell.

'That's none of your business.' Her voice sounded crisp. But then she always sounded crisp.

'It's most definitely my business if you're going to have sex with me,' I pointed out. 'And I can promise you that, if you do, it'll be a better experience than any you've had before. In fact, I can assure you that you'll never have another like it.'

She made a choking sound. 'You're incredibly arrogant. You know that, right?'

People had told me that before, though I didn't understand why. I *was* good at a great many things, and sex was one of them. I saw no reason to pretend otherwise.

'Would you rather have sex with someone who didn't know what they were doing?' I asked.

'No,' she said after a moment. 'I suppose not.'

Her answer didn't surprise me, because was there anyone who'd want to waste time on an experience that would only be disappointing? With me she'd know exactly what she'd be getting: nothing but pleasure and I could guarantee it.

'No,' I replied, satisfied. 'Of course you wouldn't. And it's not just pleasure I can give you, Morgan, but I can also promise that you'll be safe with me. You can trust me to look after you both before sex and afterwards—completely.'

She made another inarticulate noise. 'Well, when you put it like that…'

'Good.' Obviously she'd decided. 'I'll be round in fifteen minutes.' And I disconnected the call.

CHAPTER FIVE

Morgan

FIFTEEN MINUTES? WAS he kidding?

I stared at the wall of my tiny kitchen, my phone clutched in my hand.

Ulysses had disconnected before I could say a word and now he was coming here. In fifteen minutes.

Shit.

'You bloody stupid bastard,' I muttered to him, and maybe a little to myself as well, because clearly I hadn't been obvious enough. And with Ulysses I had to be obvious, since he didn't understand subtle.

If you'd wanted to tell him no, you should have said no.

But I hadn't said no. Or even, 'No, I don't want to sleep with him—not now, not ever.'

When I'd walked out of his office earlier, I'd told him I'd think about it, but what I'd actually intended to do was go on with my day as if nothing had happened. And yet I'd found I couldn't stop thinking about him, that kiss and my own intense reaction to him. In the end I hadn't been able to concentrate on work so I'd invented a headache and had taken myself off home to contemplate my life choices.

I hadn't expected him to call me. I thought he'd get distracted by work and completely forget what had happened in his office.

Apparently not.

So what now?

Good question. My subconscious was clearly up to something, as I hadn't managed the word no, which must mean that, yes, I was seriously contemplating sleeping with Ulysses.

Was I insane?

I'd never done anything outrageous or inappropriate before. I wasn't into rocking the boat. I liked my boats steady and firm underfoot, with absolutely no rocking of any kind.

My only rebellion was the occasional burst of sarcasm when Ulysses was being an utter tool.

A small rebellion. Just like my life. Small and narrow. Confined.

Safe.

Since when had I let it come to this? To long hours spent at work, living in a tiny flat in London? Going nowhere and seeing no one? The same routine, day in, day out? The only contact I had being with a man who didn't understand me?

I tossed the phone back down on the kitchen counter and paced over to the window, looking out onto the lights of the street below.

I lived in a tiny apartment in the city, a studio flat. I could have afforded bigger, given Ulysses paid me very well, but I'd never seen the point of having something big when it was just me living in it. I didn't want to rattle around in some vast space, fully aware of how on my own I was.

A safe, small little life contained in a tiny flat.

Yay, you.

I frowned at the night outside my windows.

I liked my own company. I was perfectly happy living by myself. I was perfectly happy with my job. I'd gone straight from school to London after Damian had got me a position as Ulysses's personal assistant. Do not pass go. Do not collect two hundred dollars. Sometimes I wished I'd had some time to live a little before then. But I also knew that Damian wanted the best for me and he'd worked his butt off to help me get where I was today.

It wasn't that I wasn't grateful. I just wanted something…more.

Something that wasn't safe or so confined.

Something that rocked my very stable boat just a little.

Such as sex with your infuriating boss? Passionate sex? Rough, wild sex?

A shiver slid down my spine. An excited shiver.

He'd assured me I'd have a better experience than any I'd had before. That I'd never have another experience like it, and that wasn't an empty promise. I'd called him arrogant, and he was, but only because that arrogance was thoroughly justified. Socially he might be at sea, but he knew his company inside out, saw the big picture as well as the small. He knew exactly what was happening where and at any given time. He'd told me once that he saw Black and White Enterprises like an engine, every part fitting perfectly together and moving as one. It made it easy for him to see what was going wrong and how he needed to fix it, and he did so every time, with precision.

If he does this with his company, how would it feel if he did this with sex?

Another shudder worked its way down my spine.

If I told him what I wanted, would he give it to me? Would he judge me the way one-night-stand guy had?

You know he wouldn't.

He'd asked me if I'd wanted to be forced into the kiss, which presumably meant he didn't have a problem with doing so. And if he didn't have a problem with doing that, perhaps he wouldn't have a problem with other things…

I swallowed, my mouth dry, a pulse of hunger going through me.

Perhaps that's why I didn't want to ask him for those things. Because I knew he'd give them to me and then I'd have to confront the reality of my own dark fantasies.

The lights of the city twinkled beyond the glass, a reminder that life was going on outside the four walls of my flat. Life that, if I wasn't careful, would pass me by.

I didn't want it to pass me by. I didn't want to wait

until my leave was approved or find myself another man. Not when Ulysses was offering me what I wanted *now*.

My doorbell buzzer went off, jolting me.

It would be Ulysses. He was nothing if not punctual.

My heartbeat went into overdrive as I moved into my tiny lounge area and over to the intercom, my dry mouth going even drier. I was really going to do this, wasn't I?

My fingers shook as I pressed the button. 'Ulysses?'

'Yes.' His deep, cold voice seem to fill my entire flat. 'I said I'd be fifteen minutes. Do you need me to provide you with some ID?'

'ID?' For a second I had no idea what he was talking about.

'You have no security in this building.' He sounded appalled. 'I could be anyone pressing this button.'

The offence in his voice made something tense inside me relax. It was such a Ulysses thing to say.

'I know it's you.' I smiled a little. 'I recognise your voice.'

'Someone could have made their voice sound like me. There's some very sophisticated software out there these days.'

'Ulysses—'

'I'll make a note to get Everett onto it. You can't be buzzing anyone up to your flat. In fact…' He sounded as though he was leaning away from the speaker and looking around. 'This whole building is an utter disgrace security-wise. It's not good enough, Morgan.' He sounded louder this time and three thousand times more offended. 'You need to find somewhere safer.'

'Since when have you ever been interested in the security of my flat?'

'Since now,' he snapped. 'Are you going to buzz me up?'

'I didn't actually agree, you know,' I reminded him, deciding he needed to have this pointed out. 'I never said yes.'

'Well, do you say yes now?' he asked grumpily.

Amusement soothed my jangling nerves; he did so hate it when he'd made a mistake.

'What would you do if I didn't?' Teasing him was wrong, since he didn't like it. But I couldn't help myself.

'I'd go back to the office, of course.' He sounded really annoyed now. 'Stop wasting time, Morgan.'

I *was* wasting time. And putting off the moment when I said yes. Because I knew, as soon as I let him up into my flat, that would be it. My path would be chosen and there'd be no going back.

But I was already sick of myself and my nerves, so I reached out and hit the button that opened the downstairs door.

And that was when it struck me: I was standing there waiting for him dressed in a pair of my oldest and most comfortable pyjama bottoms, a very baggy and very thin T-shirt, my hair loose and no make-up whatsoever.

Super-sexy.

I debated making a run to the bedroom and finding some decent jeans, or something to wear instead of my PJs, but I hadn't taken more than a step in that direction before the sound of knocking came from my front door.

Ulysses was already here.

Bugger it.

I took a breath then strode over to the front door and opened it.

And there he was, larger than life and twice as gorgeous, unbearably hot in the dark suit and crisp white shirt he'd been wearing earlier. He had on a red tie today and the splash of colour glowed jewel-bright against the white.

Red for passion, an inane part of my brain whispered to me as his dark gaze collided with mine.

'There you are.' His cold voice held a hot note I'd never heard him use before.

Then, before I could say another word, he strode in.

He didn't pause to look around. He didn't look around at all. He simply came for me as if I were a prize he'd been waiting for years to claim.

A hot thrill arrowed straight down my spine, a secret part of me finding his intensity unbearably exciting.

He came to a stop bare inches away, tall, dark and utterly compelling. 'First,' he said without preamble, 'We need to discuss the rules.'

My brain had gone into free fall. He was so close, making me very aware of his height, reminding me of that kiss and the heat of his mouth. The clean, fresh bite of his aftershave wove around me, a sharp piny smell that made me think of forests freshly dusted with snow.

'Rules?' I echoed blankly. 'What rules?'

'It's very important that we have ground rules and

that we both agree on them.' He frowned slightly. 'Traffic lights.'

'Traffic lights? What are you talking about?'

'Green for "go". Amber for "keep going but carefully". Red for "stop".'

'I don't…'

'Sex,' he explained. 'If you don't like something, say red and I'll stop. Green for go. Amber for—'

'Keep going but carefully. Yes, I get it.' I swallowed, my face getting hot. 'So we're getting into it straight away? You don't want a drink or something first?'

He gave me a look as if it was the strangest question he'd ever heard. 'No, why would I?'

'Some girls like a little romance, you know,' I said tartly, nervous, but annoyed with myself for being nervous.

'I don't do romance, Morgan.'

Instantly, I felt bad, because something in his face shut down. Something that had been bright and hot, that I hadn't realised was there until it had vanished.

Normally he wouldn't let one of my snarky comments bother him, but he was clearly bothered now. And that told me something: he wanted this. He wanted me.

And I wanted him to want me.

'I'm sorry,' I said. 'I don't need romance. I'm just… nervous.'

He regarded me, his black eyes cool. 'Is that a red?'

'No.' I made it as certain as I could. 'It's not.'

'If it's a red, you need to be clear.'

Of course. If this was a big deal for me, then it was

also a big deal for him. He couldn't read cues easily, which made his need for rules understandable.

'If it's a red, you'll stop,' I said, less of a question and more a statement of fact.

'Of course I'll stop. That's the whole point of rules. Everyone follows them.'

Which makes him the safest man you'll ever be with.

The flash of realisation made me blink. Yes, he *was* safe. He'd never hurt me any way, and his emphasis on rules only cemented that fact.

Where would I find another man safe enough with whom to explore those rough sex fantasies of mine? A man I trusted enough to take care of me? Perhaps I'd never find one. Perhaps I'd never be able to explore the darker corners of my imagination, the forbidden desires I tried never to think about. The ones I barely admitted I wanted even to myself…

It's him. Or no one.

I shuddered as the truth settled down inside me. And he saw, his black gaze piercing, the bright, hot thing I'd noticed in his eyes before igniting once again.

He took a step closer, now only inches away.

I caught my breath, his physical nearness hitting me like a blow. His height and the broad width of his chest were things I'd never consciously thought of before, but I was thinking about them now. And the heat of his body, warm stone on a hot summer's day. He'd feel like that too. I knew it. If I put my hand on his chest, it would feel exactly like stone. Unyielding. I wouldn't be able to push him away even if I wanted to.

He must have read my thoughts, I swear, because he took my hand, lifting it to his chest palm-down and holding it there.

Hot. He was so hot. I could feel that heat through the cotton of his business shirt. And so hard, too. I'd got that right. Exactly like warm stone.

My heartbeat was so loud I couldn't hear anything else and I felt dizzy.

His gaze on me was an intense pressure. But I couldn't meet it. Something would happen to me if I did, and I didn't know what that something would be. I was afraid of it.

He didn't say anything, only held my hand to his chest, his palm warm on my skin. Then his other hand was on my hip, sliding round to the small of my back, urging me closer, and my heartbeat got even faster. I tried to stand my ground, but he didn't let me, his strength irresistible, drawing me relentlessly up against him.

I quivered with excitement at that strength, at being pulled to him, even though I tried to resist.

'Look at me,' he ordered, a hot, dark note vibrating in his voice. 'Look at me, Morgan.'

I didn't want to, afraid of how excited I was. Of how much this whole thing was turning me on.

But then I'd always been afraid of those desires inside me, the ones that made me desperate to be held by a strong man, to fight to get away and yet not be able to. To have him hold me effortlessly and easily and to be overwhelmed by him…

I didn't want to know why I wanted those things. I didn't want to know what it was about me that liked it.

You didn't want life to pass you by. So don't let it.

That was true. And I wasn't a coward. I'd endured the fancy boarding school Damian had sent me to, then endured being sent halfway across the world to a city I'd never been to, to do a job I didn't know anything about, working for a man I'd never met.

And now here was an opportunity to explore something about myself that I'd never had the chance to before. With a man who wouldn't judge me and who'd keep me safe. Why was I even hesitating?

I lifted my chin and met Ulysses's gaze.

Blacker than pitch. The kind of black that had weight and heat. Heavy, dense. But not cold. No, not cold any longer.

Still looking down at me, he took one hand in his, then the other one that was resting on his chest, and then, with that same relentless, irresistible strength, he drew them behind my back and held them there, restraining me with pathetic ease.

And he watched me the whole time as my heartbeat accelerated through the roof.

CHAPTER SIX

Ulysses

SHE LIKED IT. I could see that by the flush in her cheeks and by how her blue eyes darkened, her pupils dilating. She was breathing fast as well, soft, breathy little pants.

All of that could have been fear, but it wasn't. I'd seen enough arousal in enough women to know the difference. I might have trouble reading people's expressions, but physiology didn't lie. I knew. I'd studied it. I'd made it my mission to overcome my own vulnerabilities, especially when it came to women.

And I'd had no complaints.

Besides, I knew Morgan very well. I'd been working with her for years and hers was a face I was familiar with.

Also, I'd told her the rules. She knew 'red' meant stop.

But what if she doesn't say it?

A thread of something I didn't like wound through me. I ignored it. Of course she'd say it. She knew how important rules were to me.

Still, I studied her carefully. She felt very good against me, very warm, very soft. It was interesting to see her like this, to see her flushed and breathing fast, obviously physically aroused.

At work she was always professional, always capable and confident. In fact, now I thought about it, I'd never seen her less than confident, which irritated me on occasion. She knew things about people I didn't and I didn't like not knowing. Being at a disadvantage infuriated me, made me feel the way I had when I'd been ten and Uncle John used to take me into the casinos, using my talents with patterns for his own ends. I hadn't understood about greed then. I'd thought it was because he liked me, one of the few foster parents who had.

But he hadn't liked me. He'd only used me. Trusting him had been a mistake and one I wouldn't repeat. I hadn't trusted a soul since, not until I'd met Damian and Everett.

Not until Morgan.

Maybe. Certainly I trusted her when it came to dealing with other people. Yet it was also good to have her at a disadvantage now. She might know how to deal with people, but she didn't know so much about sexual desire—that was clear.

But I did.

'You like this?' I kept a firm hold on her wrists, making sure her soft, warm body was pressed to mine. 'You like me restraining you?'

Her throat moved as she swallowed. A sign of nervousness. Yet this time her gaze didn't flicker. 'Y-yes.'

Satisfaction wound through me. Of course, I was right. She did like it. 'So are we green?' I asked, just to make sure.

'I…' She stopped and took another of those little breaths. 'Yes, green.'

I held her tighter, my fingers on the underside of her wrists monitoring her pulse. It fluttered, fast and frantic, against my fingertips. Her pupils dilated even further and her body relaxed against mine, her sweet jasmine scent turning musky with arousal.

Indeed, everything was green. Good.

Slowly, I began to walk her backwards.

I'd had a few plans of what I wanted to do with her tonight, thinking about them as I'd made my way to her flat. Her terrible security had irritated me, making me second-guess my initial thoughts, and then she'd been uncertain about opening the door.

But she had and I couldn't deny that, the moment I'd stepped into her flat and seen her standing there not looking like Morgan Blackwood, my PA, but someone I'd never seen before, I knew.

My initial plans, based on the kiss I'd given her, were the correct ones. And not only for her, but for me as well.

I'd liked the way she'd been looking at me, as if I was as much a stranger to her as the woman in dinosaur pyjamas rather than a pencil skirt was to me. And I liked it because I knew I irritated her, made her impatient. That sometimes, in those social situations I hated attending, she'd look at me with the same impatience that Uncle John had used to.

I didn't let that bother me with other people; I didn't care about them. But it was different with Morgan. I didn't like that irritation.

So to have her now, all wide eyes and a frantic pulse, dilated pupils and a softly open mouth… Yes, it was very, *very* satisfying.

I kept walking until I'd backed her against the wall of her small lounge. It was covered with cream wallpaper textured with patterns of climbing ivy. I wanted to look at the patterns, because the repeats were clever, but the sound of Morgan's soft gasp as she hit the wall brought me back to what was happening.

Her. Pressed against me.

A tremor shook her.

I was very hard, but I could ignore my physical needs for long periods of time, and I did so now in favour of watching her face.

'Tell me what you want,' I said, making it an order to see how she'd respond. 'I need to know what you like in order to make this experience the best it can be.'

'I…' She faltered. The fast way she was breathing made the soft curves of her breasts press against my chest. I found the sensation exquisite.

'You…what? You don't know? Or you don't want to say?'

She blinked rapidly. The heat between her thighs was very noticeable. I could feel it even through the wool of my suit trousers. 'I find it difficult to…talk about.'

'Why? What do you find difficult to talk about? Explain.'

She took another few breaths, as if she was gasping for air, the expression in her blue eyes unreadable to me. 'I've only slept with one man. And when I told him what I liked he…he told me he wouldn't do those things. That he thought they were wrong.'

That didn't surprise me. Not the part about only having one lover—I didn't care how many she'd had—but that she'd been shamed for voicing her desires. People had very strange attitudes when it came to sex.

Myself, I'd found out very early on what I preferred. As soon as I'd earned my first ten thousand pounds from some online investments when I was sixteen, I'd gone to the finest brothel I could find and paid the first prostitute I'd liked the look of to teach me. I'd been lucky; she'd been an older woman, in the business by choice because she enjoyed it. She'd been very patient, teaching me many things about myself, including that I liked rough sex.

Because it was in those moments, when I allowed sexual desire to overwhelm me, that I could almost understand people and how they felt when they were happy. When they were in love. All the good emotions I didn't understand and never would.

The woman that night had told me I had to be careful with my preferences. That I had to make sure my partner was willing and that there needed to be rules, so it was pleasurable for all. I'd listened to her. I'd also discovered that I liked making women come, so it was important to me that they enjoyed themselves.

Clearly Morgan's partner hadn't thought the same.

It made me angry to think he hadn't cared at all about her pleasure.

'Why didn't you find someone else?' I asked.

She'd lowered her lashes, veiling her gaze. 'Does it matter? It's no big deal.'

I let go one of her hands and put my fingers under her chin, forcing her head back so I could see her eyes and the expression she was trying to hide from me. 'It does matter,' I said. 'And it is a big deal. I like to make a woman come, which makes knowing what she likes very important.'

Morgan trembled, her eyes darkening. It was clear she very much liked me taking control. 'He made me feel bad about what I wanted, so I didn't want to talk about it with anyone else. And the sex we had was kind of dull anyway, and I just thought I couldn't be missing out on much.'

Anger coiled more tightly inside me at the man who'd judged her so unnecessarily and made her feel bad about what she liked.

'You are missing out,' I told her, because it was true. 'Good sex is a basic human need.'

'Not one I've never needed.'

'That's a lie. If you didn't need it, your pussy wouldn't be quite so hot and your nipples wouldn't be hard.'

Her mouth opened then shut, the flush in her cheeks becoming fiery.

'You like me holding you,' I went on. 'You like me taking control. Why won't you admit it?'

'Why do you think?' Her eyes were wide and dark.

'Because that's what he thought was so wrong. He didn't want to hold me down. He didn't want me to resist. He told me it was wrong, that women shouldn't like stuff like that in this day and age.'

'That's ridiculous,' I snapped. 'Many women like it. And some men too. Why did you believe him?'

Her throat moved against my palm. 'I…don't know. Maybe because I didn't know that. Because I was unsure. I haven't done it with anyone else.'

I could understand that. She had no points of reference. 'In that case, you can explore those fantasies with me. I like rough sex, so we should suit perfectly.'

She blinked, though whether it was with shock or mere surprise I couldn't tell. 'You…do?'

'Yes. I have those rules for a reason.'

'Oh.' Her gaze flickered and she turned her head, looking away.

I frowned. Was this a test? Did she want me to make her look at me?

I firmed my grip experimentally and felt a shudder go through her. Yes, definitely a test. Carefully, I forced her chin up and her head back, so she had to look at me, then adjusted my hold, my fingers gripping her jaw. She shivered, her breath catching audibly.

'One thing,' I murmured. 'I'd like it if you were clear with me about what you want. And, just so you know…' I flexed my fingers on her jaw, feeling her tremble '…I have no problems at all with those kinds of fantasies.'

'Oh,' she said again, though this time it was on a long breath.

'Well?'

She was silent a long time, looking at me, the pulse racing at the base of her throat. Then she said, 'I want you to hold me down, Ulysses. Even if I struggle. Even if I fight. I want you to take me roughly, overwhelm me. And I don't want you to let me go.'

CHAPTER SEVEN

Morgan

IT FELT GOOD to say it. No, more than good. It felt power-ful. I hadn't realised how bad one-night guy had made me feel until I'd looked into Ulysses's black eyes and seen no shock or disgust, just puzzlement. Then him telling me flatly how ridiculous it was that I'd even been questioned, that plenty of people liked it—and not only women. Men too.

I might have felt stupid that I'd even believed what that idiot had told me, but it was difficult to feel stu-pid with Ulysses holding my jaw firmly in one large hand, making me unable to look away. Compelling my honesty.

Isn't this wrong, though? He's your boss.

So? Did it matter that I liked this? That I wanted to be restrained and held down by a man? And not just any man. *Him.*

The thought triggered an intense, heated response, not helped by how Ulysses was holding me against the wall, his hard, hot body pressed insistently to mine.

Yes, he was my boss, and I shouldn't want to have sex with him, and certainly not rough sex. He was also Damian's friend and Damian would have an aneurysm if he ever found out.

But I wanted it anyway. Desire pressed in on me, crushing me. Pulsing between my thighs like a giant heartbeat.

Ulysses nodded once. I knew he wouldn't check that I was sure. As far as he was concerned, I'd given him a green light and he'd take that at face value.

Not that he gave me any time for doubts.

He spun me round so that I was facing the wall and then his fingers closed around the back of my neck in a dominant grip.

My heart was beating so hard I thought I was going to pass out with excitement and I was so turned on I couldn't speak. Then his grip firmed and he jerked down my pyjama bottoms in one hard movement, taking my knickers with them.

My breath caught, cool air hitting my skin and making it prickle, sensitising every inch. I barely had time to register that my butt was completely bare before he'd stepped even closer, his big, hot body pressing me hard against the wall.

All the air went out of me as I found myself trapped, my heart slamming against my ribs, my pulse deafening. A little bit of fear crept through me, adding to my excitement. It was glorious.

I swallowed, my throat bone-dry.

His big hand slid over my bare butt, squeezing one

cheek, and not gently, making me gasp, sending a hot
wash of pleasure through me and intensifying my excitement.

'Amber,' I breathed, just to test him, perhaps tease
him and tantalise us both a little.

Instantly, he stilled. He didn't move and he didn't
speak, but the hand on my butt cheek stopped squeezing. He kept it there, though, his palm hot against my
skin, warming me.

He stroked my butt, not pushing me yet not leaving
me alone either, reminding me he was still there. Definitely it wasn't a 'stop', only a 'go slow'.

'Red or green?' His cold voice shivered down my
spine, contrasting with the hot burn of his palm on
my skin.

I braced myself. 'Green,' I said, my voice hoarse.

He moved instantly, as if those were the magic words
he'd needed to hear, the grip on the back of my neck
shifting. 'You can't get away from me.' His breath was
warm on my skin as he murmured in my ear. 'Struggle
all you like. I'm not going to let you go.'

Oh, holy shit.

His voice was a hot shock, jolting me. Because
he didn't sound like his usual cold, flat self. No, this
voice was dark, deep and full of heat. Not my boss. A
stranger. Taunting me, urging me…

Adrenaline surged inside me, a wild rush of intense
excitement that for once I didn't question, and I arched,
shoving back violently against him, using the wall to
give myself leverage. I must have taken him by sur-

prise, because I heard a sharp grunt, the hot steel at my back shifting. I had no time to feel pleased with myself, though, because then he pressed harder, using his weight to keep me pinned.

'Good.' His dark, hot voice melted everywhere. 'But it won't work. You can't get away.'

I stared at the wall, panting, every bump in that awful wallpaper pressing into my front while he pressed into my back. Every sense I had was focused on him, on the belt buckle digging into my skin and the hard ridge of his cock pushing insistently against the curve of my butt. His clean, fresh scent had become more musky and his breath on my nape was faster, hotter.

I was exciting him, wasn't I?

The thought only added to my own excitement. I wanted to affect him. I wanted to pay him back for all the times he'd driven me crazy at work, obsessing about things that didn't matter or leaving me to handle difficult staff issues. For all the times he didn't see all the work I did for him, the long hours I stayed and didn't complain. For all the thanks I didn't get and the praise I didn't receive.

For all the times he didn't notice me at all.

Satisfaction twisted in my gut and I took another breath, gathering myself to shove him once more. But before I could, he moved again, kicking my legs apart. Then the hand on my butt eased down, pushing insistently between my thighs from behind.

I froze, a strangled sound of shocked pleasure escaping me as his fingers slid through the folds of my sex.

And then everything intensified as those wicked fingers began to explore with firm insistence, spreading me open, finding my clit, one fingertip sliding against it, over it.

More pleasure, white-hot and electric, crashed through me, stunning me, and instinctively I tried to get away to intensify the sensations, my hips bucking and jerking. But he only crushed me harder against the wall with his body, making it impossible for me to move. Impossible to get away from the slick glide of his fingers.

'See?' he murmured in my ear. 'I told you that you couldn't get away, but I knew you'd like to try. And you do like it, don't you? You're very, very wet, Morgan.'

Heat washed through me, uncontrollable, unstoppable. I closed my eyes, gasping as he circled my throbbing clit, making me shudder violently. I couldn't breathe, too full of sensation to move. My whole body was on a knife-edge, every sense zeroing in on that maddening finger stroking, circling, pressing, driving me insane.

I whimpered, my knees shaking, every part of me trembling as white light burst behind my closed lids. Oh, God, I was going to come so hard, and there was nothing I could do to stop it. Nothing I could do to protect myself from the intensity of it. Nothing I could do to stay in control.

I had a second where a sliver of real fear hit me. Not fear of the man behind me, but of myself and what I wanted. Fear of the pleasure that was going to rip me apart.

My hands were against the wall, my nails digging into the wallpaper as if I could claw my way through it and escape him, and the relentless movement of his fingers between my thighs, circling and exploring before pressing firmly and insistently down on my clit yet again. Pleasure was arcing through me, electrifying every nerve ending, edging me closer and closer to the edge.

I could say 'red', one tiny word, and all this would stop. This intense, devastating pleasure would be gone. But then I'd be left standing there with only the memory of it hot against my skin and the taste of my own cowardice in my mouth.

And I knew I wasn't going to say it. He could do anything to me and I wouldn't.

But even as that thought occurred to me I felt his lips brush the back of my neck again, then he bit me in the sensitive place where my shoulder met my neck. All remaining air rushed straight out of my lungs, another gasp escaping along with it. And then just as I was struggling to process the sudden burst of sensation, the hand between my thighs shifted and he thrust two fingers hard inside me at the same time as his fingertip pushed down on my clit.

The climax hit like a nuclear explosion.

I let out a hoarse scream, all thoughts of escape and traffic lights vanishing, all thoughts of anything vanishing. There was nothing but the bright burst of light behind my closed eyes and the intense, searing pleasure that echoed and re-echoed through me.

And Ulysses behind me, holding me up.

CHAPTER EIGHT

Ulysses

I KEPT MYSELF pressed against Morgan, holding her pinned as the aftershocks of her climax shook her. It was my experience that most women preferred their partners to remain close in the aftermath of an orgasm, especially an intense one, and hers would have been intense. I'd made certain of it.

Physical closeness wasn't something I required, but I had to admit that it was very pleasant to have her against me as she shivered and shook. And it didn't have anything to do with the slick feel of her pussy against my fingers, or the way her soft, hot curves were pressing against my cock. Or even the sweet muskiness of her scent.

It was something more, and I couldn't quite pin down what.

Not that it mattered right now, because right now I had plans.

As soon as I'd walked into her flat, I'd decided I wasn't going to fuck her in here. It was too small and, although she had a sofa, the arm of it was too low and that wasn't going to work for what I'd planned.

I'd need to take her back to my place, which was much larger and had a sofa with an arm the perfect height. And it was safer for her than this place, especially as I'd just now decided she'd stay the night.

A couple of hours wouldn't be nearly long enough to make sure she experienced all the pleasure I was capable of giving her, and I certainly didn't want to shortchange her. Not when it was obvious she was hungry for it.

She'd been uncertain, yes, but I'd anticipated that. It took some women a little while to come to terms with their desires, especially when those desires were what society had decided was wrong.

I'd never understand why people cared what society thought, especially when one person's sexual experience didn't affect society, only one individual. I certainly wasn't ashamed of my own sexual preferences, for example.

But then, there were a lot of things that puzzled me about people, and if I spent my time trying to understand all of them I'd never get any work done.

Morgan relaxed against me, all soft and warm, reminding me that I was still hard and in some discomfort.

I very much wanted to fuck her. She'd responded so well, giving herself over to pleasure, proving just how much she'd liked what I'd done to her. That had excited me as much as I'd told her it would, and now I was impatient to get her back to my place where we could continue what we'd been doing.

Taking my hand from between her thighs, I then touched my tongue to my fingers, licking them to get a taste of her. Sweet. Just as I'd thought.

Not wasting any time, I pulled a handkerchief from my back pocket and wiped my fingers. Then I texted my driver, tugged up her ridiculous pyjama trousers to cover her and scooped her up into my arms.

She didn't make a sound and didn't struggle, her body lax, her head resting against my shoulder. Her eyes were half-closed, a small smile curving her mouth. She looked drunk, which satisfied me very much.

A particularly intense sexual experience could make people feel like that afterwards, and it clearly was having that effect on Morgan, which meant I'd done my job well.

'Where are we going?' she asked, her voice slightly slurred.

'Back to my place.'

'Why?' She didn't sound bothered, only curious.

'Because my place is bigger and has better security.' I shifted my hold as I pulled her front door shut, making sure it had locked behind me before heading towards the lifts.

'I can walk, you know.' She sounded more like her usual cool self now.

I stabbed the button, waiting until the doors opened, and then I stepped inside. 'It's quicker if I carry you.'

'It's not.' She squirmed a little, but she felt good,

and I didn't want to let her go just yet so I kept hold of her. 'Keep still.'

She sighed and stopped squirming, her head relaxing back against my shoulder. 'Why does quick matter?'

I watched the floor numbers above the doors light up as we descended. 'Because I'm very hard right now and it's painful.'

She didn't say anything to that so I glanced down to check her expression.

Her eyes had gone a startling deep blue, the colour very obvious against her black lashes. And as I watched they got even bluer as her pale skin flushed red. 'Oh,' she said. 'Then why didn't you...um...you know?'

'Fuck you upstairs?'

'Yes. That.'

'I told you. My place is bigger.' Really, the contrast between her eyes, her lashes, the fascinating little beauty spot near her mouth and her skin was intriguing.

'Bigger for what?'

I could have explained, but it would be easier to show her when we got there. 'You'll see.'

Just then the doors opened and I stepped out of the lift, heading towards the exit of her building. Outside, my car was waiting in the street as I'd been expecting, and, as I was strangely reluctant to release her, I bundled us both inside and held her in my lap as I told my driver to take us home.

'Ulysses,' she murmured, pushing against me. 'You can let me go now.'

But I didn't want to. I'd never held anyone before,

not like this, and I'd had no idea how pleasant it would be. Her weight in my lap was painful against my aching cock, but I was prepared to bear some pain for the pleasure of holding her.

'Ulysses,' she began.

'Don't speak,' I said shortly. 'I need to concentrate.'

'Concentrate on what?'

'On not fucking you right here in the car.' I meant it. For some reason my physical needs were becoming more and more insistent, making it difficult for me to think about anything else. Which was strange. That hadn't happened to me before.

Perhaps you shouldn't be holding her?

Perhaps not. Then again, not holding her wouldn't help, as she'd still be in my vicinity and I'd still be able to smell her, still be able to taste the sweet, musky flavour I'd licked from my fingers…

Sexual heat flooded through me at the memory, my cock aching.

'Oh,' she murmured, shifting in my lap, the movement delivering a short, sharp electric shock direct to my groin. 'That bad, huh?'

I caught my breath. There was something in her voice, something in the fascinating blue of her eyes, as she stared up at me. Something familiar.

She got that look when she was annoyed with me and wanting to argue. Except all I'd told her to do was keep still and be quiet. That wasn't too hard, was it?

'Yes,' I said. 'It is that bad.'

'Hmm.' She shifted again, the curve of her butt

pressing down against my cock, sending another sharp jolt of electricity through me. 'Guess you should have done something about it up in my flat.'

I narrowed my gaze. What did she mean? And why was she squirming around? 'I told you I wanted to get back to my place.'

'So you did. But you didn't tell me why.'

'Yes, I did. Because it's bigger.'

She rolled her eyes at the same time as she gave a small wiggle. 'Another one of your non-answers.'

Once again, a bolt of intense electricity shot through me, making me excruciatingly aware of the ache in my cock.

I liked rough sex. Because the more intense the physical pleasure was for my partner and I, the closer I came to understanding and sharing all those emotions that remained mysteries to me.

Yet I'd never been so aware of the pressure of my own desire before.

It was exciting.

Morgan was studying me the way I studied her, and it came to me slowly that that was exactly what she was doing. She was watching me and gauging my response. And I didn't have to ask why; I knew.

She'd been wriggling around in my lap on purpose.

'Morgan.' My voice sounded much huskier than it should have. 'Do you want me to fuck you in the car?'

She blinked and flushed, as if the question had been unexpected. 'No, of course not.' Her attention flicked to the front seat where my driver was.

I couldn't work out her meaning. Was his presence an issue? Was that why she'd said no? Or had she said no because she genuinely didn't want to? But, if she genuinely didn't want to, why had she been shifting around in my lap? She would have felt the effect those movements had had on me.

She's pushing you.

That seemed to be the most obvious conclusion, though I was interested in why she might want to push me. Was it because she wanted me to be rougher with her? Harder? Was she trying to find my limits?

So many questions. This was why I tended to stick with the lovers I knew, who knew my quirks and my preferences—there wasn't this uncertainty. Yet the thought of going to one of my usual lovers was as unsatisfying now as it had been before.

Perhaps we didn't need to wait until we got back to my place. There was no reason I couldn't pull the car over and tell the driver to make himself scarce for fifteen minutes. Or maybe twenty. In fact, my private parking garage wasn't far—another five minutes at most. We could make it there, get rid of the driver and have all the time in the world.

Holding on to her firmly, I leaned forward and gave the man my instructions.

'What's happening?' she asked as I sat back.

'Giving him instructions for parking in my building.' I glanced down at her. 'You should have kept still when I told you to.'

'What makes you say that?'

'I had plans. But you've been wriggling around in my lap and now I can't wait.'

She flushed scarlet, yet there was a gleam in her eyes. 'You didn't have to keep hold of me. You could have let me go.'

Somehow I knew that gleam meant that letting her go wasn't what she wanted, no matter what she'd actually said.

'Yes,' I agreed. 'I could. But I didn't want to and I don't think you want me to either.' It was a small test and, when her gaze flickered away from mine, I knew my suspicions had been correct.

The five minutes it took to get to the garage felt longer than three hundred seconds and by the time my driver turned down the ramp and into the garage itself I was gritting my teeth with impatience.

The man parked the car, gave me a nod then got out, closing the door behind him.

Silence filled the back seat but for the ticking of the engine and the sound of my own rapidly increasing heartbeat. Part of me was fascinated by my own response to the prospect of more sex with Morgan and how impatient I was. How acute my arousal and how exciting the thought of fucking her was.

I'd never experienced this before, not so strongly, and I liked it.

Morgan sat up in my lap, but I held her firmly where she was. 'Red, amber or green?' I demanded, my impatience starting to show.

She turned her head, the fall of her black hair rippling

down her back as she did so. The fluorescent lights of the garage gave it a glossy sheen, like a slick of oil. It was pretty. I wanted to shove my fingers into it, hold on to it. Would she like it if I pulled it?

'What?' she said. 'Here?'

'You indicated the driver might be a problem.' I wound my fingers in her hair, staring at the black strands against my skin. It felt silky and soft. 'So I got rid of him.'

'But I said—'

'You've been squirming around in my lap this whole time, deliberately grinding your butt against my cock.' I tugged on her hair experimentally. 'I don't know why you won't just say what you want, Morgan. It makes things very difficult.'

She was quiet a moment then she said, 'Maybe I don't want to say it. Maybe I just want you to do it.'

Ah, that made sense. She wasn't being intentionally difficult; she was just trying to resist me.

'In that case...' I tightened my fingers in her hair. 'I told you that I was trying not to fuck you in this car, but you wouldn't stop moving when I told you to, and now I don't want to wait until we get up into my penthouse. I want to fuck you here and now.'

She didn't say anything. All I could see was the back of her head and the sheen in her hair. I tugged on the silky strands, slowly drawing her back against me until her head rested against my shoulder.

I looked down into her face. It was flushed and pink,

and there was a tiny blue flame burning in her eyes. That flame was familiar.

Abruptly, everything about her seemed even more impossible to ignore than it had been five minutes earlier. The colour of her eyes and that little black mole near her mouth. The slick feel of her hair against my skin. The weight of her warm body on mine and all those soft, female curves. Her scent, sweet and tinged with arousal.

More expressions moved over her face, a language I couldn't read. But with a start I realised that I *did* know what that flame in her eyes meant. It was familiar for a reason. A challenge. A dare.

She'd told me that she wanted me to hold her down, to overwhelm her, to overcome her resistance, which meant this was part of it, wasn't it?

'Red, amber or green?' I demanded, because I'd give her all those things, but I needed to hear it from her directly. 'Don't make me ask again.'

Her throat moved in a convulsive swallow, the pulse at the base of her throat beating very fast. 'Is this a… public garage?'

'No. This garage is mine.' I tugged harder on her hair again, watching the little flame in her eyes burn higher.

'So no one will see us?'

'No. Do you want someone to?'

She shook her head, unequivocal.

Public sex was a valid fantasy, but clearly it wasn't hers. Which was fine. I didn't care one way or the other.

'Tell me,' I ordered, losing what little patience I had

left. 'If you don't want to continue I need to know and I need to know now.'

'Don't make me,' she whispered. 'Please don't.'

But she wanted me to. I knew she did. Which meant that what she was saying now was more of her resistance. More of her wanting to be overwhelmed.

This was part of her fantasy.

You can *read her.*

The thought felt precarious and fragile, though, and for a brief second I wished fiercely that I wasn't the way I was. That I was normal. That I could be certain about what I saw in Morgan's face, that I didn't have to work at it so fucking hard. That I just…knew.

I hadn't felt that way since Uncle John had told me that I couldn't live with him any more, and I didn't want to feel that way now.

But I had to be certain. I really didn't want to get it wrong. 'Do you want me to make you, Morgan?'

She swallowed again, but her gaze didn't waver from mine. 'Yes,' she said. 'I do.' And then she added, 'Green.'

CHAPTER NINE

Morgan

ULYSSES'S GRIP ON my hair was very firm, making it clear that I couldn't pull away without pain, and I liked it. I liked the feel of his hard cock underneath me too, pressing against my butt, and I liked that light in his cold, black eyes, fierce and intent, and the note of heat in his voice. His harsh demand.

No, it was not just like. I loved it. Teasing and inciting him in the car. Making him fierce and hot instead of emotionless and cold.

Maybe he got that way with his other lovers, but right now the important thing was that he was getting that way with me. *Because* of me.

I was exciting him. *I* was arousing him.

Me, the girl who nobody wanted, now had this powerful billionaire all desperate and hot under the collar.

It was a powerful feeling. I suspected this was going to push me and my limits, that maybe I wouldn't be able to handle what he wanted to do to me. But I didn't care. In fact, I was excited. I wanted to be pushed, and pushed hard.

My light tonight would always be green.

Ulysses didn't say anything, only gave a sharp nod.
Then he let go of my hair, pushed me out of his lap and
stretched me face-down across the back seat of the car.

I stared at the seat cushions, my heart racing, a wild
exhilaration filling me. Part of me was afraid of what
might come next while another part was desperate to
find out.

I didn't have to wait long.

He put one heavy hand between my shoulder blades,
holding me down, while with the other he jerked down
my pyjama bottoms and my underwear in a rough
movement, dragging them completely off me, leaving
me naked from the waist down.

Hot.

I tried to get my knees underneath me so I could get
away, but his hands shifted, coming down on my hips
before gripping me hard. Then he lifted me straight
into the air. I gasped, scrabbling on the cushions for
balance as he held up my entire rear. Then came the
sound of him moving around and I felt the front of my
thighs settle on his shoulders. And I realised abruptly
what he was doing.

I flushed the entire length of my body, heat washing
through me, part embarrassment, part intense arousal.
And, when I struggled this time, it wasn't entirely
feigned, because he could not be serious. He wasn't
actually going to do…that? Like…this?

He was so relentlessly strong and he held me so tight,
wrapping his arms around my thighs, his fingers mov-

ing between them, spreading apart the slick folds of my sex from behind. The heat deepened and I realised I was panting. The feeling of his arms around my thighs restraining me, and the sheer exposure of the way he was holding me with my butt in the air and my sex right in front of his face, was incredibly exciting.

It was dirty and wrong and I sure as hell didn't want him to stop.

I struggled again, glorying in his physical strength, more intoxicating than any number of glasses of expensive champagne.

His grip on me only tightened, holding me still. And then I felt his warm breath on the inside of my thighs and across my sex, and I began to tremble.

Then his tongue pushed inside me, a deep thrust that had me gasping aloud, my hips jerking instinctively in response. Again, I tried to pull away, but he wouldn't let me, holding on, making me take the thrust of his tongue.

My one-night guy hadn't done this. He hadn't put his face lower than my breasts, let alone hoisted my butt in the air so I could be eaten out from behind. Then again, I wouldn't have let him, not the way I was letting Ulysses.

I pressed my face into the seat cushions to muffle the groan that escaped, wriggling and squirming as the wicked, dirty pleasure he was giving me flared hot along my nerve-endings. It was intense, almost agonising, making me shiver and shake in his hands.

Then that maddening tongue paused and he said

roughly, 'Let me hear you scream, Morgan. I want to know you're enjoying this.'

It felt embarrassing to be so blatant about it, but when his mouth returned between my legs, his tongue licking and exploring, pushing into my sex and making that pleasure ratchet even tighter, I couldn't keep quiet.

Moans escaped, along with a couple of choked sobs as his fingers spread me wider, allowing him greater access. My hips jerked and I tried to resist, and soon I didn't even care about the noises I was making. Not when pleasure was a great, hungry beast clawing at my insides.

He didn't stop and he didn't let up, winding that pleasure tighter and tighter until the car was full of the sound of my own hoarse cries, and then he did something with his tongue that made the tension snap like a rubber band.

The orgasm barrelled down like a freight train, making me scream into the seat cushions, my whole body convulsing as the pleasure electrified me.

It seemed to go on for ever, waves of pleasure rolling through me, my screams fading into sobs. Ulysses's grip gentled, and he held me until the intensity had faded, then I was being lowered back down onto the seat.

I slumped there, my forehead resting on the leather, my breath coming in short, hard pants, ecstasy echoing and re-echoing throughout my entire body. Behind me came the sound of Ulysses shifting and then the tell-tale noise of a zip being drawn down and then the crinkle of foil.

Oh God, he was going to fuck me, wasn't he? Right here. Right now.

A shudder went through me, the ache between my thighs beginning to build again, which was insane, considering how hard I'd just come.

Then his hands were on my hips again, he was lifting me onto my knees and I felt the warm, slightly scratchy fabric of his wool trousers against the bare skin of my thighs and butt, and then more, a blunt pressure.

I sucked in a shaking breath and, as I did so, he pushed and I felt the press of his cock spreading me open, stretching me. He was big and, though it wasn't pain exactly, the sensation was intense enough that I had to pant through it, sensitive tissues burning as they stretched around him.

My body was trembling, my thighs shaking, my hips jerking. I was still sensitive from that last orgasm, but this was a whole new level of sensation.

I saw stars. I saw nebulae. I saw whole freaking galaxies as he pushed deeper. Then I felt him move and he put his arms down on either side of my head, leaning forward, his hips flexing as he seated himself even deeper in my pussy.

He was long and thick and so hard. And he felt so good I almost came on the spot there and then.

'You can struggle,' he said, his voice so rough it was almost unrecognisable. 'But doing so will make this go quicker than I want it to, so please keep still instead.'

Keep still? Was he kidding?

I opened my mouth to protest, but then he eased his

hips back and thrust back in, deep and hard, turning my
protest into a hoarse moan as pleasure rippled through
me like a wave. He did it again, leaning forward on his
arms and using them as leverage every time he thrust.
The smack of his hips meeting mine resounded through
the car along with the harsh rasp of his breath.

It was so erotic, so incredibly arousing, I knew I
wasn't going to last long despite the fact that I'd already just come.

He wasn't going easy or being gentle, each thrust
making my body shake, and I had to dig my fingers
into the seat, holding on for dear life as he slid in
and out. He fucked me roughly, forcefully, letting his
weight rest on me so that my hips were pressed down
on the seat. And with every hard slide of his cock my
body jerked, my sex rubbing against the cushions underneath me, intensifying the whole experience almost unbearably.

I shut my eyes, the galaxies behind my closed lids
exploding into white light, stars dying and reforming
while Ulysses moved like a god inside me, creating
whole new universes of sensation.

His breath was hot against my ear and he made rough
sounds with each thrust of his hips, very obviously enjoying what he was doing to me.

I loved this. Loved the heat and the intensity. Loved
how desired I felt. How needed. And for a brief, shin-
ing moment, I wanted nothing more than to exist right
here, right now, the complete focus of this powerful
man's attention. Where I was the one making him feel

good, making him feel pleasure, not the girl who was sent away, the girl who caused pain.

Ulysses leaned down, his weight pressing me hard into the seat cushions, adding that last little bit of friction I needed to catapult me over the edge. At the same time he bit my shoulder and everything exploded in yet another blinding, annihilating orgasm.

As I screamed into the seat cushions I was dimly aware of his movements behind me, harder, faster. Then he groaned, my name coming out in a harsh rasp in my ear as his body convulsed on top of mine.

The car filled with the fast, choppy sound of our breathing, Ulysses's weight pressing me down hard. I didn't mind. In fact, there was something about it I found comforting, as if he was anchoring me. So much so that when he eventually moved I had to bite back a small protesting sound.

He didn't say anything and I couldn't bring myself to move. So I lay there as the aftershocks of the orgasm echoed through me, listening to him rustle around.

'Turn over,' he ordered, his voice raspy.

I did so, watching him as he bent to pick up my pyjama bottoms from the floor of the car. Thinking he was going to hand them to me, I reached out to take them. But instead, he bent and began to dress me.

I blinked, surprised as he carefully placed my feet inside them and pulled them up to my hips, covering me. His face had its usual cold expression on it, yet there was something burning in his black eyes. Something I was sure hadn't been there before.

'I could have done that,' I said, my voice scratchy.

'Yes, but I did it.' He reached down and picked up my underwear, staring at them for a second as if he'd never seen them before and didn't know what they were.

I put out my hand for them and he glanced at me. Then, without a word, closed his fingers over the fabric and stuck them in his trouser pocket.

'Ulysses…'

'Upstairs.' He opened the car door and got out, holding it open for me.

Clearly, he meant business.

I slid out of the car, then, without any warning at all, he scooped me up in his arms for the second time that night.

'I can walk, damn it.' I squirmed against his chest, but my protest didn't have any real power in it. My legs were wobbly and my heartbeat was still racing, and for the moment relaxing back against his hard, warm body seemed like a very good thing.

'Of course you can walk.' He turned and headed towards the garage exit. 'But I want to carry you.'

I leaned my head against his shoulder, my body going lax, looking up at him. 'Why?'

'Because I like carrying you.'

I sighed. Was there any point asking him more questions? Perhaps not. Perhaps I should lie there and let him do whatever he wanted to do. If he liked carrying me, then who was I to argue? Especially as I'd decided I liked being carried.

Actually, no, I did have one question after all. 'Are we going upstairs for more sex?'

He pressed the button for the lift. 'Yes.'

I didn't have a problem with that. 'And how long are you expecting this to…uh…go on for?'

'I suspect the whole night.' And then, as if remembering, he finally glanced down at me. 'Will that be enough for you?'

A whole night.

God. If I knew Ulysses—and I most certainly did—when he said a whole night, he meant a whole night.

'A night should do,' I said, settling against his chest.

I just hoped there'd be something left of me the next morning.

CHAPTER TEN

Ulysses

THE DAY DID not start out well. For a start, I slept in, which I almost never did, though that might have had more to do with me keeping Morgan busy for most of the night having sex.

Still, I wasn't used to it. I had difficulty sleeping most nights and, the nights I did sleep, I was awake at five a.m. Yet when I'd woken that morning I'd looked at the clock to find it shockingly late—seven.

I had a morning routine I preferred to stick to. An hour in my private gym, a shower and then getting dressed. Breakfast at six-thirty. Then my driver would take me into the office and on the way I'd read the news websites and the hard-copy dailies. I'd be in the office by seven-thirty and ready to work.

Now it was seven and my morning routine was disrupted.

I didn't have time for much more than a shower and quick breakfast, then I paused in the doorway of my bedroom, staring at the woman still asleep in my bed.

The sheet had fallen away from her shoulders, leaving her back and shoulders bare, and her hair lay black and silky-looking over my pillow.

My cock was hard, and had been hard ever since I'd woken up and a part of me wanted to go back to the bed, pull the sheet back and have sex with her again. A discomforting thought.

We'd both be very late for work if I did that and I hated being late. I also didn't like that I wanted her again, which almost never happened. Normally, once I'd had sex I didn't think about it again for at least a couple of days, and I never really wanted sex with a particular woman. I had my favourites, but they were mainly women who knew me and knew my tastes.

It wasn't personal.

But the feeling that gripped me now seemed to be about one woman in particular: Morgan. It wasn't sex per se, it was her.

That annoyed me. There was no logical reason still to be having sexual thoughts about her, considering everything we'd done last night.

I'd planned to wake her up, because if I didn't she'd be late for work, but in the end I decided not to, some part of me not wanting to get too close to her.

Instead, I settled for scribbling a quick note, instructing her to have breakfast here and to call my driver to get a lift into work. And then I left for work myself.

But the disturbed feeling didn't leave me.

Morgan was an hour late, and I thought that, once

she'd got here, the day would settle into its usual familiar routine and my odd restlessness would vanish. But it didn't.

The moment she walked in, I noticed that, though her hair was in its normal bun, it looked a bit messy, black strands falling around her ears and the back of her neck. Her light blue skirt was wrinkled and the buttons on her white blouse had been done up wrong.

I didn't know why I noticed. I certainly hadn't taken notice of such things before and it was strange that I was doing so now. I was even conscious of her sweet scent, and how it seemed much sweeter this morning, making my mouth water.

Annoyance wound through me. I tried to concentrate on my computer screen instead of on her as she smoothed her skirt, hooked an escaped strand of hair over one ear and approached my desk.

'Are you ready to go through your schedule?' She sounded breathless. 'Thanks for the breakfast, by the way. I really—'

'You're late,' I interrupted, glaring at my screen. 'By an hour.'

'Sorry, I woke up late,' she said. 'And then I had to go home and get changed.'

'You should have texted me.'

'Seriously?'

I looked at her then, a hard jolt of electricity pulsing through me as her blue eyes met mine. There were dark circles under them and I knew how those circles had got there, that I was responsible for them. And all the sounds she'd made were still ringing in my ears, the little moans and sighs, the cries of release, the sobs of pleasure.

Sexual desire hit, my cock instantly hard, and almost as soon as I felt it myself I saw a wave of red stain her skin and a familiar blue spark ignite in her eyes.

My annoyance deepened. Why was I feeling this way now? I'd had a lot of sex last night and I wasn't supposed to want more. I certainly wasn't supposed to want to bend her over my desk and fuck her hard from behind only five hours after the last time. I was supposed to give her the pleasure I promised her then think no more about it.

'Yes,' I snapped, irritated about it. 'You know I don't like lateness.'

Her cheeks were still pink, and I had the impression that she was surprised. Though what she was surprised about I didn't know. Then she glanced down at the tablet in her hands. 'Perhaps you should have woken me up before you left this morning.'

She sounded more like her normal self, which should have calmed me, but it didn't. Her voice held a chilly note that felt wrong, especially after the heat that had made it all husky and raw the night before.

I shifted restlessly in my chair. Yes, I should have woken her up. But I hadn't wanted to, and I couldn't figure out why.

'The schedule,' I said curtly, not wanting to discuss it. 'Let's go through it.'

Morgan didn't argue so we went through my schedule, normally a settling, familiar routine. But again, like everything about this morning, something was wrong.

She wouldn't look at me and I kept fixating on the cold note in her voice. I also couldn't stop noticing that the buttons on her blouse were done up wrong and there was a tiny gap, allowing me to see the white lace of her bra and her pale skin beneath it. I couldn't stop seeing the faint mark of a bruise on her neck where I'd kissed her the night before. Couldn't stop noticing the way the fabric pulled tight around her hips and how it might excite her if I were to pull it down, using it to constrict her thighs, prevent her from opening them.

'Ulysses?'

Would she like that? Would it make her eyes go luminous and dark, make her mouth go full and soft? Would she pant the way she had last night when I'd put her on top of me to test her responses?

'Ulysses? Are you listening?'

No. You're too busy imagining fucking her.

I shifted in my chair yet again, my cock painfully hard, my temper on edge. This wasn't supposed to happen but, as it was, there was only one solution. 'No,' I said. 'I'm not listening. I can't stop thinking about having sex with you and it's annoying.'

Morgan blinked, another wave of colour staining her cheeks. 'You…are?'

'Didn't I just say so?' Impatience twisted inside me. 'Last night was very pleasurable and now it's difficult for me to concentrate.'

Her mouth was open. She shut it and glanced down at her tablet. 'You enjoyed last night, then?'

I didn't know why she'd phrased it as a question. Surely that had been obvious? 'If I hadn't enjoyed it I wouldn't have been hard,' I pointed out. 'And I certainly wouldn't be hard now.'

'Oh...' The word came out on a sighing sound. 'And...you *are* hard now?'

'I just told you I was. Really, Morgan. Seems like you're the one not listening.' I shoved my chair back and stood, turning around and going to the windows so I could look out over London. Sunlight glinted off the glass of the buildings outside and I counted the glints in my head, trying to concentrate on something other than the pain in my groin. 'This will cause problems,' I went on, because it would. 'I have to be able to concentrate in order to do my job properly, and I can't. So you really have two choices. Either you stay away from me for the rest of the day or we have sex again.'

'I see.'

I turned around and met her gaze. And again it hit me, that jolt of electricity, as if I'd been punched hard in the stomach. 'Your buttons are done up wrong.' I knew this wasn't what I should have said, but I couldn't stop myself. 'And your bun is half-falling down, and your skirt is wrinkled.'

This time I recognised the definite surprise that crossed her face. 'I dressed in a rush.'

'However you dressed, it's different. You're different. You should be easy for me to ignore and you're not.'

Another expression I couldn't read flickered over her face. 'Well, thanks.'

I knew she didn't mean to thank me, that she was being sarcastic, that she hadn't liked what I'd said. 'I'm just pointing out the issues,' I said impatiently. 'And that it's a problem for me. If I can't ignore you, I can't do my job, and that includes a meeting today with the Black and White Foundation trustees. A meeting you're supposed to be attending with me and which I won't be able to concentrate on if you're in the room.'

'So,' she said slowly. 'What you're saying is that this is my fault?'

Her voice sounded neutral, but I knew from experience that she didn't feel that way.

I frowned, unsure why she should be annoyed with me. 'Well, I haven't had this problem before. It's only happened this morning, which is after we had sex. So logically—'

'Logically, yes, it is my fault.' Her mouth had flattened into a hard line and I could see what looked like anger glittering in her eyes. 'Thanks, Ulysses. Thanks for making your dick my problem.'

My muscles tightened, annoyance prickling under my skin. All I'd done was point out an issue. 'I didn't say my dick was your problem. I only agreed that you're the reason it's an issue and that there were two ways to deal with it.'

'Right. So, what? I bend over your desk so you can give it to me now? Or I leave for the rest of the day, yes?'

Again, her voice sounded very cool and calm, yet

the gleam of blue in her eyes was hot. Was she still annoyed? And, if so, why?

'Those are the two solutions I can see.' I lifted a brow. 'Unless you can think of something else?'

'I can think of something else.' She rose from the chair, tucking her tablet under her arm, her chin lifting in a familiar way. 'In fact, I can think of two other solutions you haven't mentioned.'

That lift of her chin should have warned me, but I wasn't paying attention. I was too busy looking at the gap in her blouse where the buttons were done up wrong and her skin gleamed pale. 'Two other solutions?' I muttered. 'And what are they?'

'One, you deal with your dick yourself in the privacy of your own bathroom,' she said coldly. 'Or, two, you shove it up your fucking arse.'

Then without another word she turned on her heel and stormed out of my office.

CHAPTER ELEVEN

Morgan

I STRODE FROM Ulysses's office straight into the bathroom that was for the use of his two secretaries and myself, slammed the door then locked it for good measure.

I'd never felt so angry in my entire life and I couldn't figure out why.

Ulysses was only being his normal, aggravating, infuriating self, no change there, so why was I so furious with him? Why had I lost it with him? I never shouted, never lost my cool, never was anything less than professional.

Except, apparently, for today.

Waking up this morning in his giant bed with its magnificent view over the Thames had been a shock, since I hadn't expected to stay the entire night in his massive penthouse near the river. That he wasn't there when I woke up had also been a shock, though it shouldn't have surprised me. He never missed a day of work and he was never late.

A part of me had been glad that he wasn't there, because after last night I was having a few problems adjusting to normality. And, as I'd eaten the breakfast the note he'd left me had instructed me to help myself to, I'd thought about how I'd deal with facing him across his desk on a normal work day. Which was simply to go on as normal, because that was what he'd do.

After all, it was a one-off deal. A night to explore my fantasy, nothing more.

Except he hadn't gone on as normal.

The moment I'd walked into his office, flustered after having rushed home to get dressed, I'd felt the pull of our chemistry.

He was sitting behind his desk, a tall, broad, glowering presence. Unlike me, he was immaculate in his charcoal-grey suit, pristine white shirt and silk tie in a rich, dark blue. He was also, as usual, incredibly, coldly beautiful.

He'd been staring at his computer screen with a very studied intensity and I'd been relieved, thinking that maybe the chemistry I'd felt was all on my side, that now we'd let it burn for a night there'd be nothing left of it.

At least until he'd looked up at me and I'd seen that familiar heat flaring in his black eyes. The heat I'd seen every time I looked up at him as I'd lain naked beneath him in his bed.

He'd come to the point pretty quickly, letting me know in no uncertain terms that, far from our chemistry being done, it was a problem for him, and what was I going to do about it?

Cursing under my breath, I went over to the sink, turning on the tap and running some cold water, splashing it onto my hot face.

I didn't understand it. A part of me liked being blamed for getting him hard, and also liked how he wasn't able to dismiss our night together as easily as he dismissed other things. So why I was mad, I wasn't sure.

Was it that I hadn't expected him to be thinking about it? Or was it the coldly emotionless way he'd suggested that I was the problem and that I either needed to have more sex with him or get out?

You know what he's like, come on.

I *did* know what he was like. Yet that didn't make any difference to my anger. Or my disappointment, though I didn't know what I was disappointed about.

He was a man who didn't process emotion in the same way other people did, who found it difficult to understand the emotions of others, and I knew this. So why was I even getting angry with him? And what was this disappointment about?

You wanted last night to mean something to him.

I grabbed a hand towel from the basket beside the sink and patted the water from my face, then gazed at myself in the mirror.

'You're an idiot,' I said to my reflection. 'As if a night of exploring rough sex fantasies means anything.'

I *didn't* want it to mean anything. Ulysses was my boss and, not only that, he'd never be a man I could have a relationship with. Never be a man I could have an emotional connection with.

Because that was what I wanted. Not just rough sex, but an emotional connection. Something that went deeper than physical, that gave me more. Certainly more than I had right now.

Taking a couple of deep breaths, I decided that not being around Ulysses was the best idea, so I went back to my own office, collected my laptop and went down to the HR department on the tenth floor, where I found an empty desk.

Ulysses didn't try and make contact, which was a relief, yet as the day neared its end my temper got worse.

So much for being indispensable. He hadn't wanted me to take any annual leave, yet apparently he was quite happy for me to be AWOL the entire day.

It wasn't until just before four, when his precious meeting was supposed to start, that he texted me.

I expect you in my private meeting room in five minutes.

Typical. He didn't want me until he wanted me and then I had to be there immediately. Normally I wouldn't have minded, but I sure as hell did now. Because I knew what would happen. I'd get to the meeting room and Ulysses would treat me as if nothing had happened. As if I hadn't been rude and angry and walked out on him. It would have left no impression on him whatsoever.

Like you didn't even matter.

When I'd been in high school I'd been a massive poetry fan, and I'd particularly liked Keats. I'd read up a bit about his life and had been intrigued by the epigraph on his grave: *Here lies one whose name was writ in water.*

I felt like that sometimes—as if my name was written in water too. As if I could disappear and no one would remember me, except Damian.

Ulysses wouldn't. He'd only get another assistant to replace the empty space I'd leave behind. He wouldn't think about the person who used to occupy that empty space. It wouldn't even occur to him.

Out of sight, out of mind—that was Ulysses.

I'd told him once that he had no sense of object permanence and he'd just looked at me as if I was mad.

You know what you have to do, then, don't you?

I stared down at his text again, realisation hitting me, along with a kind of certainty.

I knew why I was angry. After last night, I'd expected things to be different. I'd expected *myself* to be different. To feel that something had changed. But nothing had changed. I was still myself. My life was still narrow and confined, no matter how down and dirty I'd got the night before. I was still running around after a man who saw me as nothing but filler in an empty space.

And why should he see me any differently? When my life was a shell with no substance to it, no weight?

My name was 'writ in water' because I was water. Transparent, colourless, tasteless. And I hadn't done anything to change that. I'd expected other people to make me feel as if I was more by being a good girl, doing everything they told me. Hoping they would look and see me.

But in doing so I'd limited myself. I'd limited my life.

I'd turned myself into water and, if I wanted to be more than that, I'd have to be the one to change.

And maybe that change meant something drastic... such as leaving.

Leaving my job. Leaving London.

A drastic step, yes, but maybe it was the time for drastic steps.

Last night Ulysses had given me a taste of excitement, heat and passion, everything my life had been lacking, and if I wanted more of that I was going to have to go out and find it myself.

Or you could just get it from him.

I put my phone down without replying to his text, memories of the night before replaying helpfully in my head. His hands holding me. His strength keeping me exactly where he wanted me. His mouth exploring my body with a single-minded relentlessness that had driven me out of my mind. The hard length of his cock moving inside me, deep and hard and rough. My sex aching and throbbing, my skin sensitive.

He'd showed me that sex could be hot and intense and breath-taking, but my entire life couldn't only be great sex. I wanted more than that.

I gathered my stuff from my temporary desk and made my way back upstairs to the private meeting room that adjoined his office.

The various trustees that were meeting with him to

discuss the fledgling Black and White Foundation were already in the room.

Normally, I would have rushed in full of apologies for being five minutes late, but I didn't today. Today, I unhurriedly dropped my stuff off in my own office first before making my way to the meeting room and strolling in.

Ulysses was by the windows doing what he always did in social situations where he wasn't comfortable, agitatedly pacing up and down. Usually, when I managed meetings for him, he'd stop and sit down, relax as much as he ever could. But he didn't do that this time.

This time, as soon as I came in, he stopped behind the chair at the head of the meeting-room table and put his hands on the back of it, pinning me to the spot with his intense black gaze.

My breath caught, electricity crackling across the open space, a live current bolting straight down my spine.

It took me a moment to remember we weren't alone and I had to force myself to look away, not to let anyone else see what Ulysses's stare had done to me.

I moved around the room, shaking hands and making small talk, setting people at ease, setting the tone for the meeting. By this stage Ulysses would normally be sitting down at the table, looking as though he was going through the schedule again, studying his notes or doing one of the other distraction techniques I'd taught him to contain his impatience and his discomfort so it didn't project outwards.

Except he didn't do any of that this time.

He stood behind the chair, watching me, his expression forbidding.

It did terrible things to me, that stare. Made me forget what I was doing, forget what I was saying. Made it difficult for me to breathe, difficult to ignore the aching pressure between my thighs.

It made it impossible for me to think of anything else but that spitting electrical current sizzling in the air between us.

I did my best to ignore both that and him as I got everyone settled down around the table, then I opened the meeting.

Ulysses remained standing, and the only time he looked away from me was when he spoke. His deep voice had a rough edge to it, like fine sandpaper.

What was going on? Was he annoyed that I'd shouted at him that morning? But that couldn't be it. He was usually impervious to my moods, so perhaps he was just annoyed I'd been late for the meeting.

Or maybe he just wants you.

I reached for the glass of water in front of me, taking a sip to moisten my dry throat. That was the other explanation. Certainly I couldn't think of any other reason for him to stare at me the way he was doing now.

The pressure of his gaze was unnerving, making excitement shiver through me, even though a part of me was annoyed at the same time.

Because this wasn't exactly the most appropriate time to be having sexual feelings, and I had to work hard to distract everyone else's attention from the way Ulysses was staring at me.

Damn man. Couldn't he at least try to act normal for one bloody moment?

Of course he can't.

Anger curled in my gut, both at him for how he was acting and at myself for even getting irritated about something he couldn't help. I felt a complex web of emotions that I didn't appreciate or want to think about right now.

Then, right as I was about to finish up the meeting, Ulysses suddenly straightened and said curtly, 'Meeting's over, ladies and gentlemen. Time to leave.'

There was a ripple of surprise, people clearly not appreciating his tone or his impatience, so I had to do my usual job of soothing any ruffled feathers, which didn't improve my already frayed temper.

I was standing by the door after the last few people had left, just about to leave myself, when a long arm reached from behind me and shut the door in my face.

I stared at the wood in front of me, my heart shuddering hard in my chest as a crackle of familiar electricity whispered over my skin.

Then Ulysses said, his voice no longer cold but hot and rough against the back of my neck, 'Red, green or amber?'

CHAPTER TWELVE

Ulysses

I HEARD MORGAN'S breath catch and I wanted to press her against the door and fuck her so badly I could hardly speak.

I was also fucking furious.

All day I'd been having trouble concentrating, unable to think of anything but her, unable to stop revisiting the memories of the night before. Every time I did, I saw something new, something exciting. Something that made my cock hard and my heartbeat accelerate.

After she'd stormed out of my office that morning, I'd tried to go on with my day the way I normally did. But I had been unable to ignore those angry words she'd flung at me, nor the ache in my groin.

Working harder usually solved any uneasy feelings I experienced, but that hadn't worked. There were too many unanswered questions—such as why was she angry with me? Why had she'd shouted? And why did I want to keep touching her?

All I'd suggested was more sex and yet she'd acted

offended. I knew that the subject of sex could sometimes be difficult, that it touched on people's feelings, but I'd thought Morgan and I had gone over that: it would be one night in which I would give her pleasure and then we'd resume our normal working relationship.

All I'd done this morning was to suggest changing the agreement, since that seemed to be the most logical way to solve my concentration issues. I didn't know whether she'd feel the same as she had the night before, but I'd thought it likely, given she'd enjoyed herself.

Yet she'd got angry. She'd shouted.

Morgan had never shouted at me before and I didn't like it. I didn't like the way it made me feel. I didn't like questioning myself, wondering what I'd said, what I'd done wrong.

You don't like that maybe you hurt her.

But how had I hurt her? I didn't understand that either.

Then she'd been late to the meeting, and I'd had the sudden thought that she might not come. That I'd be left to deal with the trustees on my own.

I hadn't been able to sit still, trying not to think about what I would do if she didn't arrive. But then she had and I'd felt every muscle in my body relax as soon as she'd walked in the door. Only to tighten once again as I looked at her.

Because her blouse still wasn't done up properly and she'd done nothing to fix her messy bun. Tendrils of black hair still hung around her ears and curled at the back of her neck. And her skirt was still wrinkled.

She didn't look like Morgan Blackwood, my PA.

She looked like Morgan, my lover, whom I'd spent half the night fucking and whom I couldn't stop thinking about fucking again.

What did you expect?

I didn't know. I only knew I was glad she'd turned up to the meeting and that I was also furious she hadn't tidied herself up. That now all I could see was a woman I wanted so much that I couldn't concentrate.

It had to stop. And the only way I knew to stop it was to have sex with her again.

Right now.

Morgan said nothing, but her scent wrapped itself around me, so sweet and familiar it made my mouth water for the second time that day.

'Answer the question,' I demanded, my patience hanging by a thread. 'I need to know right now. Red, amber or green?'

If it was red, I'd have to leave.

I heard her take a little breath. 'Ulysses—'

'A colour. I need a colour.'

Her hair was curled at the back of her neck and I wanted to lean in and nuzzle the soft skin there. She'd liked it when I'd done that to her the night before and I'd got very involved in doing what she liked.

I'd got very involved watching when her eyes had glowed bright and when they'd darkened. When they'd turned glassy and when they'd nearly closed.

Before, sex had always been about giving a woman pleasure. But last night, somehow, it had become less about 'a woman' and more about Morgan.

It was Morgan I wanted to give pleasure to. Morgan I wanted sobbing with ecstasy in my arms. I didn't know when that had changed, but now it was all I could think about.

She turned around, tilting her head back against the door so she could look up at me. Her fascinating eyes were full of things I couldn't read and, not for the first time, I felt frustrated at not being able to.

But I did know what that faint spark of blue meant. That, I was familiar with.

My already tight muscles tightened even further.

I scanned her face, looking at all the things that fascinated me about it. That little mole near her top lip. The striated blue of her eyes. The silkiness of her eyebrows and the way they flicked up at the ends. The crease between those brows that deepened when I annoyed her. The full curve of her bottom lip and how it had tasted when I'd bitten it.

I put another hand on the door beside her head, caging her against it.

And still she didn't speak.

'Morgan.' Her name came out on a low growl and the pain in my groin intensified. 'Why aren't you answering me?'

'Because it would do you good to wait.' Her gaze had dipped to my mouth, the colour rising in her cheeks. 'You always expect people to do exactly what you want, when you want it, and I think you could learn some patience.'

I growled again, my anger and desire becoming more acute. I bent, brushing my mouth over hers, because I wanted to taste it and I couldn't wait. Her breath caught, her chest rising sharply as my lips touched hers.

Sweetness flooded through me and I felt something inside me relax. As if something terrible had been meant to happen but instead it was something good.

'Ulysses…'

She breathed out against my mouth and I deepened the kiss, wanting more of her sweet flavour. Letting it crowd out the desperation that filled me at the same time as it made me even more desperate.

Her head tilted back, her mouth opening, letting me in, and I took advantage, exploring her deeper as an emotion I could only identify as relief rippled through me. The only relief I'd had the entire day.

'Colour,' I demanded against her mouth. 'I need to hear it.'

'Green.' Her reply was husky. 'Very green.'

I didn't wait.

I kissed her again, deeper, harder, biting on her bottom lip the way I'd been thinking about doing all day. She shivered, her hands coming to my chest and pressing against me. But not to push me away. The pressure was slight, as if she just wanted to touch me, feel me.

Her touch felt good and I leaned into it, letting her sugary flavour wind through me like a drink of something alcoholic. But my cock was getting insistent and, no matter how I'd have liked to stand there kissing her, it wanted more.

Keeping my mouth on hers, I jerked her skirt up around her hips then insistently slid my hand between her thighs, pushing my fingers beneath the waistband of her knickers, finding her pussy all hot and slick.

She made a moaning sound and suddenly I wanted to look into her eyes, see the effect my touch had on her, watch the reactions ripple over her face.

I lifted my mouth from hers and looked down into her eyes. They'd gone that luminous blue that had so fascinated me last night, laying bare her reactions to what I was doing.

I kept my gaze on her as I slid two fingers inside her, brushing her clit gently with my thumb at the same time. Her eyes went very wide, her mouth half-open, another breathy moan escaping as her hips lifted against my hand.

Leaning my forearm against the door, I moved in closer, almost pushing against her, looking right into her eyes. Then I slid my fingers in and out of her pussy, feeling it clench around me, getting even more slippery and hot. I added more pressure with my thumb on her clit and she gave a shuddering gasp, her hips jerking.

The light in her eyes was so fascinating—the way it shifted and changed as I touched her, responding to her level of pleasure, and I wanted to spend days reading it. Days watching it. Days familiarising myself with all the things that made it glow brighter.

That made her glow brighter.

It was important to me, I realised. Her pleasure was important, not just because I liked doing that for women, but because I liked doing that for *her*. She'd had to put up with a lot because of me and I paid her well for it. Though I knew money wasn't the most important thing for her.

I'd never asked what was, because it wasn't a discussion I'd likely understand. But I could give her this and I wanted to.

I kissed her again, exploring her, tasting her, noting which things made her tremble and which things made her moan, how the stroke of my tongue against hers made her shiver.

And, as I did so, I increased the pace of my hand, giving her enough friction so that soon she was arching against me, her hips flexing, becoming demanding, the way she did when she was just about to come.

Then she did come, shaking and gasping, her eyes wide and dark in her flushed face as they stared up into mine.

It was only then that I became conscious once again of my own aching groin.

I couldn't wait any more.

Taking my hand from between her thighs, I eased my fingers into her mouth. 'Suck,' I ordered, wanting to know how she'd respond to tasting herself and her own pleasure.

She didn't disappoint. She sucked my fingers, watching my face as intently as I watched hers, licking herself from my skin.

Desire roared louder in my head.

I reached into my back pocket for my wallet, getting a condom out of it and discarding the wallet onto the floor. Then I pulled back, unzipping my fly and getting my cock out. Morgan grabbed the condom packet out of my hand and ripped it open, her hands moving to put the latex on me, and I let her, unable to stop the shiver of pleasure that rippled through me as her cool fingers brushed over my aching cock.

She did it again and I had to take her hands away, gripping her wrists and pinning them to the door above her head with one hand while I jerked her underwear down with the other. Then I reached down and grabbed her behind one knee, pulling her leg up and hooking it around my hip, opening her pussy to me.

I positioned myself, my heart beating so loud I couldn't hear anything else, and there was a minute when a part of me wondered what was happening to me. Then it was gone and I was thrusting into her, feeling her flesh stretch around me, her pussy clenching hard around my cock, taking me in.

Pleasure burst through my head and I groaned, at the same time as she made exactly the same sound. And I realised that what I felt she must also feel. The same thing. The same emotion.

I stared into her eyes. I don't know what happened, but for one instant it was as if I could read her thoughts. As if I knew exactly what she was thinking, exactly what she was feeling. And the way she stared back made it seem as if she was thinking exactly the same thing.

I couldn't move. I couldn't breathe.

I felt… I didn't know what I felt. I only knew that it was like chaos resolving itself into a pattern, letting me see it in all its glory for the first time.

Letting me understand it.

But my body wouldn't let me be still, so I moved, thrusting into her, all friction, heat and the sweet muskiness of her scent.

She struggled and arched against the door, pulling against my hold even as her hips bucked against mine. And, when I tugged her leg higher on my hip so I could get even deeper, she struggled even harder.

It was unbelievably exciting, intensely arousing, and before I knew it I was gripping her wrists hard, driving into her, shoving her harder against the door with every thrust, the pleasure climbing higher and higher inside me.

I kept watching her, seeing the glow in her eyes get brighter, feeling as if I knew her better with every thrust. As if there was something between us. Something I couldn't see or touch, but was there anyway.

'Morgan,' I growled as the pleasure drew into a tight, hard knot. Then I put my hand down between us and stroked her clit until she cried out, growling again as that knot burst apart and I was hammering into her, pleasure exploding through me, making me feel as though I'd been hit over the back of the head with a cricket bat.

I couldn't see, couldn't hear. I was conscious only of the jolts of the aftershock, the feeling of lethargy, of complete relaxation, and the sweet, jasmine scent of her body.

This has to happen again.

Yes. I couldn't have another day where I was so distracted and preoccupied. Where all I could think about was fucking her. That would be the opposite of productive, which meant that there was only one solution: she and I needed to keep sleeping together.

Slowly, I withdrew from her then lowered her wrists, chafing them to make sure her blood flow was good. Then I dealt with the condom, zipped myself up and began helping her with her own clothing. She half-heartedly tried to bat my hands away, but I didn't let her.

'Keep still,' I said. 'Your blouse is buttoned up wrong and I need to fix it.'

Her hands dropped and she let me put her to rights again. The blue glow had faded from her eyes, but I could still see the remains of it, burning like banked embers. 'You need to come back to my place tonight,' I told her. 'In fact, I think you might need to come back to my place every night for a while.'

The crease between her brows appeared and my gut twisted. Because I couldn't read her. I didn't know what that crease meant, only that it wouldn't be good.

The thing that had been between us was gone, the sense that I knew her slipping through my fingers like water.

She was as opaque to me now as she always had been.

'I can't, Ulysses,' she said quietly.

'Why not?' I didn't like the way my gut lurched, the way it sometimes did in a lift. 'You liked what we did just now, didn't you?'

The look in her eyes was a complete mystery. It was as if I'd never seen anything in them at all. 'Yes, I did. But… I'm sorry.' She didn't sound sorry. She didn't sound sorry at all. 'I'm going to have to hand in my resignation.'

CHAPTER THIRTEEN

Morgan

ULYSSES'S BLACK BROWS descended into a ferocious-looking frown. 'Your resignation?' he demanded. 'Why?'

My mouth had gone very dry. I felt a little wrecked, and also like the biggest arsehole in the entire world.

He'd made me come and, in return, I'd handed him my resignation.

But the sex up against the door hadn't changed my mind. In fact, it had only cemented it, as had his demand that I come to stay at his place at night.

No matter how intense the pleasure he gave me, Ulysses couldn't change my life. He could give me physical pleasure, excitement and passion, help me explore my fantasies, but that was all. I might sleep every night at his place but the only thing that would happen was sex.

There had been a moment just before, when he'd been deep inside me and I'd seen something ripple in his eyes, something more than simple sexual heat—something that looked like wonder and discovery—and I'd felt myself respond.

But it had only been a moment. Then I'd come, he had too and now he was looking at me the way he always did. Puzzled and angry that I wasn't doing his bidding. I was merely a physical adjunct who helped him do his job but no one he'd actually care about.

You want him to care about you?

No, that was impossible. I couldn't have a relationship or anything like it with Ulysses. For a start, he was my boss, and then there was the fact that he was a man for whom having any kind of relationship was difficult. Because *he* was difficult.

But doesn't that make you wonder if he's as lonely as you are?

Shit, I didn't need that thought either.

All my life I'd had to contort myself for other people. First, with my brother, pretending I wasn't scared or grief-stricken after our mother had died so he wouldn't worry about me. Then at school, being the good girl and doing well to make worth it all the effort he put into sending me there, not to mention trying not to make a big deal of my poor origins so I'd be accepted by the other girls.

And after that being sent to London to be a PA for a difficult man with whom I had to suppress all my emotions because he didn't understand them.

I didn't want to do it any more. Yet, if I were with Ulysses, contorting would be all I'd do since he couldn't change himself.

'I'm sorry,' I said again. 'But it's necessary.'

Real anger glittered in his eyes, the lines of his face gone hard. He stared at me, then turned away, pacing over to the desk and then to the window, going down the room before coming back again. A giant black panther on the prowl.

He only paced when he was upset or unhappy.

Guilt tugged at me and I clasped my hands, as if that would soothe it.

I hadn't thought he'd be *that* upset. Annoyed, sure, but the anger in his eyes and the way he was pacing around… It was almost as if it mattered to him.

Because he'll have to replace you.

Of course. It wasn't me, was it? It was never me.

He stopped mid-pace, turning sharply. 'Why do you want to leave?'

Would he even understand if I told him? Probably not. So I went with the simplest explanation. 'My life is all about work. I spend all day, every day, here. I don't have anything outside it. And I'm tired of that, Ulysses. I want to travel, to see different things, meet new people. Do something different.'

'I can give you a new job. Then you can meet some new people and do different things.'

'It's more than that. I don't want to just…work.'

'I'll give you a day off a week.'

'That's not…what I'm asking for.'

'More money, then? I'll pay you double.'

'I don't want money, Ulysses.'

'Triple. I'll fucking quadruple it if that's what you want.'

'No.' My chest felt tight, which was strange, because this shouldn't be difficult. 'That's not it.'

He was struggling, I could see it in his face. He was trying very hard to understand and the tightness in my chest became pain.

Why are you doing this to him?

I wasn't doing this to him. I was doing this *for me*. Because someone had to. No one else was going to care for me, so I had to do it. I'd always had to do it, hadn't I? Damian had tried after Mum had died, but in the end I had been too much for him. I'd been anxious and fearful, clinging to him in the months after her death, because he was all I'd had. He'd been a serious boy, but all that had changed once Mum was gone. Almost overnight he'd become funny and upbeat, smiling all the time. But just for me. No one else.

It was a mask he'd put on, a pretence, and I'd known he hated it so I'd tried not to be so fearful and anxious. Tried not to be so clingy and needy. But in the end he'd sent me away anyway, first to boarding school and then to London.

He'd given me opportunities and he'd done his best for me. He'd had his own very real issues to deal with too, and I'd been so young. Dealing with me couldn't have been easy for him.

But I'd never been able to shake that feeling that I'd been got rid of. That no matter how good or otherwise I'd been, no matter how hard I'd tried to change myself so I wasn't so much of a burden, I still was. He'd still had to send me away. And I'd gone without a fight because I hadn't wanted to make things harder for him.

Just as now I'd have been staying because I didn't want

to make things harder on Ulysses. Once again, I'd have been limiting myself and my life for someone else's sake.

I didn't want to do that again.

'A date,' Ulysses said suddenly. 'You said you wanted to go on a date and maybe get laid.'

'Yes, but—'

'We've had sex, but you didn't get your date.' He stared fixedly at me. 'I'll take you on a date.'

'Ulysses, that's not going to—'

'One date,' he interrupted. 'Come on one date with me and then review your decision.'

A date was a big thing for him and I knew it. He hated when he was required to do small talk or take part in the normal kind of social interaction that most people did.

I met his fierce gaze. 'Why is me leaving such a big deal when you can just get someone else to take my place?'

His eyes glittered with anger and frustration. 'Why do you think? You know me, Morgan. You know my... quirks. We work well together and I'm used to you. I don't want to have to train a new assistant. And I don't want to have to find someone who understands me the way you do.'

As I'd suspected—it wasn't about me. It was about him and how I could best not inconvenience him.

You also know that's how he thinks. You're being very hard on him.

But he was human. And he had feelings. And, though it was hard for him to understand another person's emotions, he could do it. Just as I could understand him.

'That's a you problem, Ulysses,' I said flatly. 'And it's up to you to solve it, not me.'

'Of course it's my problem.' He began to pace again. 'It's going to affect me and how I work.'

'What about me and how *I* work?'

'I've offered you many solutions and you—'

'But none of them actually solve the issue!' I cut him off, tired of the conversation. Of all the conversations I had with him. 'I want a relationship with someone. I want someone to care about me.'

His frown became even more ferocious. 'You just said that you—'

'Wanted new things and new experiences, yes. But I also want someone in my life.' I swallowed, not really sure why I wanted to tell him this, yet not stopping. 'I'm lonely, Ulysses. I've been lonely a long time and I'm tired of it.'

He stared at me in that intense way. 'Lonely,' he repeated as if tasting the word. 'You're lonely.'

'Yes.'

'But why? You work with people. You work with me.'

'You're not my friend,' I pointed out. 'You're my boss. And it's friends I want. A potential partner, too. A life outside of work.'

He'd stopped pacing now and was standing quite still. 'A date,' he said again. 'I'll take you on a date.'

'Right, because one date will magically cure all loneliness.'

'Of course it won't cure all loneliness. And I know it's not magic. But it would help, yes?'

'I can't date you,' I said automatically. 'You're my boss.'

'You said you couldn't sleep with me because I was your boss and yet you did,' he pointed out aggravatingly.

What would it hurt to go on a date? He's trying.

The tightness in my chest coiled a little tighter.

He *was* trying. But a single date wouldn't change my mind, just as money wouldn't change my mind. Then again, it wouldn't be a bad thing. Hell, maybe I could even use the practice.

Maybe he could too. Because you know you're not the only lonely one.

I didn't want the thought of Ulysses being on his own in my head. Because he had no one. At least, I'd never seen any evidence of it. He had Damian and Everett, but that was it. And, just because he never showed any signs of being lonely, that didn't mean he wasn't.

He was looking at me now and, even though he was standing still, I could feel the restlessness and impatience pouring off him. He wanted me to say yes. This mattered to him.

'Okay,' I said at last. 'One date.'

Instantly he straightened. 'I'll make the arrangements for tonight—'

'Not tonight,' I interrupted, because right now I needed a night away from him and his aggravating presence.

'Fine,' he snapped, obviously not liking my response. 'Tomorrow, then.'

'I'll need to check my schedule to see if I'm free.' No need to give him what he wanted immediately.

'No, you don't,' he said irritatingly, calling my bluff. 'You're free.'

I wished he wasn't right. I wished he wasn't so literal all the time.

You wish he was different.

But no, I didn't want to wish that. Because that would mean I felt more for him than I did, and I definitely didn't. Anyway, I didn't want to have an argument with him, so all I said was, 'Fine. Tomorrow night.'

'Excellent,' he said. 'Put it in my schedule.'

'Do you want me to book anything?' He usually left all those details to me.

But he shook his head. 'I'll arrange it.'

That surprised me and for a second my chest felt a little less tight, a little less sore. 'You will?'

'I'm the one who asked you on a date, which means it's up to me to arrange the details.' He was already striding towards the exit. 'On second thought, don't bother putting it in the schedule. I'll do it myself.' He paused by the door. 'Will you come to my place tonight?'

Even though I'd just had two intense orgasms not ten minutes earlier, my sex gave an almost painful throb at the heat I saw burning in his cold eyes.

But I had to draw the line somewhere. 'I don't think so. Not tonight.'

His gaze flickered, but he didn't say anything. He only gave a sharp nod before turning and striding out of the meeting room.

CHAPTER FOURTEEN

Ulysses

IT WAS LATE that night when I stood in front of the windows of my office, staring at the streetlights outside. But I wasn't counting them this time. I was too busy thinking about the date I'd scheduled with Morgan.

I hadn't been able to stop thinking about it since I'd put the suggestion to her earlier that day.

I'd never been on a date, not when it involved all the social things that made me uncomfortable, but she hadn't left me with much choice. The last thing I'd expected was for her to tell me she wanted to resign, so I'd had to do something. She hadn't wanted money or a different job, or even a day off per week—all easy enough things to give her. No, she'd said she was lonely. That she wanted a partner, and working for me meant she couldn't have that.

It was a difficult problem. Money was usually the best solution but it wasn't going to help me here. I'd have to solve her loneliness issue without it. Loneliness was a lack of contact with another person, and that meant a date would be the most logical answer.

It wasn't what I wanted to do, but Morgan was important to me. I needed her to stay. I couldn't do my job without her and I didn't want to find someone else to do it. No one else understood me the way she did.

Maybe someone else could. But it's her you want.

Of course it was her. I'd worked with her a long time and I...felt comfortable around her. A date wouldn't solve the issue of my sexual desire, but perhaps we could discuss that. The most important thing was that she couldn't resign. I had to convince her to stay.

So I'd spent a good couple of hours thinking about the date. I could have got her to arrange it to her liking, but a part of me didn't want her to. Dates weren't usually arranged by the person asked on the date, but the person asking, so I needed to do the arranging.

Except I'd run into an issue. I might have worked with Morgan for years but I didn't know much about her. I knew what annoyed her and what made her smile. I knew how to make her call my name. I knew how to make her come.

But I didn't know what she liked to eat, or what she liked doing. I didn't know what movies she liked or even if she liked movies at all. So many things I didn't know, things I'd never thought about before. Things I'd never thought would be a problem before, but were a problem now.

I wanted her to stay, which meant it was vital this date be something she'd enjoy.

You think your company will be enough for her?

I glared at my reflection in the glass. No, my company wouldn't be enough. I knew that already. Another reason I didn't date. When it came to women, sex was all I had to offer, so that was what I offered. Except this was going to have to be different; I'd have to organise other things to do to compensate for my lack of social graces.

Logically I should have asked Morgan herself what she liked, but again a part of me wanted to surprise her. Which meant getting help from someone else.

Luckily I knew just the person.

I scrolled through my contacts until I found Damian's name. Then I hit the call button.

He didn't answer immediately, which was irritating, but I called him another five times until at last he answered. 'What the fuck do you want now, Ulysses?' he snapped. 'I told you that I wasn't going to be around for—'

'What does Morgan like?' I interrupted, not in the mood for his excuses.

'What?'

Why did people ask these stupid questions? He'd heard me. Did I really have to repeat myself? 'What does Morgan like? What foods does she like to eat? What things does she like to do? Does she have any hobbies? Books she likes to read? Movies?'

'Why?' Damian asked.

At last, a valid question. I opened my mouth to tell him that I was planning to take her on a date and then stopped, an unfamiliar hesitation gripping me.

When Damian had first asked me to take Morgan on

as my assistant, he'd told me that it was important his sister was looked after and that he trusted me to take care of her. No one had ever asked me to take care of anything before, but because he was as close to a friend as I'd ever got I'd decided to give her the job and make sure she was taken care of.

I hadn't thought of that moment for years and it was strange to think of it now. To remember Damian's trust in me and how pleased I was with that trust.

He won't like you taking her on a date, let alone sleeping with her.

There was no reason he shouldn't like either of those things, because it wasn't as if I'd ever hurt Morgan. Nevertheless, instinct told me that it would be better that I didn't tell him the truth. Or, at least, not the greater part of it.

The only problem with that was that I hadn't had much experience at lying.

'She's doing very well in her job,' I said, which was true, but also not quite true at the same time. 'I want to take her out to thank her.'

'Huh.'

'What does that mean?'

'I thought giving people a bonus was more your style than taking them out?'

I didn't like the direction of this conversation, not at all. 'Just tell me what she likes,' I snapped. 'I haven't got time for all the ins and outs.'

'I don't know,' he said at last. 'I haven't spent a lot of time with her recently.'

Damian's voice sounded strange. Why was that? And why hadn't he spent time with her? It was true he never came to London. Not until a couple of weeks ago, when he'd turned up for the Black and White Foundation launch.

I'd never thought about why that was. It hadn't interested me. But now…

'Why not?' I demanded, something unfamiliar shifting inside me, a discomfort. Because it made me think of Morgan's face as she'd told me that she was lonely, of the thing that had glittered in her eyes, as though she'd been injured and was in pain, except the wound wasn't physical.

The loneliness hurt her and I didn't like that, not one bit.

'I have my reasons,' Damian muttered.

'And what are those?' I didn't like what he was saying. Was Morgan's loneliness somehow related to Damian? Had he made her feel lonely because he never visited? That made me angry and I wasn't sure why.

'Private reasons that have sweet fuck all to do with you,' Damian said curtly. 'If you want to know, you'll have to ask her.'

'I will,' I assured him. 'But you must know something about what she likes or doesn't like. She's your sister, after all.'

Damian let out a breath and I heard a woman's voice in the background, soft and husky, saying something to him. 'Okay, okay. When she was a little kid, I remember she wanted to visit the Eiffel Tower.'

Well, that wouldn't be too difficult for me to arrange. 'Good. Anything else?'

But this time a very feminine laugh came down the other end of the line and Damian said breathlessly, 'Oh yeah, one other thing. Remember what I told you about taking care of her. If you try anything, I'll punch your fucking head in.'

The line went dead as he disconnected the call.

Presumably by 'try anything' he meant sex, in which case it was too late. Another of those discomforting sensations twisted in my gut. Not because I'd had sex with her already, but because Damian hadn't visited her. And the more I thought about it, the angrier I became.

I couldn't imagine why he wouldn't have done so. He was her brother—wasn't he supposed to? I wasn't sure how families worked, never having had one myself, but I was sure they were supposed to talk to each other regularly or at least stay in contact. But Damian hadn't with Morgan, and now Morgan was lonely.

My fingers curled into a fist. Maybe it wouldn't be Damian punching my fucking head in. Maybe I'd be punching his.

But Damian wasn't here to punch so that wasn't helpful. I needed to concentrate on the date tomorrow, get everything planned. And if I did it well enough perhaps Morgan wouldn't be so lonely any more.

I uncurled my fingers and turned away from the window.

It took me a couple of hours to get everything set up and ready, but once that was done I put a call through to Morgan to tell her what would be happening tomorrow, as she did like to be prepared.

She answered the phone almost immediately, but she didn't sound very happy. 'Ulysses, do you know what bloody time it is?'

I stopped beside my desk and glanced out of the windows again. It was dark outside, same as it had been a couple of hours ago. 'No.'

'It's nearly midnight!'

'I needed to tell you what's happening tomorrow,' I said, annoyed with myself about the time, because I did know that most people didn't stay up the way I did. Then again, she needed to know the plan. 'If I'd left it until morning it would have been too late.'

She sighed. 'Okay, so what's happening tomorrow?'

'Our date.' I was about to go on and explain, then another of those suspicions wound through me. Perhaps it would be better if I didn't tell her.

'What about it?' Her voice was a little bit curt.

'I've arranged it.' I hesitated. 'Maybe I won't tell you, though. Maybe it should be a surprise.'

'A surprise?'

I couldn't tell what was in her voice now, couldn't tell if she was pleased or not, but I wanted her to be pleased. 'Yes, a surprise. You like surprises?'

'I don't know. It's been a long time since I've had one.'

'I could tell you if you want,' I offered. 'I'm going to—'

'No,' she interrupted quickly, 'don't tell me. I'd… like a surprise.'

I stopped beside the window again, looking out over
the lights, but I didn't count them. Every sense I had
concentrated on Morgan's voice, trying to glean meaning from the husky notes in it. Was she tired? If so, why
was she up at this time of night?

'Why are you awake, Morgan?' I asked.

'Oh… I couldn't sleep.'

'Why not?'

She was silent. It was the strangest thing, but I was
sure I could hear something in that silence. As if she
was trying to tell me something without words.

I'd never managed to pick up on the unspoken cues
that people gave to each other, never managed to read
people. And, since Uncle John, I'd never tried. Why
would I when I always got it wrong?

But I didn't want to get it wrong with Morgan. I'd
been getting a lot of things wrong with her and now I
wanted to get something right.

'Is it…because you're lonely?' I asked very carefully.

Another silence.

Her voice this time was quieter, softer. 'Yes.'

It had been a guess, and I should have been pleased
that I'd got it right, but I wasn't pleased. I didn't want
her to be lonely.

My chest felt as if something was pressing down on
it, and I didn't know what to do.

Or maybe I did.

'Morgan, do you want to…?' I stopped, unusually
hesitant. Was this the right thing to offer? I wasn't sure.

Then again, I didn't have anything else to give her. 'Do you…want me?'

Yet another silence. Longer this time, and the pressure on my chest became more intense, the sides of my phone digging into my palms as I held on to it. Why did this matter? Who cared if she said no?

But I cared and the feeling inside me gathered tighter, reminding me of sitting on that park bench with Uncle John and watching his face, wanting something I didn't understand. And afterwards feeling a heavy, painful sensation in my gut as he'd told me that he'd decided he wouldn't be adopting me after all, that I'd have to find another family.

It was a memory that made me uncomfortable so I ignored it, concentrating instead on the silence down the other end of the phone.

'Yes,' Morgan whispered at last. 'I think I do.'

The tightness in my chest released.

'I'll be there in ten minutes,' I said.

CHAPTER FIFTEEN

Morgan

I WOKE IN Ulysses's bed for the second morning in a row and for a moment I lay there, staring at the ceiling. He wasn't beside me, I could tell already, and that was probably a good thing. Parts of me were still aching and tender from the night before and I felt a bit rough around the edges.

He was a demanding partner and, though I was more than okay with his demands, I wasn't sorry for some recovery time now.

I still wasn't sure if I'd done the right thing in sleeping with him again, though. Yesterday I'd thought that some distance was what I wanted, and when I'd got home that evening I'd busied myself with a TV dinner and catching up on a romantic drama I'd been watching for the past week.

I'd tried not to think about the decision I'd made to hand him my resignation. Or about the date I'd agreed to go on with him.

Something sad settled in me whenever I thought of

those two things, which wasn't what I'd wanted at all. The decision to resign was meant to be a change for me. It was supposed to be exciting. And yet I didn't feel excited.

I hadn't felt excited about this date, either. Ulysses was only asking me out because he didn't want to get another PA. It wasn't about me. None of it was about me. And I was selfish enough that I wanted it to be.

I'd lost myself in my TV show, but once I'd got into bed I hadn't been able to sleep. The sadness felt as if it had crept into my bones and was sitting there like damp in the foundations of a house, making me feel fragile. Making my chest ache. The silence in my little flat had never been so loud or so heavy, and I'd been on the point of getting up and turning the TV on, just for some noise, when my phone had buzzed on my bedside table.

I hadn't meant to answer it, but when Ulysses's name had flashed up my hand had shot out and I'd pressed the answer button before I could stop myself. And when his deep, cold voice had come down the phone, the silence around me had felt less loud, less heavy.

I don't know how he'd guessed that it was loneliness I'd been feeling. He never picked up on that stuff face to face, let alone on a phone call. But somehow he'd known. And his question had surprised me so much that I hadn't been able to give him anything but the truth. When he'd asked me if I wanted him, I'd said yes before I could stop myself.

Of course, it was just sex he was offering, but I didn't care.

It was one of those times where I loved his straight-up impatience. That he didn't make me wait. He'd been there in exactly ten minutes and, as I hadn't wanted to be in my flat, he'd taken me back to his.

Then he'd fucked me on the floor of his living room, then over the arm of his couch, then twice more in his bed. I'd fallen asleep with his arms around me, the heat of his passion burning the sadness right out of me.

It was still there, though, I could feel the cold ache of it, so instead I tried to think about what this date would be like.

A surprise, he'd said, which itself surprised me, as I hadn't thought Ulysses was capable of surprises.

You underestimate him. There's a lot of things you don't think he's capable of, yet it turns out he is.

But I didn't want to think about that. Mainly because I had a suspicion that, once I did, I'd start thinking other things, wanting other things. Things I shouldn't be wanting from him because, not only was he my boss, he was a man who ultimately could never give me the thing I most craved.

A connection.

Pushing aside the duvet, I slid out of bed. A white towelling bathrobe was draped over the end of the bed and, as my clothes weren't in the immediate vicinity, I put on that instead then went in search of Ulysses.

His penthouse was at the top of one of the skyscrapers near the river and had the most fantastic views. It was furnished very simply, with a neutral palette of whites and greys and blacks. There was no art on the walls or knickknacks on the bookshelves. No photographs, even. Nothing at all that was personal.

It was very much like a hotel room, which made the sadness in my bones ache a little more. Because, if the emptiness of his home was a reflection of the emptiness of his life, then he was even more isolated than I'd imagined.

Did he have no likes or dislikes when it came to his environment? No friends with whom to have photos taken and pinned onto the fridge door? No souvenirs he wanted to bring back to remember different experiences by? No family?

He had Everett and Damian, but there were no pictures of them anywhere. No photos of his family. No nothing. There were books on the bookshelves, but they all looked pristine, the magazines stacked on the shockingly expensive glass coffee-table uncreased. There was no dust anywhere, but I knew he had the place cleaned every day.

And it came to me, as I paused in the doorway, that he was a man who moved through life leaving no trace of himself anywhere, except for the company he'd built. Was that a monument to something? Did he have a reason for why he'd driven himself to build that company up from nothing? Was it money or something else? A legacy? Did he even know himself?

The questions tumbled around in my head like dice being thrown, and I realised that I wanted to know. I wanted some insight into the man I'd been working for for so long.

'There are some clothes on the couch.' Ulysses's deep voice came from behind me. 'You have time for a shower, but then we'll have to leave.'

I turned around.

He was standing in the hallway behind me, adjusting his cufflinks. Again he was in one of his beautifully cut suits, a white business shirt and a gorgeously coloured tie in blue silk. His beautiful face was set in its customarily granite lines, but there was a light in his black eyes I'd never seen before.

If I didn't know any better, I'd say it was excitement.

'What's the time?' I asked, belatedly realising that of course it was a work day, and here was Ulysses, plainly ready for work. I was going to be late again, wasn't I?

'Just before nine. The plane leaves soon so I'd get dressed if I were you.'

'The plane?'

Finishing with his cufflinks, he glanced at me. 'Yes. It's for our date. We're going by plane.'

I blinked in astonishment. A plane? Did that mean no work? Unheard of. 'Going where?'

'It's a surprise.'

Was that…smugness in his face? Surely not?

But then, I didn't have much more time to wonder as Ulysses gently ushered me into the shower, bringing the clothes that were on the couch into the bathroom so I had something to put on. They weren't the clothes I'd been wearing the night before. In fact, they were clothes I'd never seen before.

'Where did these come from?' I asked as he laid them down on the stool beside the vanity. 'They're not mine.'

'A shop.'

A typical Ulysses answer. 'Yes, but why did they come from a shop?'

'I bought them for you.' He glanced down at his watch. 'You have fifteen minutes.'

'Why did you buy them for me?'

'The ones you were wearing last night weren't suitable for our date. Come on—you don't have much time.'

It was clear I wasn't going to get too many more answers out of him, so I had my shower then dressed in the clothes he'd apparently bought for me. Black lace knickers and a strapless black bra. A very pretty, but very figure-hugging, blue silk dress with spaghetti straps that fitted me like a glove. There were even matching blue high-heeled sandals to go with it.

I wasn't sure how I felt about wearing something he'd bought for me—how did he even know my size?—but when I came out of the bathroom the hot gleam that leapt in his eyes as he looked at me made warmth glow in my chest.

'It fits well,' he said, his gaze raking over me.

'Yes, it does.' I swallowed, my throat gone tight. 'Did you guess my size?'

'No. I looked at the labels on your other clothes.'

Something warmed inside me. No one had bought me things before and I'd never thought he'd be the first one to do it.

'I like it,' I said and meant it. 'Thank you. But…why are we going on a date this morning? What about work?'

'We won't be at work today.' He turned. 'Come on, the car is downstairs already.'

He was being quite mysterious for such a literal man and I wasn't sure whether to be irritated about it or not. In the end, I decided to go with it, because I liked that he was being mysterious. And I liked that he was obviously excited, too. He'd put thought into this date, which I hadn't expected.

The car took us to one of the private airfields just out of London and from there we boarded one of Black and White's sleek little private jets. Ulysses wouldn't be drawn on where we were going but, as he'd somehow miraculously managed to conjure my passport out of thin air, it was obviously going to be out of the country.

Pleasure curled inside me, leaching away some of the aching sadness in my bones, and as we sat down ready for take-off I teased him gently about how mysterious he was being and whether he was sure one day off work was allowed.

He never noticed when I was teasing him, but something told me that he was aware of it now, because he sat opposite me, staring at me, that hot gleam steadily burning in his eyes. He didn't smile—he never did— yet his beautiful mouth was relaxed, as if any minute it would curve.

He looked so thoroughly pleased with himself it made my heart tighten.

Our date turned out to be in Paris, which thrilled

me. I'd never been there, because I'd never had time, but I'd always wanted to go. And I couldn't stop smiling as yet another car took us from the airport into the city. 'Where are we going now?' I asked as we drove along the banks of the Seine.

'It's a surprise,' he said yet again.

Another half an hour and I soon discovered what my surprise was.

Brunch at the Eiffel Tower.

We had the most delicious meal in the restaurant on the first level, and then I discovered that Ulysses had somehow managed to get the whole top level closed off just for him and me.

I stared in amazement at the views as I stood at one of the rails, looking north. It was a beautiful day. The sky was the same colour as Ulysses's tie—a dense, deep blue—and the sounds of the city rose all around us.

'Do you like this?' Ulysses asked, leaning on the rail beside me.

'Oh, yes, it's fantastic.' And it was. Very fantastic. I inhaled some of the rich Parisian air. 'What made you think of this?'

'I didn't think of it,' he said with his characteristic bluntness. 'I called Damian to ask him what you liked and he said that you always wanted to go up the Eiffel Tower.'

I had? I frowned, trying to remember. Oh, that was right. Damian had got me *Madeline* out of the library and I'd been obsessed with Paris for a couple of weeks afterwards. 'When I was seven,' I said, smiling at the memory. 'How funny that he'd remember.'

'Why does he never visit you here?' Ulysses asked unexpectedly.

A cold shock pulsed down my spine.

I'd had no idea Ulysses had even noticed, let alone wondered about, the reasons Damian never came to London. Why was he interested now?

I kept my gaze on the beautiful view, looking along the Champ de Mars, the warm air whispering over the bare skin of my shoulders. 'He has his reasons.'

'That's what he said. But what reasons are those?'

I didn't want to talk about this, which was silly. Damian and I had begun to sort out our issues when he'd turned up unexpectedly at the Black and White Foundation launch. He'd texted me since then about meeting up to talk and it was plain he had things to tell me.

I hadn't replied. Why? I didn't know, because I loved my brother. And I understood why he'd put distance between us; he'd been under tremendous pressure after our mother had died because he'd had to look after me. I knew that he loved me, though. I knew that he cared.

So why are you still so angry at him?

Ulysses's hand gripped my chin gently, turning me to face him, and then all I could see was his black eyes. 'Why, Morgan?'

CHAPTER SIXTEEN

Ulysses

HER SKIN WAS soft against my fingers, warm, and the sunlight on her shoulder where the blue strap of her dress lay over it was distracting. The contrast between the deep blue silk of the strap and her pale skin, almost translucent in the light, was fascinating.

But I had to concentrate because she wasn't answering my question and I wanted to know why. I wanted to know what the strange note in her voice meant.

Her brow creased, an odd, sharp glitter in her eyes. 'Why do you want to know? What does it matter to you why he didn't visit me?'

'Because it does. When I called him last night to ask him what you liked, he initially said he didn't know.'

'Oh.' Something shifted in Morgan's eyes and I felt the muscles in her jaw tense.

'I thought he'd know, but he didn't,' I went on. 'He said it was because he hadn't spent time with you recently and then I realised that he didn't visit you. I asked him why, but he wouldn't say.'

She wanted to pull away. I could feel the resistance in her muscles. But I kept my grip on her because I wanted to look into her face.

'I don't want to talk about this, Ulysses,' she said.

'Why not?'

Her mouth became a hard line. 'Because it's personal.'

'But isn't that what happens on a date? You talk about personal things?'

'Not the first date. You don't talk about personal things like that on the first date. It's more "getting to know you" stuff.'

'I already know you, though,' I said. 'We've worked together for years.'

'Yes, "working" being the operative word. That doesn't mean you know me.'

Again, there was a hint of something in her voice that bothered me. Was it anger, irritation?

I searched her face, trying to sort out what it was. 'I do know you,' I repeated. 'You're punctual and reliable. You're conscientious. Your appearance is always immaculate and you work very hard. You have the most fascinating little beauty spot near your upper lip, and when you look at me sometimes it's like there's a flame in your eyes.' I thought a bit more. 'And I know that I annoy you, but you don't let it get the better of you. You're very patient. And your hair feels like silk when I put my hands in it.'

Her eyes widened. I'd surprised her and I liked that.

'Tell me why he didn't visit, Morgan,' I said again, making my voice softer.

She hesitated. 'Why don't you tell me something personal about you, first?'

That seemed strange. How was that relevant? 'Why?'

'For the same reason that you want to know about me.'

And I thought about that for a second, my gaze falling to her mouth and the soft curve of her lips. To the little black beauty spot that I wanted to kiss and taste, as I had last night. The silk dress I'd bought for her looked interesting against her skin, and I noticed how closely it fitted to the curves of her body…

But that was not what I wanted to know more about, was it? She'd said that her wanting to know more about me was similar to my curiosity about why Damian didn't visit her. That was…interesting. Why was she curious about me?

Whatever—I didn't want to talk about myself. That wasn't interesting to me. I wanted to know about her. Then again, telling her something about me seemed like a small thing to give.

I let go of her chin even though I didn't want to stop touching her. 'What do you want to know?'

She leaned against the rail, the breeze blowing her skirt around her knees and whipping up her black hair. 'Do you have any family?'

'No.'

'None?'

'My mother was a teenager who gave me up for

adoption and died about ten years ago. I never managed to find out who my father was.' I'd done the research for my own interest's sake after I'd met Damian and Everett in an Internet chat room. We'd had similar childhoods, in that they'd been difficult, and their experiences with their own parents had encouraged me to find mine. It had taken some doing, but I'd eventually found my mother. It had been an interesting experience.

'So what happened to you?' Morgan asked. 'Were you adopted? Fostered?'

The questions made me uncomfortable so I glanced away, putting my hands on the rails and looking out over Paris spread out before us. Thinking about my childhood always made me feel that way so I never thought about it. I didn't particularly like talking about it either, but since there was no good reason not to I continued, 'Fostered. I came close to being adopted once, but Uncle John decided against it.'

'Uncle John?'

'A foster father of mine. He took me around the casinos when I was a boy, to Europe, and the States too. Las Vegas in particular. He'd smiled at me a lot, especially when I helped him win big, and he'd told me that he wanted me to be his son. Until we were banned from every casino in both Europe and America, and then he decided he wasn't going to adopt me after all. We were barred from entry after six months or so for card counting, and so he changed his mind about adopting me.'

'Oh, Ulysses.' Morgan's soft voice was a murmur. 'Did you want to be adopted?'

'Yes. I thought he liked me.' Or at least, that was the impression he'd given me. Until I'd discovered otherwise.

'But he was using you,' Morgan said quietly.

'Yes.' That had surprised me and made me angry, because he'd told me how important I was to him. But it wasn't me who'd been important, only my gift for patterns because that had earned him money. 'I believe he was.'

'Oh…' she said, and I had to move away from her, the odd note in her voice and the warmth of her skin making the discomfort inside me get worse.

I was silent, staring out at the view; there was nothing else to say.

'That must have hurt.' Her voice slid over me, quiet and certain. 'You liked him, didn't you?'

The discomfort shifted once again. I didn't want to think about this. I didn't want to remember. It brought back feelings I didn't understand and, yes, it had hurt. But I'd never understood why.

Uncle John made me angry, nothing more.

'He used to buy me ice cream every time we went to the casino, and when we won he told me I was a good boy.' I didn't look at her because her gaze made everything worse. 'I used to like that at first, but then later I realised it sounded like he was praising a dog.' Anger gathered in the pit of my stomach, but this was familiar, understandable, so I let it sit there. 'I wasn't a dog. I was a boy. But he didn't see me as one.'

Morgan said nothing.

'I went on to other foster families after that. They were all the same. They didn't understand me, and I didn't understand them, and that was fine. But I made sure that no one ever knew about what I could do with patterns. That was for me.' And Everett and Damian. My relationship with them was the closest I had ever come to getting understanding from other human beings. Yes, they annoyed me, but they'd never used me the way Uncle John had.

They'd never treated me as if I was someone's favoured pet or performing monkey.

Morgan once again didn't say anything, which was what I preferred, but then her hand moved, shifting to mine on the rail, and she put it over mine. I'd never been one for casual touches that weren't related to sex. In fact, I couldn't remember the last time someone had touched me that way.

Ordinarily I would have pulled away, but her touch felt as if it was dulling the sharp edges of the pain inside me, making my anger less intense. So I didn't pull away. I left my hand there. I let her touch calm me.

'Damian didn't come to visit me because he felt he failed me after Mum died,' she said after a moment of silence. 'He felt he should have done something to make things better for me and he couldn't.'

Ah, so that was how it worked. If I offered her something, she'd give me something back.

'How does not visiting you help?' I asked.

'He was afraid of what I'd think of him. And he was ashamed that he hadn't come earlier.'

That still didn't make any sense to me and it probably never would, which made asking further questions pointless. So all I said was, 'He should have visited you. He shouldn't have left you here alone.'

This time, when she didn't say anything, I turned to look at her.

She too was staring out at the city, her profile one pure, uninterrupted line. Her nose was small and slightly tilted, her lips full, her forehead high.

I thought about the anger in her voice when she'd mentioned this before, and how I could understand that anger, because I was familiar with it. Both of us were angry at people who'd treated us badly.

'He was trying,' Morgan said at last. 'He was doing his best for me.'

'No, he wasn't. If he'd been doing his best for you, he would have come and visited you.'

She lifted a shoulder. 'Does it really matter why he didn't?'

'Yes, of course it matters.' Did I really have to explain this? 'I don't want you to leave. And perhaps if Damian had been more attentive to you then you wouldn't feel like you had to.'

'It's not just Damian.'

'Then what else is it?' I turned so I was facing her, her hand still on mine on the railing. It felt natural to turn my hand over and interlace her fingers with mine. 'Explain it to me.'

The muscles in her jaw were tight, but she didn't pull her hand away. 'There's no point, Ulysses.'

'Why?' I demanded. 'Because I wouldn't understand?'

She shook her head wordlessly.

'Are you going to pat me on the head and call me a good boy too, then?' It was meant to be an honest question, but it didn't come out that way. My voice had got sharp, which I hadn't intended.

Morgan went still and then she turned to me, her eyes very blue. 'No, of course not. I would never do that.' She sounded fierce. 'I'm sorry, I didn't—'

'You're right, though,' I interrupted, the discomfort inside me growing edges once more, as though I'd swallowed a shard of glass. 'I wouldn't understand.'

'Ulysses…'

'Perhaps it's best if we don't discuss personal matters any more. Would you like to hear about the Eiffel Tower?' I took my hand away. 'It was constructed in…'

Her fingers closed around mine before I could pull away entirely and I froze. I hadn't realised such a small hand could contain such strength, because I couldn't move. It was as if my feet were rooted in place.

Her gaze was sharp and it felt as if she could see inside me. As if she knew my thoughts. As if she knew me better than I knew myself.

'I'm angry with Damian because he sent me away. Because I tried to be a good girl, to not make myself more of a burden to him than I already was. To not argue with him or protest when he sent me to boarding school and then to London. To not tell him that I didn't want to go and do either of those things.'

Her fingers tightened around mine. 'I'm angry because, even though I did everything I could to make him happy, he still never visited me. And that felt like he didn't care. That, once I was out of sight, I was out of mind. I'm also angry at myself, because all I've done for years is exactly what he told me to do and I'm tired of it. I'm tired of making myself acceptable to other people. I'm tired of trying not to be difficult, of contorting myself for other people. I'm tired and I don't want to do it any more.'

Her words fell over me and I concentrated hard on them. She was giving this to me like a gift, as if she expected me to understand, and I wanted to. I wanted to make sense of what she was saying.

So I didn't ask questions, I sorted through what she said, trying to find the patterns. Trying to draw some conclusions. Contorting herself, making herself acceptable… What did she mean? Because she was always acceptable.

But maybe she doesn't know that.

I blinked, groping for the thought, catching hold of it. Perhaps she didn't know. She wasn't like me. I'd always be who I was, and I couldn't change for other people. There had been times when I'd wished I understood more, that I could be more like the rest of the world, but those times were few and far between.

Maybe that wasn't true for Morgan. She could change, and did, because she thought she wasn't acceptable as she was. Which was a lie.

'Why would you want to contort for other people?' I asked. 'You're perfectly acceptable as you are.'

'No, I'm not.' Something in her eyes glittered like a tiny diamond. 'If I was perfectly acceptable as I am, then my brother would never have sent me away like a...' She stopped and turned away, pulling her hand from mine.

My chest felt sore and I didn't like that glitter in her eyes. It looked like tears.

She didn't think she was acceptable at all.

'Morgan.' I tried to think of what else to say, to tell her that she was all I needed in a PA.

Just in a PA?

The thought was hot, glowing in my head like the lights I looked at outside my windows at night, and I stopped speaking in order to examine it. She *was* all I needed in a PA. But she was also now my lover and she was all I needed there too. She didn't need to be anything for me other than who she already was.

'What?' she prompted and I realised I hadn't finished what I'd been going to tell her.

'Morgan, you're exactly what I need in a PA. You're also exactly what I need in a lover too.'

I'd hoped that would ease the look in her eyes, but it didn't. Instead, she said, 'That's because I contort myself for you as well.'

My gut twisted. 'How? Why would you do that?'

She shook her head. 'You don't want to know.'

'Yes, I do. Otherwise I wouldn't have asked.'

'That,' she said at last. 'That right there is why I

have to contort myself. Because you're so literal. Because you don't get my sarcasm or understand some of the things I say. Because I have to explain everything down to the nth degree. Because I can't make a joke, or smile at or tease you, since every time I do you have to ask me a hundred thousand questions about why I'm doing those things.'

Her lashes swept down, veiling her gaze. 'Of course I'm everything you want in a PA. Because that's all I ever let you see. Because, if I was my real self with you, you'd probably fire me.'

I felt cold and the pain in my chest that her touch had eased returned and, along with it, my anger. Though there was no reason to be angry with her. She did have to do all those things because of who I was. Because of what I couldn't change about myself.

She was only telling me the truth.

Yet that didn't change the sick feeling in my gut.

'What about when we were having sex?' I asked, wanting to know, as this felt important to me. 'Were you yourself then? Or were you just trying to please me?'

A wave of red washed over her cheeks. 'I don't think—'

'You were,' I interrupted, knowing it was the truth even as I said it. And I wasn't sure how I knew. I just did. 'You were yourself with me then.'

She looked down, the sunlight glossing her black hair. 'I don't know. I don't even know who I am deep down these days myself.'

'I know who you are.' It felt strange to say that, when

there was no real way to know another person, not when it was impossible to read thoughts or see emotions— at least, it was impossible for me. Yet when I had her in my arms, when I was inside her, it felt as if I knew her. As if I could read her. As if she was as understandable to me as everyone else was understandable to her.

Slowly she lifted her head again and looked at me. 'How can you?'

She didn't believe me. She didn't think I would understand.

It was time to show her that I did.

CHAPTER SEVENTEEN

Morgan

THE PARISIAN SUN was bright yet it only made the darkness of Ulysses's eyes seem even darker. He had that look he got when he was intently interested in something, intensely focused on it. And right now that something was me.

It sent a ripple of sensual heat chasing over my skin, distracting me from the ache in my heart and the cold in my bones that had seemed to settle in for good.

I hadn't wanted to tell him about Damian, because I knew he'd never understand it, but I'd also been unable to refuse when he'd asked me to. He'd never wanted to know about me before, had never seemed interested, and I could see that this meant something. That he didn't want me to treat him any differently than I would treat someone else. And I knew why after hearing about his Uncle John.

He'd told me in his usual flat, inexpressive tones, but there had been a rigidity to his powerful body and a familiar tension gathering around him. He was angry, that was clear, and I could understand why, even if he didn't. He'd been hurt. That man had used Ulysses, given him promises that he would have taken at face value, because he would have been unable to see it any other way, and not only because he'd been a child.

So the eventual realisation that it was for his abilities, not himself, that he'd been wanted must have been awfully painful. I felt that pain too, even though I didn't want to, because I knew what it was like to feel that you weren't enough for someone.

Ulysses's expression was normally granite-faced, but there had been something even harder in it than usual when he'd mentioned being called a 'good boy'. Like a dog…

God, I hadn't known what to say. I'd felt angry and hurt for him, but he was a difficult man to comfort, so in the end I hadn't said anything, instead letting my hand rest over his.

I couldn't refuse to tell him the truth about Damian, about all the things in my heart, even though I suspected he wouldn't understand. I couldn't treat him like a 'good boy', as if he wasn't even a person.

He'd tried. I could see it in his face as I'd told him about how I'd never felt good enough. How I'd felt I had to contort myself to make people happy. How I had to contort myself for him too.

He was making the effort for me. And it came to me in a sudden burst of irony that, right now, it was him contorting for me, trying to understand what I'd told him.

My throat had tightened and then he'd said that stuff about sex. About being myself when I was with him. And that had surprised me. Even shocked me. Just as it shocked me that he seemed so certain about it, especially when I wasn't certain myself.

How could he know that? How could a man who couldn't read other people, and wasn't interested in reading them, who only considered his own viewpoint, know me better than I knew myself?

He put his hands on my hips, drawing me towards him, until I was standing pressed to his powerful body. He felt hot, hard, the warmth of his palms burning through the thin silk of my dress. His dark, deep gaze was full of that cold focus, yet heat as well, the contrast fascinating to me. 'Let me show you,' he said softly.

I struggled to take a breath, because the air seemed suddenly lacking in oxygen. He couldn't possibly be thinking what I thought he was thinking, could he?

'What? Here?' I looked around a little wildly. 'Right now?'

'Why not?' he asked with his usual infuriating calm. 'There's no one else here.'

'Ulysses. It's the Eiffel Tower. We can't have sex on the Eiffel Tower.'

'I'm not sure of French law around sex in a public place, and maybe legally we can't. But don't worry. I can get such things overlooked.'

Law. He was worried about the law.

'People will see. There are probably cameras and all kinds of…'

He was already turning me, crowding me against the rail with all of Paris at my back. There was a wire cage around the whole of the top deck, so there was no danger of falling, and the second deck was a long way beneath us, so in essence he was right. No one would see. So I didn't know why my heart was beating so fast or why I was feeling so nervous, especially when this wasn't the first time we'd done this.

'Colour?' he asked shortly, gripping my hips, his body pressing insistently against mine.

He was very hot, his clean, fresh scent surrounding me, arousing me. I couldn't work out what I was nervous about. Was it the fact that we were in the open or did it have more to do with what he intended to do?

He'd said I was myself when we were having sex, but what did that mean? How was I myself? I didn't even know and maybe that was what scared me—the fact that I didn't know.

So don't you want to find out?

I caught my breath.

He was still, those black eyes of his so intent, as if he saw something in me that I didn't see myself. He was so blind in many ways, yet at the same time he saw things so clearly. Without anything clouding them or getting in the way. What did he see when he looked at me? What was I to him when he held me? When he touched me? When he was inside me?

'Green,' I said in a thick voice, knowing that as soon as I said it he'd take charge.

And he didn't disappoint.

His gaze flared hot, but he didn't kiss me as I expected him to. Instead, he reached down, gathering up the front of my dress while leaving the rest of me covered. I shivered as his fingers brushed over the front of my underwear, tracing the shape of my sex through the fabric. He didn't look down, his attention on my face as he stroked me. My cheeks got hot, my breathing fast, and a sudden shyness swept over me which was strange, considering all we'd done together the previous night.

I wanted to look away but, as if he knew exactly what was going through my head, he shifted his grip from my hip to my chin, holding my head still so I couldn't turn away from him. And he kept up the gentle stroking, tracing my sex through the lace until my knees felt weak and the fabric damp.

'I don't know how this is supposed to show me myself,' I said breathlessly, trying to cover my nervousness.

His eyes glittered in the sunlight, dark and depthless. 'Are you contorting yourself for me now?'

'I…uh…' I stopped on a gasp as his finger found my clit, circling it gently, making white-hot streaks of pleasure fan out inside me.

'Well?' His gaze raked over my face, his intensity hotter than the sun above us, his finger circling maddeningly, a light, almost unbearable pressure. 'Are you, Morgan?'

I blinked, trying to think through the rising pleasure. The ache between my thighs was growing more insistent and I could feel myself getting even wetter. I wanted his finger to press harder, give me more, and my hips moved, shifting against his, encouraging more pressure, more friction.

'Answer me,' he ordered.

I realised I'd lost track of things. My hands were on his chest, gripping the front of his shirt, and my thighs were trembling. I wanted to lean back, spread my legs, give him greater access, because this wasn't enough.

'No.' The word came out thick and husky. 'I…don't think so.'

'No,' he echoed. 'You're not. You're not contorting for me at all, but for yourself. Because you want me to make you come.'

'I…' I began, only to have the words fail as his finger pressed down on my clit, pleasure flashing like lightning along all my nerve-endings.

'You are yourself now, Morgan.' He kept up with the circling, round and round, making me pant. 'Right now, all that matters to you is pleasure. Your own pleasure.'

I swallowed, my throat bone-dry, trying to get my brain to work. 'I…suppose that's true.'

'It is.' His hand on my chin shifted until he was gripping my jaw, tilting my head back so all I could see was his black eyes. 'Your true self likes physical pleasure. It likes touch. It wants passion and it wants to be free to experience those things.' His finger slid just to the side of my clit, the indirect touch making a moan gather in the back of my throat. 'Your true self is responsive and demanding. It wants what it wants, and it doesn't much care whether that's right or wrong.'

His voice slid along my nerve-endings together with

the touch of his fingers, cold yet hot, smooth yet with a rough edge. How did he understand these things? Could he really see them? Did he really know what he was talking about?

Ulysses moved even closer, pressing me harder against the rail, the feeling of being trapped by him sending my excitement sky high. 'How do I know?' he asked, as if he could read my mind. 'Because, right in this moment, I'm all those things too. Responsive and demanding. Passionate.' The pressure of his finger increased until I was shuddering, my hips trying to lift against his. 'I want to fuck you as badly as you want me to fuck you. The only difference is that I don't care so much for my pleasure. It's yours that matters the most to me.'

The words he said rippled through me and I found myself watching his face, the way he was watching mine, looking into his eyes and seeing only the heat this time, not the cold. It hadn't occurred to me that this was where we communicated perfectly. Where we matched perfectly.

Because it was true—he *was* all those things and so was I. Here, right now, we understood one another in a way I'd never understood another human being in my life. And that I would find this with my genius and very literal, enraging, infuriating boss was something I'd never expected, not in a million years.

He was right. I wasn't contorting myself, wasn't making myself more acceptable. Wasn't worried about what I said in case he didn't understand. Wasn't laboriously having to explain myself.

He understood me and I understood him.

We were so very different. Yet right now, like this, we were the same.

He stopped touching me, reaching for his wallet and getting something out of it. I inhaled as I realised that yes, indeed, he was pretty much intending to fuck me at the top of the Eiffel Tower.

My heartbeat roared in my ears, but I didn't stop him. Not when he unzipped his trousers and sheathed himself, and not when he lifted my dress again, tugging the front of my knickers aside. He lifted me, bracing me against the rail, his strength astonishing as he held me up, ready for him, and I lifted my legs and wound them around his waist.

His eyes were full of flames and I stared straight back. All the lights were green, and he saw it, understood it without having to ask, and then he was sliding into me. Not hard and fast this time, but slow and deep. I bit my lip at the agonising pleasure of him stretching me, a sweet, delicious burn that had my thighs gripping him tightly, a groan escaping me.

He made no sound except for a hitch of breath that told me everything I needed to know about what he was feeling. Not that I needed to hear it. I could see it in his face, in the rigid lines around his eyes and mouth, in the set of his jaw. In the black furnace of his eyes.

We were one in this moment and not just physically. It went deeper than that. It was elemental, almost.

A rush of emotion caught in my throat and I wanted to hold on to this feeling, hold it for ever, because it made the cold damp of loneliness vanish from my bones, filling up the space left behind with heat and pleasure. With passion.

With Ulysses.

He began to move, taking his time, drawing out of me in a long, slick glide and then easing back in. I forgot we were on top of the Eiffel Tower, forgot that all of Paris was at my back. Forgot about every single little thing except for the coal-black eyes of the man in front of me, inside me, and the leisurely flex of his hips, the spread of pleasure that was lighting me up.

I had the feeling that I knew him. That I'd always known him. And that he knew me too. He knew me better than I knew myself. Perhaps he always had.

I lifted my hands, wound my arms around his neck and leaned in, tasting his mouth, kissing him as slowly and lazily as the movement of his cock inside me. Taking my time, not rushing. And he let me explore, opening his mouth so that I could kiss him deeper, tasting coffee and a dark sweetness that had all the blood rushing to my head.

There was no hurry between us, no urgency. No fighting or resisting. This time it was the moment that mattered, the unspoken understanding that was rippling between us, the pleasure almost secondary.

His grip changed, his weight pressing me to the railing and the bars of the thin cage that protected us from the drop, his fingers gripping into the iron. He altered the angle of his hips slightly, every thrust now brushing against my clit, making me moan helplessly into his mouth.

I tightened my arms around him, arching into him, the pleasure tugging at me, urging me to go faster, harder. But I didn't want to. I wanted this sweetness to last, because I had the sense that once it was over I wouldn't have it again. I would lose him.

The thought was unbearable.

I kissed him deeper, harder, and his grip shifted again. I felt him ease one hand between us, his fingers brushing over my achingly sensitive clit, everything in me drawing into a tight, hard knot.

Tears pricked behind my eyes.

'Red,' I whispered against his mouth. 'Red, Ulysses.'

CHAPTER EIGHTEEN

Ulysses

I HEARD HER very clearly and I stopped, my pulse pounding, my cock still buried deep inside her.

I was breathing very fast and I was having difficulty getting my thoughts in order. I wasn't sure what I'd done wrong. Had I not read her correctly? I'd thought we understood each other so I hadn't asked her for her colour. I'd thought I didn't need to.

You've done that once before, though, haven't you?

Yes, but that had been with Uncle John. And I'd been ten. It wasn't with Morgan.

You didn't understand him. You'll never understand her.

I ignored that, lifting my mouth from hers and looking down at her.

Her eyes were so blue and liquid with moisture, her lips full and red, swollen from our kiss. The heat of her pussy gripping my cock tightly was undeniable, and she was wet too, so surely I hadn't got it wrong? Surely she wanted this?

'Am I hurting you?' I grated out. 'Is that why you want me to stop?'

She shook her head, her breathing ragged. 'No, it's not that.' Her arms around my neck shifted and she cupped my jaw with one small hand. 'I just…don't want this moment to end.'

But it would end. Everything did. 'Morgan…'

'I don't want it to end because I don't want to lose this feeling between us.'

A heavy weight shifted in my chest. 'You won't lose it. We can have sex again.'

'No, it's not just the sex, Ulysses.' The sunlight caught the tears in her eyes. 'I don't want to lose you.'

I stared down at her, trying to ignore the soft grip of her body, her heat and the scent of her arousal. Trying to ignore the physical pleasure so I could concentrate on what she was trying to tell me.

'How can you lose me?' I asked. 'I'm not going any-where.'

Her other hand came up so she was cupping my face between her palms. 'But you do. You go somewhere I can't follow. Where I don't understand you and you don't understand me. Where we don't have this feeling between us any more.'

I understood even as she said it. For once, I knew exactly what she was saying. The physical pleasure we shared enabled us to connect in a way that normally we couldn't. It bridged the gap that was too wide to cross when we weren't in each other's arms. But soon it would be over and the connection would snap. And once again we'd be left with a distance that could never be bridged.

I didn't know what to say, because it was true and it made something inside me hurt. Which in turn made me angry, because there was nothing I could do to fix it. I couldn't change myself. I couldn't be different.

This was the way I'd been made and, apart from that one moment back when I'd been a kid, when I'd looked at Uncle John and wished that I wasn't different, I'd always been fine with how I was.

But I wasn't now. Now, I wished I could be like everyone else.

There was nothing I could say, so I leaned down and kissed her, covering her mouth with mine, giving her the only thing I could, which was pleasure. I moved again slowly, drawing out this moment for as long as I could, until she was writhing in my arms, twisting and gasping, her thighs locked tightly around my waist.

Then I shifted again, changing the angle yet again, hitting her clit with each thrust. Soon she'd put her arms around my neck again, holding me tightly as she buried her face against my throat, her whole body convulsing as the climax hit her.

I closed my eyes as I thrust harder, deeper into the wet heat of her, finally allowing the rush of the orgasm to take me as well. The pleasure was annihilating and for long moments afterwards I wasn't able to move.

I simply stood there with Morgan pressed against the iron of the cage around the viewing deck, deep inside her, the sun on my face and my closed lids, the scent of her around me. She felt so good I could have stood there for ever.

Did she feel the same? Was this, too, something I could understand?

I opened my eyes and looked down to find her blue gaze on mine. I studied her and studied her, but I couldn't read her expression. I didn't know what she was thinking, didn't know what she was feeling. She was a mystery.

My gut clenched, the pleasant emotion that had gripped me before draining away.

'And, just like that, he's gone.' Her voice was fragile glass.

She was talking about me, wasn't she? The tightness in my gut felt like pain. 'No,' I said. 'I haven't gone anywhere. I'm here.'

But she looked away as if she hadn't heard me, making the pain deepen. Was she dismissing me? Did she not want to talk to me? What was going on?

I couldn't bear not knowing, so I gripped her tighter. 'Tell me what you're thinking, Morgan. You have to tell me.' Would she explain? Or would she dismiss it the way she'd tried to before?

She looked back, blue eyes glittering. 'Why do you want to know?'

The question felt like a test. Where the answer was important. And there'd definitely be a right answer and a wrong answer.

I didn't want to get it wrong, but right now it felt like I might.

I didn't reply immediately, trying to think of how to say this, groping for the words because it was difficult to explain. Not that I could explain it to her—I couldn't even explain it to myself.

'I want to know because the answer...matters to me,' I said. 'It feels like something I should know.' Did that explain it adequately? I had the sense that it didn't and her expression didn't give me any clues whatsoever, so I went on, feeling as though I were blundering through a jungle without a path or even a map. 'I'm interested in you. I'm interested in the way you think, and I want to know how you're feeling, because...you're important.'

I wasn't sure if that was what I should have said, because her expression twisted and she looked away again.

'Morgan.' I didn't want her to look in the other direction. I wanted her to be looking at me.

She quivered slightly then took a breath, and her gaze found mine again. 'Okay.' Her voice still sounded fragile and it made me want to get closer to her, as if somehow my physical presence would help in some way. 'I'm sad. Because I can feel you...withdrawing from me.'

I struggled to understand. 'I'm not withdrawing. I'm right here.'

'I know you are. But you...' She paused again, as if she couldn't find the words, which was odd, because she always had the words. 'We had a connection just before. A closeness. And I'm sad now it's gone.' Her hands moved over my chest in an absent, stroking motion. 'You're different when we have sex.'

Her sadness I could understand, because that connection had been important for me too. But I didn't know what she meant when she'd said I was different during sex. How?

'I'm not different when I have sex,' I insisted. 'I'm the same as when I'm not. I'm always the same.'

She took another breath and the tension went out of her. 'Yes,' she said quietly, staring up at me. 'Yes, you are, aren't you?'

It was one of those statements that I knew didn't require an answer, and I couldn't tell if she thought it was a good thing or not. But this conversation was difficult, and it hurt, and I thought that if it was more of that connection she wanted then I'd give her more. I'd booked a suite at one of the best hotels in Paris and I'd planned to spend at least one night there with her.

We'd go there now. Right now.

I let her go, dealing with the condom and then our clothing before stepping back to give her a little bit of room. 'I have a suite at the Shangri La. We can go there now and spend the rest of the day there.'

She frowned. 'What about work?'

'I wasn't intending to work at all today. Or the next.'

'Seriously?'

Why was that so surprising? 'I'm the boss. I can do what I want.'

Something tugged at her full mouth and it looked like a smile, though I didn't know what was so funny. 'Of course you can. But you know...' She stopped and the almost-smile vanished.

'What?' I prompted.

She glanced away. 'It's nothing.'

But I wasn't going to accept that. I wanted to understand her, so she needed to tell me the things she thought I wouldn't get. If she wanted that connection... Well, it started here.

And you want to give it to her.

That wasn't even a question. Of course I wanted to give it to her. Especially if it meant she wouldn't leave. I'd do anything if it would stop her leaving.

Is it only so she doesn't leave?

Again, a stupid question, and one that I didn't want to think about.

'Morgan,' I said again. 'If it was nothing, you wouldn't have said it.'

Her gaze was on my chest, on her fingers resting on my shirt. 'It was a joke. And you don't understand jokes.'

'No, but that doesn't mean you can't say them.'

She sighed. 'Does it matter?'

'Yes,' I insisted. 'You're contorting yourself for me and I don't want you doing that.'

She was quiet for a long moment and I wanted to tip her chin back so I could look into her eyes, see those indecipherable expressions move across her pretty face. But just as I was about to do so, she suddenly looked up at me. 'What I was going to say was that people don't usually sleep together on the first date. And this is our first date.'

It wasn't that I didn't have a sense of humour. I did. It

was just that it was different from other people's, which meant they didn't understand it. To be fair. I didn't understand theirs.

'But we haven't slept together,' I felt compelled to point out. 'And, yes, I'm aware "sleeping together" is a euphemism for sex.'

Morgan's brow creased and something glittered in her eyes. 'Was that…a joke of your own, Ulysses?'

'I…' I stopped, staring at her. At the curve of her mouth and how the lines of her face had relaxed. How the fragile thing in her voice had vanished. 'It wasn't meant to be one.'

'No, but it was a humorous thing to say. Because you're right. This is our first date and we haven't actually slept together.' The curve of her mouth deepened. 'We only had sex.'

I still didn't understand why that was amusing, but she was smiling, and that made the pain inside me lessen, made my own mouth curve in response.

She gazed at me. 'You don't get it, do you?'

'No,' I said truthfully.

'So why are you smiling?'

'Because you are.'

Another expression rippled across her face, but she was still smiling, so it couldn't have been bad. 'You know, I don't normally have sex on the first date.'

I frowned. 'You don't? Why not?'

'I'll explain later.' Her palm pressed down on my chest, directly over my heart, as if she wanted to feel it beating. 'But do you know what it means that I had sex with you?'

'No. What?'

The pressure of her hand increased slightly. 'It means that you're special.'

It was a nice thing to say. I understood that. So why it made the pain inside me turn sharp, I couldn't have said.

What I did understand was that I'd reached the limit of my patience with this conversation. So I put my hand over hers where it rested on my chest and held it there, for some reason needing to touch her. 'Will you come to the hotel suite? Or would you rather go back to London?'

Morgan's eyes were bluer than the sky above us. 'Hmm, sex with the hot billionaire or going back to work? I think the answer's pretty clear.'

'It's not clear to me,' I said. 'Which is it?'

For some inexplicable reason, Morgan's smile deepened even further. 'Guess.'

I didn't want to guess, because I didn't want to get it wrong. But... I had a feeling the answer was there, just out of reach, and that if I thought about it the way I'd been thinking about all her other responses it would come to me.

And, sure enough, it did.

'You want more sex with me, don't you?' I said cautiously.

Her gaze turned brilliant, tiny flames glittering in the depths, and she was still smiling, which meant I'd got it right again. Then she said, 'Do you see any other hot billionaires standing around?'

I almost turned around to look before I realised.

She was teasing me. This was her not contorting herself, wasn't it?

I felt lighter all of a sudden, as if gravity had changed somehow while I hadn't been looking. Which was impossible. But the feeling remained, and for a second I wished that I could tease her back in the same way. Again, impossible.

Then I realised something: I had my own ways of teasing her.

I increased the pressure on her hand, sliding it down over my chest and guiding it lower, over my abdomen and then lower still, until her palm was directly over my fly so she could feel my cock hardening. 'There's only me here,' I said. 'So, if it's this hot billionaire you want sex with, then I suggest you get in the lift right this instant.'

Unexpectedly, Morgan laughed.

And it felt as if my heart had turned into a bird and flown straight into the sky.

CHAPTER NINETEEN

Morgan

OUR FIRST DATE turned from a couple of hours at the Eiffel Tower to a whole three days spent mainly in the bedroom of the magnificent suite in the hotel Ulysses had booked for us.

It wasn't that we spent the whole time having sex—he'd arranged a few touristy things for us to do, such as a private tour of the Louvre, a vaguely disturbing yet fascinating look at the catacombs beneath Paris, a tour around Notre Dame and other historic sites, plus a leisurely boat ride along the Seine. But, when we weren't doing those things, we were having sex in the suite.

Because that was where we communicated best with each other, where we understood one another. Where that connection I'd felt at the top of the Eiffel Tower was renewed, again and again.

I didn't question myself as to why that connection to Ulysses was so important to me. Or why I was so bereft when I felt it slip away from me, taking him along with it. Because, as he'd pointed out, he was still here. He hadn't gone.

Yet, every time we had sex, I could feel this… understanding and closeness between us and every time, when the sex was over, I felt it vanish. And it hurt. Gradually, I realised it wasn't so much the connection itself that was important to me but the connection to him.

It was he who mattered.

Because he was right. When I was in his arms, I wasn't trying to make myself more palatable. I was simply in the moment, consumed by sensation and the raw emotion that flowed between us.

With him I was more myself than at any other time and he was the one who'd uncovered me. Just as he'd helped me explore my sexual fantasies, he'd given me the freedom to be who I was. And I loved that. I didn't want it to end.

An odd thing gradually to realise. To understand that this strange man, on the surface so cold and emotionless yet underneath burning hot, had the power to strip away my armour and make me feel so many things. In retrospect, I realised he always had, with his maddening ways and frustrating attitudes.

But now, in Paris, the way he touched me, the little things he did for me, and most of all the way he tried to understand me, even though it was hard for him, felt like bricks in a structure I hadn't even realised I was building.

Whenever I made a joke, I smiled to let him know,

and he smiled along with me. And it didn't matter that he didn't get it; he was smiling because I was and that was enough. His smiles were amazing too, softening the stern, cold beauty of his face, turning him from avenging angel to seductive devil in seconds.

I talked a lot, rabbiting on about things that he obviously didn't care about, but he didn't tell me to stop and he didn't change the subject. He just listened, even though he didn't quite understand.

He was patient when I grabbed his hand and dragged him to a department store along the Champs-Elysées to window-shop, and he didn't protest or ask questions. And, when I asked excitedly if we could go to a burlesque show, he merely shrugged a shoulder and organised it.

I asked him once if there was something he wanted to do himself, since he was organising all this stuff for me, but he only gave me a mystified look and said that we were already doing it. And it struck me then, in a way it hadn't before, that I could always take Ulysses at face value. That I didn't have to worry about whether he was enjoying himself or only doing things because I wanted to, because he wouldn't. He couldn't.

He was always himself and, if he didn't want to do something, he simply didn't.

It was a curiously freeing realisation.

Yet it wasn't until we were getting ready to leave Paris that I realised just how much I'd enjoyed the time I'd spent with him, more so than I'd ever expected. And not simply due to the connection we had with each other every time we had sex, which I'd come to crave like an addict. It was also due to his stoic presence beside me and his black gaze on me whenever we were out of the bedroom too.

There was something about him that felt grounding and sure. It was as if the world could change, mountains could crumble and the continents could shatter, but Ulysses White would be enduring. He was as certain as gravity, and just as unalterable, and I found that deeply calming. My childhood had been nothing but a series of losses and changes, and Ulysses staying the same felt like balm on an aching wound.

He stood by the window now, doing up his cuffs, his movements methodical, his attention focused on what he was doing, and it hit me that we hadn't discussed what was going to happen after this date.

We'd had other discussions, such as me asking him about Black and White and why he'd started it, and what had driven him to build it. He hadn't really been able to articulate the reason other than he'd had to do something with his life, and he liked playing with money. Also that, although money could be bad, it also had the power to do good, which was why he'd started the Black and White Foundation, to help kids in similar situations to those in his own past.

I'd loved discovering that about him, but it didn't help me now.

We should have discussed it. We'd be returning to London and what was going to happen then? Would we continue sleeping together? And, if so, for how long?

Did this mean we were in a relationship? How would that affect work?

You were going to leave, remember?

The wave of cold came out of nowhere, swamping me, and what had been so clear before we'd got here suddenly seemed shrouded in mist and fog.

My decision to leave, not to have Ulysses's presence at least nearby, felt wrong. As though I were a kid again, my brother's grief pressing in on me, not knowing why he was pretending that nothing was wrong when something was. Knowing only that when I cried, when I got afraid, it would hurt him, so I'd learned to push that all down, pack it away. Pretend that nothing was wrong for me too.

It had felt like walking over a bridge made of air while underneath lava flowed, and where one wrong step could send you falling.

Ulysses wasn't air. He was stone. And I couldn't fall while he was around.

But weren't you lonely? Didn't you want to be with someone?

Well, maybe that someone was standing just across the suite from me...

The thought gripped me so tightly I couldn't breathe. Could the someone I wanted be Ulysses? He was the last person on earth I'd ever thought could give me what I craved. This man, who didn't understand his own emotions yet who somehow managed to put me back in touch with mine.

The light came through the windows, glossing his

black hair, highlighting the masculine purity of his profile, the high forehead, the straight line of his nose, the
curve of his mouth, the hard angle of his jaw...

I didn't want this to end. I didn't want to leave.

I didn't want to leave *him*.

His head came up suddenly and he glanced at me,
his black eyes glinting in the light. 'What is it? You're
staring at me.'

You've fallen for him, haven't you? What an idiot.

I swallowed, my throat tight, my chest aching. I
could have pretended that nothing was wrong, but I
didn't want to. I was done with pretending. 'We haven't
talked about what's going to happen when we get back
to London.'

He straightened, his arms falling to his sides. 'Nothing's going to happen when we get back to London.
Apart from the all the work we still have to do on the—'

'I'm not talking about work, Ulysses. I'm talking
about us.'

'Us?'

'Sleeping together.'

'Oh.' He frowned. 'Do you want to keep sleeping together? Because I'm happy to continue doing so.'

My stomach clenched. This kind of conversation was
always going to be difficult with him and somehow it
was worse now. Somehow it hurt now.

Because you've fallen for him.

I shoved that thought away and went around the bed,
crossing the room to him. Sometimes touch helped, so I
put my hands on his broad, firm chest. 'I want what we

have here in Paris,' I said, my voice husky. 'I want us to keep sleeping together. To keep doing things together.'

His hand came over mine automatically, his skin warm. 'Oh, I expected we'd keep doing that,' he said, as if it was self-evident.

Relief made me almost dizzy.

Yep, you've definitely fallen for him.

'You're so arrogant,' I said shakily, smiling at him to let him know I was teasing, the acceptance of my emotions falling into place inside me.

'Yes,' he agreed. 'I am.'

'Were you going to ever ask me if that's what I wanted too?'

'No.' His fingers tightened around mine. 'You seemed to enjoy what we were doing so I thought we'd just keep doing it.'

I laughed. 'You're a very bad boss, you know that?'

His frown deepened and then his mouth curved faintly in the smile he'd started to give me when he understood my gentle teasing. 'I'm probably not the best boss, it's true. But that's why I have you. You make me better.'

My heart throbbed, brushing painfully against my ribs. Yes, I had fallen for him, and how could I not when he said things like that to me? 'Ulysses,' I whispered.

'Yes?' His brows twitched. 'You sound sad. Why?'

I should have told him. But this feeling felt too new, too precious. And I didn't want to have to dissect it the way I'd have to in order to explain it to him. So all I said was, 'I'm not sad. I'm happy.'

'I see.' He studied me intently for a moment. 'Have you changed your mind about leaving, then?'

I swallowed yet again. 'Yes. I have.'

'Good. And are you still lonely?'

That was Ulysses. Straight to the heart of the matter.

'No,' I said croakily. 'No, I'm not.'

His hands were so warm over mine and I could feel the beat of his heart beneath the fine white cotton of his shirt. 'Because of me?'

'Because of you.'

He didn't smile, but I'd got very good at reading the slight changes in his affect, and I could see the shift in the darkness of his eyes. That had pleased him.

'We should go,' he said in exactly the same tone of voice. 'It's check-out time.'

But I hadn't quite finished. 'And when we get back to London? Will we work together the way we always have?'

'Of course. And you'll move in with me. It'll be easier if we're living together.'

I blinked. Okay, now *this* was a conversation I hadn't expected to have quite yet. 'That's something we need to talk about more.'

'Why? Your flat has terrible security and it's very inconvenient if we're going to be sleeping together. My penthouse is better. Also, we can go to work together in the morning.'

'But—'

'We'll talk about it on the plane.' He bent and kissed the back of my hands. 'We need to check out now.'

We did talk about it on the plane and it was like arguing with a brick wall. He was adamant I should move in with him and he didn't understand why I was objecting.

I didn't understand why I was objecting either. Yes, it was fast—we'd only been sleeping together a matter of days—but his relentless logic made short work of my protests. Of course it did. Logically it did make perfect sense.

Emotionally, though…emotionally it also made perfect sense.

I didn't want to go back to my tiny, lonely flat, not now I'd had three days of being with Ulysses. The thought of having his presence around me all the time was reassuring.

You think it's all going to be easy? You should probably think about this.

But I didn't want to think about it. I'd been thinking about things for too long and now I wanted to take a leaf out of Ulysses's book and just do it. Take everything as it came and sort out problems as they arose.

You care about him, though, that's going to make it harder.

That I ignored entirely, because it made no sense. Sure, I'd fallen for him, but it wasn't going to make anything harder. No, if anything, it was only going to make things clearer, surer.

It was going to make things perfect.

CHAPTER TWENTY

Ulysses

I STOOD BY the parapet on the top of the Black and White skyscraper, the entire top deck transformed by Black and White staff into an outdoor garden, and glanced once more at my watch.

Morgan was five minutes late.

Irritation stirred inside me and I looked towards the lift area yet again.

More people were arriving for the party Black and White was throwing for the trustees of our new foundation, but Morgan didn't appear to be among the latest group that stepped out of the lift.

How bloody annoying.

A group of Foundation donors was standing close by, having a discussion about football, which I couldn't take part in because I found football pointless. I knew this was where I was supposed to pretend, or maybe turn the conversation onto something I was interested in, but I knew that talking business at a social occasion was generally frowned upon. And, as they probably wouldn't want to talk about Morgan—the only other thing I was interested in apart from money and patterns—I didn't have anything to say.

I turned around and stalked through the crowd, not knowing what else to do with myself and not wanting to stand still in case someone approached me and I was rude to them. I wasn't intentionally rude, but apparently there were things you talk about and do in social situations and things you didn't do, and because I generally forgot what those things were I'd inadvertently offended people in the past. I didn't want to do that again, not when this occasion was important for the foundation and therefore important for me, so all I could do was stalk around and wait for Morgan to arrive.

After a couple of minutes, I found a corner of the rooftop that was unoccupied and where the coloured lights that had been wound around the wooden trellises and gazebo structures especially set up for the occasion didn't reach.

It gave me a good enough view of the lift area so I waited there, more and more annoyed as the minutes ticked by. Why was she late? She knew this was an important occasion. She'd been the one organising it, after all, and had spent most of the week doing so, running schedules and plans by me, all of which I'd had no interest in, but had cursorily looked over anyway because she liked it when I did.

There were a lot of things I'd been doing the past week simply because she liked them. A lot of things I thought I'd be irritated by and wasn't.

For example, I'd thought her things cluttering up my penthouse—little cushions and small blankets, photos of her and Damian, knick-knacks that I couldn't see the point of, jewellery and clothes and all sorts of other stuff—would be very irritating, yet they weren't.

The opposite, even. I liked having them around me. Seeing them gave me pleasant little electric shocks, reminding me that she was here in my penthouse, living with me. That I woke up with her every morning and went to bed with her every night. That she wouldn't disappear when her work day was done. That if I stayed late she would be waiting for me when I came home.

Though, I found I didn't want to stay late. In fact, I gradually realised that I was looking forward to the day ending so I could go home, where I could gather her in my arms and take her to bed. And after that she'd either make food, or we'd eat what my housekeeper had left for us, and she would talk to me while I listened, watching her face, marvelling at the colour of her eyes and how there was a light in them that seemed to dance when she spoke. Watching for her smile so that I could smile too.

I could have watched her all day.

Sometimes at night, when I couldn't sleep, I wouldn't get up and look at the streetlights outside, the way I normally did. Sometimes, I would take her in my arms and watch her face instead.

I seemed to sleep better when I was holding her, when I was touching her. I hadn't realised how much the touch of another person could soothe me, though I had a sneaking suspicion that it wasn't the touch of just any person that would do it. Because, if it was, I could have slept with anyone.

But I didn't want to sleep with just anyone. I only wanted to sleep with her.

My phone buzzed and I took it out of my pocket, frowning down at the screen. There was a text from Morgan on it.

Sorry to be late. I'll be there in five.

Five what? Five seconds? Five minutes? Five hours? I scowled. What was she doing? She knew I didn't like these social occasions, that I needed her to be here to help me navigate them, so where the fuck was she?

At that moment I heard the lift doors open once again and I looked up as another group of people stepped out onto the rooftop terrace.

I recognised two of the men instantly. There was Damian, with his ridiculous haircut, and Everett, wearing inappropriate jeans. I hadn't seen either of them since the Black and White Foundation auction at least a month ago, and they'd both been extremely hard to get hold of.

Apparently they'd both got married, though that wasn't any excuse not to be around when I needed them.

Anger simmered inside me, most especially when I looked at Damian, because all I could think about was Morgan's voice telling me how he never visited her. How he'd sent her away to boarding school, and then here to London. Morgan's voice, fragile as glass, telling me she was lonely.

I shouldn't have been angry with him—not when it

wasn't anything to do with me that he'd sent her away. But that didn't stop the heat inside me, or the urge I had to go over there and punch his face in.

In fact, I'd already taken a step in their direction when I realised it wasn't just Everett and Damian. A small woman in a red dress with short dark hair and dark eyes was holding on to Damian's arm, and another woman in green, much taller with long, red hair, was whispering into Everett's ear.

I searched my memory for their names. Ah, yes— Thea, Damian's little jewel thief, and Freya, Everett's friend who was now his wife.

So they'd finally decided to come back and they'd brought their wives with them.

Then, just as I was about to take yet another step, another small woman stepped out from behind Damian, rising on her tiptoes, craning her head around the rooftop as if looking for someone.

She was in my favourite colour on her, blue like her eyes, the dress very form-fitting in a way I also liked. On her feet were silver sandals that looked like they were inlaid with tiny diamonds, making her feet glitter when she walked, and her hair was so black and glossy it looked like polished onyx.

Morgan.

When she didn't see me, she came back down onto her heels and glanced at Everett and Damian, frowning. But they weren't looking at her. Everett was smiling, and it had to have something to do with what Freya was whispering in his ear. Damian had his arm around

Thea and she was laughing, and so was he. He abruptly let her go, took her face between his hands and leaned down, whispering something. I could see his mouth move. Her smile deepened and then she rose up on her toes to kiss him.

I couldn't look away. There was something between them, between Damian and Thea, and Everett and Freya, something that had to do with their smiles and their laughter. With the way Damian held Thea, the way Freya's hand rested on Everett's shoulder.

They were smiling. They were all smiling.

They looked…happy.

Morgan smiled, and I smiled with her, but it wasn't the same and I knew it. I smiled because she did, not because I understood why she was smiling. And when she smiled it wasn't always because I'd teased her or told her something funny. I…didn't know why she smiled.

I probably would never know.

There was a cold feeling in the pit of my stomach, a cold feeling that got stronger, that bordered on pain.

Morgan wasn't smiling now, she was looking around again with that crease between her brows that she always got when she was irritated at me.

That was all I could give her. Physical pleasure and irritation.

I could never give her happiness. I could never give her joy. I didn't even know what those things were. And I wasn't sure why it mattered to me, since all the things I couldn't do didn't often bother me.

But they were bothering me now. They'd bothered me ever since I'd started sleeping with Morgan.

Why?

You know why.

I stood there in the darkness, trying to think, groping for the reason.

Yes, I did know. It was because she mattered to me. What she wanted mattered to me but the things she wanted I was never going to be able to give her. And that hurt.

Another thought occurred to me. She'd said she wasn't lonely with me, that I was special to her, but… was that true? People lied, like Uncle John had lied, so you could never trust what people said.

No, *I* could never trust what people said. Perhaps others could, but I couldn't, not when I'd never know if I was being lied to or not.

I stayed where I was in the shadows, for some reason not wanting Morgan to find me, yet I must have given myself away somehow because she turned at last and her gaze met mine. And her mouth curved in a smile.

I felt mine start to curve automatically, but all at once it felt robotic. It wasn't natural, the way Damian's and Everett's smiles were, and if I knew it wasn't then how would Morgan see it? She'd seemed to like it back in Paris, and over the past couple of weeks we'd been living together, but did she really?

Did it matter to her that I was only doing it for her? That I didn't feel the same laughter, happiness or joy the way Damian and Everett did?

'Ulysses,' Morgan said, coming quickly towards me, the others trailing along behind. 'There you are. I'm so sorry I was late.' Her hands lifted towards me, then abruptly she stopped and dropped them back at her sides, a blush rising in her cheeks as she glanced at Damian.

I made no move towards her, the cold feeling in my stomach and the pain in my chest making me scowl. 'What are you two doing here?' I snapped, glancing at my friends. 'It's a bit late to turn up now, don't you think?'

Damian lifted a shoulder, his mouth turning up in a smile. 'Nice to see you too, Ulysses. But better late than never. Besides, we were otherwise engaged.' His arm curved around Thea, pulling her in close, and he looked down at her, the expression on his face making me uncomfortable.

'Yeah, we had a few other things to take care of,' Everett muttered. 'It's all handled, though.'

'I resent being "handled",' Freya said and jabbed Everett in the ribs. He didn't seem to be offended and just smiled instead.

I didn't understand them. I didn't understand any of them.

Oh, you do. You just don't want to understand.

Ignoring the thought, I stared at Morgan instead. 'You're late. What happened?'

'I'm sorry,' she repeated. 'I was just tidying up some last minute things, and then Damian texted me, so I thought—'

'We'll talk about it later at home,' I interrupted, because, now she was here, we could start all the necessary social interactions.

'Home?' Damian asked.

I glared at him. 'Yes, home. It's a place where people live.'

His eyes were very sharp and they glittered. 'Oh, I know what home is, believe me. I'm just surprised that you have a home in relation to Morgan.'

'Damian…' Morgan began.

'Of course I have a home in relation to Morgan.' I stared straight back at him. 'She lives with me.'

There was a silence, the noise of the party suddenly very loud.

'Fuck,' Everett muttered. 'I think it's time we went and found a drink, Little.' He wound an arm around Freya's waist and drew her away.

But I didn't watch them leave. I kept on staring at Damian. He was angry, I could tell, and I'd known he would be. But I was angry too.

'Why?' Damian asked. His voice sounded quite casual, but the look on his face was not. Yes, he was very definitely angry.

Morgan stepped in front of me, facing her brother. 'Because he asked me if I wanted to move in and I said yes,' she said flatly. 'Also, yes, we're sleeping together.'

A muscle flicked in Damian's jaw and I saw Thea put a hand on his chest. It was something that Morgan did to me too, putting it over my heart, and it always made me feel calm. Was that what Thea was doing to Damian?

I shouldn't have been surprised. He'd told me if he found out I'd taken her on a date he would punch me in the face. Then, I hadn't wanted him to know the truth, because I'd promised I'd look after Morgan and had felt uncomfortable about the fact that we were having sex.

But now I'd found out how he'd hurt her. How lonely she was. And all I felt was rage.

Damian shook off Thea's hand and took a step towards me. 'You fucking—'

'No.' Morgan took a step towards him, getting right up in his face. 'Leave him alone. This was my choice, you idiot.'

He glanced down at her, then back at me, that muscle in his jaw flicking. 'You're her boss, you tool. And you were supposed to protect her—'

'I said I would and I did,' I interrupted coldly. 'But you sent her away, Damian. You got rid of her. And she was lonely. So I helped her.'

He blinked and his mouth opened. Then it closed and I found I'd taken a step too, standing behind Morgan. I knew Damian wouldn't hurt her and yet I pulled her back against me all the same, needing her close so I could protect her.

Damian stared at his sister and then at me again. 'Fucking her is helping her?'

'Oh, for God's sake,' Morgan muttered.

I didn't like the way Damian had said it, even though he was right. 'You're not protecting her any more,' I said flatly. 'That's my job now.'

Damian finally looked away from me, staring at

Morgan instead. 'I hope you know what you're getting yourself into,' he said. 'He's not like everyone else.'

'I know that,' Morgan said. 'I know that better than you do.'

The pain that had been lingering in my gut sharpened as she said the words.

'Why?' Damian asked and, again, he didn't look at me.

'I think you know,' Morgan said quietly and glanced at Thea.

He closed his eyes at that, as if that glance meant something, and then he muttered, 'Jesus Christ.'

'Damian,' Thea murmured from beside him, threading her fingers through his and tugging gently. 'Come on. Come with me.'

Morgan watched them leave and then she turned around in my arms and looked up at me. 'I'm sorry. I shouldn't have been late. I should have—'

'What did you mean, "you know why"?' I demanded, because the pain inside me wouldn't go away and it had something to do with those words 'he's not like everyone else'. Something to do with her saying, 'You know why'.

Her eyes had gone dark and there was no light dancing in them any more. 'We should probably start mingling.'

'No.' I let her go, my fingers curling into fists. I wasn't sure why I was feeling this way. I only knew I didn't like it, just as I knew I wouldn't like what she was going to say. 'Tell me.'

'Ulysses…'

'I'm not a dog, Morgan. I'm a man. And I want to know what Damian was talking about. I want to know what you meant.' My jaw ached all of a sudden, my shoulders stiff with tension. 'Tell me fucking now.'

She'd gone very pale, though I wasn't sure why. 'Damian said "why?" because he wanted to know why I'd moved in with you. Why we were…sleeping together.'

That made sense. But not her other reply. 'So why did you look at Thea and say "you know why"?'

She wasn't smiling now and her blue eyes looked black. 'I looked at Thea because Damian loves her. And I said "you know why" to let him know that, the way he feels about Thea, I feel about you.'

The cold inside me was spreading, as if I was slowly freezing from the inside out. 'You need to be clearer than that,' I said, my voice not sounding like mine. As if that was freezing too.

Morgan was silent for a long moment, staring up at me. 'I'm in love with you, Ulysses,' she said. 'Is that clear enough for you?'

CHAPTER TWENTY-ONE

Morgan

I HADN'T WANTED to say it, not here at a work party, and not after my stupid brother had arrived in the country without letting me know beforehand. And definitely not after said stupid brother had almost started a fight by being an insensitive arsehole.

Actually, I hadn't wanted to say it at all, even though it was true. Even though I felt it with every beat of my heart.

I was in love with Ulysses White and, over the past few weeks, I'd fallen deeper and deeper in love with him.

I'd thought working with him as well as living with him would have presented some challenges and, yes, it had. But not as much as I'd expected. And he was so up front and honest that it made working around those issues much easier than I'd anticipated.

Being at home with him was a joy. No, he didn't chat much, and we didn't have easy conversation. But we could talk about work and about the things that interested him. I didn't understand most of what he said about numbers and money, but then he didn't understand most of what I said when I talked about the book I was reading or how much I'd loved the art in the Louvre.

What was important was that we listened to each other. And then, when the talking was done, he was happy to sit on the couch with me as we watched TV, or fiddle around on his laptop while I read. Sometimes we went out for dinner and those nights we'd either sit there quietly, simply enjoying each other's company, or we'd talk about world events or the political situation, because he never got mad and his dispassionate, logical viewpoint was something I valued.

But it was his presence I loved the most. How he was there, solid and enduring, and that all I needed to do was touch him and he would draw me into his arms, his warmth reassuring me in a way that no amount of words could.

I knew he wasn't like other people. He was better.

I hadn't thought about the fact that I loved him. But I did now.

His eyes narrowed, blacker than the sky above our heads, the look on his face suspicious. 'Why are you in love with me?'

I tried to think of how to explain. 'Lots of reasons. But mainly because of how you make me feel.'

'Sex?' He didn't sound bowled over, relieved, thankful or any of those things. He sounded as he normally did. 'Because I make you come?'

The bluntness of the words hurt, even though it was

just another of his usual questions as he tried to understand.

'No, it's not just that,' I said. 'It goes deeper than physical pleasure. You…make me feel less lonely. You make me feel like myself.'

He scanned my face. 'I don't make you laugh, though.'

The observation was so unexpected, I had to catch my breath, my stomach clenching tight. 'Why…what?'

'Damian makes Thea laugh. I saw it just before. And Freya made Everett laugh too. But I don't do that with you. And you don't do that with me.'

'You do make me laugh.' I flailed around, trying to think of an example.

'Because I'm a joke? Because I don't get the things you do?'

The words were uninflected and yet the fact that he'd even asked me hurt.

'No, of course not.' I tried to sound calm. 'Why would you think I would?'

'Because people lie.' His voice was cold. 'People tell you what you want to hear all the time.'

Of course, that would be his worst nightmare. He wouldn't be able to tell whether people were lying to him or not. And he'd been lied to once already, hadn't he? That man, Uncle John, telling him he could be adopted. Telling him that he was a 'good boy'. Telling him things that one lonely boy was desperate to hear.

All lies.

My eyes filled with helpless tears, my heart aching

for him, for the boy he'd once been. 'I would never lie to you,' I said thickly. 'Never.'

'But you just did,' he pointed out with relentless logic. 'You told me I make you laugh. And I don't, Morgan.'

'You did. That day on the Eiffel Tower.' Thank God I could remember.

Yet that didn't seem to satisfy him. 'Did you mean it? Or were you pretending?'

I shook my head, my throat aching. This wasn't the conversation I wanted to have right now. 'Does it matter?'

'Of course it matters.' His eyes glittered with the anger I could sense rising in him. 'Because I can't tell. And I'll never be able to tell.'

'Ulysses—'

'I'll never be able to make you laugh just like I'll never be able to tell if you really love me.'

My throat closed up entirely. No, naturally he wouldn't. But that would only matter if he wanted me to love him. And I hadn't thought about that. I hadn't even considered it. Yet…it seemed as though he did want that, especially if he was asking these questions. Especially if they were making him angry.

'Do you…want me to love you?' I asked, hope slowly growing in my heart.

'I want to know if you're telling me the truth.'

'That's the thing about love,' I said carefully. 'You kind of just have to trust that I do.'

He was silent, standing tall and still in the shadows

of the rooftop. The coloured lights didn't reach here so he seemed part of the darkness. Black hair and black eyes. Wearing a black tux. A cold-eyed black angel. Not the seductive devil. Not this time.

My throat got even tighter, the pain unbearable. I didn't want to ask. I didn't want this thing we'd been building between us over the past week to break. Because, even though it was beautiful, it was fragile. So fragile.

The slightest breath would shatter it.

Yet I couldn't leave it alone. 'Do you trust me, Ulysses?'

'No,' he said flatly, taking a hammer to our beautiful structure. 'I don't trust you. I don't trust anyone.'

It hurt. Much more than I thought it would. Though what it changed I had no idea. Did it matter that he didn't trust me in this? Did it change anything?

Of course it matters. You want to make him happy.

There was a boulder lodged in my throat, another sitting on my chest, pressing down. I *did* want that. But how could I when he didn't even know what happiness was?

'Oh,' I said, not sure of what else to say and hoping I didn't sound as broken as I feared. 'Well, that's okay. That's fine. We can—'

'It's not okay,' he interrupted tonelessly. 'It's not fine. I can see that you're upset. This hurts you. And I don't like it, Morgan.'

I wanted to touch him, but I couldn't bear the thought

of him pulling away, so I clenched my fingers instead. 'I'm sorry,' I said again. 'I can try not to—'

'I don't want you to try anything,' he cut me off yet again. 'I don't want you to have to pretend. I don't want you having to contort yourself for me. And I don't want you not to laugh.' There was an intensity in his eyes now, burning bright and cold. 'It would be better if you didn't love me, Morgan. It would be better if you found someone else.'

Perhaps I'd known that he'd say something like this eventually because it didn't feel like a shock. Yet, even so, the pain that wound its way deep into my heart still had the power to stop my breath.

Again, no one wants you.

'But I can't love someone else,' I said stupidly. 'I already love you.'

'Well, don't.' He said the words as if that was easy. As if it was simply a decision about what kind of dress to wear or whether I wanted coffee instead of tea. Because of course it was easy for him. He didn't understand.

'It doesn't work that way.' There were tears in my eyes but I shouldn't have let them fall. I should have pretended that everything was fine, that he hadn't ripped my heart out of my chest, but he hadn't wanted me to pretend, so I didn't. The tears dripped slowly down my cheeks. 'You can't switch love off, Ulysses. It's there for ever. That's why it's love.'

'It can't be for ever.' He looked away from me, uncomfortable. 'People are always changing their minds and loving other people.'

'Not me,' I whispered, because I knew myself. I knew the feeling in my soul. 'It'll always be you.'

Ulysses didn't look at me. Instead, he took a step towards the crowds, a restless tension radiating from his powerful frame. 'We need to go and talk to people.'

He didn't like emotions in others and he clearly didn't know how to handle mine. And, if I'd been any kind of decent PA, I should have dried my tears, picked up the pieces and carried on.

But I couldn't. I just…couldn't.

I'd thought it wouldn't matter that he wasn't the same as other people. That he couldn't process emotions like I could. I'd thought I'd be fine with it.

Yet I wasn't fine with it. And it wasn't because of me, it was because of him.

I wanted him to be less lonely and isolated than he was. I wanted him to be happy. But he couldn't be happy with me. Not when he couldn't trust me. Not when he thought I'd lie to him.

Not when there's someone else out there who might be able to give him what he needs better than you ever will.

And that was true, wasn't it? I hadn't been enough for Damian. I'd been nothing but a millstone around his neck and, even though I'd tried hard not to be, tried not to be scared and upset and afraid after Mum had died, he'd still sent me away.

I'd never been able to pretend.

'Does this mean it's over?' My voice sounded small in the darkness. 'You and me? Are you saying you want me to leave?'

He kept his head turned away, looking towards the party. 'Yes, I think that would be best.'

Why did I think this would turn out differently? Why did I always want more?

'You'd be happier with someone else,' he went on unexpectedly. 'Someone who can make you laugh. Someone who knows what love means.'

More tears ran down my cheeks and I took a helpless step towards him, my hand outstretched to touch the heart that I knew beat inside his strong chest. A heart built like everyone else's. 'No,' I began. 'You're the one…'

'I need to have some words with the trustees.' He moved away before I could touch him. 'Are you coming?'

'Please, look at me.' I had no idea what I wanted to say, but I had to say something. Do something.

But he wouldn't, his perfect profile remaining averted.

I took another step. 'Ulysses.'

He moved away. 'People will be wondering where we are.'

'Ulysses, please…'

He side-stepped. 'We can't stand here all night.' He didn't glance at me, not once. 'I have to join the party.' There was no expression at all on his beautiful face. It was as if he didn't feel a thing.

But he did feel something. He wouldn't have withdrawn from me so completely if he hadn't. But it was inaccessible to me. He'd retreated along that bridge between us and I couldn't follow him.

I'd never be able to follow him.

My heart was a collection of glass shards in my chest held together by barbed wire, jagged and sharp. I wanted to reach out and take his jaw in my hand, turn his face towards mine and tell him that all I wanted was for him to be happy. To teach him what that meant and how that felt.

Love him the way he deserved to be loved.

But the gap between us was too far and I couldn't bridge it. He was a prince from a fairy tale, cursed to sleep in a glass case, separate from the rest of the world for ever. I could see him, talk to him. But I could never touch him. I could never lean down and wake him with a kiss. He was destined to sleep for ever.

So I let him go, standing still as he walked away, disappearing into the crowd.

My tears fell, the glass shards in my chest shattering further as the fragile connection we'd managed to build between us pulled tight.

Then snapped.

CHAPTER TWENTY-TWO

Ulysses

I WALKED INTO the party, wanting to get the social inter-actions out of the way as soon as possible. But it was too loud. There was too much light. Too many people. It was too much. I didn't want to be there.

So I went to the lifts instead and took one down, going out of the building and stepping out onto the foot-path, walking along it.

I didn't know where I was going, but I had to move. It felt as if a million ants were crawling all over me, even though there was nothing there, making me want to claw my own skin off. But obviously that would have been impossible, so I walked instead.

I couldn't stop seeing Morgan's face and the tears running down her cheeks. They'd glittered in the lights of the party, despite the shadows, and her eyes had been black. She'd been so sad. Hurt. As if someone she knew had died.

That had hurt me. A pain that felt like being stabbed, even though there was no knife. I didn't like it. I didn't want it. It reminded me of sitting on the bench with Uncle John, eating the ice cream he'd bought me even though we'd been thrown out of the casino, telling me he wasn't going to adopt me after all.

I'd hurt then too.

People always lied. They never meant what they said. They gave you something that felt good with one hand, while in the other hand was a knife you didn't see and they stabbed you with it.

Always avoid the knife.

Morgan hasn't got a knife. There's nothing in her hand.

But thinking of Morgan was too painful so I didn't think of her. I just kept walking, trying to put some distance between myself and the pain.

Yet the pain kept following. I couldn't leave it behind.

I walked and walked, the city waking up around me. The lights I used to map in my head from my office window vanished as the dawn came.

There was silence around me and yet the noise in my head was inescapable. Her voice, cracking and broken down. I could still hear it, even though the party had been loud. I hadn't been able to look at her, because the expression on her face had been too painful.

The expression on her face had been the hidden knife, stabbing me.

Damian had been right. I wasn't like everyone else. I couldn't give her what she needed so ending our affair was the only logical course. And, yes, that would upset her, because I knew she'd enjoyed being with me, but she'd get over that. She'd find someone else to love.

She loves you, though.

I didn't know why. No one else ever had.

I walked, but the pain dogged my footsteps, digging deeper, gouging a hole inside my heart. At least, that was what it felt like.

Why was I feeling like this? Where had this pain come from? Not from ending it with Morgan, surely? Because how could it? It made sense. She'd never be happy with me, and I wanted her to be happy, so ending things should have made me feel better, not worse.

This was inexplicable. I should go home, try to sleep and maybe in the morning I'd feel like myself again.

But then I remembered that her little things would be everywhere at home, and those pleasant jolts wouldn't be so pleasant now. They would be more like knife cuts. More pain.

It was her causing it. It was all her hurting me.

I should never have slept with her. I should never have taken her to Paris. Never let her move in with me.

I should never have thought she could be mine.

I couldn't have the things other people did. I'd never be able to have those things.

I kept on walking.

Dawn was over the city now and I wasn't looking where I was going. I wasn't aware of where I was. The river was on my right and I'd left the city behind me.

And then a car pulled up beside me. I didn't stop.

'Ulysses,' someone said.

I didn't stop.

'Ulysses, for fuck's sake!'

If I stopped, the pain would swamp me, so I didn't stop.

Then Damian was in front of me, scowling. I prepared to side-step him, but he put his hand out and slammed it into my chest, halting me.

'Stop,' he ordered flatly.

'No.' I tried to side-step again, but someone grabbed my shoulders.

'Ulysses,' Everett said from behind me. 'Stop.'

They were strong and they kept me still. I couldn't move. The pain moved up my legs and into my chest, into my heart. I couldn't breathe. 'I'm having a heart attack,' I said sharply. 'I need to get to hospital.'

Damian's expression flickered and then, bizarrely, his mouth curved, as if my coronary events were somehow amusing. 'You're not having a heart attack, believe me.'

But the pain was closing like a fist around my heart. 'What's happening to me, then? It hurts.'

Damian sighed. 'I think you're in love with my sister. Nothing else makes a man act like this much of a fucking idiot.'

'What?' I didn't understand a single word he said. But then that was what I'd always appreciated about these two men. They never adjusted themselves for me. They treated me as if I was normal.

'Morgan disappeared,' Everett said. 'We found her at your place, very upset.'

More pain rippled through me. I caught my breath.

I thought she'd have seen that this was the only logical thing to do and be feeling better by now, or at least have accepted it.

No, you didn't. She's not like you, remember?

I remembered her tears. She was upset. She was without me to hold her. She hadn't been able to put her hand on my heart the way she did when she needed to comfort herself because I'd pulled away. I hadn't let her.

'I...' I didn't know what else to say.

'She told me what happened,' Damian said gruffly, exerting enough pressure to keep me still. 'She's in love with you and you walked away from her, you fucker.'

There was anger in his eyes. Anger at me.

'Yes, I know she is,' I tried to explain. 'But I had to walk away. I can't make her laugh. And I can't make her happy, not the way she deserves to be happy. She has to pretend with me.'

Damian cursed under his breath. 'Look, I said a dumb, fucking thing. And I'm sorry. I shouldn't have—'

'You were right, though. I'm not like anyone else. And I can't give her the things she needs. And it hurts that I can't. She shouldn't ever have to pretend—'

'She's not pretending,' he growled.

'But how do I know? How will I ever know?' The pain felt as if it was slicing my heart in two. Of course, this was the problem. That was why it hurt. I'd never know if she was lying to me. I'd never know for sure that she meant it when she said she loved me.

And I wanted her to.

I wanted her to love me.

I didn't even know what love was, but some part of me must have had an inkling. And that part of me wanted it more than I wanted my next breath.

Damian shook his head. 'Join the club, buddy. None of us ever knows for sure.'

I frowned. 'No one?'

'No.' He let out a breath. 'We don't have certainty, Ulysses. None of us do. All we have is trust.'

You have to trust me.

But I'd told her I didn't. How could I?

'I can't trust. People have lied to me in the past.'

'Has she ever lied to you before?' Damian's expression was oddly fierce. 'Even once?'

Do you trust me, Ulysses? I would never lie to you.

'She pretends to laugh,' I said dumbly. 'She—'

'She pretends because she cares about you, you fucking idiot,' Everett said impatiently from behind me.

'But I don't want her to pretend,' I said. 'She's been pretending all her life. She shouldn't have to any more.'

Damian's expression twisted. 'We all have to pretend sometimes, man. It's part of living with someone. But, fundamentally, all you've got is trust. Which means you have to trust her, Ulysses. You have to help her, you fucking ass. You've broken her heart and I can't make it better.'

The pain coursed through me, but through it I felt something shift.

Only I could make it better. Only me. There was no one else.

It will always be you.

Did I trust her? Could I trust her? Could I trust Damian when he said that everyone felt this? That no one had certainty? That everyone had to pretend sometimes?

If you keep questioning that, you'll always be alone. You'll never have anyone. You'll never have her.

My throat closed up, a powerful emotion swamping me. I wanted to walk away from it, but Damian and Everett were holding me still, so I had no choice but to stay there until it broke over me. Drowning me.

Making me realise that I didn't want to be alone. I'd never wanted to be alone. That was why it had hurt when Uncle John had told me he didn't want to adopt me. And that was why it was hurting now.

But it was more than just loneliness. It was the craving for another person—yet not just any person.

I wanted Morgan.

Was this emotion love? Was this craving for one person and one person only love? This pain and this longing? This wanting more? I didn't like it. And yet... I couldn't escape it.

It was a choice, I understood suddenly. I had to choose it. I could choose to walk away and keep walking, choose to avoid the pain. Or I could embrace it.

'It hurts,' I said to Damian. 'I don't like it.'

Damian shrugged, his silver eyes glittering. 'Goes with the territory. You just have to ask yourself whether you want to be alone for the rest of your life and avoid the pain. Or you choose her and take the pain with all the good stuff.'

What 'good stuff'?

Think about it.

Her hand on my chest. Her smile. Her scent. The little black beauty spot near her mouth. The light in her eyes when she looked at me, as if I was enough for her. As if my company was something she took pleasure in. Her things everywhere in my penthouse. The intense feeling when I was inside her, holding her in my arms…

'I hurt her.' My voice sounded hoarse. 'I couldn't stay… I couldn't…' I stopped, then tried again. 'How can I make it better? I don't know…'

'You do.' Damian said it with so much certainty I couldn't help but believe him. 'You know, Ulysses.'

And I did.

'Take me to her,' I said. 'Now.'

CHAPTER TWENTY-THREE

Morgan

I WOKE UP the next morning curled up on the couch of Ulysses's penthouse. Damian had put a blanket over me, but it didn't make me feel any less cold. Or less empty.

It was dawn and the place was silent. As silent as my little flat had been.

He wasn't here. He hadn't come home.

Another tear slipped down my cheek. I felt as though I'd been crying all night, which was just ridiculous. I'd always thought I'd be stronger than this, that I wouldn't let a man destroy me. But turns out I wasn't. I'd let Ulysses devastate me and there was no coming back from it.

I wiped the tears away uselessly. He wasn't here and worry made everything worse. Was he all right? Where was he?

Damian and Everett had come to find me when both my absence and Ulysses's had been noted, and had discovered me in Ulysses's penthouse crying in the shower. Fully clothed.

Damian had been furious, but I'd told him to shut the fuck up, that I didn't want him getting angry on my behalf—not when Ulysses had already broken my heart. I didn't need my stupid brother kicking around the shards in my chest.

Everett had pulled him away and told me that they'd go out and look for Ulysses. Just to make sure he was okay. And presumably to give me some alone time.

But I was done with my alone time. I had too much of that already.

I didn't want to be alone. I wanted Ulysses.

At that moment, I heard the door open and I turned towards it, thinking it was Damian and Everett returning.

But it wasn't.

Ulysses came storming into the room. He looked a wreck. His hair was standing up and his shirt was wrinkled. He didn't have a jacket. His tie was gone.

His eyes were black holes in his shadowed face and they burned.

He didn't look anywhere but at me and he came towards me without hesitation.

I opened my mouth—to say what, I had no idea—but nothing came out as he came over to the couch, ripped the blanket off me and bent, gathering me up in his arms.

His heat was around me, his scent, the sound of his heart beating against my ear, and for a second I just went limp, weeping silently, because him here was the last thing I'd expected.

The relief of his presence was agony and I couldn't move. 'What are you doing here?' I forced out. 'Where have you been? I thought we were over.'

He turned and sat down on the couch with me, holding me tightly. 'Walking. I've been walking.'

'Ulysses—'

'Damian and Everett found me. And they told me you were upset and that you needed me.'

I shook my head. He'd never get it.

'And so I came back…' He stopped, and I thought he'd finished, but then he said, 'I don't want to be alone, Morgan. And leaving you hurt… It made me feel like… like I was ten again and Uncle John said he couldn't adopt me. I'd believed him when he said he would and then he said he wouldn't… I couldn't believe anyone after that.'

The confession was so unexpected, I couldn't speak. So I put my hand on his chest, over his heart, because who knew how long he'd stay here? I had to take what I could, while I could.

'But then you said I had to trust you,' he went on, sounding as if he was choosing his words carefully. 'And I said I couldn't. I can't trust people, because I don't know when they're lying. And I couldn't bear the thought of you lying to me. It hurt badly. So I had to ask myself why it hurt so much. Damian said it was because I loved you and I…think he's right. I don't know what this emotion is. It's very strong, and it overwhelms me, and it hurts. And I don't like it. I don't want to be that boy any more. But… I don't want to be without you. I want you in my arms. I want your hand on me. I want your things in my penthouse. I want your smile. It makes me feel…good. And I think the good things are worth the pain.'

I blinked in shock, my heart aching. 'What are you trying to say, Ulysses?'

He frowned, obviously frustrated. 'I'm saying that I want you. I want to have you in my life. And, more than anything, I want to make you happy.'

The jagged shards of my heart were digging in, hurting, but this time the pain had the sweet edge of hope to it. 'That's what I want for you too,' I said hoarsely. 'That's all I ever wanted for you.'

His frown deepened. 'There's some things I won't ever be able to do, Morgan. There's some things I won't ever be able to understand.' He hesitated. 'Are you sure that's what you want? I'm not like everyone else.'

I could feel the tears fall, but this time I didn't mind them. They were happy tears. Tears for us both. Because, no matter what he said, no matter that he didn't understand some emotions, he was here. He was holding me. And, whether he knew it or not, he felt those emotions, just like we all did.

'No, you're not like everyone else.' I lifted my hand and cupped his strong jaw. 'You're better.'

He would never be a typical man. But I didn't want a typical man.

I wanted him.

He stared at me in silence a long time, then he said,

'When you say that, I'm glad I'm the way I am. Because, if I wasn't this way, I'd never have you.'

My heart swelled inside my aching ribs, and I couldn't speak. There were no words for how I felt in this moment.

But I didn't need to say anything, because he went on, 'I don't want this to end, Morgan. I want us to be together. I want you to be mine.'

I swallowed. He couldn't say the words so I said them for him. 'I love you too, Ulysses.'

'Damian told me that only I could make you better and I had a thought about how to do that. So red, amber or green?'

So very Ulysses. 'Green. All the lights are forever green.'

He gave a very serious nod. 'Good.'

And then he set about making me feel better with a single-mindedness that took my breath away.

And afterwards, lying peacefully in his arms in bed, I heard him make a soft noise. 'Ulysses, are you humming?' I asked.

'No,' he said. And resumed humming.

It was strange how happiness could be painful and yet so unbearably sweet at the same time.

I put my hand on his chest. 'You're happy, aren't you?'

He looked at me, and this time, for the first time, he smiled without me doing so first. 'Yes,' he said. 'Yes, I think I am.'

EPILOGUE

Ulysses

SHE'D WANTED TO get married in Paris. I didn't care where I got married, as long as I was marrying her, so I organised it. It was one social occasion I was actually enjoying, mainly because it meant I got to hold her all day.

The previous week she'd been on a tour of a few of our head offices, as part of her new role as my second-in-command—Frankfurt, Hong Kong, New York, plus the new one in Sydney—and I'd missed her. I wasn't sure I liked her promotion—my new assistant was good, but he wasn't Morgan—yet I saw the need for it. I couldn't be everywhere at once, and I didn't want to be, so she'd do the travelling and personal interactions, supporting and encouraging staff in the other offices. She'd put together the role herself, with some input from me, and it was perfect for her, allowing her to travel and meet different people. Do different things.

It wasn't at all what I wanted to do myself, but maybe one day I'd go with her.

Today, though, we held the reception on the first level of the Eiffel Tower and there was dancing.

I didn't like dancing, but I didn't mind when it was with her.

She was in a flowing white wedding dress that felt silky when I touched it, but it wasn't as silky as the skin it covered. Skin I planned to touch and kiss every inch of later that night.

Right now, though, I had her in my arms, the lights glossing her shiny black hair. Damian and Everett were also dancing nearby with their wives. Morgan had told me she and Damian had talked a lot about the past and had cleared some things up. I was glad. I really didn't want to have to punch Damian for the way he'd treated her.

I spun her around beneath the coloured lights.

She smiled and said, 'I love you.'

I held her closer. She'd said that a lot over the past few weeks and I still hadn't said it back. I knew she didn't expect me to but I wanted to. The issue was that I didn't know what love was, so how could I say it? Was it what I felt for her? Or was it something else? Something I'd never be able to feel?

It was very important that I get it right.

'How do you know it's love?' I asked.

She opened her mouth, then closed it. Then she smiled again. 'I can't explain. It's one of those things that I don't think I'll ever be able to describe for you.'

'Then how will I ever know if what I feel is love?'

'Well, it's different for everyone.'

I stared at her, surprised. 'It is?'

'Of course. Because everyone is unique. The word "love" means one thing, but the feeling is different for every single person.' She clasped her small hands behind my neck, leaning back in my arms. 'For me, love is the feeling I get whenever I look at you. Whenever you touch me or smile at me. It's painful and sharp, and so big I feel like I'm drowning. And yet it makes me so happy I want to cry.'

'That sounds terrible,' I said.

She laughed and my heart leapt. 'I know, but that's love for me. You have to decide what it means for you.'

The idea surprised me so much that I stopped dancing. Was it that simple? Could I just decide that the feeling inside me was love?

I frowned. 'But what if it isn't love?'

'There's no right or wrong decision. You just have to trust that feeling.'

I couldn't trust my feelings, though.

But then she'd said that love was different for everyone and that I'd have to decide what it meant for me. Which meant it was another choice.

I could decide what love was for myself.

I stared down at her. She was so important to me. She'd taught me what happiness felt like and this was part of it. I wanted to give her the love that she needed.

'I thought I was having a heart attack,' I said carefully, watching her. 'When Damian found me that day along the river. I told him I needed to go to hospital.'

As I hoped, she laughed. 'Really?'

And my heart leapt again and I knew.

That was love.

Love for me.

That was the feeling I got when she laughed.

And it felt right. It felt true. So I trusted it.

'I love you, Morgan,' I said.

Her smile vanished and her eyes filled with sudden tears. But I knew the difference now. These were good tears.

So I gathered her in close, and I held her, and we danced.

I was very good at a lot of things. Patterns and money and sex.

But I was good at loving Morgan most of all.

* * * * *

DRIVING HIM WILD

ZARA COX

MILLS & BOON

CHAPTER ONE

THERE WERE CERTAIN markers I'd come to rely on over the years. Markers that signified what sort of day was in store for me.

Opening my eyes exactly sixty seconds before my alarm went off was a good starter sign. My assistant getting my coffee at ninety-one point seven degrees, not the scalding one hundred degrees most people thought was the ideal temperature for the perfect cup of java? Wonderful.

Progression from car to lift to corner office without a single one of my three hundred plus staff interrupting my seven hundred and fifty-seven steps? Utter perfection.

Precision and order equalled harmony.

There was nothing precise or orderly or harmonious about the deep rumbling voice firing off questions at my hapless crew fifty feet from where I stood, perfect coffee rapidly cooling in my hand.

No one had approached me…yet, because I'd taught my people to handle problems well.

And also, I knew deep down to my very bones, because I was who I was.

Graciela Mortimer. The woman who went by many monikers.

Billionaire heiress.

Goddess of Charity.

Queen of Cash.

Or the most frequently used—and the one I hated the most—Bitch Ice Princess.

There was some sort of irony in remembering that here, standing underneath the distant shadow of the ice-covered Alaskan Range, on a frozen lake scant miles from the Arctic Circle while surrounded by minions poised to obey my every word. But wasn't my life one giant fucked-up expression of the term? Prime example—hadn't I, in my feverish attempt to not draw attention to myself, inadvertently become the public face of a global conglomerate? That in fervently wishing to be ordinary, remove myself from the harsh spotlight of being a Mortimer, I'd somehow achieved extraordinary status, earning myself, not one or two, but *three* prestigious magazine cover appearances and a mantel full of accolades?

Nevertheless, if the frenzied media coverage over the last year were an indication, my achievements paled significantly in comparison to the man who'd arrived twenty minutes ago in a flurry of a dozen husky-pulled sleds, sleek but weathered in all-white winter gear and reflective sunglasses, and a whole hour late.

Jensen Scott.

World famous adventure photographer.

Half-English, half-Danish on his mother's side. And according to Elsa, my mostly efficient if sometimes too day-dreamy assistant, possessor of killer jawline, fuck-me hair, body and eyes.

In short, six foot five of extremely fuckable man.

From where I stood, I could confirm the six-foot-five stature.

I could also confirm that the man possessed a certain intangible…*presence*, the kind that tweaked even my jaded senses. The kind that *compelled* and intrigued.

With the ever-present threat of a snowstorm and precious few hours of remaining daylight, everyone had pressing tasks to be getting on with. Yet even those scouts tasked with looking out for unfavourable visits from curious polar bears and other Arctic wildlife were distracted by our latecomer.

That straying from procedure grew increasingly unacceptable, sparking my uncustomary *temper*. The kind normally tightly controlled and unleashed on the very deserving. Like certain members of my family.

Incomparable talent or not, right this moment, the man dressing down my project manager without so much as raising his voice higher than the cold, frozen landscape around us was jumping on my last but one nerve. Not quite the last because that was reserved. For what exactly? I wasn't sure. But the instinct I'd learned to heed told me save that last nerve.

Because I'd be needing it sooner rather than later?

Shame I didn't listen to that caution twenty-odd years

ago, back when I'd needed it most. If I had, my life would've been oh, so different than it was now.

You sure about that? You think escaping your destiny would've been that easy?

I ignored the cynical voice in my head that sounded eerily like my mother's and narrowed my eyes at the small gathering.

Larry, my normally unflappable project manager, was positively quaking. And it had nothing to do with the freezing wind blowing off the frozen Alaskan lake we currently stood on.

I discarded my coffee and forced my limbs to move, swearing for the umpteenth time to fire my stylist the moment I returned to London. Despite the five-thousand-dollar insulated winter gear she'd sworn high and low would keep me warm and toasty, I was freezing. And I was most definitely not in a mood for temperamental Nordic men whose broad shoulders looked as though they'd been hewn from the very glacier I stood on.

'Problem?' I asked as I approached.

Jensen Scott turned.

And every single one of Elsa's proclamations zinged off in my brain.

Fuck-me eyes. Tick.

I was hit with a set of eyes so glacial and blue and transparent, the hard kick to my gut took me by surprise.

Killer jawline. Tick.

His square jaw looked sharp and solid and chiselled

enough to cut diamonds, despite being covered in a dusting of dark blond stubble and snow flecks.

Fuck-me body. Tick.

Even under several layers of insulation, the Viking-god build of the man was unmistakeable. His shoulders went on for ever, as did his rangy torso and tree-trunk legs.

The *fuck-me hair* I couldn't verify on account of the snow-white beanie covering him from forehead to nape. Not many guys managed to pull off a beanie. Jensen Scott managed to pull it off with extra aplomb.

Suck-me lips.

My own addendum to Elsa's list.

Tick.

A thinner upper and slightly overfull lower, his mouth was the perfect ingredient for wet-making sex fantasies. The kind you could imagined latched onto your clit for hours while his tongue went to work.

A flash of heat blazed through me, welcome only because of its life-saving purposes. The rest of it—that sweet sting to my clit, that plumping of my labia, the slow slide of hot liquid I hadn't felt in a while and almost convinced myself had become unimportant—I intended to ignore the same way I'd been ignoring the demands of my libido for the better part of a year. It wasn't worth it any longer to go against what I'd denied for the better part of a decade. What I now knew went deeper than a mere proclivity—my utter and unapologetic need for complete control. A hunger I'd attempted to feed with the wrong men and the wrong choices until I'd decided, no more.

Those eyes that looked as if they were sparked with sky and snow narrowed at me. 'And you are?'

I chose not to be offended. Hell, I was even a little glad to not be instantly recognised. 'I'm in charge here,' I stated.

To his credit, he didn't do that subtle double-take some men did when confronted with a woman in charge. Nor did he look to Larry for verification. He simply accepted my word, even while his nostrils flared with his displeasure.

'The problem is that Larry here has been less than candid with me, haven't you, sir?' he accused. His deep, low voice held the faintest Scandinavian accent, probably from his Danish motherland. The kind that made my ears prickle with a need to hear him speak more, just so I could hear the inflexions in that beautifully modulated accent.

Or perhaps it was that *sir*?

I kicked myself into touch, tightened my hold on control before even the mere *idea* of indulging in scandalous thoughts strayed into my consciousness.

'How exactly have you been deceived?' I pressed.

I trusted Larry implicitly. He'd been with me almost from the beginning of what had been a throwaway job cobbled together by my family to shut me up. A project they'd hoped would occupy my time and stop me demanding an active seat in the boardroom. Little had they known that I would breathe my very life into it until it was an equal force in its own right on the Mortimer Group business radar.

That the award-winning charitable foundation *Fortune 500* companies clamoured to be a part of and the associated *Mortimer Quarterly* magazine named the number one for three years running would become an integral part of the family company.

These days I turned away more requests from family members eager to promote their own sectors of the family business almost as much as I turned away other public business requests.

In content and advertisement alone, the magazine was scheduled almost twelve months in advance. Which was why nothing could be allowed to get in the way of its smooth running.

Not even the man lauded as a genius with a camera. The man currently casting a disdainful eye over the assembled crew, the two heavy-duty glacier helicopters standing two hundred feet away waiting to transport us away from this beautiful-but-deadly frozen tundra once we were done, and the half-dozen tents set up around the camp, before meeting mine.

His eyes lingered a second or two longer, a touch of sensual awareness stealing into his face when his gaze dropped to my mouth. And stayed.

Two of the huskies began yapping at each other. A sharp whistle from Jensen silenced them immediately. He blinked and shifted his gaze, and that tight little frisson of awareness dissipated. 'This isn't what I signed up for.'

'Let me get this straight. You turn up an hour late only to inform me that you won't be doing the job you've been contracted to do?'

Everyone around us grew still.

'I despise subterfuge, Miss…what did you say your name was?'

'I'm Graciela Mortimer.' I held out my hand.

Recognition finally dawned as he slowly tugged off his thick glove. His gaze left my face, travelled down my body to my feet before rising again. His large hand engulfed mine and his expression heated up by a degree or two. Not the kind of instant appreciation I was used to but even that sent another spark of awareness through me. Drew my attention back to those lips. To everything I would've let myself imagine they could do. If I were interested.

Which I most definitely was not, I told myself, ignoring the slight surge of disappointment when he dropped my hand and tugged his glove back on.

'Miss Mortimer. I wasn't aware you would be here.' His tone suggested what most did. That the Ice Princess of Charity only got involved with her work when it was time to throw another gala to raise money for her various causes. That, like most, he also believed not every project I put my name to was mine from inception to execution. That I merely *dabbled* until boredom led me elsewhere.

I glanced at Larry, who was writhing in discomfort. 'I know you've been dealing with Larry, but I'd appreciate you explaining to me what exactly is going on here. What exactly were you told?'

'I was led to believe this would be a *wildlife* shoot.'

His emphasis didn't go unnoticed.

'And that's exactly what it is.'

His eyes narrowed. 'Excuse me, but if that's the case, why do I see two helicopters and supermodels and stylists all around me? I'm not sure what your definition of wildlife is, but it's certainly not supermodels in the wild.'

That untamed urge rose, the one I'd been fighting to tamp down or ignore for most of my life. The need to put him in his place in a way he would never forget. To have him on his knees. To *dominate*…

I chose a different route. 'Like it or not, beauty sells, Mr Scott. Each of those models you object to is attached to a company and an article in my magazine that seeks to promote awareness of global warming. And while you might find it distasteful, together with the Mortimer Group, we're raising almost a billion dollars for the cause. Surely the ultimate goal is what matters in the end?'

'No, it's not. Because all this—' he cast a wide, irate arm at the crew '—does nothing but disturb the very wildlife you claim you're here to protect.'

Irritation swelled to annoyance. 'My people did their research and chose the course that would have minimal impact on this location. Had you turned up when you were supposed to an hour ago—'

'It wouldn't have changed a thing. Bears. Seals. Melting glaciers. The occasional bald or golden eagle if you're lucky. That's what Larry hired me to photo-graph. And I was late because the huskies needed a rest. Four of them are in training, a process which requires patience and time. Not unlike the very wildlife you're here for. Turning up an hour ago wouldn't have been a guarantee of a wildlife sighting. Especially not with the kind of commotion you and your crew are creating.'

Again, my gaze flicked to Larry. He avoided my gaze, confirming that something had gone seriously wrong, somewhere.

'Excuse me, Mr Scott. I need a word with my PM.'

Jensen Scott held my gaze for several seconds, then he nodded and strode several steps away. Again, that urge fizzled, alerting me to the fact that it was merely dor-mant, not dead. I pushed it away and focused on Larry.

'I'm sorry, Gracie,' he blurted before I could speak. 'All the guys I interviewed either didn't come close to what we wanted or were booked months in advance. I heard on the grapevine that Scott had a very rare can-cellation and I—'

'You thought you'd lie your way into signing him?'

He grimaced. 'I didn't think he'd object this strongly. After all, he did the thing with the Danish royal family and a few high-profile people recently—'

'We've known each other for almost ten years, Larry. That's the only reason I'm not firing you on the spot. Pull another stunt like this and it'll be your last. Are we clear?'

He paled further, then nodded gruffly before glanc-ing over to where Jensen was petting one of his huskies.

He murmured to the dog and the creature responded with rapt adoration. The few words that drifted over in the chilled breeze didn't sound like English.

'Do you think he'll stay?' Larry asked. 'Do you want me to—?'

'No.' My objection emerged much stronger than I'd anticipated. 'I'll deal with Mr Scott. Just alert the crew that there might be a change of plans.'

He nodded immediately, his certainty that I'd get what I wanted infusing me with confidence as I approached Jensen.

Sensing my approach, he straightened and speared me with those glacial eyes. 'Well?'

I shrugged. 'It does appear a few…liberties were assumed about your hiring.'

His lips firmed, but he didn't reply.

'So, what will it take for you to stay?'

Something glinted in his eyes. Something that tugged at a vicious need inside me. Then he shook his head. 'Nothing. I would never have signed up for this.'

I swallowed a swell of irritation. 'Seriously? You're that opposed to what I'm doing?'

'Not what you're doing. Just the way you're going about it.'

Patience. Don't lose your shit on him.

'There are sixteen-wheelers trundling along the highways of this state every hour of every day of the year so deeper mines can be excavated and more oil can be drilled. Amongst other things. And you have a problem with a twenty-four-hour shoot over a small area to bring more awareness to a growing problem? A shoot that you've delayed by turning up late, I might add.'

He shrugged, his lips twitching as if he wanted to smile before he grew serious. 'I have a problem with those trucks too. And the mining and drilling, if that makes you feel better.'

'Let's talk hypothetically. Or better... I'll give you one minute to pitch me your version of how this would go if you were in charge.'

Perhaps it was a trick of the light. Perhaps I was imagining it. Or perhaps that lance of searing awareness that tunnelled through me was really a result of that look I'd caught on his face. The look that tugged at that desperate need again. The one that said were I to put him on his knees, Jensen Scott wouldn't mind. That perhaps he would even...welcome it?

My heart leapt, even as I tried to throttle down its wild sprint. What if my instinct was wrong? It wouldn't be the first time I'd misjudged a potential suitor. Wouldn't be the first time I'd wholeheartedly trusted my instinct only to end up with ashes.

Still... I stared at him. Watched his face tighten with rejection. But not before I caught a look that treacherously resembled...*longing*.

Perhaps longing he resented me for?

He turned away, breaking eye contact to lean down to pet the nearest husky. 'I'd pick one person to be the face of your campaign. Find a way to feature everyone else in another capacity. Your cause might mean something to every one of your crew, but they don't all need to be here to make it count. One person can represent a million.'

For some reason his sound argument made my mouth dry, my heart beat just a touch faster. 'And who would you pick—again, if you were in charge?'

This time I saw a tangible reaction to my deliberate choice of words. His jaw clenched, his nostrils thinning. 'You want to make an impact. Pick the person who has the biggest voice.' He stared at me in that direct and pointed way that left me in no doubt *who* he meant.

'Me.'

He shrugged. 'You decide.' Glacial eyes met mine. 'I'm not in charge.' *You are.*

It was a silent gauntlet thrown at my feet. A brief relinquishing of his control as his eyes deliberately dropped.

Was this a *test*? Would he dare?

Something heavy and profound unfurled inside me, threatening to unleash that forbidden yearning I'd kept in chains. Again, he turned away, this time to check the reins attached to his sled.

Look at me when I'm talking to you.

I bit back the words, took a steadying breath. 'I've spent a considerable amount of time and money to make this shoot happen. Leaving empty-handed would make me very unhappy.'

He tensed for a moment, but he didn't look up.

My heart beat faster. 'Do you want me to be disappointed, Mr Scott?'

'Jensen,' he offered with a low but distinct rasp, still without looking at me. 'Call me Jensen.'

A surge of blood roaring in my ears made me dizzy for a moment. Then a peculiar elation rushed through my veins. One I desperately wanted to deny but found I wasn't quite ready to. Not just yet. Not until I was absolutely sure this man who effortlessly blended into this landscape as if born to it was what…*who* my instincts were screaming him to be.

A submissive.

'Here's what I'm going to do. I'm going to send everyone but the most essential crew away. And you're going to stay and deliver the shoot you promised me.'

He stopped toying with the reins and turned around. When his gaze met mine, his face was carefully neutral, making me doubt my instinct. 'You don't have the right equipment to travel over long distances and different terrain. Your PM was very vague with my agent—now I know why. I came here to find out more about what you need from me…from this project before I started. Even with what you deem an essential crew, you'll have to wait for more sleds to arrive from Utqiagvik. That'll take the better part of half a day.'

I raised my eyebrows as, for whatever reason, my heart banged even harder against my ribs. 'So you're suggesting no crew at all?'

'At the most, I can make room for one more on the sled. Any more means more weight on the sleds and more weight for huskies to pull.'

Just you and me... 'You want me to stay here on my own. With you?'

His eyes glinted before they blinked back into careful neutrality. 'Have you been keeping an eye on the weather reports?'

Someone on my crew had. 'Of course.'

He looked sceptical. 'Then you'll know that in less than three days' time the sun will set for the next couple of months. Today and tomorrow are your only chances to get the variety of photographs you want.' He waited a couple of beats, no doubt for his words to sink in. Then he took a breath. 'What's it to be, Miss Mortimer?'

Call me Graciela.

It was an automatic invitation to new acquaintances and potential donors. *Call me Graciela* was so I wouldn't be reminded that I was a Mortimer. That the blood of an unfeeling, dysfunctional dynasty ran through my veins. It reminded me of the many times I'd attempted to correct that dysfunction, when I thought I knew better, believed I was different. A misguided, cruelly awakening time I would wipe my brain clean of if I could.

The words hovered on my lips but never emerged.

Because I wanted clear, definitive boundaries between myself and this man.

Boundaries I was curious to see whether he would breach. Whether he would prove me wrong.

Or...*right*.

Dangerous, forbidden boundaries. The kind that had

the power to wreck my sleep, turn my daydreams inside out with dark yearning.

'Larry,' I called out without taking my eyes off Jensen. His gaze stayed on my face, dropped to my mouth for a charged moment before returning to mine.

I heard Larry hurry over. 'Gracie?'

'Tell the crew to pack up.'

'We're leaving?' The disappointment in Larry's voice was distinct.

I gave a single shake of my head. 'Everyone else is. I'm staying.'

'Oh? For how long?'

'As long as it takes. What will I need, Mr Scott?'

He didn't correct me this time or invite me to use his given name. 'I have a satellite phone, but if you wish to keep yours, two is better than one. A couple of changes of clothes, in case you get wet.'

'Food? Water?'

He shook his head. 'I have enough to get us through the day.' A hint of hard smile tilted the corners of his lips. 'Be warned, it's more utilitarian than gourmet.'

I let the mild insult bounce off me. If my instinct was correct, he'd learn his lesson soon enough. 'I can rough it for a day or two without expiring from the horror of it all.' I looked past him to the covered trailer attached to his sled. 'Speaking of roughing it, where will I be sleeping?' Thoughts of my warm hotel suite back in Anchorage filled me with longing for a short moment before I pushed them away.

Did he just swallow? 'I have a tent if we decide to

stop for the night. Or my cabin is a couple of hours'
sled ride away.'

Larry cleared his throat. I glanced at him to find
him frowning. 'Are you…you're really staying here on
your own?'

The veiled *'Are you mad?'* in his tone drew equal
amounts of irritation and amusement. But more than
that, it drew intrigue and possibilities directed at the
man standing tall and delicious in front of me. Twin
emotions I hadn't allowed myself to experience in a
long time. Because inevitably both had led to painful
disappointment.

'There's a chance to salvage something from this de-
bacle. Or would you rather I scrap it and call it a failure?' I asked Larry.

'Of course not. I just meant…' He paused, casting a
dark glance at Jensen.

'I think your PM is worried about your safety,' Jensen said with a trace of amusement.

I didn't smile back. I was a Mortimer after all. And
as with most individuals with nine or more zeros attached to their bank balances, I'd been at the receiv-
ing end of a few security scares. I couldn't afford to be
blasé about it, even in an icy wilderness like Alaska.
'Should he be?' I tossed at him.

Every trace of humour vanished. 'I won't let any
harm come to you. You have my word.'

For a taut stretch our gazes locked, unspoken words
arcing between us. 'Instruct the crew,' I told Larry without taking my eyes off Jensen. 'No need to freeze here

if you don't have to. Tell Elsa to pack me a change of clothes and get going. I'll check in tonight.'

He knew better than to argue with me. Barely ten minutes later the small camp was all packed up and aboard the helicopters.

The apprehension I should've felt at being alone with this…captivating stranger was curiously absent as I watched my crew leave. Behind me, Jensen stashed my bag under the tarp covering the trailer then approached. I didn't look his way as he stopped next to me.

'I spotted a mother bear and her cubs feeding about half an hour from here near a broken ice floe. We can start there if you want?'

I shifted my gaze from watching the choppers turn into dark specks in the sky. 'You've had that information since you got here and chose not to share it?'

He shrugged, drawing my attention to one broad shoulder. 'It wouldn't have helped if you hadn't been inclined to see things my way. In the time it would've taken to gather your crew to get there, they'd have been gone.'

Neat answer while delivering the punch he no doubt intended to. 'You don't think very highly of me, do you?' There was a distinct sting to that knowledge, one quite different from the dull throb of pain I'd experienced over decades of holding my emotions inside.

'I don't know you. I'm only going on what I've seen so far.'

'Are you? Then why do I get the impression you've already made up your mind about me? Is it perhaps because you believe you *know* me despite us having only just met?'

'Are you accusing me of something, Miss Mortimer?'

I studied the profile he insisted on presenting to me. There was a tightness around his mouth and jaw that spoke to more than the face-value conversation taking place. 'Yes, I am.'

His delicious lips pursed for a second. Then he exhaled. 'The dogs are rested; we can probably make it in time if we leave now.'

'Aren't you going to ask me what I'm accusing you of?'

His gaze finally turned my way, and the endless depth of icy emotion swimming within nearly made me sway. 'No. My statement goes both ways. You don't know me either, so whatever you think of me is most likely flawed.'

'Ah. So that's how we're going to proceed, is it?' I asked softly. But he caught the steel I hadn't disguised. 'First, we skirt each other warily, assessing weaknesses before we land the first punch?'

This time his lips twisted in a cynical twitch. 'I'm sure you have far better things to do than to waste time delving into what makes me tick.'

His tone suggested he applied a very heavy vice versa to his statement. And despite the icy weather, my blood heated up. I reined in sweet, exhilarating control with a subtle clench of my fingers.

'You're right. But I wouldn't have needed the time anyway. I know exactly who you are, Mr Scott.' This time the gleam in his eyes was fairly mocking. But before he could tailor words to that look, I added, 'And I also know exactly *what* you are.'

The gleam faded as if extinguished, his face settling into an inscrutable mask. And even though his gaze stayed on mine, everything about him bristled with restlessness. An almost visceral need to…*deny.*

Except he couldn't. Not without denying a vital part of himself. Not without perhaps…letting himself down? But he strained against exposing his true self to me until his struggle was as real as the snow beneath his feet.

God, what had happened to him?

An equally visceral need to know attacked me, punching right through my defences to that secret vault I'd sealed shut once and for all.

Five seconds ticked by. Ten.

After twenty, his head snapped forward, his jaw jutting out with aggression that spoke of his turmoil. An aggression I wanted to wield beneath my fingers. To test and twist and mould into something sublime.

My breath shuddered out, astonishment at my train of thought nearly overwhelming me.

'The day needn't be wasted. Or we can waste time and your money on a hypothesis that leads nowhere.'

I allowed myself a small laugh, saw a slight tensing of a different kind in his frame as he heard it. 'My hypothesis is definitely leading somewhere. Otherwise why else would you be so wound up? But by all means let's change the subject.' I waved a hand at the vast white tundra. 'Take me to your mama bear, Mr Scott.'

CHAPTER TWO

SHE WAS A SPOILT, overindulged princess.

The kind who watched a few episodes of a reality show about surviving in the wilds of Alaska and suddenly decided they wanted to *dabble in nature.* The type who got it into their heads that stroking a seal or two and posting a selfie with the Arctic wildlife or atop the odd ice floe automatically granted them environmental activist status.

I didn't need to look back at where she was perched on the sled behind me to visualise her clutching her collar, grimacing at the intensifying wind. I was surprised she hadn't whipped out her sleek satellite phone and ordered her chopper to come pick her up.

The bear family might have moved in the time she'd been ordering her staff about.

The time she'd spent *analysing* me with those stunning hazel eyes, deciding whether to toy with me or not.

Muscles jumped in my stomach. As hard as I tried to ignore the sensation, what I'd seen in her hooded, sultry eyes still sent fresh waves of apprehension through me. Not the kind that had anything to do with the work she'd hired me for. That I could do with one hand tied behind my back and one eye closed.

No, the kind of sensation that look had elicited… that fucking *craving*.

I shook my head, partly to clear it, partly in denial.

Dammit, she'd seen it. Then she'd spotted my efforts at denial…

I gritted my teeth and unnecessarily flicked the reins attached to the dogs. The huskies were highly trained, would respond to the softest whistle or voice command, which made the reins largely superfluous.

Or, hell, was that particular symbolism for me? Was I so hard up, I was now expressing myself through my bloody dogs?

Dammit.

I didn't need this. I should've left Graciela Mortimer's little ice circus the moment I confirmed her project manager had lied to my agent in order to secure my services.

More than any other flaw, *I hated lies.* And the people who told them.

Large. Medium. Tiny white lies. Every single one of them came with wrecking balls that altered lives, changed the dynamics of relationships, no matter how much we fooled ourselves into believing otherwise.

How many had my mother told my sister and me in order to avoid facing the glaring truth?

I'm all right. It doesn't hurt. He'll change. And the worst lie of them all: *he loves us.*

Even before my fifth birthday, I'd known that statement for a lie. And for the decade after that, that fabrication had been exposed time and again until, like poisonous acid, it'd begun to erode my relationship with my mother.

Of course, I knew now it'd been her way of coping, the delusion her own form of security blanket. Hadn't I risked falling into that same pattern of delusion until I'd wised up as a grown man? Hadn't I made allowances for Stephanie's lies just to hang on to what I thought was a solid relationship, all the while knowing that trust, once broken with lies, never—

'How close are we, Mr Scott?'

Of course her voice would have to melt my insides. Visions of heated honey…no, more like the anticipation of watching melted wax in the moment before it hit my skin. The sharp burn before the breathless, sizzling warmth.

That was what Graciela Mortimer's voice had evoked the moment she'd spoken the words *I'm in charge.*

Lort!

I should've left after imparting my thoughts on what she was proposing to do. Which would've been easy considering I hadn't wanted to do this gig anyway. Regardless of the fact that my own company had been driving me insane. Regardless of the fact that I hated myself a little for not being able to stay the course of what was left of my month-long self-imposed hermitage.

I should've left.

Instead, here I was, secretly yearning to hear that

voice again. To do that, though, I'd have to engage her in conversation.

'Ten more minutes. Give or take,' I threw over my shoulder. The GPS co-ordinates I'd noted on my watch would see us there in less time, but I'd learned to make allowances on unknown terrain.

Silence greeted me. Against my will, I looked over my shoulder.

Despite the stylish shades covering her eyes, I felt her gaze boring into mine with unapologetic direct-ness that tunnelled lightning straight into my veins. It singed me into life, making me aware of every inch of my skin, and especially the rush of blood to my groin.

This was why I hadn't walked away.

Yet.

'Give or take what?' she asked with a slight arch of a silky eyebrow.

Good question. My sanity? Another sign that my screaming instincts were right? That she wasn't merely toying with me?

But fuck, where the hell did I get off trusting my in-stincts when they'd let me down spectacularly so very recently with Stephanie?

'Mr Scott, while I have a thing for the strong, silent type…on occasion, this isn't one of them. I will need you to actually engage with me here.'

The dry amusement in her tone should've raised my hackles further. And yet it drew a wry smile. And what was it with that *Mr Scott* when I'd invited her to use my first name?

Perhaps because she didn't need invitation. *She commands it.*

My senses jumped, dark need clamouring through me so hard every inch of my body tightened with anticipation.

Futile anticipation. I had no intention of even probing possibilities. Not after the fucking fiasco with Stephanie.

There was a reason I'd retreated to my remote cabin in Alaska. A reason I'd welcomed the last-minute cancellation to my tight work schedule. When it came right down to it, the need to escape my thoughts and immerse myself in my work were the reason I'd grudgingly accepted what I thought would be a solo assignment.

Which was why I should've left Graciela Mortimer where I found her.

'We're here.' I tugged on the reins with a sharp whistle and the dogs immediately slowed to a stop.

The mother and her three cubs were still on the large floe about a quarter of a mile away, finishing off the last of a fish meal. One of the dogs barked and the mother bear raised her head warily, eyeing us from across the distance.

I sensed Graciela approach, felt her invasive presence when she stopped next to me. The very fact that my every sense clamoured to look into those hazel eyes once more made me avoid her gaze.

'Are they… We're not disturbing them too much, are we?'

The question was soft enough to have fooled me had

I not witnessed the circus I'd convinced her to dispatch. 'Do you care?'

Stephanie would've inhaled sharply at such a blunt question, then, depending on whether she was in her false role or not, would've delivered icy condemnation or tears on command.

Graciela met my question with another imperious lift of her brow and a steady regard when I flicked a glance her way. 'You really don't like me, do you?'

There was another hint of a smile in the question, a suggestion that she didn't care either way. It should've confirmed every impression I'd had of her. Instead, it disconcerted me. Did my opinion of her count so very little?

'You don't care whether I do or not so why bother asking?' I countered.

Her sigh was long and exaggerated, another indication that she found me…vastly amusing. That she could grind me underneath those expensive snow boots she was wearing without a second thought.

Just as Stephanie had believed she could.

Another spoilt little rich girl, this one with a few billion to play with, who believed she could buy anything and anyone in sight.

More than a little vexed that I couldn't detach as easily as I'd hoped from the events of the past few months, I headed for the sled, pulled back the tarp and lifted out my treasured camera and slotted a fifty-millimetre lens to it to capture the close-ups I wanted to start off with.

'You want shots for the print magazine and videos for the digital version, correct?'

'If it's not too much to ask, yes.' Again she sounded amused.

And I couldn't help it. I paused in the process of unscrewing the lens cap and looked her way to find her glasses sitting on top of her head and her stunning eyes fixed on me.

Not a single picture I'd seen of the heiress had done her justice. She had a face that just begged to be photographed. As for her body, despite being under wraps from neck to toe, I'd seen enough pictures of her in the glossy rags Steph used to devour to know just what was beneath the outfit.

Graciela was taller than average for a woman but even though she only reached my shoulder she seemed…taller.

Larger than life.

But while I wanted to believe it was mostly entitlement—because, let's face it, that shone from her eyes and bristled from every pore—there was more. Which again made sense, since she was the very definition of a wild child and went out of her way to prove it with her various antics.

Skydiving in nothing but a string bikini over Rio.

A three-day sex party with a premier league soccer team in a hotel in Mali.

The rumours that she kept a string of lovers across the globe…

The icy wilderness landscape of Alaska was the last

place I'd expected her to turn up, thinking she, like Steph, was the kind to leave all the hard work she'd later take credit for to her minions.

I finished adjusting the exposure to compensate for the darkening sky and took an initial short burst of photos of the polar bear family. Then I swapped the lens for a sixteen-millimetre, for wide-angle shots, and took another burst.

Surprisingly, she remained quiet throughout, didn't fill the silence with mindless chatter, which I appreciated.

'Can the cubs swim at their age?' she asked when I lowered the camera after five minutes.

'If they're more than a few months old, yes, for short periods. But with more distances between icy landscapes some bears have been seen swimming with their young on their backs.'

She nodded, her gaze on the ice floe. 'Is it dangerous for them?' she asked.

'Danger comes from all angles in this environment. This is a slow-moving floe and surrounded by frozen land on three sides. The mother would be on the lookout to ensure they don't drift too far.'

'That's great, but it's moving…towards us.'

I curbed a smile as I swapped cameras and grabbed a tripod to set up more stills. 'We'll be gone before it gets to us.'

She nodded again, but her gaze grew speculative, shifting from the bears to the other floes. They varied in size from a few metres to ones the size of football fields, all broken away from the mass that would nor-mally have stayed solid well into the new year.

'Can I get a short video of the floes, too?'

'Sure.'

She didn't interrupt or badger me with questions once I got into the flow of things. Hell, she even took herself off a short distance away, taking out her phone to take pictures of the distant Alaskan Range and the beginning of the spectacular orange on white sunsets that graced this stunning part of the world.

She returned in time to witness the bears' floe touch another one and the mother supervising her cubs jump-ing from their floating platform onto a larger one.

With one last warning look over her shoulder, the mother bear escorted her cubs away towards a jagged mountain peak.

'How long before they go into hibernation?'

'Another two or three weeks.'

She frowned. 'They don't look nearly padded up enough.'

I shrugged. 'Probably because they have to travel farther distances to feed.'

As if on cue, a loud, sharp crack sounded. Camera poised, I swung around in time to capture the tower-ing wall of ice break away from a glacier to crash into the lake.

The sound seemed to echo for ever, bouncing off the icy landscape in perfect surround sound. Beside me, Graciela gave a soft gasp. 'God. That's…'

I lowered the camera and glanced at her. 'It's breathtaking and awe-inspiring until you remember that it shouldn't be happening?'

Her face shuttered, her brows creasing in a frown.

I wasn't sure whether she didn't like that being pointed out or whether she didn't want to admit she was affected by what was unfolding before her eyes. Wasn't she here after all because money had been thrown at her charity by people who could afford to contribute ten times more?

'Do you want to be included in the video?' I asked.

She remained silent for several seconds, then shook her head. 'I'll let the environment speak for itself.'

I throttled back my surprise. She'd just passed up the perfect opportunity to get in front of the camera. A camera manned by me. According to my agent, her PM hadn't shied away from tossing his boss's name into their phone conversations at every opportunity in an attempt to sway me. While I knew now he'd bent the truth to suit his purposes, I also knew most people wouldn't pass up an opportunity to be photographed by Jensen Scott.

I came within a whisker of being impressed before I reminded myself this was just the beginning. Women like Graciela Mortimer wouldn't overplay their hand with over-eagerness. If anything, she'd expect *me* to talk her into it.

She'd be waiting a long time for that. I ignored her, shooting a three-minute video in sharp focus, the white landscape capturing the stark story.

'Are you ready to go?' I asked once the echoes had receded and the equipment was packed away.

She nodded. 'Where to next?' she asked briskly.

'Depends. Do you want to show all the gloom or is your piece aimed towards reminding people of the glory too?'

'The aim is for more shock than awe but I'd like to use the time efficiently. So whatever's closest.'

'How about we kill two birds with one stone, so to speak?'

'As figures of speech go, I wouldn't have reached for that one. And for some reason I think you wouldn't have either. Now I'm totally convinced you're trying to get a rise out of me, Mr Scott.'

I was, and a small part of me cringed at the pettiness. 'It's Jensen.'

Again, one corner of her mouth tilted, drawing my gaze to the overfull lower lip. Its juicy plumpness and far too lickable curve. Almost in slow, torturous motion, a perfect picture slid into my brain of those lips wrapped around my cock, drawing sweet torment with every suck. I didn't have a single doubt that Graciela would know just how to suck me off. She was far too confident in her femininity not to be an expert in all things coitus.

'Is it?' she taunted in answer to my offer.

I might have been attempting to rile her, but she was having a ball reciprocating.

'Is there a reason you refuse to use my first name?'

'I think we both know why.'

Why the hell was this friction turning me on? This wasn't the type of interaction that got me off. 'Look, I think we got off on the wrong foot—'

'No. I think we got off on the exact right foot. I remind you of the baggage you're attempting to shed by running off and hiding in the icy wilderness next to the Arctic Circle, and you don't like it.'

Anger fired up inside me, even while I was thrown by her near-accuracy. 'I'm not running anywhere,' I bit out.

'Aren't you? Sorry, my bad.'

I snapped the tarp over the equipment with more force than necessary. 'You don't sound sorry at all.'

She shrugged. 'I'll work on my sincerity while we head for wherever you're taking me next. Shall we?'

We stared each other down, with the friction and tension increasing with every moment that ticked by.

I'd had enough of that with Stephanie, each moment with her spent on the uncertain edge of judging a mood that could veer from icy indifference to volcanic.

Walk away.

The faster I completed this assignment, the quicker I could be rid of Graciela and the unsettling emotions she evoked.

Slowly, as if she'd read my intentions, her expression changed to one of steady assessment tinged with boredom.

Absurdly, that only riled me further, the need to ruffle feathers she'd effectively smoothed with a dismissive thought firing through me.

'You get a kick out of being contrary?'

She shrugged. 'Maybe. Or perhaps you simply don't like the truth pointed out to you. Either way, we can still talk while we…sled. Is that what you call it?' She gestured at the animals.

'You know exactly what it's called,' I replied, noting absently that my heart was beating faster, my senses more fired up than they had been in weeks. 'Pretending you're less intelligent than you actually are may be a turn-on for other men. Not me.'

'And you think that's what I'm trying to achieve here? To turn you on?'

God, the way she said that, with the exact cadence engineered to stroke my cock. Did she practise it to get that perfect degree of hotness and craving?

I had a feeling she knew the exact effect she and her voice were having on me.

'I don't think you utter a single word or make a move without calculating the exact effect you wish to achieve.'

Like a switch her expression grew icy, her eyes dimming to a dull brown before she blinked and cast a disdainful glance at a spot over my shoulder.

I'd struck a nerve. For a moment I wanted to take back my words, but then I wanted to know just what I'd done. To explore that nerve, get to know it better. So I might know this woman better?

She's only here for another day. You don't move in the same circles so if you don't want to, you won't need to see her ever again.

That thought…dissatisfied. I wanted to know Graciela. If for nothing else, to satisfy myself that my instincts weren't wrong about her. That my craving was misplaced. That she was another wannabe, unworthy of the name…

Dominant.

My senses jumped. Harder than before, my gaze falling once more to those biteable lips. To her clothes and what lay beneath. To how it would feel to receive her command to unwrap her, lay my hands on her bare skin, feel her silky pulse jump beneath my touch. Hear her voice hitch with arousal as she revelled in controlling my every desire.

Even if it was a matter of losing myself in a woman just for the hell of it, with no agenda or deeper meaning, I was up for that.

'I don't believe I'm paying you to stand around and work out my IQ, Mr Scott.'

Keep your money. This one's on the house.

I swallowed the words. I was richer than I'd be able to spend in one lifetime, courtesy of a life-changing photograph taken on a faraway continent. I'd been doing well before the photo that had propelled me to fame and fortune had set me up for life. I didn't need her money, true. But I suspected a gesture like that would impress her even less. Not that I was out to impress her. And really, why the hell would I want to cut my nose to spite my face?

More axioms, Jensen?

I cursed the mocking voice and gestured at her to get back on the sled.

Disdain and designer sunglasses firmly in place, she hopped back into her seat.

The next destination was forty minutes' sled ride away and, save for a quick stop to water the dogs, we completed it in silence.

Killik Falls was a natural waterfall cascading from a tiny blue lake cradled in one of the many glaciers situated between Prudhoe Bay and Utqiagvik. The sight of the blue water bursting through a wall of ice was a stunning phenomenon, a fact evidenced by Graciela's gasp when I pulled the sled to a stop near a flat plateau on one of the glaciers.

'Wow, that's breathtaking.'

I let out a relieved breath, noting annoyingly that I'd hoped the sight would please her as much as it'd pleased me the first time I saw it. 'Yeah.'

She stepped off the sled, sliding off her shades to get a closer look. When she glanced at me there was only curiosity in her eyes. 'It all looks great. So why here?'

'It should've frozen over two months ago.'

Her face cleared, leaving behind a solemn look. 'Ah. I see.' She took in the snow-dusted fauna around the lake while I took out my equipment. 'How long has that been happening?'

'Steadily for the past ten years.'

Her lips tightened, but she didn't answer, her gaze flitting over the landscape to pause thoughtfully on the waterfall. 'That's…disturbing.'

Suddenly, I didn't want to film the waterfall. I wanted

to capture her reaction, the way the failing light teased shadows and light over her features.

She would be an interesting subject to photograph. My fingers clenched around the camera, the insane urge to aim my lens at her, zoom in close and catch every emotion, swelling higher with each moment. It grew strong enough to zap alarm through me.

'Perhaps we should get on with it?'

I didn't reply. Wasn't sure I wanted to interact with her while in the throes of…whatever this was. Instead, I went to work, getting a vast array of shots so I didn't miss a thing. When I was satisfied, I put my equipment away and glanced at my watch.

'Gloom or glory?' I asked. I had a site for either in mind I could squeeze in tonight, and her brief had called for five location shoots. While the cracking glacier earlier had been a bonus, I was technically required to do three more. I glanced over at her, caught the shiver she tried to hide. 'Or are you ready to call it a day?'

Her gaze shifted to the covered equipment at the back of the sled. 'Did I spot a tent in there?'

I frowned, inexplicably tensing. 'Yes. Why do you ask?'

'Did you plan on spending the night on the snow?'

'Not tonight.' And certainly not with her in tow. The last thing I needed was her kind of distraction.

'When?' she pressed.

'At some point. When you're not here,' I added pointedly.

Again she surprised me by smiling where I'd expected her to be offended. She approached, not stopping until our bodies were six inches apart.

'Guess what my favourite game is, Mr Scott,' she murmured, her voice low, husky and sensually loaded enough to achieve its aim of curling tight around my cock.

'Winding people up?'

'Wrong,' she breathed. 'That's my *second* favourite. My first is Tug of War. Care to know my percentage on wins?'

'Sure. Enlighten me.'

She leaned up and in, until our condensed breaths mingled. And fuck if that didn't heat my blood. 'It's high, Mr Scott. *Very* high.'

'Very high doesn't mean one hundred per cent. Which means on occasion you lose.'

Her smile widened. 'Perhaps. But you're contractually obliged to give me what I want.'

'Or what? You're going to fire me? I'm the best,' I answered, with a tinge of well-earned arrogance. 'Your PM told you that or you wouldn't have hired me.'

'Nothing as melodramatic as firing you. More along the lines of thinking you wouldn't want to deny a client's reasonable request. Would you?'

'I've yet to hear what this reasonable request is.'

'You want me to spell it out?'

'Just so we're clear, yes.'

'You. Me. In the tent. Tonight. Doing whatever you were planning to do.'

Her words were deliberately phrased to get a rise out

of me. And fuck, did they just. My cock hardened at the imagery, my gaze unable to shift from the perfect curve of her lips. No wonder she had men in a lather all over the globe.

She already had me in a lather, all over the innocuous idea of spending the night in a tent under the Alaskan sky. Time to defuse this before it got out of hand.

'I always travel with a tent. You don't know when the weather will turn. Or when a night shoot will reap rewards.'

'What particular reward were you hoping for?'

I shrugged. 'The forecast is for a clear night. I was hoping to score a borealis on video as part of the project.'

I caught the faintest hitch of her breath. She didn't outwardly show her excitement, but the thought of witnessing an *aurora borealis* was a phenomenon most people rhapsodised over.

She slowly lowered her heels and slipped her shades back on, but even with the shield, I felt the power of her hypnotising stare. 'In that case I'm going to have to insist on staying,' she said after several seconds.

My pulse tripped, then raced at full speed. The thought of spending the long hours of the night with her in a tent, a woman even the most red-blooded alpha males feared, filled me with equal measures of dread and anticipation.

Overlay that with the persistent thought that she could be a Domme...

Again, where I should've refused, I found myself

shrugging, moving to the back of the sled to grab a thicker anorak. Returning to where she stood watching me, I held it out. 'It's a bit of a trek, sometimes over rough terrain. Bumps and bruises are unavoidable but wear this and you won't freeze to death.'

She took the anorak and shrugged it over her suit, then sent me another spine-tingling smile. 'Thanks. And when we arrive at our destination, you can tell me what her name is.'

I froze. 'Excuse me?'

'The name behind the baggage you're running away from. I'm sure she has one. I'd love to hear about her.'

CHAPTER THREE

I WATCHED HIM attend to the dogs, his movements efficient, capable, and yet sexily streamlined in a way that made me want to watch him on an endless loop. Which was absurd in itself, because I was used to beautiful men, wealthy, filthily pampered men who strutted about, cushioned by power and privilege.

Even hardened men like my brothers, Gideon and Bryce, who had been through their own versions of hell and back but had somehow managed to rise above, didn't hold as much interest for me as this man did.

You should've paid more attention, because they both seem to have found answers to love and acceptance that you haven't.

I pushed the thought away, my gaze lingering on Jensen as he petted his dogs, his back turned decidedly on me.

Why was I pursuing this? Why was the urge to needle and probe sliding like a narcotic through my blood? Something about the man had captivated me from the first, even *besides* the strong possibility that he was a sub. While I'd had my own versions of *no* in the past—

my parents delivering the most gut-wrenching one of all—I wasn't sure why this particular reluctance from him made me even more determined.

Determined to do what, precisely?

Exactly how did I expect this to go? I was emotionally bankrupt, according to myriad blood relatives, past lovers and strangers. I had nothing valuable to give, save my money, of course. After years of tossing those opinions away like so much chaff, I had finally been forced by my innate stubbornness to admit that perhaps they—and my mother—were right.

Every relationship was doomed to failure. Hell, even my brothers were avoiding me, my bitterness and emotional inadequacy making them run for the hills rather than spend time with me.

I couldn't even blame them any more. And it certainly didn't help that I was the spitting image of my mother. The mother who'd callously abandoned us decades ago and never looked back.

The urge to grab the satellite phone, summon my helicopter and get the hell off this barren landscape pulled at me.

I reached for the phone just as Jensen rose and pivoted towards me. Thoughts of leaving evaporated. Something about this man captivated me, made me want to dig deeper beneath the thick layer of concrete he wasn't shy about putting up.

I would've admired his resolve, if he hadn't ignored me for the better part of an hour and a half.

We'd arrived at his chosen site twenty minutes ago

and set up camp on a flat landscape with nothing but snow for miles around. Being born into wealth and spending most waking minutes in the lap of luxury where every whim was catered to had inevitably cultivated healthy jadedness about most things well before I hit my twenties.

But looking around now, I couldn't help but be overawed by the stunning beauty around me. And as much as I wanted to dismiss it, Jensen was a big part of that draw.

I'd perused his portfolio on the plane ride to Alaska. He was unapologetically talented at his job and had no modesty or pretensions about it. Sure, it grated that he was pretending I didn't exist at the moment. I would've been amused had it not been for the wicked little thrill that tunnelled inside me every time he glanced my way. It pleased me that he was fighting this connection between us. And failing. The man couldn't help but look at me every few minutes.

He hadn't answered my question, though.

His gorgeous face had grown taut and forbidding, warning that my question about who had treated him badly wasn't going to be answered.

Yeah, I'd probably stepped over the line with that one. But, hell, wasn't that one of my many flaws, according to those who branded themselves experts on me?

I summoned one of my 'ice princess' smiles as he approached. 'Is this going to be an exercise on who blinks first? If so I'm happy to throw in the towel. You don't have to answer the question if you don't want to. I'm happy to let it be.'

He stopped at the entrance of the tent, his gaze pinning me where I sat in the folding chair he'd provided when he'd started setting up the tent. He'd firmly refused my offer of help, a move that'd stung a little more than I cared to admit. So what if I was out of my depth in this whole…snowy outdoors thing, and I'd probably have got in his way more than helped? I could follow instruction. On occasion.

'Are you?' he asked, his voice a little stiff and that edgy look still on his face.

'Not really,' I admitted. 'I still want to know.'

'Why?'

'I'm a hopelessly curious creature, Mr Scott. I can't help but wonder why a man like you would consign himself to this wilderness for weeks on end.'

'And you automatically assume it's because of a woman?'

'Isn't it?'

Something flickered in his eyes, something that sparked a kindred light inside me. One that burned brighter with every second he held my gaze.

'Maybe it was, maybe it wasn't,' he muttered eventually. 'But that's all you're going to get.'

I didn't tell him, of course, that his little addendum had only fuelled the need for satisfaction. That need for resolution born of stubbornness and desperation that had brought me more heartache than I cared to catalogue.

He ducked into the tent, emerging a minute later with a weatherproof bag he set down a dozen feet away. In silence, he lit a camp stove and started dinner. When he handed me a cup of coffee five minutes later, I answered with a smile. He stared down at me for a second longer than necessary before returning to his task.

I sipped the coffee, groaning as the warmth chased away the worst of the cold.

That drew his gaze again, as if he couldn't help himself. I hid a smile and finished my coffee, just as the aroma of pasta carbonara drifted towards me. Jensen dished out two bowls and held one out to me.

'Thank you.'

He nodded, went into the tent and brought out a thick rug, which he tossed onto the ground. Watching him fold his six-foot-plus frame before me, a cross-legged position that placed him at my feet, punched a deep longing that made my breath catch.

Perhaps he was aware of what he'd just done—that right up there on a Dominant's most cherished wish was a willing submissive at their feet—because he froze too, his eyes holding mine for a charged moment before returning to his bowl.

We ate in silence, eerie white darkness gathering around us as night fell and the moon rose.

'Her name is Stephanie,' he volunteered grudgingly.

I nodded, torn between satisfaction that he'd answered of his own free will and a peculiar dart of jealousy that I now had the name of the person who'd contributed to Jensen's wary reserve. I concentrated on eating, attempting to ignore the latter emotion.

'Not going to push for more?' he asked after a long stretch. 'Now you know, you're no longer interested?' he added with a trace of snark.

'You used the present tense just now. I may be many things, but I'm not a woman who encroaches on another woman's territory. Not even to satisfy simple curiosity.' I was lying, of course. I was way more interested than simple curiosity dictated.

'She's no longer in my life. Feel free to encroach away.'

Why did that invitation make my heart jump? Make temptation surge high? 'Are you sure?'

He shrugged.

'Maybe I won't encroach. Maybe I'll simply sit back and savour the mystery of you, like a fine wine.'

The lamps he'd set outside the tent illuminated enough for me to catch the slight flare of his nostrils at my words. The strong movement of his throat as he swallowed.

He wasn't unaffected by me. Far from it. And the longer we stayed out here under the star-dappled sky, for all the world the only two people left on this planet, the more I was tempted to discard the vow I'd made to myself.

The vow of no more relationships.

The vow to focus on the things I could control, like my charity work. So why the next words tripped from my lips, I would never fathom. 'Do you like the idea of being savoured, Jensen?'

He tensed at my use of his name, but it wasn't affront that bristled from him. It was something far more potent. Hot and wicked and carnal, it reached out in the space between us, wrapping itself around us the way only two people dangerously attracted to each other could be affected.

In the silent landscape disturbed only by intermittent faint cracking ice, he stared at me, want and need and lust building in his eyes until his chest rose and fell with rapid rhythms.

Beneath the thermal layers, my skin tightened, heat pooling as my body answered with equal fervour.

But slowly his face hardened again. 'I'm not one of the men you can toy with and discard when it suits you.'

Needles of hurt stung deep. I pushed the sensations away, telling myself it was better this way. Better that he thought he knew enough about me to believe the lies and make judgements for himself. That meant he was interested *despite* his better judgement. That meant neither of us would be seriously invested.

'The last thing I want to do with you is play, believe me.'

His fingers tightened around his bowl, the last bite forgotten. A second later, his jaw gritted. 'My bedpost-notching days are behind me. Sorry.'

'Are we talking about my bed or yours?'

'Yours is purportedly far more interesting than mine.'

This time the grating lingered longer, sharp disappointment lancing me as I stared at his averted profile. 'I'm surprised. I wouldn't have pegged you for a tab-loid chaser.'

'I'm not,' he said tightly.

'Really? Because I could've sworn you just judged me by the contents spewed out on a regular basis in gossip rags.'

His gaze returned to mine, digging, attempting to see far more than I was willing to show him. 'I'm an experienced adventurist and can easily prove that there can be the smoke without fire. Is that what you're ask-ing me to believe?'

I could've responded in a great many ways, bat-ted him away with sarcasm and flippancy. But when I opened my mouth, only one raw, unguarded word emerged. 'Yes.'

His gaze was sceptical and probing, but it wavered for a moment to reveal another expression.

He wanted to believe me.

My heart leapt, a foolish action that I immediately condemned.

There was nothing to be excited about here. Bitter experience insisted that, regardless of how it started, inevitably every relationship ended with acrimony and pain. Trust wasn't a commodity I gave away freely; lately, I wasn't sure I possessed it any more.

That bracing reminder cooled some of the heat ram-paging through my blood. It drove me to my feet, and I glanced around for somewhere to put the bowl.

Jensen rose too, once again towering over me as

he reached for it. With quick, efficient movements, he rinsed the bowls out and tucked them away.

Within a minute he was back, tall and mouth-watering, in front of me. But the past remained a hard reminder, a harsh voice that said I couldn't even explore, out here in the middle of nowhere, without further risking the last of my emotional reserves.

But does it have to be that heavy? You could just no-strings fuck him.

Temptation slithered inside, quickening as my gaze dropped to his sensual lips, slowly parted as he stared at me. The air thickened between us, his eyes darkening with every second that ticked away.

'Careful there, Jensen,' I murmured. 'Or I'll think you want me to truly savour you.'

One corner of his mouth tilted in a sexy little smile that jerked the strings attaching my brain to my pussy. 'Better that than being downed like a shot and forgotten about.'

'That's what you're worried about? That you'll be forgettable to someone?'

A shadow cast over his features, indicating I'd hit near enough to a bullseye. The urge to probe deeper surged through me. But then his gaze dropped, to rest somewhere near my throat, possibly at the frantic pulse beating there. Or, as I suspected, the submissive nature screaming out to me was rising, despite his attempt to ignore it. Need flared again, intensifying with each second.

'What if I am?' he murmured.

Unable to resist, I raised my hand, brought it close without touching his taut jaw. 'False modesty doesn't become you. You're as far from unforgettable as it's possible to get and I'm pretty sure you know that.'

He smiled, but the shadows remained in his eyes. And because I'd exhausted the willpower to remain this close to him without touching him, I ignored every last reservation, leaned up and pressed my lips against his.

He tensed for a frozen moment, and then his lips were clinging to mine, opening up beneath the pressure of my kiss, a grunt escaping his throat as he leaned down, granting me access to better explore him.

He was delicious. Heady, in a way that made my senses swim even before I'd taken my next breath. I swept my tongue over his slightly parted lips, and he groaned, pressed closer, wanting more. That fierce connection, that need to have my instincts satisfied, drove me to kiss him deeper, start an erotic dance with him.

Gloriously, he followed, met me stroke for stroke, intensifying the kiss. His teeth nipped, nibbling and tasting. My clit swelled, need building till the slickness dampened my panties.

Through it all, Jensen held his hands at his sides, adding another degree of certainty to my instincts that when it came to all things sensual and sexual, Jensen Scott would truly submit, wouldn't proceed without express permission.

My permission. My *domination*.

My heart and senses raced at the thought, saturating me with a sense of promise until I swayed under the strength of it. But it was short-lived, my spirits deflating. In less than twenty-four hours, the real world would beckon, and with it the knowledge that nothing this good ever withstood the pressures of a Mortimer life.

If we were really going to do this, all I had was this one night to savour him as I'd loftily offered.

I'd warned him about believing everything he read in the paper. Was I really about to embark on a one-night stand, my very first with a mysterious but intriguing man I'd only just met?

Why not? If that's what we both want?

But was it?

I trailed my hand over his jaw, neck and down a chest ridged with his rock-hard muscles. He jerked, reacting to me despite the layers of clothes between us. Insanely thrilled by his response, I took my time with him, fingers lingering as I headed south.

I disengaged from the kiss just before I reached his belt. I watched him, absorbed the almost haggard arousal etched into his face; took in the lowered gaze resting on my breasts. Pulling my lips between my teeth as anticipation blazed through me, I trailed my hand the last scant inches and gripped his hard length through the layers of clothes.

'Fuck,' he breathed.

I bit back a moan of my own, unwilling to admit how much his unguarded reaction pleased me. Despite the warnings shrieking in my head to slow down, think this through properly, I continued to stroke him, learning his length and girth and glorying in the heat and power of him. After a minute, I leaned closer, brushed my lips against his in a light kiss. 'Do you feel savoured yet?'

He gave an abrupt shake of his head, his tongue flicking out to taste my lower lip. 'More. Please.'

I curbed my smile, even as my heart jumped. This was so foolish. Disappointment surely lurked around the corner. But for the life of me I couldn't stop touching him.

A harsher wind swept over us, and, despite the insulation of clothes keeping the worst of the chill out, I shivered. Immediately, he unzipped the opening to the tent.

'Let's go inside. It's freezing out here.'

He held back the flap of the tent, and I went inside.

The large sleeping bag stretched out over a waterproof mattress was more than adequate for one person. Not two. I turned to comment on the feasibility of our situation.

The raw, ravenous look in his eyes stopped me.

That look became the deciding factor.

He was an adventurer. Used to taking risks and reaping stunning rewards.

Wouldn't it be a kick to take a leaf out of his book?

I reached for the zip fastening my suit. His gaze dropped to trail the movement, his harsh breathing so insanely sexy, my nipples beaded harder. Within the atmosphere of the closed tent, with double space heaters warming up the space, arousal bit harder.

'You want to help me with this?' I asked, my voice sultry with excitement.

With a firm nod, he stepped forward, taking over my unzipping. 'It'll be my pleasure.'

He was way taller than the tent and had bent his head when he stepped inside. Still, my heart lurched when he dropped to his knees. But his position in no way diminished him. Jensen was overwhelmingly large, his sheer size making my mouth water as I stared down at him. I dug my arms out of my outer suit, then held onto his shoulder as he manoeuvred the material down my legs.

I'd just stepped out of them, leaving my thermal all-in-one underneath, when he inhaled sharply. 'Shit. The aurora.'

I wanted to laugh, weirdly amused by the notion that the phenomenon was enough to distract him from what we were doing. 'Is it happening now?' We'd been in the tent only a handful of minutes.

He shook his head. 'No, but I don't want to miss it if it does.'

Even as he sprang into action, his gaze locked on my body, eyes heating up as it lingered on the twin diamond-hard points of my nipples, brazenly outlined in the thermal suit. After a thick swallow, he veered away, his movements graceful yet efficient as he dug through his equipment, took out three powerful-looking cameras and tripods and then swiftly exited the tent.

Minutes passed as he set up the cameras outside the tent. Then he was back, sealing the flap closed behind him. Need clamoured through me. Impatient to be naked, to feel his hard body and hands upon mine, I swivelled away from him, exposed my nape where the zip of my thermal suit rested.

Eagerly, he went back to work, his expert fingers lowering another zip, this one exposing my naked back to him. His sharp intake of breath made me smile, eroding a few more layers of doubt.

Jensen's reaction gratified, salved a wound I didn't want to admit needed soothing and I revelled in the warm hands that undressed me, pleasure gliding through me as I looked at him over my shoulder, watched his eyes linger on my behind, where my thong dissected the globes of my ass.

'You're beautiful,' he breathed, his hands shaking as they trailed up my legs, pressing into my calves on the way to wrapping around my hips. He leaned forward, pressed his face into the gap between my legs, shamelessly breathing me in before letting out a thick groan. 'And you smell amazing, *min elskerinde.*'

The foreign words were almost whispered against my skin, under his breath. I wanted to ask what they meant, but he was nipping at my flesh, using his teeth to wreak havoc.

Doing things I hadn't quite given him permission for.

I twisted in his hold, braced my hands on his shoulders. 'You've seen me. Now I get to see you. Undress.'

His hands reluctantly left my body, pulled at the fasteners securing the neck of his snow suit, but his movements were slow. Perhaps because his lust-dark eyes were fixed on my breasts, still encased in the burgundy bra that matched my panties. Lingerie was an expensive weakness of mine.

It was partly why I'd kept in touch with Bryce's childhood friend and now girlfriend Savannah Knight, and ordered a new selection from each of her Voluptuoso lingerie collections the moment it hit the stores.

Perhaps lace and silk that barely covered my intimate parts were impractical for sub-zero weather temperatures, but it was a decadence I didn't feel bad about indulging.

Judging from Jensen's reaction, it was well worth it.

'Hurry up, or I might change my mind about all of this.'

He attacked his zip without taking his eyes off me, hissing when it went over his engorged cock. He wore the same thermal under gear as I did, but in a blinding white two-piece trousers and long-sleeved T-shirt combo to my black one-piece. I was sure there were some Freudian connotations in our colour preferences but all I could absorb in that moment was the way the material moulded his sculpted shoulders and chest, the way it outlined his mouth-watering abs. With each movement as he shrugged out of the garment, I was exposed to even more of Jensen Scott's perfection.

I wanted to lick him all over. Then devour him in large, choking chunks.

The strength of that need alarmed me. But the sight of him on his knees, ready to surrender to me, overpowered the apprehension.

I was a grown woman, perfectly ripe for my first

one-night stand in a tent somewhere in the Arctic Circle if I wished it. Empowered by the thought, I cupped his strong jaw, leaned down and pressed an open-mouthed kiss to his lips. Before the flames could leap out of control, I eased away, walked past him to where the sleeping bag was laid out.

Like everything else around here, it held a chill as I lay back on it, but it warmed quickly. I let out a pleased sigh, watched as he swivelled to follow my movement, kicking away his suit as he did.

I beckoned him with a finger, and he rose.

He was gorgeous. Built like a true Viking with thick thighs, chiselled calves and lean hips, he was fantasy made flesh.

A fantasy I intended to make reality before the night was over.

'Come and show me what else those talented hands are capable of,' I invited sultrily, moving my arms to rest them above my head.

'Just my hands?' he asked, his voice a thick rasp.

'No, Mr Scott. Not just your hands. Every inch of that delicious body is definitely on my to-do list.'

My fingers brushed the side of the tent, and the brief contact with the cold sent a delicious shiver through me, making my nipples harder.

He groaned, then, erupting into movement, he dropped onto the sleeping bag, dark blue eyes devouring me as he started to reach for me.

'Wait.'

He stilled, his nose flaring in the silence I let drag out for several seconds.

'The beanie. Take it off. I want to see your hair.'

The white cap—he really had a thing for white, didn't he?—slid off easily, and I suppressed a groan. Hell, even his hair was magnificent. Burnt gold, threaded with hints of dark honey, it was enough to make a woman weep with envy. And a shampoo manufacturer scream with joy. But it was still tied at the back of his neck.

'All of it, Jensen.'

With an impatient tug, he freed the length from the simple elastic band. My breath caught as the heavy mass fell over one shoulder. With movements that were perfunctory rather than exhibitionist, he dragged his fingers through the thick strands, tossing them off his neck. They fell well below his shoulders. And while I wasn't into the whole man-bun craze, I couldn't deny there was something wildly sexy about a guy with the confidence to wear his hair this long.

Eyes darkened with arousal raked over my body again, unfettered lust parting his lips. 'What do you want, *min elskerinde*?'

'For you to finish undressing me,' I instructed.

He fell on me, callused fingers grazing my skin as he reached behind me to unclasp my bra. At the first sight of my breasts, he groaned. 'God, you're so fucking sexy.'

I arched my back, silently inviting him to touch.

He touched. Squeezed and caressed me until he dragged a moan from my throat. The thought of the frozen tundra right outside the tent and the sizzling effect of his hands on me was one of the headiest encounters I'd experienced.

I wanted more of it.

As if he'd read my mind, his hands tiptoed down my ribs, leaving a trail goosebumps, to catch and drag my panties down my legs.

In the dim light, I saw a flush stain his chiselled cheekbones. It was a unique enough reaction to elevate me from mere lust to…something else. Something that was exclusively mine.

Something that didn't remind me of my uncanny resemblance to my mother, a fact many chose to comment on, either with reverence or with cruelty. While these days I'd stopped reading the tabloids, I'd once spent a useless, soul-shrivelling month scouring newspapers and magazines for mentions of my name that didn't involve my mother. Not a single one had been entirely about me. Because of course I wasn't my own person. I was a churned-out product, a means to an end dictated by a few lines scrawled in a centuries-old trust, discarded at the very first opportunity.

If only I could look into the mirror and not see the exact replica of just who had done the discarding—

Callused hands tightened on my inner thighs, dragging me back to the present. To the man who crouched before me, his eyes fixed on me with complete, unwavering focus. 'I feel as if I'm losing you,' Jensen said, a displeased little light in his eyes that absurdly thrilled me. The idea that a man who barely knew me would fight for my attention, when my own mother had—

Dear God, enough already!

'Well, you've got my clothes off. Now what do you want to do?' I asked, momentarily content to let him make the decision. I was merely loosening the reins, not handing them over.

He swallowed, his gaze darting from my breasts to my pelvis, hunger etched deeper on his face. His grip grew even firmer, subtly nudging my thighs apart. I was shamelessly wet, could feel the hot dampness in the cool air.

'I want to taste you. Devour you. Make you come,' he said.

Breath hitching, I spread my thighs wider. 'Then we're in accord, Jensen, because I want the same thing.'

With a rough grunt, he lurched forward, wrapped both hands around my breasts and sucked a nipple between his lips. Expertly, he rolled the hard nub between his teeth, nipping and sucking until my back arched clear off the sleeping bag. He showered attention on the twin peak, then utilised his hot and skilful mouth on a trail south.

Jensen didn't tease and titillate his way into a slow build-up. He wanted to devour me, and that was exactly what he did.

With a full-on, dirty French kiss, he launched a spine-melting assault on my sex, tasting and licking with unashamed pleasure that made me gasp in shock.

'You taste so good,' he growled, his gaze rising to

clash with mine for a second before it dropped to my sex. Minutes ticked by, the only sound in the tent the decadent acoustics of wet, aroused flesh and pleasured moans.

Then his fingers parted me wider, exposing my engorged clit to the wicked assault of his tongue. Pleasure piled high, drawing wild tremors through me. Like a freight train, my climax bore down on me. Relishing the added friction of his stubble against my thighs, I gathered the long strands of his hair in one hand, the other cupping my breast to squeeze a nipple as I prepared to surrender to rabid lust.

It arrived in flashes of wild lightning, jerking my hips in hard spasms. Jensen's hand slipped beneath me, effortlessly holding me up as he continued to taste my climax. When it all grew too much, I tightened my grip in his hair.

With endearing reluctance, he diverted his attention from between my legs, dropped kisses down the length of my inner thighs before prowling his way up my body.

The decadent kiss tasted of my musky satisfaction. Eventually, he drew away, and I saw the building tension on his face.

I forced myself not to tense in response, despite the less than euphoric sensation moving through my stomach at the thought that he already regretted what had happened. 'If you're annoyed by the lack of accolades, I'd say give me a chance to catch my breath, then I'll—'

A sharp shake of his head halted my words. 'It's nothing like that.'

'Okay.' I waited.

His gaze rushed over me, as if he couldn't help himself. And call me vain, but it eased my tension a little.

'I'm not sure how far you want this to go…' he paused, jaw gritted, as if he didn't want to say the words '…but I don't have a condom.'

I froze, mildly stunned that the need for protection hadn't occurred to me. While I was on the Pill, and fairly certain pregnancy wouldn't be an issue, I'd never *not* used the extra layer of protection. The last thing I needed with my various issues was to add a baby to the mix. Or a different type of health issue.

In a way, this was the perfect get-out clause. A moment of reprieve to rethink this insanity before it got out of hand.

So why was I reaching for him, bunching my fist into the front of his thermal T-shirt to pull him closer? 'I'm sure we can find middle ground that works for both of us. Take this off, please. And kiss me again,' I said, reclaiming my true nature now the first hazy orgasm was out of the way.

He pulled the T-shirt over his head, and I barely managed to stop from gaping. He was glorious, a perfect synergy of sleek musculature and light golden skin.

I wanted to touch him, but he had other ideas. As per my instruction, the moment he tossed the clothing away, he fused his lips to mine. My hands went to his hair, gathered it in one hand. He gave a rough groan.

I used the pressure to draw him back, revelled in his wild shudder. 'You like your hair pulled?'

His rabid gaze remained on my mouth. 'Yes.'

I tightened my fist, applied pressure until his head bowed back, exposing his delicious throat to me. Unable to resist, I trailed a kiss down one side of his Adam's apple. 'What else do you like?'

'Everything.'

I laughed. 'That's too broad a spectrum. I deal in specifics. I'm a woman in a position of power and responsibility. I have a burden of literal billions in donations on my shoulders. I can't afford to waver or prevaricate over my decisions.'

His eyelids flickered, but he didn't lift his gaze. His submissiveness was so ingrained it was breathtaking. 'It's more than that, *min elskerinde*, and we both know it.'

My heart banged against my ribs. 'I should punish you for arguing with me.'

'But you won't because it's the truth. Being in control is who you are.'

It was my turn to shudder. But not with arousal. It was his recognition of my true self that threatened to move me. 'I'm still waiting, Jensen.'

'I'd very much like to fuck you. But since that's not on the table, I'd love to make you come again.'

As generous as the offer was, it reeked a little too much of pandering to the desires of the spoilt little rich girl, in the hope of banking brownie points. 'Why that, Jensen? Why not ask for a blow job?' My gaze dropped to the thick outline of his cock, straining about his thermals. 'I'm sure you could use a little relief?'

He shuddered against my lips, but still he shook his

head. 'The taste of you is…intoxicating. I want more,' he confessed thickly.

And what the hell…who was I to refuse such a request?

'Wake up, *elskerinde*.'

I snuggled deeper into the warm sleeping bag. 'What…why? Is it morning already?' It felt as if I'd fallen asleep minutes ago into what had surprisingly been restful sleep.

'No, it's not. But the borealis is happening. I don't think you want to miss it.'

My eyes popped open. 'Seriously?'

Jensen's eyes were amused as he nodded. 'Seriously.'

About to launch myself out of the bag, I remembered I didn't have a stitch on. The thought of piling on layers of clothes, while necessary, made me grimace.

Silently, he held out my thermal under suit, the jacket he'd given me on the last leg of the sled ride, and a blanket. 'This should be enough to keep you warm for a short time.'

I reached for the clothes with a grateful smile, something sharp and profound lurching in my chest. I was just his client. A client he didn't want to freeze to death on his watch. No big deal. Certainly no reason to read any more into this than a mere kindness.

I accepted the items, tugging the leggings of the all-in-one on without bothering with my panties or bra. As I punched my way into the jacket, I noticed that he was already dressed.

'How long have you been up?'

'About five minutes. I stepped out to check on the cameras and saw the lights.'

I hurriedly zipped up the jacket and searched for my shoes. Again, he produced them, the laces in my boots eased apart and ready to be tugged on. 'Am I going to miss it? How long does it usually last?'

The moment I stood he eased the blanket over my shoulders. 'Each one is different. If we're lucky, it'll last for a good while.'

He held open the tent flap for me. And I stepped out into the most spectacular sight.

Against a black velvet sky pierced with brilliant stars, breathtaking swathes of coloured light swirled and danced. Greens, blues, purples and yellows, they looked close enough to touch.

'Oh, my sweet Lord.' The cold Arctic slap of wind forgotten, I stared, my breath held at the wondrous sight. 'It's…indescribable.'

Ja,' he concurred, his tone a little gruff. 'No matter how many times I see one, it still takes my breath away. Each one is unique enough to make me feel like I'm seeing it for the first time.'

I could believe that. 'How many times have you experienced this?'

I sensed more than saw his shrug. 'Not as often as I'd like.' There was a wistfulness to his tone that almost distracted me from the sight.

Almost.

The beauty displayed above me was too powerful, too sacred to take my eyes off it.

So I watched, even as I sensed Jensen's subtle movements around me. Even as I heard the soft, shuttered clicks of his camera, circling. Stopping. Circling some more.

It was only as the spectacular display started to fade several minutes later that I paid attention to what Jensen was doing.

His camera was going off a mile a minute, his movements near balletic as he leaned in, then leaned back, dropped a few inches, then rotated the camera while adjusting the lens. There was something deeply hypnotic and breathtakingly beautiful about watching him at work, which was why it took several seconds before, alarmed, I realised that I was the focus of his attention, and not the spectacular display electrifying the sky around us.

Years of being photographed without my permission had engendered a hatred of having cameras trained on me, triggering a knee-jerk response. 'I hope you're not thinking of selling pictures of me to make a quick buck.'

He froze, then slowly lowered his camera as he rose from a deep crouch. In the pool of light from the lantern he'd brought with us, I watched shock and fury chase across his face.

'I get by well enough on my own hard work without the need to peddle images of celebrities, princess. I leave that kind of asshole move to pond scum who aren't familiar with concepts like respect, privacy and basic human decency.'

The bite in his voice rivalled the Arctic wind sweeping against my skin.

For a moment I was ashamed at my harsh rebuke, but even that emotion was swept away by the wild panic at the thought of having offended him. I stepped forward. He turned away, his back stiff as he went to check on his equipment.

I opened my mouth to say what I wasn't exactly sure just as the name he'd called me struck hard and deep.

Princess.

He called me *princess*. A predictable insult from someone who claimed not to read the filth and lies the media wrote about me. The world's favourite derogatory term for me, but searingly painful coming from Jensen. Anger mounted, and I stewed in my righteous fury, but beneath all that I was totally confounded by how much his slur had affected me.

Why?

Because we'd rolled around in a tent for a few hours?

It was supposed to mean nothing. And it *did*, I insisted to myself.

As passing time and work went, it hadn't been a bad day. I'd seen three spectacular sights, been the recipient of two mind-blowing orgasms, and could now tick a traipse to the Arctic Circle off my bucket list. Not bad for a twenty-four-hour jaunt.

First thing in the morning I'd order the chopper to come back and get me.

Jensen could complete his assignment on his own. If his work produced a less than satisfactory outcome, I'd hire the next best person. He might think himself the best, but surely there was someone out there equally qualified.

With that thought in mind I turned towards the tent, but at the last moment, unable to resist, I looked over my shoulder. In his white gear, he should've blended into the landscape, but there was an aura about him, the type that made him impossible to miss. Impossible to ignore. Even in these final moments of seeing Jensen Scott in this environment, I knew he'd be as unforgettable as he'd wanted to be.

The thought irritated as much as it disturbed.

Enough to trigger another unfettered response. 'This ice princess needs her beauty sleep. I'd appreciate not being disturbed when you come back in.' Yes, it was a cheap shot, but I didn't care.

Not when I zipped myself into the bag and immediately felt the lack of hard male body warmth that'd helped me sleep soundly only a few hours earlier.

Not when he didn't return for the better part of an hour, leaving my mind whirling, making me wonder where he was, whether I was that loathsome that he would stay out in the cold rather than share a tent with me.

Not when I felt another clench of my heart at the thought I'd screwed up something as simple as a one-night stand.

The same way I'd driven my brothers away.

The same way I'd screwed up and sent my mother away from me at the age of nine.

CHAPTER FOUR

THINGS WENT FROM bad to worse between Graciela and me while I was in the middle of kicking myself for over-reacting the night before.

Now I'd had time to cool down, I couldn't blame her for assuming the worst. The British media were notorious for privacy invasion, and with a family like the Mortimers, with their well-documented clashes with the tabloid press, it didn't surprise me that she'd be wary.

So what if we'd shared a few intimate moments the night before?

Everything about our encounter reeked of *temporary*.

Regardless of certainty, though, a hard bite caught me every time I thought of this project being over, that what happened in the tent last night would never be repeated.

Fuck, if I wanted the blood to relocate from what felt like its new permanent residence in my groin, I needed to stop thinking about last night and concentrate on the real threat of the snowstorm heading our way.

It'd caught me unawares, much like a lot of things had since meeting Graciela Mortimer.

Jaw clenched, I resisted yet another urge to glance behind me. To catch another glimpse of her face. She'd been asleep, thankfully, when I eventually returned to the tent last night. Knowing I couldn't join her inside the sleeping bag, despite being sorely tempted, had been another unpalatable lesson in self-control. Common sense had been little comfort as I'd shivered in the blankets on the other side of the tent.

Breakfast had been predictably chilly, and I wasn't surprised when she treated me to haughty silence as we packed up and reloaded the sled. Nor could I stem my disappointment when she informed me of her plans to cut short her involvement in the project.

There was no avoiding talking to her now, though.

I glanced over my shoulder. 'There's a storm headed our way. We're not going to make the rendezvous point to meet the chopper.'

Her eyes narrowed before leaving mine to scour the landscape and sky. 'The sky is clear. I don't see anything resembling a storm.'

I curbed a smile. 'This isn't a trick. We have about half an hour tops to find shelter before the storm hits. Your pick-up point is ninety minutes away.'

'Can't we hunker down somewhere, wait for it to pass?' she asked.

I shook my head, feeling almost sorry for her. Almost. Her hurry to get away from me rankled. 'No, we can't. It's better to find solid shelter rather than camp out.'

She reached for her satellite phone. 'I'll call my pilot, and you can redirect him here to pick me up,' she said.

'If the storm's as bad as I think it is, he won't be allowed to fly out at all. And if he does, you'll be risking everyone getting stranded—' The sound of her phone ringing interrupted us. 'I bet that's him now calling to tell you the same thing.'

With an icy glare at me, she answered. 'Hello?' She listened, her expression growing tighter by the second. Any moment now, I expected her to snap at her pilot to come, regardless of the procedures. But, surprising the hell out of me, she nodded. 'Fine. If you can't fly, you can't fly. Let me know as soon as you're given the all-clear.'

She hung up and, for a moment, I caught a lost expression in her eyes. And then she was back to glaring at me. 'So what now?'

A low hum of electricity vibrated through my bloodstream. 'My cabin is ten miles away. Provided the dogs cooperate we might beat the storm.'

Wariness crossed her face. 'And if we don't? What happens if we get caught in the storm?'

'We might catch a bit of it, but don't worry, if we need to stop, I'll keep you safe.'

Again, a raw expression crossed her face, but it was quickly stifled. 'If that's our only option...'

It wasn't exactly a ringing endorsement, but it was enough. I was prepared to risk getting us inside four solid walls rather than braving the elements, no matter how many sparks had flown in our tent. Before I'd ruined it.

I checked my watch's GPS tracker to make sure

we were headed in the right direction and whistled at the dogs.

They responded immediately, eager for brisker exercise, and turned east, towards the isolated cabin I'd been using for the last two weeks. The thought of Graciela in my personal space, alone with me under my roof, heated my blood, hardening my cock despite the possibility that she wouldn't move from her stance of clearly not wanting anything to do with me.

For a moment, I mourned refusing the blow job she'd offered last night. Bloody hell, how I wish I'd taken her up on it. Then I wouldn't be so fucking wound up tight, repeatedly dwelling on how incredible she had tasted, how snugly my tongue had fitted into her. How much I was dying to hear those control-wrecking little noises she made when she came.

I'd passed up the chance and I only had myself to blame for my state of raging blue balls.

The storm hit much quicker than I'd anticipated, catching us out a good ten minutes before we reached the copse of fir trees that signalled the beginning of the woods leading to the cabin. The dogs, sensing the turning weather, strained at the leash, barking excitedly at the thought of being given leave to go even faster. The moment I loosened the reins, they were off.

I checked over my shoulder. 'Hold tight.'

She nodded stiffly, although I caught a hint of excitement in her eyes as her hand tightened around the iron handlebar in front of the seat. She probably wouldn't admit it, but she was enjoying this, being at the mercy of the elements. I knew I was.

There was something raw and unfettered about pitting oneself against nature and coming out on top. It was mostly why I'd chosen my profession.

That and the freedom it gave me once upon a time to immerse myself in something else other than the turmoil going on at home. Turmoil that had ended up shaping my life.

I relished the icy wind lashing at my cheeks, making my eyes water as the wind picked up speed. The snow came, thick and furious, falling horizontal with the force of the wind. I checked on Graciela every few minutes, confirming that she was indeed enjoying this by the hint of a grin toying at her lips. Which stunned me a little.

The only time I took Stephanie on a shoot after her endless badgering for me to bring her with me, she'd complained the whole time, demanding to go back to *civilisation* at the earliest opportunity.

While I wanted to enjoy Graciela's pleasure for a few minutes, I was still relieved to spot the familiar treeline that signalled the boundary to the cabin, grateful to see an end to enduring what was quickly turning into a white-out.

Minutes later, I pulled to a stop in front of the compact log structure that comprised my cabin.

I hopped off the sled and helped Graciela off. 'Wait for me on the porch. I'll get the dogs squared away and bring in the equipment.'

She shook her head. 'It'll be quicker if I give you a hand.'

I nodded, located my camera bag. 'Okay. Take this up with you. I'll just be a minute.'

She grabbed the bag, lifting the heavy load without complaint onto one shoulder. Then she grabbed the blankets and sleeping bag and hurried onto the porch. I grabbed the rest of the equipment and followed.

The key was tucked into a nook specially created in one of the overhead beams on the porch. I unlocked the door and held it open for her. A full day with no heating meant the interior was icy-cold but, luckily, the electricity was still working. I turned on a couple of lamps and activated the portable space heaters we'd used in the tent. She set the stuff down next to the fireplace, and I disposed of my own load before waving her towards the wide, comfy sofa. 'Take a seat. I'll be back in five minutes.'

She nodded, but didn't sit down.

When I paused at the door and looked back, she was gazing around the cabin, inspecting the large open-plan space. It was rustic, far removed from the luxury she was no doubt used to. Nevertheless, as basic as it was, something about having her here in the space I'd made my own appealed to me.

I turned away, berating myself for getting carried away. She'd be gone as soon as the weather cleared. Besides the pictures on my camera, there'd be just my memory to evidence her brief presence in my life.

What the fuck is wrong with you?

I shut the door behind me, concentrated on relocating the dogs to their habitat in the heated shed where they slept. Ensuring they had food and water and that their blankets were dry, I returned to the cabin, grabbing Graciela's small weekender from the sled on the way.

She'd lowered the zip on the outer snowsuit, but hadn't taken it off. Which was a blessing, I supposed. The memory of her insanely beautiful body, smooth skin and the sweet flesh between her legs was vivid enough without a visual reminder.

I held up her case. 'I brought your stuff. I'll get the fire going if you want to change clothes?'

'I do, thanks,' she said, her voice a little stiff.

I sighed. Did I even have the right to be disappointed that she was giving me the icy princess treatment? What did it even matter? I'd come out here specifically to get away from women like her; taken this assignment because I'd believed I'd be alone, working while licking my wounds.

Trust-fund princesses with entitlement issues were supposed to be permanently off my menu.

What about trust-fund princesses with pussies that tasted like fucking honey?

Blood surged into my cock at the reminder, and my legs felt a little stiff as I went to the fire and tossed in a couple more logs onto the half-burnt ones I'd put out before leaving the cabin yesterday.

I lit the fire purely from muscle memory, what with my brain stuck back in that tent, reliving every second of how it'd felt to make her come, wring those insane sounds from her throat, to feel her fingers in my hair as she'd directed me on how to maximise her pleasure.

And that's what's right and so fucking wrong with this picture, isn't it? You got a taste of her and now you can't get her out of your head?

I ignored the voice, stayed right there on my knees until the fire was in full rage. The sound of a zip lowering made me turn. She was freeing her arms from the outer suit and tugging her hair loose.

I'd been so blinded by her body last night I hadn't quite clocked the long strands of her raven hair cascading halfway down her back. The urge to sink my fingers into the silky mass made me clench my fists. Realising I was staring at her like some hormonal fool, I busied myself by shrugging off my own suit.

Since I didn't want to risk her seeing her maddening effect on me, I unzipped to the waist and left the arms hanging down. Hell, she'd see the bulge below my waist soon enough if I spent any more time standing around staring at her breasts, thinking about how good she tasted.

Thinking about what else to do brought up a different dilemma, though. I eyed the sofa and hid a grimace.

She followed my gaze, but before she could speak, I grabbed her case. 'There's not much to the cabin but I'll show you around,' I offered. 'Let's start upstairs.'

I headed up the stairs and down the short hallway leading to the bedroom tucked in the eaves of the cabin. I heard her following and opened the bedroom door as she reached me.

The huge king-size bed took up most of the room because, what the hell, I liked my comfort when I slept. Besides that, though, I had very little else in the way of creature comforts. A dresser, bedside table, and closet that held a handful of clothes were all I needed when I used the cabin. I set her bag down beside the bed. 'You can have the bed. I'll sleep downstairs.'

'Why? Because I'm a spoilt ice princess?' she bit out, her face cold once again.

I gritted my teeth, regret and irritation warring inside me. 'You want me to apologise for what I said last night?'

'I wouldn't want you to waste your breath, since we both know it would be false.' She was back to using that snippy, upper-class voice.

As much as it came naturally to Graciela, it reminded me a little too much of the posh voice Stephanie had adopted to impress clients—and me—when we'd first met. It'd turned out to be as false as everything else about her.

With Graciela, I was beginning to recognise the snippiness as a facade. I'd caught enough glimpses of her vulnerability to guess the truth. Last night, for instance, even as she'd ordered me not to disturb her beauty sleep, I'd caught the hurt in her voice. Seen the way she'd held herself stiff and closed, as if she didn't want to show her vulnerability.

And, dammit, something about that made me want her more.

Perhaps even more than I yearned for the sultry creature who'd raised her arms above her head last night and invited me to use my hands on her.

'I see you're not bothering to deny it.'

I sighed, dragged my beanie off to run my fingers through my hair. She followed the movement and I did it again, a shockingly large part of me wanting to preen for her. Wanting to reawaken the Dominant I'd received an oh-so-brief taste of last night, just so I'd experience the unique pleasure of surrendering to her once again.

She seemed nowhere in sight now, though, and, for whatever reason, I wanted another glimpse of her. Wanted to test her authenticity. Wanted to—

What? See if she was real or a fake as Stephanie turned out to be?

Why?

I ignored the far too difficult question and focused on answering. 'Maybe I could've been a little less... spiky about it.'

One sleek eyebrow arched. 'Maybe?'

I hid a smile at the tight demand. She was one hell of a ball-breaker. 'Fine. I definitely could have been.'

The icy disdain didn't leave her face. I sighed again, then waved at the window, indicating the snowstorm raging outside. 'I've no idea how long this thing is going to last. I'd rather we didn't spend the whole time being at each other's throats.'

'Oh, you don't have to worry about me, Jensen. Ice princesses are experts at maintaining a dignified silence.'

My jaw gritted. 'I don't want that either.'

Her head tilted, her hazel eyes mocking as they met

mine. 'Let me guess, you want a cosy conversation by the roaring fire?'

No, I wanted to growl.

Conversation could come way later, after we stopped playing games and she showed me her true self. Long after we established a baseline of trust and she let me surrender to her from my rightful place at her feet. Long after I'd undressed her again and given her everything she wanted from me, which I hoped involved long hours spent between her thighs.

Then I wouldn't mind a conversation or two with her. A chance to discover what else lay beneath those dense layers besides the vulnerability I'd occasionally caught glimpses of yesterday.

Since even the thought of that was making me hard again, I forced a shrug. 'If that's what you want. But first you really should get out of those clothes. And you can have the bedroom. I insist.'

The barest hint of a smile ghosted her lips. 'Oh, you do, do you?'

I nodded. 'Call it my peace offering for offending you.'

A layer of iciness receded, and something tight eased inside me. 'Where are you going to sleep? Don't tell me you're going to take the sofa. It's barely long enough to accommodate me, never mind you.' She waved a hand at me.

I shrugged again. 'There's an air mattress around here somewhere. Or I can use the sleeping bag. I'll be fine.'

She didn't answer, but her gaze swung to the bed and she approached it. A smile playing over full, sensual lips, she sat down and dragged her fingers over the comforter. I bit back a groan, locked my knees as a punch of lust knocked the breath out of me. I wanted those fingers on my body, caressing me.

Before things got out of control, I waved at the door. 'You want to continue the tour?'

'It's more or less a two-room cabin, isn't it?'

'Yep. The bathroom's next door, and I have a dark-room downstairs next to the pantry, but yes, that's about it.'

Her eyes stayed on mine. 'That's all I need to know, thanks.'

'Okay.' I turned towards the door.

Her voice, firm, sexy, minus the icy disdain, stopped me. 'Jensen?'

I looked over my shoulder. 'Yes?'

'Apology accepted.'

Another knot unravelled inside me, disconcerting me as much as the smile that took me by surprise. I wasn't going to examine either right now. 'Great,' I said. 'Coffee will be ready in five minutes.'

Before I did something else insane, like beg her for another kiss, I hurried down the stairs and crossed the living room into the kitchen. I busied myself measuring coffee beans into the coffee-maker—another perk I'd allowed myself—while ignoring the noises from the bathroom and thoughts of a wet, naked Graciela. The coffee was brewing when I heard her footsteps behind me. I turned, unable to help myself.

My breath flattened in my lungs.

Dammit. She was fucking gorgeous.

Black leggings showcased long, shapely legs and feminine hips. Above that, a waist-skimming grey cashmere sweater, designed in a wide-necked sexy way to reveal one shoulder, left a creamy expanse of flesh I couldn't help but devour with my eyes as she moved towards me. 'Why the bedroom upstairs?'

'What?' I forced my brain to track.

'Why not attach a bedroom to the living room downstairs?' she elaborated.

'To conserve space. The initial plan was to make it one big room, get a big sofa that converts to a bed to use when I needed it, but I realised I'd need to make room for a bathroom down here too. I wanted to reduce the square footage so I went up rather than out and split the extra room downstairs into a pantry and darkroom. Rustic is one thing, but I draw the line at an outside bathroom.'

The barest hint of a smile curled her lips, and I was struck with the wild urge to see her truly smile. 'Surprisingly I do too.'

'Then we're in agreement.'

She looked around again. 'So, you own the cabin?'

I nodded. 'Built it with my own two hands three years ago.'

Her gaze dropped to my hands and for some reason I wanted to spread them out, offer them to her.

Get a grip, Jensen.

The coffee machine beeped, giving me the perfect excuse to use my hands on something other than supplication.

'How do you take your coffee?'

'Black. No sugar. Thanks.'

Damn. Girl after my own heart.

Woman.

Graciela Mortimer was all woman. A woman I wanted more with every passing minute. I poured two cups of coffee and handed one to her. She lifted the cup to her lips, gently blew on it before taking a sip.

Her gaze lifted, boldly spearing mine for one tight little second. I wondered if she'd seen my desire. If she had, what would she do with it?

Nothing, I told myself firmly.

I'd sworn off entanglements, remember? I took a large gulp of coffee, wincing when it scalded my mouth and throat. But it brought a modicum of common sense, enough for me to exhale somewhere near normally as her gaze swung from me to the window.

'Is there any way to find out how long this thing is going to last?'

My insides dipped, mocking the mental slap I'd just handed myself. 'In a hurry to get somewhere?'

Hazel eyes returned to clash with mine. 'Of course I am. Even charity magazines don't run themselves.'

'I don't want to start an argument, but don't you have people to ensure things run smoothly in your absence?'

'Doesn't mean I don't enjoy being in charge.'

My next breath strangled in my chest. I'd got a small taste of her being in charge and it'd sparked a red-hot fire in me. But there was something else, something she wasn't quite saying. I decided to leave it be. For now.

'You've got your satellite phone. That's enough to stay connected for the time being, right?'

Her gaze lingered on my face. 'I like to be fully present in every situation. Phones are one thing, face to face is quite another.'

Yep, we were definitely talking about something other than her business. Something that charged the blood in my veins triggered feral hunger inside me. My cock hardened. 'I get that.'

'Do you?'

My throat dried, words taking a little while to form in my brain before I replied. 'That you like being in control. Relish being in charge? Yes, I do. Am I wrong?' Fuck, I hoped I wasn't. Being taken for a fool by Stephanie was one thing. Getting it wrong *twice*…

'You really want to know the answer to that?'

I shifted as the ground beneath my feet lurched. We were straying into forbidden territory, slipping beneath the roped-off cordon and into space I'd designated off-limits since that last, soul-wrecking showdown with Stephanie. Where she'd admitted the depth of her duplicity. Admitted, *finally*, her interest in me had been mere facility, that I—and my celebrity—was a stepping stone to the bigger pool of clients she'd wished to cultivate. That she'd only *pandered to my proclivities* because she thought I'd grow out of it eventually.

I wanted to set my cup down, walk away from this subtexted conversation before it got any more dangerous. Before Graciela's sizzling gaze compelled me to disregard every reason why this was a bad idea.

'What if I said yes, Jensen? What if I told you that being in control is everything I live for? That I'm the Domme your senses are screaming at you that I am?' she stated, her voice deep, firm. Totally controlled.

My stomach went into free fall, my heart hammering a wild, feral beat as we stared at one another.

End this now. Don't risk another Stephanie episode when you know how it'll end.

What if I was leaving myself open to a new, untested form of hell?

But even as the warning shrieked inside my head, I knew this wouldn't be like that. For one thing, this would be temporary.

I was looking at hours, maybe a day with Graciela, rather than the months Stephanie had wormed her duplicitous way into my life.

Everything with Graciela Mortimer was already on a countdown clock controlled by the weather. It would end and we'd go our separate ways. So why not indulge in whatever open-ended proposition blazed in her eyes? Experience an epic adventure right here in my cabin?

And if it turned out not to be as epic… I mentally shrugged. I couldn't be more disappointed than I'd been in the last few years.

But if it was…

If she was offering me another chance to fulfil the deep craving, a chance to be rid of this hard-on threatening to cut me in half, no fucking way in hell was I to deny it. I swallowed another mouthful of coffee to buy myself some time; unable to deny the clamouring in my blood, I answered. 'Prove it.' The words fell from my lips before I could stop them. 'If you are who you say you are, prove it to me.'

She sucked in a sharp breath. 'You want me to…' She stopped.

And right before my eyes, her gaze sharpened, her features tightening with calculating purpose. Purpose that wouldn't be denied.

'For starters, you know I would never allow a sub to address me that way. Don't you?' Soft, menacing words that pounded the locked door to my soul ajar, demanding entry, demanding a glimpse of what lay beyond it.

I knew the moment she saw it. Her nostrils flared, her lips parting for just a second before she pulled the reins of the control tight.

'Yes.'

'And you are a sub,' she breathed. 'One who's yearning to find his freedom in surrender in a way he hasn't for…a while. Aren't you, Jensen?' It wasn't really a question. It was a searing acknowledgement.

Something shifted inside me. Something wild and elemental.

A key finding a lock.

Turning. Turning. Turning.

I couldn't halt my response.

'Yes, *min elskerinde*.'

CHAPTER FIVE

FIRE BLAZED IN her eyes at my answer, the flames raging as she continued to stare me down. 'How long?'

Flashes of shame and regret tore through me. 'Not as long as I've wanted to.'

'What does that mean? Explain yourself clearly to me.'

Shit, was I really doing this? Letting her open that door wider when I needed to be more circumspect? Graciela wouldn't be the first woman to profess she understood what I needed when she didn't have the first clue.

Case in point—Stephanie. First-class liar and con artist. She'd taken my trust and warped it without second thought to progress her career. Had been prepared to go even as far as *marriage*.

While I'd once upon a time made allowances because I was finding my own feet, I wasn't prepared to do so any more. Submitting to a worthy Domme for a night, or for however long we both wanted, wasn't something to frivolously toss around. I wanted a woman who knew what she was doing in the bedroom. Who understood my needs without flinching from fulfilling them. Part of that involved honesty. And openness.

I exhaled my apprehension. 'I didn't fully embrace my needs until a few years ago. Don't get me wrong, I'm not ashamed of who I am.'

'That's good to hear,' she murmured.

'I just choose not to be a raging advertisement for the lifestyle. But I know what I want in the bedroom and I'd rather not have to settle for a diluted version of it.'

She nodded. 'Again, good to hear.'

'Because?' I asked, my insides jumping, the need for confirmation running amok inside me.

She didn't answer immediately; her gaze drifted to the snow falling hard outside the window. 'Because I have a proposition for you, Jensen.'

'Ja?' I replied, slipping into Danish. My mother tongue was comforting, I'd found, in times of stress. Probably something to do with it irritating the bastard who I'd had the misfortune of calling my father. The bastard who'd made his wife and children's lives a living hell for a decade and a half before doing a disappearing act.

Sure, this was stress of a different kind, but it didn't make enduring it any easier as I waited for Graciela to respond.

Her gaze pinned mine, resolute. Commanding. My fingers tightened around my coffee mug, anticipation rushing through me.

'As long as that storm rages just outside, you will be mine.'

'Yes,' I responded immediately. Without reservation.

It was temporary. A start and end date. What could be better?

'You don't want to know what being mine entails?' she asked, a little amused.

'I do. Very much,' I said thickly, barely able to get my vocal cords to work.

'Put that coffee down and come here, Jensen.'

I set the cup down without taking my eyes off her. But I didn't move from where I stood. I needed something from her first. 'Before we start…whatever this is, I want you to promise me one thing.'

A flash of a grimace twitched her nose, but I suspected it was a flippant gesture to hide a deeper reaction. 'People break promises all the time. What makes you think I'll keep mine?'

'I'll give you the benefit of the doubt and accept you at your word.'

She seemed momentarily startled. Then she shrugged. 'Fine. What do you want?'

'That whatever you're feeling, be truthful with it.' I'd had enough of lies and half-truths to last me a lifetime. Refusing to face up to reality was the reason my relationship with my mother was still strained, even now, years after the stain of my bastard father should've been erased from our lives, Stephanie's conniving ways and betrayal the reason I'd ended up here in Alaska. With my past and my present riddled with deception and duplicity, I was one hundred per cent sure I wouldn't take it well if Graciela Mortimer fucked with me that way.

Her head tilted in that way that said she was tunnel-ling furiously towards the truths and wounds that re-sided in my very core. And sure enough… 'Is that what she did to you? She lied?'

'Graciela…'

She didn't even bat an eyelid at my warning tone. Man, she was fearless. Not that she needed to fear me, but one day she was going to poke a wounded bear and get herself in a whole world of hurt.

'Gud hjælpe mig.'

'What was that?'

I inhaled slowly. 'Nothing.'

'Are you sure? Only it sounded like you said, "God help me".'

I stiffened. 'You speak Danish?'

She shook her head. 'Not one of my many talents, sadly.'

I exhaled. Sure, the words were similar enough to translate.

Note to self—watch yourself in future.

I snorted under my breath. What future? The sharp rip of something in my chest told me it wasn't as laugh-able as I was attempting.

'I gave you a command, Jensen.'

I took the vital step that brought me close to her.

'Take my cup,' she instructed.

I took it, turned and set it down next to mine.

With a soft snap of her fingers, she pointed to the floor.

I dropped to my knees, my heart threatening to

burst out of my chest as I lowered my gaze. She inhaled sharply and moved closer until only inches separated us.

She placed her fingers beneath my jaw, nudged my gaze up before leaning in even closer. 'I've seen you out there in your element, owning and bending nature to your will. That's great. Out there, you can be in charge all you like. But in here, you hand over control to me. I own your every move, your every breath. Do you understand?'

The knot I'd carried since Stephanie's lies unravelled, the raging need for the thick promise in Graciela's words shocking me to my soul. 'Yes, *min elskerinde.*'

She gave a brisk nod. 'Let's establish rules. You have my word that I'll be truthful. That I won't do anything to degrade you. We're both free to end this any time we want, storm or no storm. Agreed?'

Relief washed through me. Something else threatened to unravel, but I kept a tight hold on it. I wasn't ready to trust. Not just yet. 'Agreed.'

'Good. Safe words. Do you have one for me?'

I wanted to tell her I didn't need one. That I'd willingly follow her every instruction. But that was a slippery slope. Checks and balances were in place for a reason. I couldn't go into this ignoring rules right from the start. Besides, if she truly was a Domme, she would insist upon it.

I cast around for a suitable safe word as she stared down at me, eyes blazing.

And then it became laughably clear. The *only* thing it could be. 'Hazel,' I said, the word ringing inside me.

'Hazel,' she repeated, a smile curving her lips. 'I can work with that.'

Her gaze swept up and down my body, lingered on my hair. I couldn't quite read her expression but I could tell she wanted to touch me. More specifically, drag her fingers through my hair the way she did last night in the tent. And, boy, did I want her to.

I didn't vocalise my need, however. The words would remain locked in my throat until she gave me permission. She didn't give it.

Instead, she stepped back, casting a critical eye over the cabin. She paused at the fireplace and glanced back at me. 'I'd like you to set up the bedding you spoke about in front of the fireplace. Then undress and wait for me there.'

I rose to my feet, barely able to think through the wild roar in my ears at the thought of pleasing her. The blankets we'd brought in from the trek still lay in a heap next to the fireplace but I went to the supply cupboard to grab fresh, more comfortable ones.

Made of thick merino wool, three would do the job of providing adequate cushioning, I judged. If things went the way I hoped they would, we'd be there for hours. If we needed it, I'd blow up the air mattress later. Or, better still, Graciela might decide on the king-size bed going to waste upstairs.

Adding a handful of pillows, I silently thanked Mrs Percy, the old lady in the small town twenty miles away, who I paid to keep the cabin cleaned and fully stocked. When I'd told her I was coming, she'd filled the pantry and fridge with enough food and essentials to last for weeks.

Keeping Graciela warm and comfortable for as long as the storm raged wouldn't be a problem at all. Suddenly, I didn't want the snowstorm to end. Not for a long time, at least.

I crossed the living room to the fire, resisting the strong urge to glance over to where she stood next to the sofa, her arms crossed. I was head and shoulders taller than her, but her presence filled the room, filled my senses in ways that I was a little too scared to describe. Unfurling the blankets, I laid them down, tossed the pillows onto them.

A little too eagerly, I attacked the snow suit, stepped out of the thermal set and boxers, grimacing at the rock-hard erection that bobbed eagerly, excited at being freed.

I wrestled the insane need to wrap my fingers around my cock, ease the ache tearing through me, and slowly sank to my knees at the edge of the blanket.

I heard her approach but kept my gaze fixed on the fire. She stopped behind me and for the longest time didn't move, although I felt her gaze on me, hot and possessive, tracking every inch of exposed skin.

'You're beautiful, Jensen, do you know that?' she murmured.

'If you say so, *min elskerinde.*' I was used to women admiring the outer package, but knew that, when it came right down to it, it was what was on the inside that mattered. My father had been one handsome bastard with a heart as black as tar, proof that beauty was only skin-deep.

Fuck, I wasn't going to think about him. Definitely not right now.

'You don't like compliments?'

'I like whatever pleases you.'

'I'm not sure if that's a nice save or a cop-out I need to punish you for.'

'It can be whatever you want it to be.'

She circled me once and then stopped in front of me. 'This man bun thing you've got going on. What's that all about?'

I managed a smile despite the strain in my groin. 'A six-month assignment in the Amazon. Barber shops were a little thin on the ground there. I've grown rather attached to it. Plus it keeps me warm in the cold.'

'Hmm, I'm getting rather attached myself. You're not allowed to cut it while we're here. Is that understood?'

'Yes, *min elskerinde.*'

'Is that Danish? I don't know what it means but I'd prefer you call me mistress when you address me.'

My smile widened. 'I already do.' I hesitated for a moment and added, *'Min elskerinde.'*

She inhaled sharply and her eyes widened. 'That's what it means?' Mild shock echoed in her voice.

'Yes.'

Her eyes narrowed. 'You started calling me that last night.'

It wasn't a question, so I let my gaze speak for me.

'Jensen?' she pressed.

'I wanted you like this before our encounter in the tent. But you knew that already.'

'So you started calling me your mistress even before this thing was established between us? Do you know how dangerous that is? Some woman out there could take advantage of it.'

My heart lurched. She sounded almost protective so I didn't tell her I'd sworn off entanglements before I met her. That no other woman would be given the leeway I was giving her. 'Does that displease you?'

Several emotions flitted across the face, but eventually she shook her head. 'People are far too predictable, but you're not one of them.'

A layer of tension eased out of me. 'Is that a compliment, *min elskerinde*?'

'You can take it however you want to,' she answered with a wispy smile, then slowly her face grew tight, controlled arousal settling over her. 'Undress me, Jensen.'

I didn't even care a little bit that my hands shook as I caught the hem of her sweater and tugged it over her head.

She was lovely. She had on a new set of underwear, a deep night-blue that accentuated the smoothness of her skin and the luscious globes of her breasts. Reaching behind her, I unclasped her bra. Her breasts fell free, heavy and gorgeous, tantalisingly close to my hungry lips. I resisted the urge to pull one pink tip into my mouth, instead concentrating on removing her leggings. Unlike last night, she didn't touch me to steady herself, exercising control that only made me harder.

I'd always had a thing for delayed gratification, which was probably another reason my soul yearned to submit. She wouldn't reward me until she deemed it appropriate, and every minute she withheld it, the promise of release became that much headier.

This gloriously naked, insanely gorgeous creature before me already knew how best to satisfy me. And we'd barely got started.

She placed her hands on her hips and stared down at me, her gaze imperious. 'Tell me we have condoms in this cabin, Jensen.'

I flipped back one corner of the blanket near my feet to reveal the box of condoms I'd grabbed from the supply closet.

She smiled, and my breath caught at the lusty fire reflected in the hazel depths. My cock bobbed in excitement as she examined the box and dropped it between my knees.

'We'll get to that in a little while. Right now I want you to place your hands on your thighs. Don't move them until I say so. I've been dying to lick you all over and I'm going to do just that.'

Shuddering with anticipation, I did as instructed.

She stepped behind me, depriving me of the joy of seeing her beautiful body. Moments later her fingers delved into my hair. She caught it up in one fist and before I could take the next breath, her teeth sank into the skin at the top of my spine.

Pleasure rained through my body and I groaned.

'You like that?'

'Yes, *min elskerinde.*'

'Hmm, I think those two are becoming my favourite Danish words.'

I smiled, pleased. 'I'll teach you Danish if you like.'

Her small teeth grazed over my skin again. 'Yes, Jensen, I'd like that very much.'

My eyes squeezed shut of their own accord as she continued to taste me, tongue and teeth and hot breath wreaking havoc all over my skin, following my spine down my back as she explored me.

Fists bunched on my thighs, need pummelling me hard, I glanced down at the thick swell of my cock. Teeth gritted, I fought the urge to touch myself. To surrender to the need to blow my load. But I couldn't come. Not yet. Not until she commanded it.

The freedom in being shackled and under her control made my senses soar.

That need to step outside myself, hand the reins to someone else—a need absurdly born from having to be in control, to keep my family safe from the monster who called himself father—was like nothing else I'd ever experienced, not even the thrill of climbing the world's highest mountain.

I shuddered as her grip tightened in my hair, as she bent low behind me. One hand caressed my butt, squeezed and released at leisure then strutted back to my front. She leaned in, her breath feathering my face without her lips making contact with mine.

'Where was I?' she demanded sultrily.

My breathing grew frantic, erratic as her lips worked

her way down my throat, nipping and tasting my hard nipples, then my abs, until, with one long look at me, she crouched lower and licked the head of my cock.

A tight groan erupted from my throat, my fists bunching harder until my knuckles bled white. Fuck, I was one breath from erupting.

As if she knew the strain I was under, wanted to test my control, she sucked me deeper into her mouth while her fingers crept under my cock to take hold of my balls.

After a few swirls of her tongue, she straightened. 'Look at me, Jensen.'

I wasn't aware my gaze had dropped to the blanket until I lifted it at her bidding.

'Would you like to come?'

'Only if you want me to.'

She smiled. 'I'd love to see you lose that iron control for me.'

'Keep doing what you're doing to my balls and you'll find out soon enough,' I croaked.

Slowly, only one hand crept down her front, two fingers sliding between her legs. I wasn't aware of the strength of my opposition until the sound erupted from my throat.

She stilled. 'Problem?'

I breathed deep, the need to vocalise my need scrambling through me. We were in this thing, for better or worse. Why deny my true nature? Nodding at the fingers moving erotically between her legs, I rasped, 'I want to do that for you.'

Her smile was a pure strain of power and femininity. 'But you're not in charge here, are you?'

'No, *min elskerinde*.'

'So if I want to touch you, while touching myself, you won't have a problem with it, will you?'

'No, but it'll torture the fuck out of me,' I confessed raggedly.

She laughed, the sound wickedly sexy. But gradually, humour died, taken over by need and insistent lust. She released my balls, took hold of my cock, and, her gaze on my face, stroked me up and down.

'I want to suck your cock, and you're going to come when you're ready but you're still not allowed to touch me.'

I jerked out a nod, my lungs struggling for air as her strokes grew tighter. Faster.

She spread her thighs wide and leaned forward, bending over with her bottom in the air. The sight of her luscious cheeks sent me to a whole new stratum of frenzy.

'Fuck, fuck, *fuck*!'

Her sweet lips wrapped around my engorged head, drew me deeper into her hot mouth. Raw shouts left my throat and my hips pumped involuntarily. My head dropped back for one fast second until the need to avidly watch her suck me off redirected my gaze.

Control shredded to nothing within minutes. My vision hazed as she pumped my cock faster. I started to unravel. Undone with a raw shout, I let go, erupting into her mouth. She made pleased sounds of approval at the back of her throat as she sucked me deeper for endless minutes.

Eventually, she rose, sultry satisfaction on her face as she stared at me. 'Thank you, Jensen. That was beautiful.'

I didn't want the words to touch my soul, but they did. And it unsettled me a whole lot more than I cared to admit. Not enough for me to consider putting the brakes on this thing, though. Not enough to stop me from leaning closer, staring deep into her eyes. 'May I touch you now, *min elskerinde*?'

'I'd like that very much, Jensen.' She sank back against the bedding and, like last night, lifted her arms high above her head. 'Come here. And bring the condoms with you.'

CHAPTER SIX

MY VOICE MIGHT have been calm and masterful, but inside I was anything but. I was shaken down to my core, terrified of the emotions sweeping through me.

I hadn't expected Jensen to readily admit to being a submissive, nor had I been prepared for the profound awe his admission would make me feel.

My mood had swung from being disgruntled about the snowstorm stranding me here to wanting it to last for a few hours. Maybe a whole day. Or two.

I wanted, no, *needed* the freedom to explore him. Explore myself in a way that I hadn't truly been able to in a very long time. But even as greed and lust and anticipation built inside me, so did a knot of tension. I couldn't afford to get carried away with this. Not when I had enough baggage to fill this cabin a dozen times over.

Not when he had his own baggage, in a Stephanie-shaped form specifically, that I couldn't help but resent even though I knew it was unfair. I had no claim on him, nor he on me.

But for as long as the storm raged outside, he was mine.

I watched him roll the condom between his fingers,

his eyes on me. At my nod, he tore it open and glided it down his long, delicious cock. Because it seemed as if I'd waited for ever, I didn't beat about the bush. And he either had amazing recovery skills or he was just as desperate as I was. He positioned himself between my thighs, and I looked into his eyes. 'Fuck me, Jensen. Fuck me hard.'

'It'll be my pleasure, *min elskerinde.*'

My mistress.

Power and gratitude surged through me, coated with the soul-deep yearning that threatened to break the leash I'd kept on it. I slackened the tight reins on my emotions, coaxed into almost feeling safe in this isolated cabin in the middle of nowhere. It was the least I could do considering Jensen had gifted me with his sublime submission. Wasn't it?

Rationale ceased to matter as his cock probed my entrance. Like the confidence with which he'd gone down on me in the tent last night, he slid in with one firm stroke, powerful, stretching me with enough friction and pressure to make me gasp. Pleasure rolled through me, intensifying as I saw it reflected in his blue eyes.

He muttered something in Danish.

'I like it when you speak in your mother tongue,' I said, my voice not quite steady.

He gave a strained smile, his nostrils flaring as he withdrew and thrust hard inside me.

'Talk dirty Danish to me,' I commanded.

Bracing himself on his elbows, he brushed his lips against mine. Then the sexy torrent began. Lyrical, alien words spilled from his lips, saturating my skin as he pleasured me with his cock and his tongue.

And, simply because I couldn't resist, I dragged his head down for a deep, tongue-tangling kiss. Our breathing turned harsh, the sizzling act of our coming together pushing us both to the edge far too soon. The urge to reward him ramped through me. That meant not giving in to climax too quickly. I needed to push him to the edge without making him go over, so I broke the kiss.

'Slow down,' I mouthed against his lips. 'Now.'

He gave a jagged little groan, but his movements slowed, his thrusts turning shallower, and his eyes squeezed shut in his effort to control his arousal. My fingers slid through his hair, caught the tresses at his nape and tugged.

He shuddered, a sheen of sweat breaking out over his sleek muscles. When he next pushed inside me, I tightened my muscles, gripping him as best I could despite the slickness of my sex. Fine tremors began unravelling over him and, heaven help me, but I loved seeing him on the edge, vulnerable and utterly lost in his pleasure.

Greedy need and the soul-deep yearning to unleash my true self prowled through me. Before I could withhold it, I pulled his earlobe between my teeth, bit lightly and relished his deep groan.

'I'd love to keep you like this for ever. Right here on the edge until you lose your mind for me. Or you beg me to end the unbearable pain. Maybe I will. Maybe I won't.'

Slowly, his eyes dragged open, intoxication drenching them as he stared down at me. 'Whatever pleases you, *min elskerinde*.'

My heart lurched wildly, the leash slipping another terrifying fraction.

This was too good to be true. *He* was too good to be true. Every single relationship I'd invested in since childhood had crashed and burned.

Whether initiated with childlike abandonment or after careful introspection and tending, each one had eventually turned sour, mocking my every effort to cultivate and maintain a sustainable connection. I couldn't need him this much, crave him this deeply.

The reminder threatened to dampen my spirits, caution seeping into my blood, cooling a layer of the frenzy triggering my yearnings. His fine tremor focused me, fine-tuned my pleasure so I could concentrate on him.

He really was perfect. Despite hard arousal etched on his face, he still moved inside me to the steady rhythm I'd instructed. I leaned up again, nipped at the skin beneath his jaw, revelling in the shudder that racked his frame.

'Beg me to make you come. Beg me to let you fuck me harder,' I whispered in his ear.

'Please, *min elskerinde*,' he said hoarsely.

'Please what?'

'May I fuck you harder? Make you come?'

'That wasn't quite what I ordered, was it?'

He shook his head. 'No, but I'll come harder for you if you go first.'

'Satisfying me gives you pleasure.' It wasn't a question. More like a shaken realisation that cracked another layer of the foundation I'd striven to safeguard myself with.

'Yes.' A simple, gruff admission that floored me. And intensified my hunger for him.

He registered the fresh wetness between my legs and his eyes lit with pleasure.

Jensen Scott might be a submissive, but he was a clever, powerful one who knew exactly which buttons to press. The thought of him doing this with another woman, somewhere in the hazy future away from this warm and toasty cocoon, drove my fingers into his flesh.

He gave another sexy growl, his hips jerking for an uncontrollable second. He righted himself immediately, his strokes measured as he awaited my command. Keeping my grip on his hair, I slid another hand between our bodies, beneath where we were joined, to grip his balls.

'Christ!'

Despite his harsh breathing, he kept up the steady pace. Impressive.

'How much longer can you hold out?' I taunted.

His jaw gritted before he replied, 'For as long as you need me to.'

I wanted his complete surrender, for the beautiful body poised above mine to drown in utter bliss along with me. The sweat drenching his skin said he was close. I wrapped my legs tighter around his hips, clenched him deep within me. 'Give it to me, Jensen. Give me everything you've got.'

Like a lion uncaged, he scooped a hand beneath me, angled my hips up, and then pounded me deep, hard thrusts that stole the breath from my lungs. Sounds of our decadent fucking filled the quiet cabin, adding another layer of erotic desire that drew me closer to the edge. Within minutes, I was mindless, a scream ripping from my throat as my orgasm hit with earth-shaking force. My internal muscles milking him, I heard him growl against my throat as he followed, coming with endless shudders until we were both spent.

Minutes passed with his arms wrapped tight around me. I floated in stunned euphoria, unable to form sensible words to fill the silence. The realisation that I didn't need to, that this wasn't another artificial encounter where I needed to deny my true self, filled me with an alien emotion that suspiciously resembled… contentment.

For however long this lasted, Jensen was my willing sub and I was his mistress. I could do with him as I pleased. If that included silence, it was my right.

Again, the thought shook me to my core. Enough to make me avert my gaze when he eventually eased up to look down at me. When there was enough space between us, he glanced down. 'May I?' he asked gruffly.

I nodded.

He eased out of me, rose and went into the kitchen. The supply closet door opened and a minute later he was back at my side, a towel in his hand. He cleaned me up, then himself, then tossed the towel away and resumed his position next to me.

It took a few minutes to wrestle my emotions under control. Striving to lighten the mood, I cast a deliberate gaze around the cabin. 'No TV. I'm assuming no Internet either?'

'In good weather my satellite phone's reliable enough to keep me connected but in this weather it's probably non-existent.'

It was a little disconcerting to be so cut off. Well, I still had my satellite phone for however long the battery lasted, but the thought that I wasn't in touching distance of a ringing phone felt…strange.

Admittedly, in a way that wasn't…awful. The lack of urgency to be in the centre of everything I'd built was freeing. Enough to trigger a smile. 'I'm assuming no board games either?'

He shook his head, his eyes twinkling. 'I wasn't exactly planning on entertaining when I came out here.'

I wanted to ask him why he'd come out here when, like mine, his professional life was booked solid for months. But the emotional wind tunnel I'd gone through a few minutes ago made me shy away from the personal. 'So what do you actually do here to occupy yourself?'

He smiled, an open, carefree smile that melted my insides as he caught a strand of my hair and toyed with it. 'We didn't get around to the full tour. My darkroom doubles up as office and studio. Most times I bring my work with me. When I'm not working, I hike the woods or take the dogs out for a run.'

Great, he was one of those healthily outdoorsy types.

He caught my expression and grinned. 'Yep, I'm one of those. I find it difficult to sit still for long.' His fingers left my hair, drifted over my shoulder and down my arm. 'Unless I have suitable distraction.'

I nodded, understanding him perfectly. After all, I was one of those. But, sadly, *my* restlessness had nothing to do with the need to be at one with nature and everything to do with running away from the demons haunting me.

'Why adventure photography?' I asked, despite my intention to steer clear of anything personal. But this wasn't personal. We were professionals exchanging professional courtesies. He was working on a project close to my heart and I had every right to know the man behind the camera.

Yeah, keep telling yourself that.

'My stepfather bought me a camera for my seventeenth birthday, a peace offering for sending me off to summer camp when I wanted to spend the holidays at home. I had every intention of hating it, along with everything and everyone at the camp,' he said with a grin.

'But you didn't?'

He shook his head. 'I fell in love with it. I photographed everything I could. When I returned and had the pictures developed, I realised I didn't suck at it, so I stuck with it.'

'And don't tell me, since you'd suddenly gone crazy about the outdoors you decided to throw a few risks in there?'

'It was easier to convince my mother that the purpose behind climbing mountains to get one unique picture out of thousands was worth it rather than climbing just for the hell of it. Although that was a seductive draw too.'

'And she was okay with that?'

His face tightened. 'She wasn't. Not for a long time.'

'Why not?'

His gaze shifted away from mine, reluctance in the fingers that absently caressed my wrist. Clearly his relationship with his mother wasn't smooth sailing. 'She found it difficult to let go, generally. At least she did before my stepfather.'

There was much more to that story and I probably should've changed the subject then. Hell, hadn't I earned a reputation for interfering where I shouldn't, pushing when I needed to step back? 'What about your father?'

He froze, his fingers sliding away from my skin. 'He's no longer in the picture,' he said tightly, his jaw clenching as his gaze swung to rest on the fire.

Was he dead? Had he abandoned Jensen as my parents had abandoned me? Questions teemed in my head, but I reluctantly accepted that he'd given me more than I intended to give him.

Minutes passed. When he looked back his expression was cordial enough to display no hard feelings but wary enough to warn me my probing questions were no longer welcome. The brief flare of disappointment and anxiety threw me. I throttled them down as he spoke.

'I'd very much like to feed you, *min elskerinde.*'

Hunger pangs immediately registered in my stomach, deciding our next activity. Summoning a smile, I nodded. 'I could eat.'

His smile returned. 'Do you have any preferences food wise?'

I shrugged. 'I don't mind, as long as it's hot and tasty.'

His gaze slid down my body and I could tell he was thinking about something entirely different from food. Nevertheless, he answered, 'I can rise to that challenge.'

He caught my hand in his, trailed kisses on my knuckles before rising. 'Stay here. I'll be about half an hour.'

I shook my head, reaching for my sweater. 'No, thanks, even princesses have to take a break from endlessly lounging about, waiting to be adored and pampered.'

He grimaced. 'I'm not going to live that down, am I?'

'Not for a long time, buster.'

He watched me pull on my sweater, disappointment in his eyes as I covered myself from chest to hip.

'Would you like some socks?' he asked, holding out a hand to help me up. 'There's underfloor heating but it's patchy in places.'

The cabin was warm enough. 'I'll be fine. I want to explore the pantry.'

Again, he smiled. My heart tripped foolishly.

'It's right through there.'

I left him to tug on his boxers and headed for the pantry. The room was about eight feet deep, with shelves that stretched from floor to ceiling, and packed with enough food and supplies to last a good few weeks. Even months.

How long had he been planning on staying here? What had Stephanie done to make him retreat from the world?

Questions lingered while I clocked the types of food Jensen liked. I was reaching out for a packet when he materialised in the doorway.

I couldn't help myself—I gaped at his delicious body. Watched him watch me as I adored him with my eyes, his cock thickening behind the stretchy fabric of his boxers. When my gaze returned to his face, his eyes were dark, gleaming in a way I'd learned signalled his arousal.

'I make a mean chicken fettuccine. Will that work for you?' he said, his voice a husky rasp.

'Good to know. The question is can you make a mean chicken fettuccine…naked?' I countered.

He delivered another one of those insanely sexy smiles, right before he yanked his boxers down his thick legs and kicked them away. I suppressed a gasp, my heart racing as he prowled towards me. 'Whatever my mistress wants, my mistress gets.'

He plucked the packet from my nerveless fingers, calmly collected the rest of the ingredients and left the pantry. I followed, worried that I was seriously in danger of becoming addicted to Jensen Scott.

It became clear very quickly that he was a maestro in the kitchen. He diced vegetables and smashed garlic

with shameless aplomb. I wasn't even annoyed that I
was reduced to simply fetching and carrying, the joy of
watching him enough to dissipate my disgruntlement.

'Like a glass of wine?'

I hadn't spotted any wine when I fetched groceries
from the fridge. He wasn't storing it outside the cabin,
was he? 'Not if I have to venture out in that storm to
get it, no.'

He laughed. 'There's a cooler in the pantry. I can't
promise the vintage will meet your high expectations,
but it's perfectly drinkable.'

My spirits plummeted, that stain of *spoilt little rich
girl* cooling the atmosphere. I sensed his gaze on me as
I went to the pantry. I'd missed it the first time round,
probably distracted by a near-naked Jensen, but there
it was in the back, a slimline cooler filled with a dozen
bottles of white, and a wooden shelf next to it, holding bottles of red. I grabbed a white without reading
the label, irritation warring with hurt as I returned to
the kitchen.

He was leaning against the centre aisle, naked as
the day he was born with his cock at half-mast. 'Look,
I didn't mean—'

I stopped him with the dismissive wave of my hand.
'If you're going to throw another apology at me, don't
bother. I know I come with a few unsavoury labels. It's
not your fault if you can't help but go with the evidence
bandied about.'

'You're upset, so I'm guessing they're not just meaningless labels?' he pressed.

'Is this just curiosity or do you actually want me to prove to you that I'm not what the media label me as?'

He shrugged. 'I want to know you. To see the woman behind the labels for myself.'

My fingers tightened around the bottle, a profound shaking starting inside me I was loath to outwardly display.

It stunned me how deftly he continued to pull the rug from under my feet. First with his unguarded admission of his sexuality and now with this. I dragged my gaze from his, but only strayed as far as the window, at the snowstorm raging harder with no signs of stopping.

The wind picked up then, and a loose branch smashed against the window, echoing the elemental force churning inside me. There was too much going on here, deep waters I was scared to wade through.

Ignoring him, I went to the drawer and searched for an opener.

Behind me, another drawer opened. A moment later, he appeared beside me, holding out the corkscrew. I took it, keeping my gaze on the bottle as I worked the screw into the cork. Tension vibrated through the cabin until a pop echoed in the silence. I'd spotted glasses in a cupboard earlier and I went towards it.

Jensen beat me to it, reaching up to the tall shelf to hand me a glass.

'Aren't you having one?'

Silently, he handed me another glass. 'I will if you want me to, *min elskerinde*,' he murmured, darkened eyes rapt on my face.

He was too much. Everything I was scared to desire.

I poured two glasses, handed him one and downed half the contents of mine.

An expression flitted across his face, too fast for me to decode as he raised his own glass and took a moderate sip. The sight of him, sipping wine while he stood there stark naked, comfortable in his own skin, yet with his eyes a little troubled as he stared at me, made me want to laugh. Or scream. Or hide.

From the first moment I'd laid eyes on him, he'd commanded extreme emotions from me. As if *he* were the Dominant.

Topping from the fucking bottom.

Well, if he wanted personal, he was about to get it.

I forced a shrug. 'No need to go on an extended expedition. I'm everything the media proclaims me to be. Spoilt. Rich. Some would even label me a ball-breaking bitch.'

A smile ghosted over his full lips. 'I can refute that last one. My balls were in your hands only a short while ago and I can attest they're still whole.' He cheekily glanced down at himself and I couldn't help but follow his gaze. Hell, he really was too perfect to ignore.

I wanted to end all of this by jumping him again, to dilute the heavy emotions with soul-drenching sex. I resisted the urge. 'Don't you need to look after the food?'

He shook his head. 'We're good for another ten minutes or so. Enough time for you to answer one question.'

I met his gaze with a deliberately sceptical one. 'Just the one question, is it?'

'Satisfy my curiosity. Just one innocent question.'

'I can order you to shut up. You know that, don't you?' I taunted softly.

His nostrils flared, but despite the mournful look in his eyes, he nodded. 'I'm aware of that. Do you want to?'

Emotion, thick and charged, arced between us, tugging tight and pulling me towards him. Several feet away from him, I stopped, bracing my hip against the centre aisle, wondering what the hell was wrong with me. Why my heart raced with alarm and anticipation of what his question would be. Why I was even considering answering in the first place. 'Ask.'

'Who's your favourite person in the world?'

I blinked in surprise. 'That's what you want to know?'

'I find the company one keeps says a lot about a person.'

'What if my person is not a person but a cat?'

His lips twisted and he shook his head. 'I'm willing to bet my favourite camera it's not. You don't strike me as a cat person.'

He was right. I actually preferred dogs, but I was a little miffed he could read me so easily. He continued to watch me in expectant silence, his hand casually twirling his glass.

We were straying into forbidden territory.

Heartache territory.

The branch slapped against the window once more, pushing me to answer.

'When I was younger it was my brother, Bryce, but

then…shit happened.' I shrugged, attempted to lighten the mood, alleviate the heaviness around my heart that reminded me of my inability to sustain relationships. My own brothers barely spoke to me, and when they did it was only to discuss Mortimer Group business. 'Right now, I'd say my aunt Flo is it for me. She doesn't take any shit, doesn't mince her words. She can be funny as hell with it, but she shoots from the hip and I…like that.'

Jensen nodded, his eyes locked on me as he took another sip. 'When was the last time you saw her?'

Technically, he'd used up his free pass. I wanted to tell him to stop. Opened my mouth to do exactly that. 'Why? What does it matter?' I asked instead.

'Humour me,' he replied.

I didn't see where he was headed with this, couldn't spot any real danger, so I responded. 'On her birthday, a few months ago.'

'So you're birthday, Christmas and anniversary friends?'

'How is this relevant to anything?'

'Is she a good person?'

A shaky sensation filled my chest. Aunt Flo was as close to love as I could manage, considering my issues. 'She's the best,' I said, my voice strangely tight.

Jensen smiled. 'She's your emotional compass. You go to her when you need centring. That means you hurt when someone causes you pain. You act spoilt when it suits you, but it's just that, an *act*. It means you may take life by the balls, but you'll never break them. Am I right?'

I set the glass down with a sharp click. 'What the hell is this?'

He shrugged, setting down his own glass to walk past me to the stove. 'Simply getting to know you, *min elskerinde*.'

He lifted the lid on the sauce, bent forward to stir it. As he did, thick strands of his hair parted at his nape. The glimpse of ink drew me to him.

'What is this?' I asked, parting his hair to reveal a dark blue tattoo etched into the skin between his shoulder blades.

Given our conversation just now, I gasped at the sight of an elaborate compass. It wasn't a common one. For starters, the lettering that should've clearly indicated correct points were different. Instead of N, S, E and W there was A where south should've been, D for east, M for west and the space for north left blank.

He stirred the pots for another few minutes before setting down the ladle. Then he faced me. 'We all have our ways for centring ourselves. This is mine.'

'What does the lettering stand for?'

'Family, for the most part,' he said a little tightly, reiterating my suspicion that things weren't warm and cosy on the family front for him either.

Nevertheless, his family seemed to be his guiding light. A compass guiding him when he needed it. I couldn't help the searing jealousy that lit through me before the curious burst of joy that immediately followed.

Even more confused by my jarring emotions, I let his hair fall back into place. 'Are we done with the interrogation? I'm hungry.' I was aware that my voice was several shades cooler, but couldn't seem to help myself.

The glance he sent me over his shoulder held empathy I didn't want.

'I don't want to risk being ordered to shut up so, yes, *min elskerinde*, we're done. And the food is ready.' His voice was even, bordering on gentle, which absurdly riled me up even further.

Feeling out of sorts, I busied myself gathering plates, cutlery, and setting the table. In silence, we dished out the food, took stools on opposite sides at the far end of the island that doubled up as a dining area.

I poured more wine while Jensen spooned mouthwatering fettuccine, sauce and lashings of grated cheese.

He stared, not touching his food, as I took the first mouthful. Grateful that we'd moved on from emotional subjects, I happily gave my verdict. 'This is good. Really good.'

He smiled, picking up his cutlery to dig into his own food. By mutual agreement, we stayed on safe subjects.

Why anyone would choose to risk life and limb the way he did as he described his most adventurous shoots was beyond me. I told him as much.

He laughed. 'Training reduces the risk of injury. Working with people you trust and will have your back also helps.'

Reminded of his question earlier, I asked, 'So you have your own group of friends you work with?'

His smile dimmed a little. 'I wouldn't call them

friends exactly. They're just a team I've worked with over the years. When we're done, we go our separate ways until the next assignment brings us together.'

'So who is your one true friend?' I pressed, tossing his question back at him. His gaze swept down, and he feigned interest in the contents of his plate. After a moment he shrugged. 'No one fits the label. Not any more.'

The finality of his statement tugged something inside me. 'Stephanie?'

His eyes narrowed, displeasure bristling from him as he stared at me across the island. He opened his mouth, but I pre-empted his reply.

'You can tell me to mind my own business if you want to. I'm just as curious as you were about me.'

His lips pursed, the last bite forgotten as he set down his fork. When he shrugged, his shoulders were stiff. 'We were lovers. But I thought we were friends too. I was wrong.'

'Was she a Domme?' I asked boldly.

He gave a bitter laugh. 'She went all out to fool me into thinking so, that's for sure.'

I gasped, unable to help my shock. 'Why…how?'

'Same way con artists fool people. She studied her craft, learned to imitate until she'd convinced herself she was an expert on the lifestyle. We met shortly before I went away on a three-month-long shoot. She made all the right moves, made me think she was what I wanted.' His eyes captured mine, boldly spearing me. 'But the truth always comes out, doesn't it?'

I wanted to snap back, punish him for daring to question me. But didn't his experience reflect mine? How many times had I fooled myself into thinking I was in a committed relationship only to discover differently? 'Yes, it does,' I found myself replying, my voice nowhere near sharp or scolding.

Understanding passed between us. Then memory etched harsh lines into his face. 'Unfortunately, Stephanie's little performance went beyond trying to fake her way into my bed.'

I looked around the cabin. 'So you came here to lick your wounds?'

I was poking the bear. Regardless of his submissiveness, he wouldn't appreciate his emotions being dissected, especially if the wounds were raw.

'Once I accepted your assignment, this was the logical base to work from.'

It was a half-truth. We both knew it. But when he stood and collected the plates, I let it go. In the space of twenty minutes we'd navigated landmine subjects with the power to blow us apart. I was all for taking a breather. Rising, I gathered the remaining dishes and joined him at the sink.

We cleaned up in companionable silence, and in ten minutes we were done.

I dried my hands as he headed for the freezer compartment of the fridge, pulled it open and peered inside. 'What would you like for dessert? We have…ice cream, ice cream and…ice cream. But in different flavours, I'm pleased to report.'

I grabbed the hem of my sweater and yanked it over

my head. 'I'm in the mood for something hot,' I said, adding sultry notes to my voice.

Slowly, he straightened. My gaze moved hungrily over his body, lingering longest at the cock rising to attention beneath my gaze.

He slammed the freezer door shut, prowled towards me with a mouth-wateringly virile swagger that made me suck in a breath. 'Your wish is my bidding, *min elskerinde*. You need only ask.'

'Return to the fireplace and lie back down. I'm in the mood to sit on your face.'

CHAPTER SEVEN

WE SAT ON the sofa, Graciela's feet in my lap, my thumbs digging into the soft arch of her foot as she sipped a half-decent glass of Merlot.

Turned out she wasn't as snobbish about her wine as I'd insinuated.

Outside the snowstorm powered on, showing no signs of abating. We'd been snowed in for two full days. The only time I'd ventured out was to feed and water the dogs, make sure they were warm. They weren't exactly thrilled about being cooped up inside, but it couldn't be helped.

Despite it being well into the night, the wall-to-wall white-out cast a brightness over the landscape.

Winter had well and truly arrived in Alaska and I couldn't be happier.

I watched her watch the fire, enjoyed the dancing flames reflected in her hazel eyes. I'd almost fucked this up with that conversation in the kitchen on the first afternoon.

Since then we'd both avoided deep, personal issues, mutually choosing other forms of entertainment. Surprisingly, we'd found a few. Graciela loved hearing tales of my adventures. Her eyes lit up with almost childlike anticipation with each recounting. As much as I wanted to downplay it, having her hang on to my every word was a thrill I could get used to.

Turned out my mistress had a not-so-secret hankering for danger. As for the sex, it was beyond fucking sublime. Graciela was unapologetically demanding while generous in return. She was extremely sensual, breathtakingly intuitive, knowing exactly what I needed when I needed it. Her demands were equally challenging, a spine-melting edge to her dominance that led to the most intense climaxes I'd ever experienced in my life.

Besides the sex, touching her was my second favourite thing. In those moments between conversation, when the only sound between us was the quiet warmth of the cabin, the crackle of the fire, and the storm raging outside, my soul felt…right. My heart as close to contentment as I could manage.

I hid a smile as she moaned—I'd hit a particularly tight muscle.

'If I didn't hate the idea of robbing the world of your unique talents, I'd seriously consider hiring you as my full-time masseur.'

'I'm that good?' I smiled.

'You know you are,' she murmured, a small smile curving her beautiful lips.

My gaze dropped to the luscious curve of her lower lip reddened from wine and kisses, my blood heating up. She clocked the look and gave a wider, smug smile in return. Arching her beautiful body, currently clad in one of my white T-shirts, thong and nothing else, she leaned forward, ran her fingers down my jaw. 'I'd love to shave you,' she murmured, a definite savouring in her tone.

The stubble I'd kept when I arrived at the cabin had grown into a short beard and, just like my hair, she loved to play with it. Now she wanted to shave it off?

'I thought you liked the friction between your thighs?'

'I do. But I like the idea of shaving you even more. I'd use one of those old-fashioned blades, take my time with you.'

I stared at her, trying to work out which kink she had in store for me next. Much more than delayed gratification, she liked to keep me guessing. Not that I minded anything she'd done to me so far. Everything we did culminated in a wild and new experience. I was swiftly becoming addicted to it. *To her.*

I glanced out of the window, sending out a silent plea for the storm not to end just yet. I needed a few more days of this. Hopefully by then, this wild fever in my blood would've abated. Enough for me to let her go with no hard feelings?

My gut knotted, a hollow sensation taking up residence in the pit of my stomach.

'Tell me another story,' she softly commanded, relaxing against the cushions again and taking a sip of wine. 'Tell me about your very first assignment.'

I grimaced. 'I'd rather tell you a different story, *min elskerinde*.'

Her eyes sparkled, intelligence scheming in her eyes as she stared at me. 'You know evasion merely triggers my curiosity, right?'

Yes, I'd discovered that about her. But I didn't want to delve into this particular subject.

Her eyes narrowed. 'Why don't you want to tell me?'

'Because my first assignment was professional and also deeply personal.'

Her eyes widened. 'And you can't tell one without the other?'

I shrugged. 'I could, but it wouldn't be much of a story.'

She waited, one finger trailing along the rim of her glass.

And against my better judgment, the words tumbled from my lips anyway. 'I was hired by the owner of a sex club in Copenhagen to take shots for her revamped website.'

Her smile turned a little wicked. 'A different sort of adventure, then?'

I didn't return her smile. 'An enlightening one, yes.'

Slowly, her smile switched off, her face getting serious. 'How personal?'

'Helga, the owner of the club, became my first Dominant. She took one look at me and she knew.'

'How old were you?'

'Twenty-four.'

Something close to envy flashed in her eyes. 'How long did it last?'

'Six months.' I let out a wry smile. 'Then she moved on to somebody else.'

Sympathy shone in Graciela's eyes. 'She broke your heart?'

I shook my head. 'I thought so at the time, but in hindsight she was breaking down my barriers so I could accept myself.'

Graciela nodded, understanding brimming in her eyes. 'Why does that make you sad?'

'Because even after all of that I was still searching.'

'Searching or denying?'

I shrugged, the memory painful to vocalise. It'd been both. After the nightmare of my father, and the need to take control and keep my mother and sister safe from his abuse, surrendering that control had felt like a betrayal. One I'd struggled with for years before accepting the freedom of submission.

'So she was your first. Who was your second?' she asked after swallowing a mouthful of wine.

Shit, it looked as if we were doing this after all. 'No one memorable.'

One sleek eyebrow arched. 'Your third? Fourth or fifth?'

'All imitations of the real thing that have disappointed more than satisfied. Till…recently.'

She gave a soft gasp. 'Jensen…are you saying…?'

Fuck, I didn't want things to slip into hot and heavy territory, didn't want this perfect flow we'd found to hit the skids. But she was looking at me, expectant. And I was helpless to deny her any damn thing.

'You're the first to make a meaningful impression since Helga? The verdict is still out.'

She looked a little…relieved, and my stomach churned.

Damn, maybe I'd laid it on too thick?

Dial it back a notch, Jensen.

She held the glass against her lips, eyes spearing into me. 'Tell me about Stephanie.'

Fuck no.

'Graciela…'

She reached out, laid her hand over my arm. 'It's not an order. I just really want to know.'

I took a deep breath, wrapped one hand around her delicate foot. Then I lifted it, placing a kiss at the soft pad of flesh beneath her toes. She gave a soft gasp, her eyes darkening momentarily before she pulled herself out of my grasp. Great, that distracting technique wasn't going to work either.

I sighed, sifting through the torrent of memories I didn't really want to relive. 'We met at a party in London. She's an event planner, but her clients tend to be more on the risqué side of entertaining.'

'She throws sex parties?'

'Not always, but yeah, some of the time. She said all the right things, made all the right moves. We went out a few times and then things got…serious.'

'How serious?'

'I asked her to move in with me.'

She nodded, encouraged me to go on.

'Then the cracks began to appear. It started off by her telling me she didn't want to role play any more.'

Graciela frowned. 'Role play?'

'That's what she called it.'

'She thought it was a *game*?'

Bitterness drenched my mouth. 'Apparently. She'd been biding her time, hoping I'd snap out of it. When I pushed her on it, she confessed she'd read a few books, watched videos and used what she'd seen at her parties to expand her knowledge.'

'Bloody hell,' Graciela muttered under her breath. 'Where the hell did she do her research? The fucking children's library? Because the first real Dom or sub she met would've told her this isn't a damned game! That you don't simply play at it.'

'She was convinced she could make me happy. As long as we had regular sex like a *normal couple* and only did the Dom/sub thing on occasion.'

'My God. I kinda want to do…bodily harm,' she bit out, her breath hissing before she regained control. I was touched by that reaction. Ashamed to admit that I'd been looking for those signs of outrage, signs that she understood that this was as vital and necessary to me as breathing. Seeing her reaction only made me want her more.

'You trusted her?' she asked, her tone gentle with sympathy. 'Enough to surrender yourself to her? You must've or you wouldn't be…' She stopped and I was grudgingly grateful she didn't spell out what a fool I'd been taken for.

Still, bitterness flayed me, gouging deep at the soul-searing betrayal. 'Like I said, she walked the walk, convincingly enough to believe she had enough to achieve her ultimate goal.'

Graciela frowned. 'Which was what?'

I paused, unwilling to admit that last piece of Stephanie's deplorable intentions for the simple fact that I'd never seen it coming. But…what the hell? 'She ingratiated herself into the lifestyle merely to land herself a meal ticket either through a husband with a fat wallet or blackmail.'

Graciela jerked upright. 'She blackmailed you?'

My nod felt jerky, my emotions ragged and raw. 'Her next move after I threw her out was an email threatening to expose our sex life unless I paid her a million pounds.'

'I… Why would she—?'

My smile was crooked…off. 'She believed I would be too ashamed. Real men didn't submit. Her words.'

Graciela's jaw tightened. 'Now I definitely want to do harm. What did you do?'

'I called her bluff.'

Fire lit in my mistress's eyes. 'That's…ballsy.'

I basked in her quiet admiration, meeting her gaze, mine unwavering. 'I'm not ashamed of who I am. I may have taken a while to embrace that part of myself, but once I did, I was all in. *Am* all in.'

'I understand that, but there's a difference between moving on and having your business displayed all over the streets. Especially a man in your position. That's what she was counting on, right?'

'Yes. Her business was doing okay, but she had far loftier aspirations. She craved prestige, and she was willing to do anything to achieve it. Unfortunately for her, she thought threatening to expose me to my family would be the way to go. She was wrong.'

My mention of family drew a watchful look. 'So your family knows?'

I shrugged, unwilling to admit the undercurrent of tension between my mother and I meant that while I'd protect her to my last breath, inhabiting the same room for a long period of time was a strain. One I avoided until it became unavoidable. Like at Christmas. I pushed the looming visit from my mind and answered. 'We haven't had an open conversation about it, no.'

'You think they'll be okay with it?' she asked, a touch apprehensive as she awaited my answer.

'I am what I am and that's not changing. They'll have to be.'

'Even your father?'

'Stepfather,' I gritted out. 'My father is no longer in the picture. Hasn't been for years.'

Questions blazed in her eyes, but she didn't press me for answers.

Which was redundant because I confessed anyway. 'He was a deplorable human being.'

Her eyes softened in sympathy. 'I know a thing or two about deplorable human beings.'

'Yeah?' I encouraged.

She remained silent for several seconds and then she shrugged. 'My parents. They were probably as deplorable as your father.'

Despite the warmth in the cabin, icy fingers danced down my spine as memory pounded like a tide against rocks, battering my need to keep them on a tight leash.

'I really hope not.' Just the thought of Graciela being subjected to what my sister and I had gone through made my insides ice over with cold fury. 'Did your father batter your mother every damned chance he got for no fucking reason? Did your mother make excuses for his behaviour, lie about the true extent of the abuse, even though it was plain to see?' I didn't blame my mother for her inability to end the cycle of abuse before I took matters into my own hands, but it sure as fuck made trusting her an issue.

Her mouth dropped open, eyes filling with raw pain. 'No,' she whispered. 'Not to my knowledge, anyway.'

'Did he lay his hands on you or your brothers?'

She paled. 'He did that to you?'

I nodded, memory scraping over wounds still raw despite the passing years. 'Until I was tall and strong enough to stop him. But I didn't know why then and I sure as hell don't know why now. Some people are wired that way, I guess.'

'Jesus, Jensen, I'm so sorry.'

I laughed, the bitter sound grating my throat. 'How the hell do you do that?'

'Do what?'

'Slide so easily beneath my skin?'

She looked startled for the moment and then she shifted her gaze to the wine glass, examining its contents before she took a sip. 'It's a unique talent not everyone appreciates.'

'By everyone you mean…?'

She lifted her gaze. 'It's got me into more trouble than it's worth.'

'What kind?'

Her nostrils flared, more with pain than the discomfort of laying her secrets bare. 'I drove a wedge between myself and my brothers, for one.'

'How?'

She averted her gaze again, staring long and deep into the fire.

I recaptured her foot, massaging her instep as she tapped a finger restlessly against the glass. 'My parents didn't abuse us physically, but they didn't think twice about abandoning us when we were young. I was too stubborn to accept that. Hell, I believed I could single-handedly fix our dysfunctional family. So I pushed and I pushed until it broke us.'

I opened my mouth to ask, but she sent me a look that drove the words back down my throat. 'Tell me another story,' she commanded.

My mistress was fully back in residence and I wasn't allowed to deny her.

I didn't want to.

I raised her other foot, kissed her in exactly the same spot. This time she didn't pull away.

And it scared me shitless how pleased that made me.

* * *

My euphoric state lasted for another mind-melting twenty-four hours.

Another day filled with sex, conversation, good food cooked together and more sex. We barely slept for more than a couple of hours.

No surface within the cabin was left un-christened by Graciela's sizzling demands. More than her blinding, more frequent smiles and the intelligence that shone from her eyes when we discussed the diverse topics that captivated us both, it was the siren-like fire in her eyes just before she ordered me to fulfil a desire that stoked a craving in my soul I was beginning to suspect would never be equalled once this thing was over. It was the reason a knot of dread had taken up residence in my stomach at the thought of it ending.

The force of the storm had lessened, snow falling with less frequency in the last half-day. I'd taken the coward's way out and avoided checking the weather forecast.

We couldn't stay here for ever, but I could sure as hell enjoy whatever hours we had left. Her favourite setting for fucking was in front of the fire, but, for the sake of extra comfort, we'd relocated to the bed last night and promptly fallen asleep.

Our limbs were tangled together, her head on my shoulder as she breathed, deep and steady. I was turning into one of those corny idiots who even enjoyed the way his woman slept, unable to help my smile as I stared down at her.

Even in slumber, Graciela Mortimer remained a Dominant. One leg rested over both of mine, her arm firmly anchoring my middle. If I weren't miles stronger than her, I'd remain pinned in place until she decided to let me go.

And fucking hell, I liked her wanting to keep me close even in sleep. I glanced at the window, willing the snow to start falling again.

But after an hour of lazing about in bed, when my prayers weren't answered, I eased away from her. Restlessness that usually drove me outside for a walk in the woods or exercising the dogs, regardless of the time of year, sent me downstairs to my office.

Sitting at my desk with my camera, I scrolled through the pictures I'd taken for Graciela.

The perfectionist in me was pleased to see there were several exceptional ones she could use for her magazine, with more shots on autofocus that I could use to make an interactive video for the digital version of her magazine if she wanted. I was confident I had everything she needed.

But my reason for coming to my office had nothing to do with work right now. I scrolled until I reached the one I wanted. Connecting the camera to my laptop, I sent the image to print, my breath stalled as the machine spat out a single portrait, glossy photo. On a wild impulse I printed off another five in various exposures to make an even half-dozen.

I placed them up at vantage points in my office, playing with the lighting and scrutinising each one critically from a different angle.

As I experimented, an idea began to form in my head, excitement building in my chest.

Graciela Mortimer was without doubt the most beautiful woman I'd ever seen. Her unique beauty, the light she tried to hide needed to be stoked. Kept alive.

I sat down at my desk, fingers flying over the keyboard as I activated my emails. As suspected, there were over two dozen emails from my office and a handful from my agent. I ignored them all, typing up an email of my own. The Internet was patchy and probably wouldn't send for a good few hours, but I didn't care. It would take a few emails to get this project under way, but I set the ball rolling, smiled as I slammed the laptop shut. My agent would be thrilled. She'd been pushing me in the direction of holding another exclusive show, since my first and only show had become a runaway hit.

That show, purely based on a series of photos I'd taken, had snowballed into a wild, insane juggernaut, with awards, book deals and insane amounts of money thrown my way to add to the small fortune I already had in the bank, guaranteeing I wouldn't have to work another day in my life if I didn't want to. It'd been more than a little disconcerting, truth be told. The only reason the furore had eventually died down several months later was because I'd taken an assignment to Papua New Guinea, one I knew would last three months. My absence had done the trick of granting me a modicum of privacy and normality.

The memory sobered me.

Was that what Graciela went through on a daily basis? As a child born into a powerful and influential family, she'd been the cynosure of rabid, relentless interest probably before she could walk. My interaction with social media was selective, getting involved only where it pertained to my work, but technology made blaring headlines impossible to ignore. I knew the kind of hellish media attention she and her family garnered, the kind of invasion of privacy that dogged her every waking hour.

She'd lived with it all her life, so was it any wonder she was wary and instantly suspicious of anyone wielding a camera?

Would she think of my burgeoning idea in those terms?

No. This was different. It would be special. A celebration rather than an invasion. Hopefully a prelude to…something else.

I drew back from putting a label on it, though the curious churning in my gut wanted to delve headlong into dissecting just what it was I felt for her.

The last three days had been illuminating. I'd caught more frequent glimpses of the woman beneath the powerful surname. Discovered her previous relationships had been just as ultimately unsatisfying as mine. That she hadn't taken a submissive in a while. Selfishly, that'd pleased me. I wasn't magnanimous enough to be the kind of guy who made accommodation for other prospects when it came to the woman I was interested in.

She had no entanglements in London. Or New York. Or wherever it was she was heading back to once we left my cabin. As primitive as it sounded, I wanted to be the only man occupying her thoughts while she was with me.

And when she left? What then?

I clenched my fist at the hollow in my belly at the thought of it.

Yeah, I was dangerously straying into obsession. Had probably done so already. Yet the thought didn't terrify me as much as it would've a handful of days ago. My gaze fell back on her pictures. Maybe we could make this work outside this wilderness bubble.

Shit, I was licked if I was already factoring her into my future.

Would that be so bad?

The answer never formed, the door creaking open redirecting my thoughts to the present.

She stood in the doorway, a blanket drawn around her body, her hair sexily dishevelled. Lips I'd feasted on repeatedly last night were still swollen and the sight of her bare feet curling into the wooden floor was seriously arousing.

Fuck me, but she was breathtaking.

'I don't remember giving you permission to leave me alone in bed.'

The firm, hot dominating voice immediately triggered a fever inside me, fire licking through my blood. Before I took my next breath, my cock was hardening, my fingers tingling with the need to submit, to please, to hand over my surrender to her.

'I would be very happy to return there if that's what you wish, *min elskerinde.*'

She started to answer but then her gaze fell on the pictures. Eyes widening, she stepped into the room. 'What is this?'

The stiff note in her voice made me tense. 'I was going through the images on my camera and—'

'And you decided to print out pictures of me?' Her voice was hushed but stiffer with growing wariness.

I spread my hands to lighten the mood. 'Hey, it's no big deal. I just wanted to see the images in different lights.'

She turned from the one propped up on the shelf, her eyes suspicious. 'Why? Your project isn't about me, remember?'

I bit the inside of my cheek, reluctant to share my idea with her just yet. In this mood, I suspected she'd say no out of ingrained habit.

Once I presented the full picture, she'd know my intentions were honourable. I took the most direct cop-out. 'I'm aware of what my brief is. This is the way I work, Graciela.'

A trace of suspicion receded from her eyes, but she remained wary as she glanced at the pictures. It was part of the set I'd taken outside the tent as she'd stared up at the aurora borealis. The naked awe on her stunning face had needed memorialising. The instinct that few people, if any, were granted the privilege of seeing this powerful woman overcome with childlike wonder compelling me to take the photos.

I wasn't about to tell her any of that, of course.

While the past few days had revealed she'd push for the personal on occasion, she wasn't one for prolonged introspection or subjects that dwelled on her or her family for too long.

The snippets I'd gleaned formed their own story.

She wasn't exactly estranged from her brothers or the rest of the family, but her interactions with them were few and far between, instigated by both sides in equal measures. It was a situation that hurt her, regardless of how much she tried to deny it.

I started to gather the pictures, intending to put them away. But a wild urge stopped me.

Besides the wariness and suspicion, there'd been something else in her expression when she'd looked at her pictures just now.

An expression of...surprise.

As if she was seeing herself in this light for the first time. I wasn't letting the opportunity slip me by. I wanted her to rediscover whatever she'd had taken from her by her family or the world at large. And hell, I was playing with fire, risking whatever time we had left with this impromptu experiment that could blow up in my face.

But wasn't taking risks part of my life? My soul?

Her voice certainly called into question my sanity as she trailed me out of the office. 'What the hell are you doing, Jensen?'

She could stop me at any time, command me to destroy the pictures, and I would do it. I was still hers to command; had a feeling I would be far longer than the snowstorm lasted.

But even that disturbing admission didn't stop me from walking across the room to place one picture over the fireplace. The second one I attached to the fridge door, the next on the fourth step.

The fourth I pinned to the front door, the fifth on the coffee table next to the sofa, where she tended to place her wineglass. The last one I was saving for the bedroom.

'Jensen.' Her voice shook with warning as she watched me.

Hands empty, I faced her. 'I want you to see yourself the way I see you.'

She refused to look at the pictures. 'And how's that?' she sneered.

'Beautiful. Breathtaking. Full of wonder.'

Her hands bunched tightly over the blanket until her knuckles turned white. 'Instead of? Just how do you think I see myself?'

Crap, this had turned way heavier than I'd anticipated, but I didn't back away from it. 'The labels you call yourself are other people's opinion of you. And yet I think deep down you believe them, don't you?'

Her lips firmed, mutiny in her silence.

'You're not spoilt. If you were, you wouldn't have sent your team away and braved the elements with me with nothing but a phone and a change of clothes. You hate sitting back and being waited on hand and foot even though it's my privilege to serve you like that.'

Her hazel eyes darkened. 'I like control. That's all this is, nothing more.'

I shook my head. 'No, it's not. Control is one thing. *Consideration* is another. Beneath all that bristling you're a good person, Graciela. I just wish you would see that yourself.'

'I'm not. If I was, I wouldn't be alone,' she grated in a harsh whisper, her jaw tightening as she attempted to hold herself together.

More than anything I wanted to go to her, take her in my arms, but I suspected this would end very quickly if I moved from where I stood. 'You're not alone. You're here. With me.'

'For how long?' She glanced out of the window. 'In case you haven't noticed, the storm is over.'

'That doesn't mean we have to be.'

She inhaled sharply. 'That wasn't what we agreed.'

I shrugged. 'Agreements can change. Nothing is set in stone. The beauty of being adults is that we can change our minds. What's to stop us from making a new one?'

A light glinted in her eyes, but a moment later she shook her head. 'You're deluded. Or probably suffering from cabin fever or some such nonsense.'

My gut churned harder. 'Don't trivialise my emotions.'

Her face hardened. 'You're disappointing me, Jensen.'

'Am I? Why?' I dared.

I could tell I'd stumped her. That made me smile. 'I may be submissive, *min elskerinde*. But I'm not weak.'

She frowned. 'I never thought you were.'

'Are you sure? Were you not hoping to discover some flaw that would make it easier to end this?'

'Is that what we're doing right now? Ending this? Because I could've sworn you were pushing for more.'

'While you're simply trying to push me away.'

'Stop it, Jensen. Just…stop.'

'Is that an order, mistress?'

'Yes,' she snarled. 'It's an order.'

I moved then, reluctantly walked past her into the kitchen. 'The coffee is just about ready. Would you like some?'

I could tell my obedience was throwing her. Heck, this morning wasn't going quite how she had expected it to go.

Join the club.

I was feeling pretty damn raw and exposed myself. But what had I expected? In pushing her to accept a different version of herself, I'd bared my own needs. That I was way too invested in what was happening in this cabin.

Preparing coffee gave me something to do, and I gleefully ignored the yearnings rampaging through me as I grabbed the mugs and poured the beverage. Turning, I caught her gaze on the picture above the fireplace.

She presented me with her profile as I handed her the coffee, waves of displeasure emanating from her. But then, she surprised me by taking a seat on the sofa, right next to where her other picture lay face up on the coffee table.

Her gaze swept down to it for a moment before she sucked in a long breath and took a sip of coffee.

'Would you like some breakfast?' I asked.

She shook her head. 'No, thanks. I'm not hungry.'

My hands clenched around my mug.

The thought that I'd triggered an early end date for us slashed panic through me. I held it together, joining her on the sofa. I intended to sit next to her, but at the last-minute I sank lower to the floor.

My arm brushed her leg. Breath held, I waited for her move.

Seconds ticked into minutes. We drank our coffee. Then I felt her fingers, whisper-light against my temple. I stilled, barely breathing.

Her fingers slid deeper into my hair, brushing against my scalp in that firm, insistent way that sent shivers down my spine. As I predicted, she gathered the mass at the base of my skull, gripped it in her fist and used the pressure to tilt my head.

Our gazes met. Locked. She pushed. I parried.

She exhaled. 'Whatever it is you're doing, it's not going to work, you know.'

'I disagree.'

Her grip eased a fraction and I was absurdly terrified she was about to let me go.

'Tell me about the whales,' she said.

The whales. My life-changing underwater experience. The most profound moment of my life thus far.

I denied the deliberate distraction, nudged my head

at the picture. 'Tell me about the last time you felt like that before two nights ago.'

Searing pain clouded her eyes and she shook her head.

'Tell me,' I insisted. 'Lighten your burden by sharing it with me, Graciela.'

She stared at me for several seconds, her expression wavering. She released my hair. And a dark, thick hollow invaded my stomach. It lingered only for a moment because she touched me again, this time nudging my head onto her thigh.

I held myself stiff, instinctively sensing she needed the silence to delve beneath the surface of her pain.

CHAPTER EIGHT

HE WAS ASKING the impossible.

Demanding the forbidden. Asking me to rip my chest open, show him my shredded heart? When had that ever helped?

I had literal proof that it didn't. Every effort I'd made to connect, to *correct*, had turned to dust.

His hand wrapped around my calf. Warm. Solid. *Present.* Grounding me for the first time since I came downstairs.

I'd woken up in a wild panic and before I could put my finger on why, my heart was racing. It'd taken half a second to realise the primary reason for my anxiety. It was because Jensen wasn't beside me. The secondary because the snow had stopped. I was torn right down the middle between accepting that this wasn't just a casual fling and grasping the out that Mother Nature was handing me.

The latter had diminished within seconds, leaving a searing sense of loss.

The weight of it had compelled me out of bed, the need to see Jensen driving me.

Only to come downstairs to this stomach-hollowing situation.

He gently massaged my muscles, intent on grounding me in the present when I wanted to flee both it and the pain-ridden past.

And go where? Into a future filled with uncertainty? God, when had my future become so bleak?

When he knelt at your feet and gifted you with possibilities you knew you'd have to walk away from.

The raw, soul-shaking admission turned my insides out even more than the last few minutes had. My gaze lifted to the picture propped up above the fireplace. My breath caught; I barely recognised the woman in the photo.

He wanted to know when I'd last experienced that kind of…joy?

'It was the last time I saw my mother before she left me for good.'

I wasn't aware I'd spoken the words aloud until his fingers moved again, gliding up and down my leg in silent reassurance.

But with the words out, I couldn't hide any more. 'I didn't know it was the last time, of course. She was getting dressed to go to some function or other. I didn't ask because I was so surprised she'd let me into her bedroom at all, never mind her dressing room. Both were strictly off-limits to every one of us. But that day was different. She was…strangely indulgent, didn't berate me when I played dress up with the diamonds she'd expressly forbidden me from touching.'

'How old were you?'

'I'd turned nine a couple of days before.' The recollection brought a small smile, my mother's presence at my ninth birthday a wonderful phenomenon in itself that'd made my small heart burst with joy, the belief that my fractured family was on its way to becoming whole again, a sacred conviction I'd nurtured for days. A wish I'd refused to let Gideon's condescending sneers ruin. I'd later discovered that he'd somehow known it was a foolish dream. My clever brother, perhaps the cleverest one of us, had seen what was coming, used his trademark sarcasm and icy indifference to safeguard himself against hurt. He'd known what was coming but had kept it to himself.

I hadn't been so lucky…

Jensen's hand wrapped around my ankle, infusing warmth into me, as if it would lessen the pain of the recounting. Nothing could. But I appreciated the gesture.

'I was tall for my age and my mother and I were of a similar build.' We were more than that. My mother had given birth to a near replica of herself, the only differences between us the hazel eyes inherited from the Mortimer gene and my black hair to her chestnut waves.

'So she let you play with her stuff…' Jensen coaxed.

'Normally it took her hours to get ready. This time she took even longer. And I got to spend every minute with her.' My heart stuttered and my fist tightened at the recollection. 'I don't even remember what we talked about. I really wish I did. I wish I'd paid better attention…'

'The time spent was more important than the words said.'

'Was it, though? Because she left for her party and I never saw her again.'

His fingers tightened on my skin. 'What?'

'She was done being a mother. She wanted to live her life. Those hours in her dressing room may have been her way of saying goodbye. Or maybe it was just a meaningless indulgence for her. Thing is, I never got the chance to find out.'

Jensen exhaled slowly, then turned to drop a kiss on my knee.

I was glad he wasn't looking at me. I didn't think I could bear him witnessing my pain. Not that he didn't have a very good idea. He was far too clever for that.

'My brothers and I found out later that it'd been their intention all along. To leave that night and never return.'

Jensen frowned. 'Both your parents left?'

'Yes.' My throat was clogged with ravaging pain. 'It became sort of a recurring theme. My cousin Damien's parents did the same thing too.'

He cursed under his breath. 'Who told you?' he asked.

'My aunt Flo knew. Hell, she probably tried to stop them because…well, that's the kind of person she is. She didn't succeed, obviously. So a day after spending what I thought was the start of the mother-daughter bonding I'd dreamt about, I was effectively an orphan, despite my parents still being alive.'

'Min Gud,' he muttered under his breath.

My fingers weaved through his hair, anchoring myself. He made a thick, pleased sound at the back of his throat, leaned into my touch.

'Was that what drove you and your brothers apart?' he asked after a minute.

Fresh anguish washed over me. 'No. That was all me.'

'How?'

'I got it into my head that I could make things right, get my mother to come home. I begged and badgered my way into getting them to agree for us to write letters to my mother. It took a few months but I finally got them on board.'

'Did she reply?'

I laughed again, but the sound broke apart, catching the sharp edge of my grief. 'Oh, yes, she did.'

'Graciela...*kæreste*...'

I didn't know what the endearment meant, but I shook my head, eager to dispel the threat of tears and unlock the lump lodged in my throat. 'I'm fine. It's fine,' I insisted.

His fingers drifted up my calf. 'It's not. You know that as well as I do.'

'You're supposed to agree with me.'

'I do, for the most part. You did what you needed to try to make your family whole again.'

'No, I pushed and control-freaked my way into making things worse.'

'What did she say in her reply?'

That knot built in my throat again. 'In a nutshell? That I wasn't worth it.'

He inhaled sharply. 'Graciela...'

I didn't look down, didn't want to see sympathy or pity or embrace any form of gentleness. I was too scared my lacerated heart would fracture into a million pieces if I succumbed to the promise of empathy. Did I deserve it? When I'd dragged everyone down with me into the pits of despair?

'No one blames you for trying—'

I laughed again, my fingers tightening in his hair to stop his words. 'Oh, believe me, they do. Gideon most definitely did. He didn't hold back. Bryce was soft-hearted enough not to hurt my feelings with his words, but I could see in his eyes that he totally blamed me. I ruined us, Jensen. He went from being a loving and carefree younger brother to avoiding me every chance he got. I was a pariah in my own home. I'd enter a room and they'd leave. In the end I begged Aunt Flo to send me to boarding school. Then I charmed my way into mid-term breaks and school vacations with any friend who would have me because I couldn't face going home. And it worked. I didn't go home for two years, was terrified of returning home to the same hatred. It was why...' I pressed my lips together, holding in the last, heart-wrenching confession. But still he pressed.

'Why what?'

'Why I hated myself even more when I found out later that she came back.'

Blue eyes found mine. 'She returned?'

'For unannounced visits. She'd breeze in, drop off presents, then breeze out again. Or so I was told.'

'Maybe she wanted to reconnect?'

I shrugged. 'I wouldn't know. She never asked for me. She knew where I was but she never came to see me in school. She never reached out. It was almost like… I was dead to her. And that made me angry, Jensen. Angrier than I've ever been in my life.'

'That's understandable. She hurt you.'

'Yes, she did. But was it enough for me to wish her dead? Because that was exactly what I did. I wished her dead, and a few months later she died.'

The cold jagged pain of that admission froze me from the inside out.

I barely registered Jensen twisting around, his strong arms lifting me off the sofa and into his lap and wrapping around me. The tightness in my throat unravelled, dissolving into hot, gulping tears that shook the very foundations of my soul.

Through it all, he held me close, running his fingers through my hair and down my back without saying a word. When I was wrung dry, he brushed a kiss against my temple.

'You were heartbroken and lashed out. That makes you human. If wishing ill on someone actually guaranteed a desired result, my father would've been six feet under the first time I saw bruises on my mother and little sister. Life doesn't work that way, *kæreste*. Sometimes the assholes who cause pain get to live long, hopefully miserable lives.'

I raised my head, saw my pain reflected in his eyes. 'Your father?'

He nodded. 'I don't know where he is, but only because I've never bothered to find out. The third time I stood up to him, he went out drinking and never returned. So you see, I was responsible for driving my parent away too, but I don't regret it. I'd do it again in a heartbeat. I wanted him gone with every fibre of my being.'

I remained silent, unable to do anything but absorb his warmth, his sheer perfection. With his lips still trailing down my face, he reached for the box of tissues sitting on the coffee table.

I plucked out a few, blew my nose and scrubbed away the remainder of my tears. I didn't feel whole, would probably never be whole again, but I felt less... tormented, less burdened. The fact that it was Jensen who'd done this to me, for me, triggered a whole new layer of panic. The weight of what I felt for him terrified me. Everything I'd dreamed of had broken up beneath the pressure of my yearning.

Like a butterfly held too tight, I tended to crush the wings of things that were precious to me. And he was fast becoming precious, right up there with things I didn't want to lose.

Which brought its own bracing demand. What right did I have to him?

His lips drifted down my cheek, lingered at the corner of my mouth, and I conveniently sidestepped the questions teeming inside. 'I look a mess.'

He kissed me firmer, his lips more demanding. 'No, you look beautiful.'

Blind panic made me turn to him, seal my lips against his. I didn't want to hear the words. Didn't want to open my heart to a promise that would never be fulfilled. The contents of my mother's letter blazed through my mind, reminding me that I wasn't enough. I would never be enough.

His arms tightened around me, his eager lips surrendering to mine as I deepened the kiss. I wound my arms around his neck, repositioned myself so I was astride him on the floor. The blanket gaped open and his hands slid beneath, gliding down my side to grip my hips, hold me close as we leaned into the kiss.

Between my legs, he was rock-hard, a thrilling reality, a consuming storm I could drown in, forget about my emotional turmoil. I shrugged off the blanket completely, my fingers dancing down his muscled chest to stroke the bulge that promised oblivion.

'Fuck me, Jensen.'

He shuddered against me. Then he pulled back, just enough to meet my gaze. 'I'm dying to, *min elskede,* but we don't have a condom down here.'

I didn't want a reprieve from this madness; didn't want time and space to thrust me back into the emotional grinder I'd just been through. So I took a breath. 'It's fine. I…' *trust you.* I barely stopped myself, my heart lurching wildly at the dangerous words I'd almost uttered.

I'd only known him a matter of days. This was the proximity talking. We'd been cooped up in this cabin with no other outlet than to fuck and bare ourselves to each other. I was letting my emotions get carried away. Another mistake I'd regret if I didn't rein myself back in. 'I'm on the Pill. It's fine.'

His eyes lingered on mine, delving beneath the matter-of-fact words to find their true meaning. I rocked my hips over him, and the distraction worked like a charm. His fingers tightened on my hips and his gaze fell to my breasts. With a deep groan, he dipped his head and sucked one nipple into his mouth. I clutched him to me, throwing my head back in wild abandon as I drowned in the unique passion he invoked.

This was…should be…just sex. Good sex I was in danger of sullying with emotion.

Again my heart shook at the half-lie, another fastening tearing itself from my control. It was almost as if it wanted to free itself, soar where I couldn't allow it. I couldn't risk the responsibility of him, couldn't risk turning another person against me.

Thankfully thoughts ceased to matter as ecstasy took over.

He bent me backwards until my hair brushed the floor. Then he rained kisses down my front to the top of my mound. I revelled in the heat of his hands and mouth, in the thick Danish words he whispered over my skin.

His thumb strummed my clit and I cried out. He toyed mercilessly with the swollen bud, didn't stop until I was mindless. Until sating this insane need was all I could think of.

Repositioning myself back on top of him, I speared

my fingers through his hair and dragged his gaze to mine. His face, powerfully lust ravaged, was the most perfect image I'd ever seen. 'I want you inside me. Now.'

He raised his hips off the floor just enough to yank down his jogging bottoms. The moment his erection was freed, I braced myself on my knees, spread my thighs wide. Jensen gripped his cock, his other hand clutching my hip, and with his eyes rapt on my face, absorbing my every action, I lowered myself onto him.

'*Min elskede.* You feel so good,' he groaned.

The gruffness in his voice made me wonder if I'd misheard the word, but I didn't care. He was inside me. I was mindless with bliss, free from memories and pain. The lack of a condom's barrier was equally thrilling, adding a layer of intimacy I'd never imagined. It was probably that, and not the lightened weight in my heart. Or the hushed voice at the back of my head suggesting I wasn't quite as hopeless, quite as deplorable, that I might be worth something if this formidable creature possessing me believed so...which brought tears to the act. Which made me want to burrow inside this bubble and never emerge.

Whatever it was, it culminated in soul-searing pleasure that made me scream with the sacredness of it. My orgasm went on for ever, my whole body shaking, my heart hammering as fresh tears formed behind my eyelids.

I wrapped myself around him, rejoiced in his shout of release and the power of him pulsing inside me. We shuddered uncontrollably in the aftermath, clinging to each other, our breaths ragged as we slowly came down from the highest high. His hands trailed down my back, over my hips and thighs until our breaths returned to normal.

'I'd like to shower with you. And then I'd very much like to feed you. May I?' Jensen asked, his breath brushing my ear.

Normality. Or a semblance of it.

I wanted to kiss him for not making a big thing out of this. Instead, I nodded. 'Your mistress would like that very much.'

I felt his smile against my jaw as he adjusted me in his arms, then lithely rose from the floor without dislodging me.

God, that was sexy.

I managed a smile as he raced us up the stairs.

We were both wrung out, didn't speak as we entered the large shower stall. Jensen washed me from head to toe, his hands firm, adoring. When he was done, he sank down to his knees, silently offered the shower gel to me.

I returned the favour, lingering longest in his glorious hair before washing his sculpted, mouth-watering body. After dressing, we returned downstairs, where I was confronted with my images. For a panicked moment I wanted to order him to take down the pictures. I could tell he was bracing himself for it. The words never came. I'd revealed the worst of my secrets to him. What was a picture or six?

When he realised I was going to leave them be, a smile broke out on his face. A smile that made my heart bang hard again. Dear God, I was in danger of expiring from heart failure if this continued.

And it couldn't really continue...

As we ate breakfast mostly in silence, that thought solidified. After what he'd been through, Jensen needed someone unbroken. Someone not quite so...flawed. Twisted and riddled with dysfunction. Someone who didn't live in torment or trail bitterness and disappointment behind her.

So in a way, I accepted fate's decision when the unfamiliar sound disturbed the silence. We both started, Jensen's gaze narrowing as it swung upward to where the sound emitted from the bedroom. 'It's your phone,' he said, his voice dark and subdued.

My satellite phone. My route out of here.

I hadn't used it for days, not even to check in with my staff because I'd been wholly enraptured and encapsulated in this delusional bubble we'd created for ourselves. But now, my life was stridently calling. I ignored the ashen taste in my mouth at the thought of leaving, stood and went up the stairs to retrieve it.

'Hello?'

'Miss Mortimer? It's your pilot. I've been given the all-clear to fly. The forecast predicts another storm later today, so this is our only window.'

I heard a noise behind me and turned around.

Jensen stood in the doorway, his piercing gaze

pinned on me. For a long stretch, we both remained frozen.

'Miss Mortimer? Would you like me to pick you up?'

My gaze darted wildly around the bedroom, the place I'd experienced fulfilment such as I'd never known. When I glanced back at him, Jensen was striding forwards, his jaw set, but appeal in his eyes. It wasn't a request I could grant. Not without disappointing him eventually, hurting us both.

'Yes. Please come and get me. Hold on a second.' I held the phone out to Jensen. 'Can you tell my pilot how to find me, please?'

He took the phone from me, but didn't raise it to his ear. 'I thought we were going to talk about this?' he hissed. 'Make other plans—'

I shook my head. 'No, we weren't. The storm was going to let up eventually. And I was going to leave. You know that.'

'Graciela,' he gritted out, stormy shadows moving over his face. 'This isn't done. Stay.'

Every cell in my body screamed with the need to say yes. I shook my head harder. 'What's that going to achieve? You've wrung me dry. Be content with that.'

'Content? You think downstairs was about me being content?'

I stopped him before he could carry on, my gaze shifting to stare pointedly at the phone. 'I'd rather not do this with someone eavesdropping.'

A muscle ticced in his jaw, but slowly, he lifted the phone to his ear and coolly recited his coordinates to my pilot. Then he disconnected the line, tossed the phone onto the bed and fixed determined eyes on me.

I pre-empted him before he opened his mouth. 'I'm not going to change my mind, Jensen.'

'We have at least an hour before the chopper gets here. Are you planning on not talking to me in that time?' he taunted.

'Don't be ridiculous.'

I hurried to the closet where he'd placed my weekender. Snatching whatever personal items I could locate within easy reach, I mentally dismissed taking things like my toothbrush and the toiletries scattered around his bathroom. They were easily replaceable.

Plus, moving around meant I didn't have to acknowledge the hard, painful knot in my belly that grew tighter with every second.

'Why the sudden hurry, Graciela?' Jensen asked, his voice deep, throbbing with challenge.

I didn't want to look his way, but, God, I couldn't help myself. His arms were folded as he lounged against his bedroom wall, his stance deceptively calm. But his eyes gleamed with purpose that stated he wasn't about to let me leave with a dismissive wave and a hollow promise.

'What are you talking about?'

'I'm talking about you, attempting to shut the door after the horse has bolted. What happened downstairs was unsettling, I know, but—'

I forced a laugh, one so false it grated my throat. And made his face tighten with irritation. '*Unsettling?*

Why, because I shed a few tears? Don't make it a bigger deal than it was, Jensen. Sure, I was due a little… catharsis, but it was hardly life-altering…'

My words trickled away when his face grew tighter, the warmth leaving his eyes. 'That's the second time you've attempted to dismiss something significant as nothing—'

'Because it was nothing!'

His arms dropped, his jaw rippling as he took a slow breath. 'It wasn't nothing. What happened with your mother was shitty and traumatic. You shame yourself by trivialising it now because you let your guard down. Did you forget what you promised me?'

My thundering heartbeat threatened to drown out everything. 'I warned you people break their promises all the time.'

An emotion that closely resembled bleakness filmed his eyes for a moment before he blinked it away. 'Yes, you did. But I chose to believe you when you said you'd be truthful about whatever you were feeling. About what happened between us.'

'And you think I'm not?'

His pointed look spoke volumes. 'I know a little bit about denial and the people who practise it, Graciela. My mother was an expert at it. And *you* are so fully immersed in it, it's any wonder you can fucking breathe,' he scythed at me, cold fury drenching his features.

The searing accusation, and the caustic acknowledgement of its truth, made me turn away from him before he saw his effect. I silently willed my pilot to hurry before I did something foolish, like beg Jensen not to be disappointed in me, to help me see myself the way he wanted to see me. But that was a road fraught with even more disappointment. After all, wasn't what I'd predicted already unfolding before my eyes?

Zipping the bag, I lifted it and blindly headed for the door.

'Aren't you going to say anything?'

I forced a shrug. 'What's the point? You seem to have me psychoanalysed inside and out.'

Without asking my permission, he stepped forward and took the bag from me. But he made no move to leave the room. His presence surrounded me, his beautiful masculine scent invading my every pore. 'And you're just going to take it?' he jeered.

Fear and frustration shook through me. 'Jensen...'

He exhaled, long and loud. Then he jerked towards me.

'Min elskerinde...'

The fury and mockery were gone, his voice low. Gentle. Coaxing.

'Stay. Take a day, let's sort through this.'

With every fibre of my being I wanted to scream *yes*.

My heart dropped to my stomach, acceptance that our agreement was officially over, that I was no longer his mistress, or he my sub, blinding me with pain so acute, I nearly gasped.

It if hurts this much, then why are you leaving?

Because what I wanted didn't matter. Because...

You're not enough. You'll never be enough.

My mother's words echoed and re-echoed in my head. And the heart I thought had shrivelled to uselessness after being steeped in years of pain and bitterness started to bleed.

'I'd stay if there was something worth staying for,' I forced out. 'It's been fun, but we both know that was all this was ever going to be.'

Gentleness evaporated and the cold scorn returned. 'Bullshit. Cut the lies and say it like it is. You're going to board your chopper and run away because you're scared.'

He waited, eyes fixed on me as a minute ticked by. Two.

I remained silent, holding my tattered emotions inside because I was terrified of opening my mouth. Petrified I would scream that, yes, everything he said was true.

With a tight curse, he left the room and jogged downstairs with my bag. I followed, mourning the sight of my bag propped beside the door. Avoiding the taunting images of a Graciela who apparently lived inside me but wasn't strong enough to reach for what she wanted, I perched on the farthest end of the sofa, staring into the fire and fighting the tears that threatened.

Stealthily, I watched Jensen prowl around the room, tugging on his thick coat and boots. When the ominous sound of a helicopter approaching shattered the silence, he strode to my bag, picked it up and opened the door.

A chill wind blew in, but it was nothing compared

to the cold seizing my insides at the thought of leaving this rustic cabin. Leaving Jensen.

'You'll hear from me shortly,' he said, his voice stony.

My heart leapt, then the true meaning sank in. He was talking about the project. The work I'd given just fleeting thought to over the past three days. 'My assistant will put you in touch with the editorial team.'

His jaw clenched and he shook his head. 'You're not fobbing me off on your assistant. You hired me. You're going to deal with me. I won't have my time wasted going back and forth with subordinates who'll feed me second-hand information. I'll be in London next week with the finished project. We'll meet, then hopefully we can be rid of each other.'

His words were firm, forceful, any hint of the earlier pleading and deep craving gone. I wanted to step back in time, accept the extra day, see where it led. But I already knew the outcome. Two more broken souls. More anguish that would keep me up at night. I couldn't take that. Not any more.

And yet, I couldn't make my feet move. Couldn't step off his frozen porch and climb the chopper patiently waiting thirty feet away.

'That's what you want, isn't it?' he pressed, his voice harsh.

I swallowed, forced my head to nod. 'Yes. Elsa will check my schedule and let you know.'

His lips tightened, assailing me with an urge to see him smile one last time that was so unbearable, I turned and hurried out onto the frozen tundra, my feet sinking into snow, towards the pilot who alighted and came to escort me.

Jensen handed him my bag, then stood, feet braced, cold eyes boring into my back as I climbed aboard.

He didn't back away or go inside as the rotor blades churned up snow.

Even when his white jacket was pelted with snow, he didn't leave. He stood there, his glorious hair whipping around his face, jaw set as he stared up at the helicopter.

Unable to help myself, I stared back, my eyes watering as he blended into the blinding white landscape.

Only when the chopper banked steeply did I look away, my heart already thudding with deep dread at the enormity of the misery that awaited me.

CHAPTER NINE

'OH, MISS MORTIMER, you're back! I wasn't expecting you till later this morning...'

Elsa's surprise registered hollowly in my head as she entered my office. I heard her stop a few feet from my desk, but didn't turn from my position at the window.

'Can I get you anything? Your usual coffee?' Her voice trailed hesitantly when I continued to stare at the window, glaring miserably at the view I didn't want to see.

It was the wrong view. For starters, London was wet and dreary and had been since my return two days ago, the rain unable to make up its mind whether to turn to sleet or mizzle.

I wanted a white-out, thick snow covering everything in sight and cutting off the world.

But more than anything, I wanted the man who I'd been snowed in with. As much as I appreciated her, Elsa's presence was just another reminder that I was half a world removed from where I wanted to be.

I forced myself to turn around, to paste a half-decent smile on my face as I sat at my desk. 'I came in a little early.' Understatement of the year. I'd abandoned sleep at two a.m., my queen-sized bed suddenly feeling like a wide, endless ocean of misery, determined to swallow me up.

The longer I'd lain there, staring at the ceiling, the deeper my despair and panic had taken hold. With the business day beginning, I'd decided to call it quits where sleep was concerned, and get a head start on my work.

In hindsight, I realised leaving the perfectly adequate loneliness of my Mayfair mews house to place myself in the operating hub of the Mortimer Group empire wasn't my finest decision.

Because the more the hive of activity moved around me, the deeper my loneliness had steeped.

The inter-family group email that someone industrious had set up a while ago was the first of many joy-shrivelling emails waiting to pounce on my vulnerable state when I fired up my laptop. Every single one of them involved some family member crowing about their personal success.

Apparently Gideon and his wife, Leonie, Damien and his new wife, and Bryce and Savannah were planning on spending the holiday season cruising the Mediterranean on the family's yacht. The invitation had been extended for anyone who wanted to join, of course, but last thing I wanted was to be a fifth, sixth or seventh wheel.

There was another email from Bryce, mildly berating me for my unavailability, and informing me of his engagement to Savannah. Apparently he'd tried to call several times in the last few days but had been unable to reach me to give me the good news.

Even while my heart had soared with happiness for him and Savvie, the depth of my despairing loneliness intensified. When we'd met up in Singapore a few months ago at the opening of Savannah's flagship lingerie store, he'd looked just as miserable as I felt. But evidently, he'd worked through his differences with Savvie.

Christmas was less than two weeks away. The thought of spending it with my dysfunctional collection of back-stabbing, acid-tongued family members filled me with dread.

...run away because you're scared...

My fingers shook over the mouse as Jensen's words struck hard and deep.

I'd been burned more than a few times, but...had some of that been of my own doing? Had I deliberately held myself up to the flame, just to see if I'd burn? For once, would it hurt to see what happened if I stepped back? Perhaps feel warmth instead of flames?

Before my courage deserted me, I pushed away thoughts of Christmas in a cabin in the wilds of Alaska and fired off emails to Gideon and Bryce, tentatively accepting their invitation to join them for New Year. I could always change my mind later.

'Give me five minutes, I'll grab your coffee,' Elsa said.

I shook my head. 'I don't want coffee, thanks.'

Her eyes widened at the uncharacteristic refusal. 'Are you all right?'

'Yes, I'm fine, thank you.' She didn't need to know that I only wanted coffee from one person. I didn't even care that Jensen hadn't given a shit about achieving the optimal temperature for his coffee. He'd served it with a blinding smile, a mouth-watering, naked torso and eyes filled with the desire to please his mistress that touched my soul.

Elsa frowned. 'Are you sure I can't get you anything? Maybe tea?' she said hesitantly, anxiety filming her eyes, as if she was afraid I'd say yes and confound her further.

'No, thanks. Do you have any messages for me?' I said, striving to keep my voice calm.

She looked down at the leather binder she always carried and back up at me. 'Nothing that can't wait—'

I held out my hand. 'I'll be the judge of that.'

She passed it over. I flipped it open, my heart racing as I perused the three neatly typed sheets containing my packed daily schedule. There was nothing about a meeting or call with Jensen Scott.

Bleak disappointment thudding through me, I handed back the binder, aware Elsa was staring at me.

'Is there something specific I should be looking at?' she asked.

'No.'

'Okay,' she said. 'Well…your first meeting is at nine. I'll give you the usual ten-minute heads-up.' She started to walk away.

'Is Larry in? Do you know if he's heard from Jensen Scott?' I blurted before I could stop myself.

Elsa turned around, her eyes flaring with interest at the mention of Jensen's name. I tightened my fist in my lap, attempting to breathe calmly so as not to give myself away.

'Larry left for Jo'burg last Thursday. He's taking his annual leave before he starts the next project. I emailed you about it last week.'

'Can you liaise with his assistant and let me know the minute Mr Scott gets in touch?' I said briskly, partly because I didn't want Elsa to linger, and slip into one of her girly chats about Jensen.

It worked, my solemn mood filtering through to her. With a nod, she left my office. My hands shook as I laid them back on the desk.

Jensen had said he'd be in touch next week. It'd only been two days, for heaven's sake. And yet it felt like a lifetime. I turned back to the window, irritated the rain was still falling, that it hadn't turned into snow while my back was turned.

I was still standing there, fighting a losing battle with dejection, when Elsa returned with the promised ten-minute warning.

Get your head back in the game.

But my performance was perfunctory at best, only years of experience seeing me through the busy day. The magazine I was so passionate about, nurtured from an often disregarded five-page newsletter into an award-winning mechanism for charity, had lost its lustre. And

I wasn't sure whether to be terrified or shocked at my apathy.

In between meetings, I rabidly refreshed my inbox, hoping for an email from Jensen.

It didn't arrive.

I held my breath each time Elsa entered my office with a message, each time a new email hit my inbox and I experienced a bolt of excitement, only to deflate when it wasn't the one I yearned for. By Friday afternoon, I wanted to hate him for sticking to his word. For cutting me off so clinically.

But how could I when nothing had changed for me, except the searing sense of loss every time I thought about him? How selfish did it make me to long this desperately for a moment of joy on what should be a conclusion to a business transaction for the sole purpose of alleviating my loneliness?

An email pinged and my heart leapt. It wasn't from Jensen, but Bryce's name caused a different sort of excitement.

I know you're thinking about joining us on the yacht for New Year's, but do you fancy Christmas Day with us as well?

My fiancée insists you join us if you don't have plans.

I would love to see you too.

Bryce

I read and re-read it, unable to stem the expanding hope in my chest.

In a moment of weakness a year ago while in New

York, I'd had lunch with Savannah, and blurted out my desire to reconnect with Bryce. Her store opening had been the perfect opportunity to fly to Singapore to attempt to salvage things with Bryce. I'd come away with a suitcase full of exquisite lingerie and a growing hope that my relationship with my brother would be rekindled.

I fought back tears that sprung out of nowhere, daring to accept that things weren't so hopeless with my brothers after all. I was dashing away tears when Elsa knocked and entered. She looked flustered, her eyes a little too bright. 'Umm, sorry to disturb you, but Mr Scott's just turned up. He says he has a meeting with you, but—'

I jumped up to my feet, despite the sudden nerves and the memories of our parting. 'Where is he?'

'I'm setting him up in the conference room, but you have an appointment in fifteen minutes.'

'Cancel it,' I blurted.

Her eyes widened as I rounded the desk and headed for the door. 'Which of the conference rooms is he in?' I asked, my heart slamming against my ribs.

'Conference Room Three.'

I nodded, pleased. It was the most secluded one, the one with the best soundproofing. Which we wouldn't need, of course, because this was purely a perfectly civil business meeting. A last meeting before we parted ways.

If you are so unaffected, then why is your heart racing? Why are you shaking?

I ignored the taunting voice, walked with measured strides to the door.

'Umm… Miss Mortimer?'

'Yes?' I answered, impatience and anxiety ramping high. 'Was there something else?'

Elsa nodded at my face. 'You might want to fix your make-up.'

I grimaced and reversed direction, tossing my thanks over my shoulder as I headed to the private bathroom adjoining my office. When I saw my reflection, my jaw dropped in shock. I looked a mess. No wonder Elsa had been casting me concerned looks all day.

My mascara was smudged to clown-like proportions, my lipstick non-existent from stress nibbling. My hair looked as if I hadn't brushed it in days.

Who cares? He's seen you without make-up for three straight days.

That didn't mean I wanted to present myself looking like a scarecrow.

I repaired my make-up, tugged a brush repeatedly through my hair until it fell in acceptable waves over my shoulders. My suit was professional but stylish, uniquely edged with purple stripes against black adding an unapologetic touch of femininity to the outfit. After gliding nude gloss over my lips, I left the bathroom.

My heart banged harder against my ribs, my palms growing sweaty as I approached the conference room and opened the door.

Jensen looked up from where he lounged in the seat

at the head of the table, eyes just as chilled as the last time I'd looked into them.

Despite the cold reception, I froze, my senses needing a moment to absorb him.

He wore a dark navy suit, clearly bespoke, gloriously highlighting every superb physical attribute.

His hair was combed, but it still achieved that sexily dishevelled look. The stubble he'd cultivated during our time in the cabin had now grown into a short, sexy beard, making his face even more wickedly handsome.

'Good afternoon, Miss Mortimer. I hope I'm not disturbing you too much?' His deep, gravel-smooth, desperately missed voice slid over me like silk.

Ice-cold silk.

My fingers tightened on the door handle as I shifted my gaze to where Elsa stood frozen next to him, her eyes wide with interest as they flicked from Jensen to me and back again.

'You can leave now, Elsa.'

Her lips drooped with disappointment, but she nodded. 'Oh…er… Okay. Sure thing. The projector for your presentation is all set up for you, Mr Scott.'

His smiled warmed for her but turned frigid a moment later. 'Thanks, Elsa.'

I shut the door behind her and approached, only then taking in the leather case that contained his trays of photos before my gaze swung back to him.

In time to catch a flash of hunger before he checked his expression.

I wanted to pepper him with questions, demand that

he tell me everything he'd done since we last saw each other. But wouldn't that be prolonging the agony?

I took a deep breath, forced my gaze away from his face to the photos laid out on the conference table. 'Shall we begin?' I said briskly.

'Yes. Let's,' he rasped, his voice brisker, perfectly emulating the Arctic wind I yearned to feel against my skin. Because, absurdly, it suddenly symbolised bliss and freedom I was terrified I'd never experience again.

A different sort of shudder moved through me, a forlorn little forecast of what my future held. Desperately, I pushed it away. 'Is this everything?' I waved my hand at the tray.

He laughed, harsh and bitter. 'Are we really going to do it like this?'

'Do it like what, Mr Scott?'

Without answering me, he rose, strolled down the length of the conference room to the door and turned the key in the lock.

A million butterflies fluttered in my belly. 'What the hell do you think you're doing?'

He ambled back to me, looking sleek and delicious in his suit. 'I thought giving you a week to think things through would work,' he repeated.

I deliberately raised an eyebrow, despite my heart leaping at that fixated look in his eyes. 'Then you obviously don't know me well.'

He stopped a few feet away, his gaze not leaving my face. 'And whose fault is that? One of us ran away the moment things got a little too personal, and that person wasn't me.'

Shame engulfed me but years of staring opponents down weren't easy to dismiss. 'Is that why you've locked the door? To physically restrain me?'

Distaste washed over his face. 'That's so we're not disturbed, not so you can't leave whenever you want to. I'll never keep you prisoner, Graciela. Not unless you specifically ordered me to.'

A fever started in my belly, heating me up from within. I fought to deny it. 'Not going to happen.'

Briefly, his nostrils flared, his expression dimming before he turned to the table. He shrugged off his jacket and tossed it over a chair before curtly nudging his head at the tray. 'Fine. Looks like you want to keep hiding from reality, so let's get on with this, shall we?'

He started the projector. I grabbed the remote and dimmed the lights and took a seat, forcing myself not to glance his way. Not to breathe him in.

He negated all of that by dragging his chair closer, until he was a tempting arm's length away. For the next long while hundreds of pictures scrolled across the screen, each one stunning enough to make paring it down to the essential twenty-five I needed for the magazine near impossible.

When we reached the images he'd taken on the night of the borealis, fine tremors shook through me, memory attempting to shake free everything I needed to hold inside. Every frame he'd captured was overwhelmingly breathtaking, unique enough to draw a gasp.

I felt him lean in close but couldn't move away. Didn't want to.

'I'll never be able to experience another borealis without thinking of you,' he breathed in my ear. 'You know that, don't you?'

I didn't answer. I couldn't. A lump had lodged in my throat; with selfish pleasure I took from his words. Yes, I didn't want him thinking of anyone else but me.

Abruptly, he moved away, hit the button again, and we scrolled through the last of the images. When Jensen activated the lights, I blinked, still awestruck by the power and beauty of the pictures.

'How the hell am I going to choose?' I blurted.

His smile was stiff and cold. 'I'll take that as a compliment.'

I stared at the display on the table, at a loss as to where to start.

Impatient fingers drummed on the table, then, 'Do you want my help?' Jensen offered.

I hesitated, the idea of handing over such an important decision to him stopping me for a moment.

The drumming stopped. He lounged back and folded his arms as he watched me back. 'Don't worry, Graciela. You're still in charge. I'm merely lending you support.'

My heart fell at the mild sneer in his voice. And again, I wanted to throw caution to the wind, rewind to the blissful moments on his cabin sofa. To the intense, transcendental hours spent before his fireplace. But I needed to stay in reality. *My* reality, not the one Jensen believed I needed to face. Anything besides strict professionalism would only be adding to the heartache I'd experienced in the last week.

If that meant letting this animosity ride out for the duration of our meeting, then so be it.

I nodded my consent. He didn't move immediately. His arms remained folded, his piercing gaze narrowed at me for a stomach-tingling stretch.

Then, lips firmed in a line of displeasure, he went to work, sorting out forty pictures with jaw-dropping efficiency. 'I think these will work for what you have in mind. They have an element of each topic you're discussing, and, together with the interactive video in the digital version, I think your message will be heard.'

I stared down at the pictures he'd chosen, added another ten of my own, and, refining down again, halved the photos and rearranged them in the order I envisaged them laid out in the magazine.

We both stepped back and admired the mock-up, and he nodded. 'That's even better.'

I wanted to preen at his compliment, but I couldn't even give myself that little leeway. 'I'll leave them there for now, and come back to it in a while. See it with fresh eyes.'

He nodded. 'Good idea. You don't want to saturate your senses before you make a decision.'

I turned to the rest of the images, totalling over eight hundred. 'It seems a shame for all of these to go to waste.'

'They're yours. Do with them as you will.'

Again there was a distinct timbre in his voice that

caught me on the raw. I looked over and he was staring straight at me.

Hunger tore through me. I licked my lips and his eyes darkened, his gaze rapt on my gliding tongue. Face tight, he took a half-step closer. I averted my gaze from him, back to the photos, terrified of the wild leap of my heart. 'I can make a coffee-table book, donate the proceeds to charities in Alaska?'

I felt his gaze linger on me for a few seconds more before he answered. 'You have enough here for two books, easily. Even make it an annual thing.'

The idea thrilled me, but even more was the thought of a possible future collaboration with Jensen.

Terrified of the frenzied leap of my senses, I focused on the pictures, killing the idea of an extended connection with Jensen. There wouldn't be a different outcome in the future. I would always disappoint and fall short.

He joined me, handing me images on one subject, then the other. Within a short time, I had over three hundred photos for the first coffee-table book. He reached for the last set of photos at the same time I did. I jumped back, the electrifying effect of his touch lighting through me.

His face froze over and he reached for his jacket. 'It's getting late. I need to be somewhere else.'

'Where?' I asked before I could stop myself.

He shrugged. 'I have a prior engagement.'

A vice clamped around my heart. Was it business or pleasure? Was he seeing someone else? So soon?

What right did I have to be distressed by it? I'd

pushed him away. Still, the thought of him leaving strangled my insides. 'We're not done here.'

He paused, raised a mocking eyebrow at me. 'Aren't we?'

'We have an executive chef in the building. I can order something for us to eat while we finish up here.'

If anything, his expression grew more remote. 'You sure you want to risk indigestion by spending more time with me? Aren't you afraid I'll want to get *personal* again?'

'It's a professional courtesy, Jensen. That's all.'

His smile lacked any trace of warmth as he leaned forward, right into my personal space. And, God, he smelled so good, looked so mouth-watering, I wanted to leap across the gap between us, press myself against him and never let go.

'What makes you think I'll play by your rules of professional courtesy?' he rasped.

Because he brimmed with integrity. Because not a single time during our cabin seclusion had I had reason to call his character into question, the way I did so many people in my life. 'Because I know I can take you at your word.'

He hissed in a breath. 'What the fuck do you think you're doing, Graciela? I won't let you toy with me.'

My heart kicked hard. 'I'm not—'

'Did you decide some time in the past week that you weren't quite done with me as you purported to be? That perhaps I'm good for one last fuck, maybe two?'

Until I witnessed it for myself, I would've deemed

it impossible but Jensen's gaze was both sizzling and frigid as it swept over me, lingered on my face, my breasts, my hips and legs before returning. He wasn't bothering to hide his hunger and each look triggered, until I couldn't stand it any longer.

When I stepped back, he followed. I didn't order him away, couldn't even get my tongue to work, the electricity zapping through me freezing my vocal cords.

My hip bumped the table, halting my momentum.

Slowly, he raised his hand, brushed the pulse leaping at my throat with his knuckles. My nipples immediately puckered and I bit back a moan.

He tossed his jacket away, and captured my wrist. Holding my hand within his, he turned my wrist, his gaze on the fingers he was running over my racing pulse. 'So tell me, did you miss me, *min elskerinde*?'

I gasped, my senses cartwheeling at hearing those two words fall from his lips even while I was searingly aware I was foolish to open my heart up to it. 'Don't call me that,' I forced out. I wasn't worthy, not if I couldn't be what he wanted me to be. Open. Wearing my pain on my sleeve. Vulnerable to seismic emotions that would eventually consume me whole.

He exhaled long and deep. 'Why not? You're my mistress, whether you want to acknowledge it or not.' His gaze still downcast, he raised my hand and placed an open-mouthed kiss on my wrist.

I sucked in a sharp breath, arousal lighting through me as he slowly tasted my skin.

'Staying in the cabin without you was fucking hell,'

he confessed roughly. 'For the first time since I built it, I couldn't wait to leave. Return to London.'

Something deep, profound, moved through me. 'Jensen,' I attempted again, my heart hammering hard.

'I'll stop calling you *min elskerinde* if that's what you truly want. After today, you don't need to hear it again, anyway, right?'

I didn't pull away. I loved what he was doing so much more than the bleakness that awaited me once I ended this.

He trailed erotic kisses down my arm, drawing closer with every caress.

Something cracked open inside me, letting a flood of hope and desperate craving rush in.

'Not going to answer?' he mocked as he bit the sensitive skin. 'I'm afraid I'll need an answer to my next question, though.'

I cleared my throat, forced my voice to work. 'What question?'

Glacier-coloured eyes met mine, blazing lust and censure fighting for supremacy. 'Despite the bullshit we're rolling in, I want you. Fucking badly. So may I have you one last time, *min elskerinde*?'

I should've said no, of course. Should have snatched my arm away, shown him the door, tossed whatever temptation he was dangling out with him. But of course, I didn't. Because this was Jensen. Gorgeous. Wickedly talented. Pure sex on two legs. As close to a perfect sub as my jaded heart and broken spirit could appreciate.

So I cupped his jaw, caressed my fingers over his nape before sliding them into his hair.

My fist tightened around a handful of glorious hair.

He sucked in a sharp breath, his eyes squeezing shut as a hot shudder shook his towering frame. His hands stayed at his sides, his breath panting as he waited for my next move.

'Maybe I won't let you have me. Maybe I'm just going to make you watch me come.'

Harsh, razor-sharp need twisted his features. 'If—'

'You're not allowed to say *if that's what you wish*. You're so big on being real, then tell me what you truly feel. Not what you think I want to hear.'

His Adam's apple bobbed. 'Fine. I want to be the one to make you come, *min elskerinde*.'

'Why?'

Stark need darkened his eyes, transformed his beautiful face into a mask of pure masculine arousal. 'Because you can't hide from me then.'

Another rivet yanked free, a slither of hope flaring high before despair doused the flame. 'Did you stop to think that maybe I'm protecting you, Jensen?'

His nostrils flared. 'What from?'

'From me!' I released him, started to step back.

He yanked me close. 'Why the hell would I need protection from you?'

'Because I'm not enough! You think you want the whole, sordid truth? I haven't sustained a single relationship in my life. Not a single one. Everything I touch turns to fucking dust. I may be successful in business but I'm a mess in private.' The unfettered confession snagged several emotions inside me, twisting up into a knot of need so acute I feared the power of it. 'You think I'm hiding? Maybe I am. But I'm hiding for a reason. You judged your mother for living in denial. Did you stop to think she may have been protecting you? That she didn't want you to witness every single sorry detail of her trying to hold it together?'

His face tightened into a taut, angry mask, his skin losing a trace of colour. 'We're not talking about me. Or my mother—'

'Why not? Because you feel *exposed* when we do? Maybe even a little unsure about that high horse you're perched on?'

Anger slowly dissipated, leaving behind a poleaxed look I'd never seen before. He dragged a hand over his mouth and jaw, and his gaze shifted from mine as he processed. Frowned as he turned his back on me and strode a few paces away. A different sort of tension rode him as the minutes ticked by in silence.

'Could you have got her wrong, Jensen?' I pressed softly.

He whirled back, traces of alarm and uncertainty in his eyes. 'Whether I have or not, that's for me to deal with,' he gritted out. 'Right now, we're talking about you, Graciela—'

'No. I don't want to reason this out. I've lived with this for years, Jensen. The promise of my mother's love and her abandonment wrecked me for any relationship.

I've tried. Believe me, I've tried everything. Nothing works.'

And the end result had turned me inside out, raw with anguish and guilt because not only had I brought pain on myself, I'd dragged my brothers into that dark hellhole. I'd ended up ruining not just my childhood, but theirs.

Silence stretched, tight and fraught. 'Fine. So what now?' Jensen demanded, eyes narrowed.

I shrugged, surprised my shoulders could move beneath the heaviness weighing me down. 'I'm more than done with this crazy emotional roller coaster you seem determined to make me ride. So we can end this right now. Or we can end this an hour from now on condition the hour is spent the way we intended ten minutes ago.'

I held my breath, praying he wouldn't take the first option. Praying for a precious sixty minutes more with him before I had to let him go.

He stepped forward, paused for an infinitesimal second, then lifted his hand to my cheek with a wry smile. 'I'm not idiotic enough to walk away given those options. But know this. We might be fucking instead of talking, but we'll still be having a conversation, *min elskerinde*,' he said with quiet confidence that angered me, even as my heart wept at the gift of those two words.

A gift I didn't deserve, but was too selfish, too greedy to turn away. 'I hope you're not awfully disappointed if that conversation is one-sided,' I sniped, distressed by the dominion he seemed to have over my emotions. 'Undress,' I ordered, kicking my shoes off before stepping out of my own clothes.

Naked, I pulled out one of the conference room chairs, sat down and then slowly cupped my breasts and toyed with the peaks as I watched him tear off his clothes.

His cock jerked, a drop of moisture already beading the tip of the broad head. Tugging, twisting, tormenting the hard tips, I opened my senses to self-pleasure, intensified by the rapt look on his face as I arched my back.

My pussy throbbed and clenched around the promise of his cock. When I moaned, his lips parted on a harsh pant.

Abandoning one tight peak, I trailed my hand down my midriff, my fingernails drawing shivers over my skin and trailing goosebumps down my navel to my hairless mound. There I rested for a moment, revelling in the agitated rise and fall of his chest and my own dark pleasure.

Slowly, I parted my thighs. His gaze zeroed in on my wetness, and I spread my legs wider. He groaned and licked his lower lip.

Stark, anguished need intensified on his face and his thighs shook beneath the force of his desire.

I slid two fingers on either side of my wetness, pinching my labia tight. The zap of lust was nearly my undoing. Jensen growled beneath his breath, and I knew he was on the verge of begging.

Except he wouldn't. He had his instructions, and,

sublime sub that he was, he would obey to his dying breath.

Enjoy this while you can.

I refocused on him. His gaze was still riveted to the fingers gliding up and down my folds. 'Do you want to taste me, Jensen?'

He groaned. 'Yes, *min elskerinde.*'

I slid one finger inside. Then two. Deep. Deeper to my second knuckle. Rolled my hips to get them deeper, then drew them out. Held them up in front of his face.

He inhaled long and deep, licked his lips again. But he didn't move. Didn't even beseech me with his eyes. He simply...waited.

Flooring me with his control. Making me want to reward him. 'Taste.'

The words were barely out of my mouth before he grasped my wrist, wrapped his mouth around my fingers, drawing deep. The strength of his suction made me flinch. He felt it and immediately eased, his eyes flashing an apology as he glided his tongue over my digits, eagerly lapping up my essence. His deep grunt of satisfaction trebled my need. Hunger flaring wider, I dropped my other hand between my legs and slowly fucked myself.

He followed every movement, cock bobbing up and down. A thicker bead welled, then trailed down the underside of his cock. Veins stood out in hungry relief. I knew he was suffering.

'Would you like to come with me, Jensen?'

Again, he hesitated a fraction. 'I would like to fuck

you, *min elskerinde*. It would be a privilege to come inside you. But…'

'But what?'

Pure torment darkened his eyes. 'I don't have a condom.'

'I feel like we've been here before.'

He jerked out a nod.

'Has anything changed since then?'

His eyes narrowed, a gleam I couldn't decode lighting the depths. 'Not sexually for me, no.'

'Nothing has changed for me, either.'

His gaze swept down, and I got the feeling my answer had pleased him. More than anything I wanted to know what he was thinking…feeling.

I didn't ask. I didn't have the right. Never would.

Best keep this to just sex. Pure, unadulterated sex.

'If we're agreed, then what are you waiting for?'

He insisted on taking me home afterwards, dismissing my driver with a few words when we exited the building. Words that seemed to be the last he was going to utter as we rode through London in charged silence. Maybe it was the after-sex endorphins zipping through my blood I didn't want to deplete by acknowledging the dark, bleak finality racing towards us. Or worse, that Jensen had finally accepted it too.

At my door, he stared down at me for tense seconds, his eyes inscrutable.

I opened my mouth, but words refused to form, thoughts fraying to nothing because there was nothing to reach for. Hell, even uttering *goodbye* felt insurmountable.

'Goodbye, Graciela,' Jensen murmured heavily, apparently having no trouble with the word.

I didn't respond. Couldn't.

Could only watch as he sauntered back to his car.

I thought I knew what pain was.

The days that followed Jensen's departure introduced me to a whole new level of desolation.

So when Elsa slid the envelope addressed to me on my desk, I barely glanced at it. Barely had the strength to lift it.

When I summoned the energy to open it, the power of my need floored me.

Hands shaking, I read and re-read the words.

Don't fire her, but Elsa tells me you have no firm plans for Christmas.

Join me for a private event in Copenhagen next week.

I guarantee a misery-free and unforgettable adventure.

Spend a day or a week. Your choice.

Come and I'll tell you about the whales.
Jensen

CHAPTER TEN

I SHIFTED AGAINST the soft leather of the town car, my booted foot bouncing on the foot well carpet.

Nerves threatened to turn me inside out. But my gaze remained fixed on the entrance to the airport's arrival hall. Jaw clenched, I tried to regulate my breathing.

Adrenaline was good in any situation. It kept you sharp, focused. Nerves, on the other hand, were…bad. And since I couldn't remember the last time I'd been *this* nervous, I was lost as to how to deal with it.

I laughed under my breath. That seemed to be the recurring theme when it came to dealing with Graciela.

She'd kept me in suspense for six long days, refused to give me an answer to my invitation, drawing out my nerves until I'd thought I would snap. When she'd eventually answered, she'd done so through Elsa, giving just a date and time of her flight and nothing more.

I'd wanted to meet her inside the airport but decided against it.

The last thing I wanted was to set the tabloid press after her. And while I could fly under the radar in most countries, I was as recognisable here in Denmark as the Mortimers were around the globe.

I'd fucked things up, not once, but twice with my righteous bullheadedness. I wanted, no, *needed* to get this right this time.

But what if I didn't even get the opportunity? What if she didn't turn up?

I'd replayed our conversation in her conference room countless times, each recount a little more eye-opening. Each one shaming me a little.

Did you stop to think she may have been protecting you? That she didn't want you to witness every single sorry detail of her trying to hold it together?

A handful of words that had rocked me, more than she knew. She'd changed something fundamental inside me during those three days at the cabin, then completely shifted the axis of my world in her conference room.

A saner man would flee from such a seismic shift. But what the hell kind of adventurer would I be if I didn't explore to see where it led?

A surge of travellers heading for their holidays ebbed and flowed out of the entrance, but there was no sign of Graciela. At this time of night only two flights were supposed to land. As the last of the passengers trickled out, my insides plummeted.

She wouldn't leave me hanging like this. Would she?

My fingers gripped my thighs, then immediately un-clenched to tap a wild beat, in direct contradiction to the dull thudding within my chest. I was so intent on debating whether to call her mobile or not I didn't see the figure walking up until a knuckle rapped sharply against the window.

I jumped, then waved the driver away as he made to alight, yanking on the door handle and stepping out. She was dressed in the sort of classy chic I'd come to associate with her. Dark glasses despite the time of night, dark designer denims, black cashmere sweater and thick parka, and a stylish scarf with slashes of colour wrapped around her neck.

Thigh-high boots that were totally impractical for winter in Denmark adorned her feet but, of course, she carried it off effortlessly, looked seriously sexy.

'You're here,' I said uselessly.

Her smile was wary, her eyes apprehensive. Unlike the confident Dominant I knew. 'I hate mysteries. I had to come and see what that second line was all about.'

I reached for her suitcase, a little disconcerted by how small it was.

She either intended to stay for a short visit or she didn't intend to wear many clothes while she was here. I fervently hoped it was the latter. I tossed the case into the boot and joined her in the back seat. She unwrapped the scarf from around her neck and ran her hands through her hair, and I searched her features as the car joined traffic. I was willing to admit my approach hadn't been the most risk-free. I'd titivated and cajoled without knowing what the outcome would be.

'So when do I get to see my surprise?' she asked.

'The day after tomorrow.' I held my breath, waiting for her to tell me she only intended to stay one night.

She didn't, but a curious look crossed her face. 'Tomorrow is Christmas Day.'

'I know. The idea was for you to spend Christmas with me.'

She shook her head. 'We never agreed on where I spent Christmas. I'm supposed to be in the south of France.'

Chains tightened around my chest. 'The south of France?'

She nodded, naked emotions shifting over her face before she expertly masked it. 'Gideon and Bryce invited me to join them.'

I wanted to be pleased for her. But I wanted her here with me more. 'Are you going?'

She shrugged. 'I haven't decided yet. The idea was for me to come here and for you to show me whatever it is you want to show me.'

'I would've elaborated if you'd bothered to answer me directly. You spoke to me through your assistant.'

'Is that an accusation?'

I sighed. 'Are you going to allow me to be a charming host or are you going to turn this adversarial?'

Her eyes widened, surprised at my daring. 'Your insinuation that I was a charity case was not appreciated,' she snapped.

I frowned. 'I never said that.'

A sad little smile curved her full lips. 'That's what you meant, though, wasn't it?'

'If I recall, my exact words were, *I guarantee a misery-free and unforgettable adventure.*'

She waved her hand out of the window at the twinkling lights strung up in festive cheer. 'So what is this? An experiment to see whether you can cheer up the poor little rich girl at Christmas time?'

'If your brothers are reaching out, then things aren't as hopeless as you think, surely? Self-pity is not a good look on you.'

She gasped, hurt reflected in her eyes. After several tense seconds, she looked way. 'I don't think this is going to work.'

'Giving up already?' I pushed.

'How dare you?'

'No, how dare *you*, Graciela? How dare you waste your beautiful life?'

'I'm not—'

'You are and you know it or you wouldn't be here. You're curious. If you want a different experience, let me give that to you. You can start by letting me give you a proper welcome to Copenhagen.'

She arched a brow. 'What, with a visit to a sex club?'

'A kiss. I was simply offering a hello kiss.'

Nostrils flaring, her gaze dropped to my lips.

Silently, I held out my hand. After a beat, she put hers in mine.

I pulled off her gloves, warmed her chilled fingers between mine before brushing a kiss over her knuckles. Then, leaning close, I pressed my lips to hers.

It was all I permitted myself. All I could control against the need clamouring to rip free. It was gratifying to see her disappointment when I pulled away.

But then a determined little light glinted in her eyes as she glanced at the window. 'Where exactly are we?'

Despite the nerves eating me up again, I played the tour guide for her, answering questions until we drew up in front of my apartment building. I ushered her into the lift, my hand on her waist as we soared up to the penthouse suite I bought five years ago.

I watched her look around my apartment. Watched her take in the countless pictures documenting every project I'd worked on. She ignored the million-dollar view, her interest sparking as she went from frame to frame. 'These are amazing.'

A layer of nerves settled inside me. This could work. Either way I was going to give it my best shot.

'Thank you.' I set her case down, and went towards her.

Another wary little look crossed her face.

'There's no need to fear what's coming, Graciela. I promise you it's all good.'

Defiance replaced wariness, her eyes snapping with irritation that did a shoddy job of covering the alarm beneath. 'I'm not afraid. I just don't like surprises.' Her head tilted, fire sparking in her eyes. 'Give me something at least, Jensen, or all we'll be doing is making meaningless conversation while I wonder what you have in store for me.'

I smiled. I couldn't help it. She challenged and terrified me. Brought me alive in ways that I could never have imagined a short while ago. Ways I didn't want to have to do without. 'How about instead of telling you, I show you?' I offered.

Her gaze started past me, down the wide hallway that led to my bedroom. It was the only hallway in the apartment. So I'd correctly guessed her thoughts. I laughed.

'Hopefully the sex will come later. I need your clothes on for this one. Or we'll risk shocking a few people.'

'People,' she echoed, tensing.

I reached for her hand. 'I know we only just arrived but we need to leave again. We're expected.'

She opened her mouth, most likely to demand I tell her. But a different light shone in her eyes. One that thrilled me far too much. It was a light of trust. It said she was willing to take this small step.

She nodded, and my hand tightened around hers. We took the lift to the underground garage. She looked around, curious as I led her to the late-model sports car. She remained silent for the twenty-minute journey to our destination, but every now and then she'd glance at me, bite her lip, the first sign of nerves I'd ever seen on Graciela. It was endearing. But also a little sad that she'd be so afraid of the unknown. Sad that she didn't know her strength or underestimated her worth.

I was equally nervous when I pulled up in front of the large, familiar suburban house. The past few days had been enlightening, and Graciela was about to find out how instrumental she'd been.

I took her hand and kissed the back of it.

'I'm beginning to associate you kissing my hand with something that'll freak me out.'

I smiled. 'You liked something about my invitation or you wouldn't be here.'

She shrugged. 'It beats spending the night listening to my cousin Jasper drone on about our family feud with the Binghams, that's for sure.'

'The fondness in your voice tells me he's not all bad.'

She shrugged. 'I tolerate him, probably because I hardly see him.'

It was more than that and we both knew it, but I let it slide. We stepped out and I walked her to the red-painted front door decorated with garlands and Christmas lights. As we approached, sounds of festive music filtered through the air.

'You brought me to a party?' There was no disappointment, but neither was there anticipation. She was guarding her feelings and I couldn't blame her.

The door opened before I could knock, a woman of slim, tall build throwing her arms wide.

'Jensen! You made it.' Her wide smile didn't cover the wariness I glimpsed in her eyes but the tight band that usually gripped my chest when I was in my mother's company had loosened. Enough that I could return her smile.

Beside me, Graciela tensed. I tightened my fingers around hers, infusing reassurance. 'Mor, meet Graciela Mortimer. Graciela, my mother, Agnetha.'

Graciela held out her hand, but her face remained politely neutral as she greeted my mother. 'It's lovely to meet you.'

My mother's smile widened. 'You too. I was thrilled when Jensen said he was coming home and bringing a guest with him. Usually I have to beg and plead.' She threw the door wide open. 'Come in, meet the rest of the family!'

As we entered, I slanted a glance at Graciela, gauging her reaction.

Her face gave nothing away, not even when the rest of my family descended en masse. Not when Dag, my gregarious stepfather, enfolded her in an embrace. She remained coolly polite, upper-class and boarding-school-honed manners fully in place.

Dread slithered down my spine; the notion that my plan had backfired, that I'd probably killed any chance I had with her, became a reality when she cornered me in a quiet alcove while pre-dinner drinks were being served.

'I was right, wasn't I? I'm just some guinea-pig experiment to you!' she hissed with quiet fury.

Frustration boiled inside me. 'Only you would see it like this.'

Her face tightened. 'What's that supposed to mean?'

'Look around you, Graciela. We're not perfect. Hell, some of us have been through a lot of shit. But we don't wallow in it.'

I knew the words coming out of my mouth were wrong the moment I said them. 'Dammit, I didn't mean it like that.'

Pain dulled the fire in her eyes. 'No, I think you meant it exactly like that. You either meant to show me what a fuck-up I am or to rub my face in your idea of happy families,' she said.

'Or maybe there's a third option? How about gratitude? Wanting you to feel affection? Warmth? Conversations that didn't start and end with who could hurt whom worse or whatever version of hell you were too scared to face this Christmas?'

Her eyes grew bright with unshed tears. Furiously, she blinked them away. 'I don't need you to deliver whatever message you feel you need to deliver. I've survived holidays with my family for the better part of two decades.'

'And you still choose to accept things the way they are? What are you, Graciela? Deluded or coward?'

The blood drained from her face, her eyes turning into twin pools of torment.

I dragged my fingers through my hair as my words replayed in the shocked silence.

What the hell was wrong with me?

Showing her that her powerful words had changed my relationship with my mother was one thing. But this…?

Hell, I hadn't even got around to telling her why we celebrated Christmas on the twenty-fourth instead of on the traditional Christmas Day we used to celebrate in England.

She started to walk away. I held on. 'Wait. There's something I need to tell you…'

'You want to give me more of the same, you mean?' Her voice was ragged, her face still tight.

'I'm sorry. Dammit, that came out wrong. So fucking wrong.'

She held my gaze for a blazing moment. 'I can't leave without appearing rude. I can't order you to take me away from here because that would make me a bitch who's stealing the precious son away at Christmas. So I guess I'm fully immersed in your little experiment, aren't I?'

Without waiting for my response, she darted into the living room, the centre of revelry. For the rest of the evening, she placed at least half a room width between us, finding an excuse to distance herself whenever I got close.

If my mother and stepfather noticed, they decided on diplomatic silence. Merete, my sister, however, repeatedly shot me questioning glances, which I silently warned her not to vocalise.

Merete tended to shoot her mouth off before she engaged her brain. As much as I loved her, I wasn't in the mood to accommodate her adorable foibles tonight.

Not when I could feel the woman who'd gained monumental importance in my existence slipping through my fingers. The loud, obnoxious gong sounded for dinner. I rushed to my feet, crossed the room towards Graciela.

She ignored me, turning instead to Mikkel, Merete's five-year-old son, who'd spent most of the evening gazing at her in wide-eyed adoration. 'Would you like to show me where I'm sitting, Mikkel?'

He nodded eagerly, and I couldn't help the bite of

jealousy I felt towards my nephew. I followed, my spirits sinking lower when I clocked the place-settings.

I was seated as far away from Graciela as possible, next to Merete. I gritted my teeth, suspecting my sister had been instrumental in the arrangements.

Short of making a scene, I had to let it go.

Dinner was a loud, boisterous affair. But Graciela picked at her meal, offering a shallow smile as my sister peppered her with questions. I wasn't surprised when she excused herself the moment the second course was cleared away, to go to the bathroom. I stared at her back as she disappeared down the hallway, refocusing on my family when the throat cleared loudly. My mother was staring at me, her gaze a mixture of curiosity and sympathy.

'Whatever's going on, son, you need to fix it. Fast.'

I nodded, a curious little lump in my throat as I contemplated hunting her down again. Going down on my knees to beg forgiveness. I didn't give a fuck who saw me. But perhaps it was best to give her a little time to cool down?

Five minutes later she hadn't returned, and my foot was bouncing again.

Bloody hell.

Was it supposed to be this complicated? Was reaching for the most perfect thing I'd ever experienced supposed to be this hard?

I snorted under my breath. Of course it was. I'd nearly lost a couple of fingers climbing mountains all over the world. But regardless of how treacherous and agonising the climb, it was worth it every single time once I reached the summit. That kind of euphoria was indescribable.

It might have backfired spectacularly today, but there was always tonight. And tomorrow.

Cold, misery-filled shivers rippled down my body as I sat through the rest of dinner. They continued to surge, drowning out the sound of merrymaking until only my mother's voice remained in my head.

He's trying to prove his point. You're a charity case. The poor little rich girl he's taken pity on because he's got nothing better to do. You read his invitation and allowed yourself to dream. Deep down you know you're not enough. You'll never be enough.

I barely heard Jensen making his excuses to his family. Barely registered that we were leaving when he approached, my jacket in his hand. I held myself stiffly as he helped me into it. Desperately holding onto the last reserves of composure as I said my good-byes.

In silence, we walked out to the car in the freezing cold.

I felt his penetrating gaze on my face as I slid into my seat, through the tense drive back to his apartment. My heart thudded dully as I walked through his front door.

A few hours ago, I'd been elated that he was sharing his private space with me. Just as he'd shared his cabin in Alaska. This was a bigger deal, of course. And, contrary to the guard I'd wanted to place around this whole visit, I'd fallen in love with his apartment the moment I walked in.

It wasn't so much the stunning view outside the glass windows, but the testaments to his brilliance scattered everywhere. He loved what he did and wasn't afraid to show it. He didn't need to brag about his talent. The evidence was everywhere. His apartment felt like home in a way that I hadn't felt at home anywhere else for a very long time.

But…it turned out I was deluded. I glanced at my case, sitting there on the floor, waiting to be scooped up again sooner rather than later.

Stomach in miserable knots, I went towards it. 'I'm going to stay in a hotel tonight.'

He grunted an angry sound, one of the first I'd heard him make. 'No, you're not. This is insane. You don't need to leave, Graciela. Let's talk about this.'

I turned on him, anguish and fury boiling inside me. 'Again with the talking? Fine. Admit what you hoped to achieve by taking me to your parents' tonight.'

He stalled for a moment and then his lips firmed. 'For most of my childhood we celebrated Christmas the English way, until my mother decided to revert to the Danish way of celebrating the day before. Do you want to know why?'

I shook my head, impatient with his deviation.

'It's because my father ruined every Christmas for us, without fail, for as long as I could remember. He'd pick a fight over the smallest thing, use it as an excuse to ruin the whole fucking day. One time, my mother stood up to him, and he destroyed all the presents. Smashed everything to pieces with a fucking baseball bat.'

I flinched, my heart going out to him despite my own despair.

'When she met Dag, they decided to revert to Danish tradition, head off the day before bad memories ruined it.'

'Well, I guess it was a good way to counter what your father did, but by not celebrating both days, wasn't he winning?'

'Don't get me wrong, we still celebrate Christmas Day, but over the years, the Danish celebration has become a bigger deal.'

'A bigger deal you wanted to throw me in at the deep end of, to see whether I sank or swam?'

His face hardened. 'You really think I would do that to you? Deliberately sabotage your happiness?' His voice was rough. Ashen.

'I don't know. Tell me why you did it.'

'Because I wanted you to be happy!' he all but bellowed.

'Why? Why does this mean so much to you?'

He exhaled harshly. 'Do you remember what my mother said when she opened the door?'

I frowned. Shrugged. 'Something about bringing a guest?'

'No, the bit about having to beg and plead for me to visit.'

'Yeah. So?'

'So I avoid going home as much as I can. Excuses were easy to find and I wasn't ashamed to use them.'

'Sorry, you've lost me.'

'I walked you to your door last week, then drove straight to the airport. Because something you said pulled the rug from under me. Made me see what a selfish bastard I'd been to my mother.'

My heart kicked. 'Something… I… What did I say?'

'That she was trying to protect me by keeping the painful details of what my father was doing to her from me. I'd secretly blamed her for years for staying, failed to see her choices were limited. It's easy to stand back and judge. And I'd judged her harshly until you forced me to face the truth. Taking you home with me to-night… I wanted you to see what you'd done for me. Show my gratitude. Instead, I fucked it up.'

The different, enlightening slant to the whole eve-ning shook my world. He'd invited me here to witness something beautiful. Something wonderful *I'd* helped create.

The haggard sob caught me by surprise. Jensen too, from his stunned expression. Then he cursed. 'What the fuck did your mother do to you?'

Instantly, a vice tightened around my heart. 'Jen-sen…no,' I warned.

'No, I really want to know. What did her letter say?'

'It's none of your business,' I bit out through lips gone numb with pain.

'Oh, but I think it is. Because here you are, on the

verge of throwing away something precious because you can't or won't move from the past.'

More icy shivers drenched me. 'God, you're really in full flow tonight, aren't you?'

He dragged desperate fingers through his hair, his eyes spearing into me. 'I have to. Because I want you, Graciela, *min elskerinde*.'

My heart shook, as it did every time he called me that. 'You will not call me that again,' I said, my voice firm enough to make him freeze.

For a moment, stark bleakness darkened his eyes. 'You have my word. I won't address you like that again until you ask me to. But I meant it when I said I want to know what she said to you.'

With compulsion I couldn't stop, my gaze darted to the handbag I'd dropped on the sofa when we arrived.

His gaze followed mine, enlightenment and shock sharpening his eyes. 'Jesus, you carry it with you?'

I glared at him. 'So what if I do? What's it to you?'

His lips flattened as he strode across the room.

'Don't you dare—!'

He grabbed the bag and held it out to me. 'Show me,' he growled.

'No.'

Tense seconds ticked by, then he dropped the bag on the coffee table. 'Fine, if you won't show me, then get rid of it.'

Anguished ravaged my insides. 'I beg your pardon?'

'You heard me. I'm not sure how long you've been

carrying that toxic thing around with you, but you need to get rid of it, Graciela.'

'I don't know where the hell you get off—'

'I get off where I fucking love you so much it kills me that you won't give yourself a chance to be happy!'

My heart dropped to my toes, my brain ceasing to function. 'You...*what*?'

He reached out, seizing my wrists and dragging me close until we shared the same air. 'I love you. I've loved you since the second day at the cabin when you ordered me to tell you a story.'

I shook my head wildly. 'I... You can't.'

'Is that an order? Because if it is, I'm afraid I'm going to have to disappoint you by declining.'

My mouth dried so hard I feared I'd never form words again. So instead, my soul unfurled, eager to absorb the promise of his words.

'I can't, I'm no good for you.'

His fingers caressed my jaw. 'Oh, but you are, *min elskede*,' he insisted thickly. 'You're everything I will ever want in this lifetime and the next. And before you give me some excuse about not knowing you, or you not being right for me, remember that I'm a risk taker who's been diving headlong into dangerous situations since I could get away with doing it. Whatever you think you're hiding underneath this strong, beautiful heart that will scare me away, don't bother. I feel like I've been preparing all my life for this chance to win you.'

A rough, shocked laugh took me by surprise. 'So I'm just a challenge to you? While you tell me you love me?'

He grimaced, then shrugged. 'Shock therapy was part of my game plan in bringing you here.'

His admission should've angered me but, dear God, he wasn't taking any of it back. He wasn't grabbing my suitcase and tossing me out of the door with it.

Because he loved me...

Slowly, he released my hand and sank onto his knees.

I gasped, the act shockingly blunt, cutting through the noise in a way his words hadn't been able to convey. His hands curled around my calves, glided up slowly until he was gripping my hips. He leaned forward, laid his cheek against my stomach.

'With everything that I am, everything that I will ever be, I am yours, Graciela Mortimer. *Min elskede.*'

'I thought you weren't going to call me that until I gave you permission?'

I felt his smile against my stomach. 'You're *min elskede*—my love. I intend to do whatever is necessary to earn the right to call you *min elskerinde* again.'

The tremor started from the depths of my soul, rolling out like a tsunami until I was shaking and he was clutching me harder. The tickling on my chin I absently registered as tears pouring down my face. My hands sank into his hair, my grip loose as I nudged his face upward to meet my gaze.

'I don't know that I can love you, don't know if I'm capable.'

He nodded, pure understanding in his eyes. 'For now,

I'll be confident for the both of us. But you will. I believe in you.'

Dirty, soul-racking sobs seized me then, as they had at the cabin. He caught me when I broke, held me until I was wrung dry, then he rose, swung me into his arms. The bedroom was on the minimalist side, from the little I spotted before he crossed over to lay me down on the bed. He went to the bathroom and returned a minute later with a towel. After drying my tears, he tossed it aside. Then he climbed on, fully clothed, and folded me in his arms. Silence reigned for a few minutes and then he nudged my chin up.

'Why do you carry the letter around with you?'

Shame and pain twisted my insides to knots. 'Because it's the only thing of hers that I've got.'

He frowned. 'What do you mean?'

'Remember when I told you I was very angry with her for a very long time?'

He nodded.

'After she died, the lawyer told me I'd inherited all her clothes and any jewellery that didn't belong to the Mortimer family trust. I told the lawyer I didn't want any of it. Aunt Flo talked me into getting them. I don't think she believed me when I said I *really* didn't want it. Anyway, her things arrived a few days later. Boxes and boxes of pretty things I'd only been allowed to touch the day she left me. I set everything on fire that night, staying to make sure everything was turned to ash. But the letter, I kept. It's the only thing I have that's truly…hers.'

He gave a grim nod. 'I understand why you want to hang on to it, *min elskede*. But I still want you to destroy it.'

I tensed, ready to launch myself out of his arms, but he held me tight. 'You won't truly move on and heal until you do.'

I kept mutinously silent, my heart shaking at the enormity of what he was asking.

But…what if he was right? What if I was chaining myself down by dragging that letter through life? I'd kept it partly as a reminder not to make the same mistakes I'd done with her. Not to hope or love or reach for happiness in case I proved the failure she'd predicted I'd be. But that had happened anyway, hadn't it?

Until Jensen had battered through that toxic fortress, taken the chance on me I was too afraid to take for myself.

What if… *I was enough*?

My breath shuddered out of me.

His piercing eyes were fixed on me; he knew the moment I reached for courage and made the decision. He vaulted out of bed and held out his hand to me.

Together we walked into the living room and crossed over to the coffee table. Wildly shaking, I dug through my purse until my fingers brushed the corners of the worn, folded paper.

The words were seared in my memory, trickled through as I held it…

You'll never be enough for any man, woman or child.

You cling too hard, love too deep.

We Mortimers have an addiction problem.

Yours is emotional addiction.

Wean yourself off it or you'll be nothing but a disappointment.

You already are to me, and I suspect to your brothers.

I'm not coming back, Graciela.

One day you'll see it's for the best. You might even thank me for it.

I held it out to him. 'Do you want to read it?'

He shook his head. 'I don't need to. Whatever it says in there, it's not true. Very soon, you'll believe it too.'

With quick strides, he went into the kitchen and returned with a large ceramic bowl and a box of matches. Heart in my throat, I dropped the paper into the bowl. He handed me the matches, and when my fingers shook too badly, he cupped my hand, steadied me.

When I struck it, he released me.

I held the flame to one corner of the paper, my heart in my throat as it immediately caught fire. In less than a minute it was gone.

He gently cupped my face, dropped a reverent kiss on my lips before catching me in his arms once more. I refused to look into the bowl.

Couldn't mourn a mother I'd never really had.

With each step away from the blackened remains of words that had weighed me down all my life, the tightness in my chest eased, smothered hope breaking through the fog of doubt.

A clock chimed somewhere within the apartment as he walked us back into his bedroom. This time he set me down next to the bed, his face lighting up in a smile.

'It's Christmas Day and I would very much love to unwrap you.'

My heart hammered hard enough to power up a small city, yet I still managed to raise my chin, to stare him down despite our height difference.

'I may just allow you to, but only if you address me the way you crave to.'

I'd bared myself to him, admitted that I wasn't sure how capable I was of returning the feelings he craved from me. But *this* I could give him. He dropped to his knees, and I was awed all over again by how magnificently comfortable he was in that position. How magnificent he was, full stop.

With reverent hands, he took my clothes off and then, at my nod, he undressed himself, pulled back the coverlet and helped me into bed.

Sliding between my thighs, he wrapped his arms around me. '*Jeg elsker dig.* I love you.' He dropped a long kiss on my lips. 'Merry Christmas, my heart. *Min elskerinde.*'

'Merry Christmas, Jensen.'

We spent Christmas in bed making the most sublime love I'd ever known.

Jensen was searingly sweet, attentive and generous

with his love. With every second that passed, my soul healed.

When Bryce called out of the blue, I bit back tears as I wished him and Savvie a merry Christmas. A text from Gideon an hour later *daring* me to spend New Year with him and Leonie brought on another emotion bout.

I'd never discovered what my mother had written to them in their letters, and I didn't need to. Not any more. Somehow we'd all found happiness despite the abysmal odds, and that was enough for me.

I was a little apprehensive when Jensen strode into the room the next night, breathtaking in his tuxedo. I was also formally dressed in a strapless gown, with shoes and a matching clutch. Diamonds sparkled at my throat and in my ears, and my hair was slicked back and down my back, a simple enough style that'd surprisingly taken more time than I'd anticipated, making me a little late and a lot flustered when Jensen halted in his tracks.

'Holy fuck, you look incredible,' he breathed, his voice rough.

'All this wasn't achieved without huge effort, I'll tell you that.'

He shook his head, his hands sliding over my waist to grip my hips. He loved gripping me there, and I loved his big, callused hands on me.

'The outer package is merely the support act to the real diamond beneath that shines through your eyes, your smile. I taste it when I kiss you. Feel it when I'm inside you.'

I fanned my face, swallowing more than once before I could speak. 'You're going to make me cry again and ruin my make-up and make us late to wherever we're going.'

He gave a wicked smile, kind enough not to point out how many times I'd dissolved into tears in the last twenty-four hours. It was as if all the grief, anger and bitterness I'd bottled up inside had needed an outlet immediately. He'd never once complained.

He'd simply gathered me in his arms and held me until the storm passed. That simple act of kindness had helped me heal faster, enough to tentatively embrace the phenomenon of his love.

He held out his hand and I slipped mine into it, my heart flooding with joy as he walked us out of the door and downstairs to his car.

The bright lights of Copenhagen flashed by as we headed into the inner city. When he stopped in front of a futuristic-looking glass building, I stepped out, looking for clues as to where we were.

'If you're trying to guess where we are, don't bother. Unless you've become fluent in Danish in the last day and a half?'

I shook my head, laughing. 'I'm good, but not that good.'

Jensen tossed his keys to a valet and held out his arm to me. I slipped mine through and we walked together into the building that turned out to be an art gallery.

My eyes widened. 'It's your exhibit?' I guessed, thrilled.

He nodded with a smile. 'My agent thinks it's about time for another one.'

'I wholeheartedly agree.'

He mock-winced. 'I hope the two of you never meet. My life would become unbearable.'

'It's because we both believe in you. Your work is magic.'

He leaned down, his lips brushing my earlobe and making me shiver. 'That's what you keep insisting in the bedroom. And I might just start to believe you, *min elskerinde*.'

I was laughing when we walked into the first, largest room.

My laughter died, my senses overtaken by a different sort of pleasure.

The space was filled with Jensen's work, starting from the first time he'd picked up a camera to his latest project, which happened to be mine. The whole place was hushed, the guests admiring his work in reverent silence.

We walked slowly through the gallery, stopping every now and then when a guest stopped him to congratulate him or express their wonder at his talents. He accepted accolades with a simple nod and smile, but as we drew closer to the end of the exhibit, he grew apprehensive.

'Something wrong?'

He flashed a smile. 'I hope not.'

About to ask what he meant, I held my tongue as his mother, stepfather and sister approached. His mother was smiling, her smile a little tearful as she addressed her son. Dag simply beamed, the proud father.

After a quick exchange in Danish, Agnetha turned to me. 'Your lovely presents arrived this morning, Graciela. Thank you so much, but you really shouldn't have. You've given me the best Christmas present.' Her gaze veered to her son, fresh tears filming her eyes.

Tears clogging my own throat, I waved her away. I'd woken a slightly disgruntled Elsa and had her raid the emergency presents stash I kept in the office. Agnetha's scarf, Dag's vintage bottle of red, and Merete's crystal bracelet had been hand-delivered this morning, along with Christmas cards and a present for Mikkel.

'Excuse us, please,' Jensen said to his family, then smoothly led me down a short, darkened hallway.

'Where are we going?' I asked, excitement mixing with a touch of anxiety.

'You'll see,' was all he said.

I was learning that in some things Jensen was immovable. He was mine to command and cherish in the bedroom. But it was equally fulfilling for both of us for the reins to slacken a touch. It was all the more rewarding and thrilling when I pulled them back and took control.

I watched him grow more tense as we approached a set of double doors. With one last, furtive look at me, he threw them open.

Every surface, from floor to ceiling, was covered

with images of me. All taken on the night of the borealis. There were easily over two hundred, but I could
swear each frame had captured a different expression.

I turned to him, my heart in my throat as I stared at
him, my soul bursting with feeling I couldn't quite describe but wanted to embrace.

'This, *min elskerinde*, this is how I see you. This is
how you should look every day for the rest of your life,'
he said, his voice thick with emotion.

'Thunderstruck?' I croaked.

He smiled. 'Starstruck. Awestruck. Filled with wonder and joy. Beautiful. Hopeful. Breathtaking. Fulfilled.
Beautiful.'

'Your already said *beautiful*.'

'I know. It deserves repeating.'

His fingers interlocked with mine, I slowly spun
around, my gaze lighting on each picture, tears brimming in my eyes as his words nurtured my soul, watered
it and helped it sprout wings of belief. And as I came
full circle, he was waiting, arms wide open.

I flew into them, my heart full. 'I love you,' I confessed, the words a vow I knew I'd never doubt or break.

His body shook, his breath expelling long and deep
as he held me tight. 'I know, my darling. I got there a
little faster than you, but I knew you'd catch up.'

I laughed. I cried, uncaring that I was becoming
emotionally wrecked again as I basked in his love.

'We can enjoy this just between us, or you can show
it to the world. You direct the narrative of your life from

now on. I'll merely provide the support. But I'd like the world to see the real Graciela Mortimer.'

Eventually, I dragged my head from his chest and looked up into his eyes. Watched him slowly sink down, uncaring who saw him on his knees in front of me, waiting patiently for my reply.

'I want what you want, Jensen. Today, tomorrow, for always. If you see me like this, then I would be proud to show myself like this to the world.'

I leaned down and kissed him, my fingers gliding through his hair, catching the knot at the back of it and gripping it tight. He groaned into my mouth, then drew back for a spell. 'I love you.'

'Jeg elsker også dig,' I repeated back to him, watched his eyes light up and knew that within that light my soul had been reborn.

EPILOGUE

'TELL ME ABOUT the whales, Jensen.'

He gave a thick groan and I hid a smile. 'You want me to tell that story right now?' he asked, his voice strained.

It might have had something to do with the fact that I was completely naked and astride him, and he was deep inside me, doing everything in his power to hold absolutely still at my command. Or perhaps it was the old-fashioned folding razor I was using to shave off his stubble that made him a little nervous. I had a feeling it was the combination of edgy danger and surrendering himself to me that gave us both the ultimate thrill.

I carefully scraped the sharp edge beneath his firm jaw, the sandpapery rasp curiously making me wetter. 'It's been a crazy couple of months. But I think we have a little time now?'

He snorted. 'By a little time, you mean you plan on being fashionably late to your launch party?'

I couldn't hold back my grin. Hell, I'd been smiling so much lately, I was surprised my face hadn't fallen off from the well of happiness growing inside me.

My life had changed in the space of a few weeks.

First, Jensen and I accepted Gideon's invitation and joined him and Leonie on the family yacht in the south of France a few days into the new year. My apprehension melted away within minutes when my hitherto fearsome and formidable brother greeted me with a wide smile and swept me off my feet into a bear hug. The second surprise, in the form of Bryce and Savvie stepping onto the deck, was equally heart-warming, starting what had become the best family time I could remember. That they were coming to the party tonight filled me with warmth I wouldn't have believed possible a short time ago. My heart swelled as I acknowledged that it all had to do with the man beneath me.

'Don't change the subject,' I said, projecting sternness into my voice.

'I wouldn't dare. Not when you've literally got me by the throat and cock,' he joked, but he swallowed hard nonetheless, a fine tremor shivering through his body as I slowly rolled my hips. 'Christ,' he swore thickly under his breath.

'The whales, Jensen.'

'What do you want to know, *mit hjerte*?'

My heart. I loved the Danish endearments that fell so effortlessly from Jensen's lips because I knew the wealth of emotion behind them.

'Everything. Start from the beginning. Did you know they were going to be there?' I finished with his left side and angled my body to his right.

The movement dragged my inner heat over his

length and he gave a deep groan. Then took a shuddering breath. 'I wasn't going to shoot any underwater stuff that day. We were in Tonga to film the active volcano. I spotted a couple of whales on my morning swim, grabbed a few of my guys and headed out on the boat for a closer look.' He stopped. I paused, overawed by the transcendent look on his face. 'There were dozens of them, just…frolicking. Mothers with newborns. Older ones. I couldn't get into my scuba gear fast enough.'

I smiled. 'Tell me about that picture.' The one that had made him famous. The iconic one everyone raved about when they spoke about Jensen Scott.

His throat moved as he swallowed again. 'Until very recently, it was the most profound thing to happen to me.'

'Tell me how it felt. In that moment. Were you terrified?'

'The smallest was easily the size of a bus so, yes, I was plenty terrified going into the water. But…all I know was that one moment my chest was pounding, then the next all I felt was…incredible, soul-quietening peace.' The last word was gruff. 'I don't know why they stopped playing or why they came close the way they did.'

The picture of seven sperm whales surrounding him in a perfect circle with Jensen suspended in the middle had rocked the world. The perfect synchronicity of giant tail fins moving as one while the whales all stared at Jensen had moved millions. Thousands had believed the picture was fake. When it'd been authenticated, Jensen Scott had shot to fame, winning a clutch of awards both for the stills and for the ninety-second video he'd shot with the camera pointing up.

'What made you leave the camera where you did?'

He exhaled. 'That was nothing new. I always dive with multiple cameras. You never know where the perfect shot will come from. Everyone thinks there was just that one camera but there were three, set up on the ocean floor on tripods. The one I released captured the best angle.'

I gasped. 'There are others? Can I see them?'

'They're in the Denmark apartment. You'll have to come back with me next week if you want to see them.'

I leaned close and brushed my lips over his. 'I was planning on coming with you anyway.' We hadn't quite worked out where or when we'd move in together. All we knew was that we were rabid about spending every spare moment together.

I leaned back again, watched his eyes fall to my breasts before darting back up to meet mine. His cock jerked inside me, and he sucked in a desperate breath.

'How many times has your video been watched?'

'According to my agent…two and a half billion times.'

'God, that's incredible.'

He made a pained sound and squeezed his eyes shut for a moment. He was almost at breaking point, just where I loved him to be.

'Last question,' I murmured as I passed the razor along his taut cheek, shaving the last bristled spot.

'Ja, min elskerinde.'

'You said it was your most profound moment until recently?'

Ice-blue eyes met mine, blazed with steel-forged love, before dropping in submissive surrender. 'It was. At the time I thought nothing would ever equal it. Then I met you.' His voice was hushed and solemn, reflecting everything he felt. An expression I was still finding hard to fathom belonged to me and only me. 'Now I simply accept that it was a moment that was destined to happen just so it would bring me to you.'

I heard the razor clatter to the floor without fully taking it in. I gripped his nape, nudging his head up until I captured his gaze with mine. 'You can't say things like that to me.' God, was that mess my voice?

His nostrils flared. 'Why the hell not?'

'Because there's only so much room in my chest for how big my heart gets when you say things like that.'

The most dazzling smile stretched across his face, making my heart swell even bigger. 'Will you punish me if I say I'm not sorry?'

I slowly circled my hips, biting back a moan at the scalp-tingling sensation. 'I most definitely intend to punish you. Later. Right now I'll reward you for sharing your beautiful story with me.' I pressed a kiss to his lips. 'And for loving me,' I added in an even thicker voice.

His smile altered, weighted by emotion as he bared himself even further. 'I intend for us to have many beautiful stories to share, *min elskede*,' he vowed.

'Then share one with me right now, Jensen. Touch your mistress. Show her how much you love her.'

The words were barely out of my mouth before he was switching his death grip from the chair to my hips, slamming me back down on his steely length.

I held on tight for a moment, then simply let go as I was swept under a torrent of love. One I was beginning to believe would stand the test of time.

An hour later, after a quick but carnally eventful shower, we stepped hand in hand out of the lift ten floors below, in the tallest building in London, which just happened to have the Mortimer name stamped on it, and into the glitzy affair that was the ice-themed party to celebrate the latest release of *Mortimer Quarterly*. The climate-conscious theme had resonated powerfully, with many media outlets running features off what Jensen and I had put together.

We circulated, holding on tight to one another.

A loud wolf whistle cut through the music and chatter and I turned to see Bryce, grinning, with one arm slung around Savvie, the other waving me over. Next to him, Gideon also kept his wife close, as if they were both afraid of letting the women they loved stray too far.

My fingers tightened around Jensen's, my own possessiveness engulfing me.

'Everything okay?' Jensen murmured, sensing my emotions.

I swallowed the lump in my throat. 'Yes, Jensen. Everything's great.'

He smiled, kissed my hand again.

'This is some shindig, Gracie,' Gideon said when I reached him.

'The whole thing's amazing,' Leonie, his wife, added, looking stunning in a green sequinned dress.

More accolades flooded in from Savvie and Bryce. Inexplicable tears prickled my eyes. Perhaps the women sensed my surfacing emotions. They excused themselves to go to the ladies'. Jensen kissed my cheek, then headed to the bar to get us drinks.

An easy silence settled between my brothers and me. Bryce broke it. 'What the fuck is wrong with Jasper? He looks like he's about to deck someone.' He nodded his head towards the opposite corner of the room, where our cousin was staring daggers at his drink while ignoring the tall, stunning woman next to him.

Wren Bingham.

Daughter of the late Sheldon Bingham, brother of Perry Bingham, the man currently fuelling the flames of the decades-old family feud between the Binghams and Mortimers.

I was surprised when Jasper listed Wren as his plus one to my party. Reading the fiery undercurrents between them now, my thoughts echoed Bryce's.

'Maybe he's in the mood for a little self-flagellation,' Bryce answered his own question with a smirk, then his face grew serious. 'Fuck me. Would you have ever believed we'd get here?' he said gruffly.

Gideon lifted a snarky eyebrow. 'Here?'

Bryce slugged him on the arm. 'Yes, *here*, and with

other halves who tolerate us for more than five minutes rather than, I dunno, in the bloody nuthouse.'

'And why the hell wouldn't they?' Gideon demanded. 'Beneath all the bullshit, we're fucking awesome.'

I laughed.

Bryce joined in.

Gideon chuckled.

In that flawless moment, I realised I did indeed have more room.

For infinite love.

* * * * *

COMING SOON!

We really hope you enjoyed reading this book. If you're looking for more romance, be sure to head to the shops when new books are available on

Thursday 26th June

To see which titles are coming soon, please visit

millsandboon.co.uk/nextmonth

MILLS & BOON

MODERN

Power and Passion

Prepare to be swept off your feet by sophisticated, sexy and seductive heroes, in some of the world's most glamourous and romantic locations, where power and passion collide.